"*The Heart's Shelter* is another sweet, wholesome story that readers are sure to enjoy. Kira and Jayden's journey of healing and love is a delightful treat!"
—KATHLEEN FULLER, *USA TODAY* BESTSELLING AUTHOR

"This is such a sweet story! Savannah and Korey were both hurting so much and needed some time to work out their angst. I love how their friendship and their plan to end all the speculation about both of them still being single turned into something more for both of them. And Korey's kindness to Savannah's brother Toby was a gracious example of God's love for all children. This prodigal son story touched my heart and gave me such hope. A perfectly sweet and touching story that will touch any heart!"
—LENORA WORTH, AUTHOR OF *PINECRAFT REFUGE*, ON *BREAKING NEW GROUND*

"*Breaking New Ground* is a beautiful story of heart, hope, and healing. You'll feel the warmth and emotion of this book long after the last satisfying page."
—JENNIFER BECKSTRAND, *USA TODAY* BESTSELLING AUTHOR OF *THE AMISH QUILTMAKER'S UNCONVENTIONAL NIECE*

"Amy Clipston once again entertains us with a story that reaches all the way to the heart."
—VANNETTA CHAPMAN, *USA TODAY* BESTSELLING AUTHOR, ON *BUILDING A FUTURE*

"Clipston kicks off the Amish Legacy series with a heartwarming romance . . . It's a tender romance, precisely the kind that Clipston's fans expect."
—PUBLISHERS WEEKLY ON *FOUNDATION OF LOVE*

"Amy Clipston has once again penned a sweet romance that will have her readers rooting for a heroine who deserves her own happily-ever-after. Crystal Glick is a selfless, nurturing woman who has spent her life caring for others—to the detriment of her dream of a family of her own. Duane Bontrager is a much older widower with three nearly grown sons. Readers are in for a treat as these two overcome one obstacle after another to be together. The real stars of the show, however, are Crystal's nieces and nephews. They're enchanting.

Grab a cup of coffee, a piece of pie, *Foundation of Love*, and settle in for a lovely Clipston story."

—KELLY IRVIN, AUTHOR OF *THE BEEKEEPER'S SON* AND *UPON A SPRING BREEZE*

"A heartwarming story that works as both a standalone romance and a satisfying series installment."

—PUBLISHERS WEEKLY ON *THE COFFEE CORNER*

"Clipston always writes unique and compelling stories and this is a good collection of light reading for evenings."

—PARKERSBURG NEWS AND SENTINEL ON *AN AMISH SINGING*

"Amy Clipston's characters are always so endearing and well-developed, and Salina and Will in *The Farm Stand* are some of my favorites. I enjoyed how their business relationship melded into a close friendship and then eventually turned into so much more. *The Farm Stand* honors the Amish community in the very best of ways. I loved it."

—SHELLEY SHEPARD GRAY, *NEW YORK TIMES* AND *USA TODAY* BESTSELLING AUTHOR

"This series is an enjoyable treat to those who enjoy the genre and will keep readers wanting more to see what happens next at the Marketplace."

—PARKERSBURG NEWS AND SENTINEL ON *THE FARM STAND*

"Clipston begins her Amish Marketplace series with this pleasing story of love and competition . . . This sweet tale will please fans of Clipston's wholesome Amish romances."

—PUBLISHERS WEEKLY ON *THE BAKE SHOP*

"Fans of Amish fiction will love Amy Clipston's latest, *The Bake Shop*. It's filled with warm and cozy moments as Jeff and Christiana find their way from strangers to friendship to love."

—ROBIN LEE HATCHER, BESTSELLING AUTHOR OF *WHO I AM WITH YOU* AND *CROSS MY HEART*

"Clipston closes out this heartrending series with a thoughtful consideration of how Amish rules can tear families apart, as well as a reminder that God's path is not always what one might expect. Readers old and new will find the novel's issues intriguing and its hard-won resolution reassuring."

—*Hope by the Book*, BOOKMARKED review,
ON *A Welcome at Our Door*

"A sweet romance with an endearing heroine, this is a good wrap-up of the series."

—*Parkersburg News and Sentinel* on *A Welcome at Our Door*

"*Seasons of an Amish Garden* follows the year through short stories as friends create a memorial garden to celebrate a life. Revealing the underbelly of main characters, a trademark talent of Amy Clipston, makes them relatable and endearing. One story slides into the next, woven together effortlessly with the author's knowledge of the Amish life. Once started, you can't put this book down."

—Suzanne Woods Fisher, bestselling author of *The Devoted*

"With endearing characters that readers will want to get a happily ever after, this is a story of romance and family to savor."

—*Parkersburg News and Sentinel* on *A Seat by the Hearth*

"[*A Seat by the Hearth*] is a moving portrait of a disgraced woman attempting to reenter her childhood community . . . This will please Clipston's fans and also win over newcomers to Lancaster County."

—*Publishers Weekly*

"This story shares the power of forgiveness and hope and, above all, faith in God's Word and His promises."

—*Hope by the Book*, BOOKMARKED
review, on *A Seat by the Hearth*

"This story of profound loss and deep friendship will leave readers with the certain knowledge that hope exists and love grows through faith in our God of second chances."

—Kelly Irvin, author of *The Beekeeper's Son* and
Upon a Spring Breeze, on *Room on the Porch Swing*

"A story of grief as well as new beginnings, this is a lovely Amish tale and the start of a great new series."

—*Parkersburg News and Sentinel* on *A Place at Our Table*

"Themes of family, forgiveness, love, and strength are woven throughout the story . . . a great choice for all readers of Amish fiction."

—*CBA MARKET MAGAZINE* ON *A PLACE AT OUR TABLE*

"This debut title in a new series offers an emotionally charged and engaging read headed by sympathetically drawn and believable protagonists. The meaty issues of trust and faith make this a solid book group choice."

—*LIBRARY JOURNAL* ON *A PLACE AT OUR TABLE*

THE HEART'S
SHELTER

OTHER BOOKS BY AMY CLIPSTON

THE HEART'S SHELTER

An Amish Legacy Novel

AMY CLIPSTON

ZONDERVAN

The Heart's Shelter

Copyright © 2024 by Amy Clipston

Published in Grand Rapids, Michigan, by Zondervan. Zondervan is a registered trademark of HarperCollins Christian Publishing, Inc.

Requests for information should be addressed to customercare@harpercollins.com.

Library of Congress Cataloging-in-Publication Data

Names: Clipston, Amy, author.
Title: The heart's shelter / Amy Clipston.
Description: Grand Rapids, Michigan: Zondervan, 2024. | Series: An Amish Legacy novel ; 4 | Summary: "Kira Detweiler does not plan to be in Lancaster County for long. She's left her family in Indiana to help her aunt after the birth of her fourth boppli. Or at least that's what she tells people. Deep down, she's trying to escape the heartache of a broken engagement and has no plans to date again anytime soon. Jayden Bontrager watches his older brothers with admiration, and he prays that someday he'll have the kind of life they do. Even so, he's only twenty-three and not in a hurry to marry and start a family. He's content to watch from the sidelines and is happy to see his brothers enjoying a close relationship once again. When Jayden and Kira strike up a friendship, they are each drawn to the other's gentle and humble demeanor, and they feel things for one another unlike anything they've felt before. But Kira is torn between her heart and her home. She sees no point in pursuing a relationship with Jayden when she doesn't plan to put down roots in Pennsylvania. The last thing she needs is another heartbreak. Will Jayden and Kira be able to overcome the obstacles in their path to find the future they both dream of?"--Provided by publisher.
Identifiers: LCCN 2023032981 (print) | LCCN 2023032982 (ebook) | ISBN 9780310364443 (paperback) | ISBN 9780310364474 (library binding) | ISBN 9780310364450 (epub) | ISBN 9780310364467
Subjects: LCSH: Amish--Fiction. | BISAC: FICTION / Amish & Mennonite | FICTION / Small Town & Rural | LCGFT: Christian fiction. | Romance fiction. | Novels.
Classification: LCC PS3603.L58 H44 2024 (print) | LCC PS3603.L58 (ebook) | DDC 813/.6--dc23/eng/20230724
LC record available at https://lccn.loc.gov/2023032981
LC ebook record available at https://lccn.loc.gov/2023032982

Printed in the United States of America
23 24 25 26 27 LBC 5 4 3 2 1

For my mother, Lola Goebelbecker,
with love, appreciation, and admiration.
You're my partner in crime, my movie buddy,
my binge-watching pal, my cheerleader, my company
while I write, my rock, and my best friend.
Thank you for all you do for our family.

GLOSSARY

ach: oh

aenti: aunt

appeditlich: delicious

Ausbund: Amish hymnal

bedauerlich: sad

boppli: baby

bopplin: babies

bruder: brother

bruderskind: niece/nephew

bruderskinner: nieces/nephews

bu: boy

daed: father

danki: thank you

dat: dad

Dietsch: Pennsylvania Dutch, the Amish language (a German dialect)

dochder: daughter

dochdern: daughters

dummkopp: moron

Dummle!: Hurry!

Englisher: a non-Amish person

fraa: wife

Frehlicher Grischtdaag!: Merry Christmas!

freind: friend

freinden: friends

froh: happy

gegisch: silly

gern gschehne: you're welcome

grosskinner: grandchildren

Gude mariye: Good morning

gut: good

Gut nacht: Good night

haus: house

Ich liebe dich: I love you

kaffi: coffee

kapp: prayer covering or cap

kichli: cookie

kichlin: cookies

kinner: children

krank: sick

kuche: cake

kumm: come

liewe: love, a term of endearment

maed: young women, girls

maedel: young woman

mamm: mom

mammi: grandma

mei: my

narrisch: crazy

onkel: uncle

Ordnung: the oral tradition of practices required and forbidden
in the Amish faith

schee: pretty

schtupp: family room

schweschder: sister

schweschdere: sisters

sohn: son

Was iss letz?: What's wrong?

Wie geht's: How do you do? or Good day!

wunderbaar: wonderful

ya: yes

zwillingbopplin: twins

THE AMISH LEGACY SERIES FAMILY TREES

Crystal m. Duane Bontrager

Tyler (mother—Connie—deceased)
Korey (mother—Connie—deceased)
Jayden (mother—Connie—deceased)
Kristena Mae

Michelle m. Tyler Bontrager

Connie Elaine

Savannah m. Korey Bontrager

Ryan

Celia m. Lamar Detweiler

Abigail m. Victor "Vic" Raber
Kira
Leah
Maribeth

Ellen m. Stanley Lapp

Ruby
Liesel
Mimi
Austin

A NOTE TO THE READER

WHILE THIS NOVEL IS SET AGAINST THE REAL BACKDROP OF Lancaster County, Pennsylvania, the characters are fictional. There is no intended resemblance between the characters in this book and any real members of the Amish community. As with any work of fiction, I've taken license in some areas of research as a means of creating the necessary circumstances for my characters. My research was thorough; however, it would be impossible to be completely accurate in details and description since each and every community differs. Therefore, any inaccuracies in the Amish lifestyle portrayed in this book are completely due to fictional license.

CHAPTER 1

KIRA DETWEILER PUSHED THE GROCERY CART DOWN THE CE-real aisle and stopped and studied her aunt's list. "Cheerios, oatmeal, and apple juice," she muttered before slipping the list into the pocket of her apron. Then she smiled down at her little cousin perched in the seat of the cart. "Let's find the cereal your *mamm* wants, okay, Liesel?"

"Baby!" Liesel, her three-year-old cousin, held her cloth doll up in the air and dropped it onto the ground. "Baby go boom!" She giggled, and her dark-brown curls bobbed with the motion of her laughter.

Ruby, Liesel's five-year-old sister, sprang into action. "I've got it!"

"*Danki*, Ruby." Kira touched her little cousin's dark-brown braid. "You're a *gut* helper."

Ruby beamed, her dark-brown eyes sparkling in the fluores-cent lights humming above them.

"Will you help me find the Cheerios and the oatmeal?" Kira asked.

Ruby scampered down the aisle. "*Ya!*"

"*Ach*, don't run," Kira called after her as she navigated past another Amish woman with a toddler sitting in the seat of her cart. She nodded a hello and followed Ruby to the display of cereal boxes.

Ruby stood up on her tiptoes and reached for a box of Cheerios. "There it is."

"*Danki*." Kira took the box and then leaned down toward her little cousin. "Please don't run. I don't want you to fall and get hurt."

Ruby nodded, and her long braids bounced off her little shoulders. "Okay, Kira." Then she pointed. "There's the oatmeal *Dat* likes. I'll get it." Kira watched closely as Ruby pulled a box from a display a few feet away.

Kira smiled. She loved her little cousins. She was so grateful when her aunt Ellen invited her to come from Indiana to Pennsylvania to spend some time helping her with her three older children after giving birth to her fourth child last month. Kira was thrilled at the opportunity to spend time with her mother's youngest sibling. Her sweet aunt felt more like a sister since she was thirty-five, and only ten years older than Kira. Although they lived in different states, Kira felt a kinship with her aunt through letters and phone calls. She had arrived nearly a week ago, and she planned to stay for as long as her aunt needed her help.

Coming to Pennsylvania gave Kira a chance to get to know her little cousins. But Kira had another reason for wanting to escape her home in Shipshewana, Indiana, for a while. She also needed a chance to mend her broken heart after her former fiancé, Philip, called off their November wedding, saying that he wasn't ready for marriage. She was grateful her aunt had extended the invitation so that she could flee from the shame and heartbreak of her broken engagement.

"What's next?" Ruby's question brought Kira back to the present.

Kira pulled the list from her pocket. "Apple juice and cranberry juice."

"I'll get it!" Ruby took off toward the next aisle, and Liesel giggled, holding her doll above her head.

Kira steered the grocery cart past other shoppers and into the juice aisle, where her five-year-old cousin stood by the shelves. "Slow down, Ruby!"

"Here it is!" Ruby bounced up and down on her black sneakers and pointed toward the bottles of apple juice. "This is the juice Liesel and Mimi like."

Kira turned toward an Amish man loading a large pack of bottled water into his grocery cart. With sandy-blond hair and bright hazel eyes, the tall man gave her a warm smile. She nodded, and he returned the greeting before smiling at Ruby and pushing his cart down the aisle.

Ruby balanced on her tiptoes and grunted while attempting to grab the bottle. "Can you reach it?"

"I'll get it." Kira chose a bottle of apple juice and then found the cranberry juice before they continued their journey through the store.

Liesel hummed and Kira crossed more items off her list, adding milk, cheese, eggs, butter, cream cheese, and yogurt to her cart. By the time they reached the frozen food aisle, Liesel's humming had transformed into wails as she twisted in the seat and her little face turned red.

"Shh, *mei liewe*," Kira cooed, doing her best to ignore the looks from fellow shoppers. "We're almost done."

"No. Go home. Now." Liesel shook her doll over her head.

Ruby touched her little sister's arm. "Let's sing. *Jesus loves me, this I know . . .*"

"No!" Liesel shook her head. "No sing!"

Kira squared her shoulders. She needed to finish her shopping and get her little cousin home before she had a full-on temper tantrum in the middle of the grocery store. Her aunt had warned her not to take Liesel out shopping so close to her nap time, but Kira had been determined to help her aunt by offering to leave only Mimi, the eighteen-month-old, at home with the newborn.

But as Liesel's whines transformed to sobs, Kira knew her aunt had been right, and she should have left Liesel home. She needed to finish this shopping trip as soon as possible.

After examining the list, Kira pushed the cart over to the shelves of meat and then turned to Ruby. "You stay here with your *schweschder* while I get what your *mamm* needs," she instructed, speaking over the three-year-old's whimpers.

"Okay."

Kira found ground chuck, pork chops, and steak and dropped them into the cart, where Liesel continued to whimper. Kira examined a package of ground turkey and then stilled when she realized Liesel had stopped crying.

She spun and found the blond Amish man who had smiled at her earlier standing by the cart and holding Liesel's doll out to her. His grocery cart contained a few bags of chips and a pack of paper towels, along with the large pack of water she'd seen him lift in earlier.

Kira hurried over to the cart, where the man spoke softly to Liesel, and Ruby smiled up at him.

"What's your doll's name?" he asked her.

Liesel wiped her eyes and sniffed. "Baby."

"Baby." The man looked at the doll. "What a nice name. Hi, Baby. I'm Jayden." When he turned to meet Kira's gaze, he flashed that warm smile. "She'd thrown her doll. I thought I'd hand it to her and try to calm her down."

Kira smiled. "*Danki.* You seem to be a natural with *kinner.*"

"Not really." His expression became sheepish. "I just like to play with my *bruderskinner* and baby *schweschder.*"

Ruby stood up taller and patted her chest. "I'm Ruby, and I'm the big *schweschder.*"

"Is that right?" Jayden grinned. "I bet you're a helpful big *schweschder.*"

Then Ruby pointed to Kira. "She's Kira, my cousin."

"There you are, Jay. I thought you ran off on me." A tall man with dark-brown hair and a matching beard sidled up to Jayden. His bright hazel eyes resembled Jayden's. Perhaps he was a relative? Maybe a brother? The man with the beard grinned at Ruby and Liesel. "Who do we have here?"

Ruby stepped forward. "I'm Ruby. This is *mei schweschder* Liesel and my cousin Kira."

"So nice to meet you." His eyes seemed to light with amusement. "I'm Tyler, and this is *mei bruder* Jayden." Then he turned to Jayden. "We need to head out. We're going to be late for that job."

Jayden nodded. "I know." He glanced over at Kira. "Have a *gut* day."

"You too," Kira told him before he and his brother walked toward the front of the store.

She quickly chose a package of ground turkey, along with two packages of lunch meat, before pushing the cart toward the cashiers. She sighed when she found a long line at each of the three open registers.

Liesel hugged her doll and stuck her lip out, and Kira touched her curls. "Just hold on, little one. I promise we'll be home soon."

"Look!" Ruby announced, pointing to Jayden and Tyler. "Our *freinden* are in that line! Let's go there." Then she rested her hand on the front of the grocery cart and steered it toward their line. "Hi, Jayden! Hi, Tyler!"

Jayden turned and grinned at her. "Hi, Ruby."

Tyler waved.

"Are you going to work?" Ruby asked Jayden.

Kira shook her head. "Ruby," she began, her voice holding a hint of a warning, "don't be nosy."

"It's okay." Jayden laughed as he bent down to Ruby's level. "*Ya*, we're heading to work. Our large water cooler has a crack in it, and water leaked all over the bed of our driver's truck."

Ruby gasped. "Uh-oh!"

"*Ya*, that's right. It was a mess too."

Tyler leaned forward on their grocery cart and pointed to the paper towels. "And Jay expects me to clean it all up too."

Ruby chortled.

Jayden's handsome smile brightened even more as he focused those glorious hazel eyes on Kira. She was certain she mirrored his amusement.

The middle-aged *Englisher* woman in front of them paid for her groceries, and Tyler began loading the conveyor belt with their items.

"Are you going to eat all of those chips today?" Ruby asked.

Jayden chuckled. "I'm sure we'll have some of them during lunch, but we'll take the rest home. Do you like chips?"

"*Ya.*" Ruby nodded with emphasis. "*Mei dat* loves chips. *Mei mamm* and *schweschdere* do too." She faced Kira. "Do you like chips, Kira?"

"Doesn't everyone?" Kira asked, and they all chuckled. She was struck by Jayden's easy rapport with Ruby. She wasn't sure she'd ever met a young man who communicated so well with children. It was . . . charming.

After loading their items on the conveyor, Jayden and Tyler turned their attention to the cashier, a young *Englisher* woman with blond hair and bright blue eye shadow. Tyler pulled his wallet from the back pocket of his trousers.

The woman rang up their items and moved the conveyor down, and Kira and Ruby began loading their groceries onto the belt.

Jayden turned toward them. "Do you need help?" He picked up the meat and added it to the conveyor.

"No, it's okay." Kira shook her head, and she felt her cheeks heat. "But *danki.*"

"All right." His eyes seemed to linger on hers and then he nodded and faced his brother once again.

Tyler paid for their supplies and pushed the receipt into his pocket before nodding at the cashier and then looking over at Kira. "Bye now."

"Bye!" Ruby waved vigorously. "Bye, Jayden!"

Kira smiled as she continued to take her groceries out of the cart.

Jayden graced each of them with a smile. "It was nice meeting you."

And as he walked away from them, Kira felt a strange spark of disappointment that she'd most likely never see him again.

———— ❧ ————

Tyler ripped open the package of paper towels while Jayden hopped up into the bed of their driver's gold Dodge pickup where the water had spilled out of the cooler that they kept at their roofing job sites.

"Well, this was an unusual start to our Thursday." Tyler pulled off a handful of paper towels and held them up to Jayden.

"At least we got an early start this morning." Jayden pushed their toolboxes and boxes of supplies back and stared down at the river of water running toward the tailgate. He had noticed the water gushing out of the cooler when they had stopped at the hardware store for nails on their way to their job site that morning.

He took the paper towels and started mopping up the mess. It was a beautiful morning with a bright blue sky, and the warm early-September sun beat down on his straw hat and back as he worked.

Jack Damon, Tyler's driver, climbed out of the driver's seat. "You really don't need to worry about cleaning it up, Ty. I can take care of it later."

"We don't mind," Jayden insisted.

Jack tapped the side of the bed. "It's water, Jayden. It will dry on its own."

Jayden gestured toward their supplies. "I don't want our boxes to get ruined either."

"True." Jack drummed his fingers on the bed. "Thanks."

Tyler went to work wiping down the tailgate. "That little girl in the store was adorable." He grinned. "And she seemed to really like you."

"*Ya.*" Jayden peeked toward the store in search of Ruby, but secretly hoped to get another glimpse of her cousin, Kira. Ruby was cute and funny, but if he was honest with himself, he'd been mesmerized by Kira the moment he'd seen her walking down the aisle pushing the grocery cart.

With her dark-chocolate-colored eyes, high cheekbones, long neck, ivory skin, and dark-brown hair peeking out from under her prayer covering, Kira was a natural beauty. And when she had smiled at him, her face and eyes lit up, making her even more attractive.

At first he'd assumed she was a young mother, and he definitely assumed her husband had fallen in love with her the moment he'd seen her. Both little girls had her similar coloring with their dark hair and eyes, and he was almost certain they were her children. But when Ruby explained that she was their cousin, it all made sense, especially once he noticed the shape of her prayer covering, which indicated she was from a western Amish community—possibly Ohio or even Indiana. The prayer coverings in Lancaster County were heart-shaped, and hers was round. He wondered if she was visiting or if she planned on staying in Pennsylvania for a while.

But that was something he'd never know. They'd met in a grocery store and would most likely not see each other ever again.

"Jay?" Tyler's question broke through his thoughts. "Hello? Did you hear me?"

Jayden's eyes snapped to his brother's curious stare. "I'm sorry. What did you say?"

"Are you all right?" Tyler leaned toward him. "You seemed lost in thought."

Jayden balled up the damp paper towels and snuck another

peek toward the front of the store before focusing on his oldest brother again. "What were you saying?"

"We need to get going. We have to finish this job so we can start on that strip mall in Paradise by Saturday."

"I know." Jayden jumped down from the truck and dropped the damp paper towels into a nearby trash can while Tyler closed the tailgate.

Jayden had worked on his oldest brother's roofing crew for nearly five years now while his middle brother, Korey, had run his own crew for more than two years. The three of them were grateful that their father had expanded his company, Bontrager and Sons Roofing, allowing Tyler and Korey to run their own crews. Although Tyler ran a tight ship, constantly reminding Jayden and their other two crew members how important it was to stick to the schedule, Jayden enjoyed working for him, but deep down he wasn't sure roofing was his calling. He felt the urge to learn another trade. If only he could figure out what that might be.

While Jack returned to the driver's seat, Tyler jogged around the front of the truck. Jayden spun toward the store once more, hoping to get one last glimpse of Kira and her cousins, but she was nowhere in sight. He imagined her still waiting to pay for her groceries.

"Jay!" Tyler hollered from the front seat. "Let's go!"

Sighing, Jayden trotted toward the back seat and climbed in beside the large pack of water and the grocery bag of chips.

As Jayden buckled his seat belt, he grinned and imagined Ruby enjoying chips with her parents, sisters, and cousin. He would relish a chance to share a bag of chips and another fun conversation with them.

CHAPTER 2

"I THINK I GOT EVERYTHING ON THE LIST," KIRA SAID AS SHE SET the box of Cheerios in the pantry. She was grateful her uncle's driver had helped her load the groceries into the back of her minivan since Liesel had started crying again as soon as she'd finished paying for the groceries with the stack of cash her aunt had given her.

While Kira and Ruby carried in the groceries, her aunt had taken Liesel upstairs to tuck her in her crib for a nap, which was what the toddler had desperately needed.

"I'm sorry if I missed anything, but Liesel was a bit cranky in the store," Kira added.

Her aunt gave her a knowing glance as she slipped the meat into the freezer. With dark-brown hair and eyes, *Aenti* Ellen always reminded Kira of a younger version of her mother. Kira had often been told that she resembled her mother, and she imagined she also favored her aunt. "I told you that you should have only taken Ruby with you. She's a *gut* helper."

"*Ya*, I am." Ruby beamed and carried the lunch meat over to the refrigerator, while Kira brought over the bottles of juice.

"Ruby was a very helpful big *schweschder* when Liesel started crying," Kira said.

"I tried to calm her."

"*Danki*, Ruby." *Aenti* Ellen touched Ruby's head. "Why don't you go play while Kira and I finish putting away the groceries?"

Ruby trotted toward the family room. "Okay!"

"Not so loud, *mei liewe*," *Aenti* Ellen cooed. "Your *bruder* and *schweschdere* are sleeping."

"Sorry!"

Aenti Ellen chuckled and shook her head, causing the ties on her prayer covering to fan over her slight shoulders. "How I long to have her endless energy."

"*Ya*, I know." Kira set the eggs in the refrigerator and then the cheese and butter.

"Did Liesel have a tantrum in the store?"

"She cried, but an Amish man actually helped calm her down."

"Oh *ya*?" *Aenti* Ellen handed Kira the bag of yogurts. "How?"

"I was looking at the meat and asked Ruby to help me console her. When I realized Liesel had stopped crying, I turned and found an Amish man talking to her about her doll. He knew just what to say to get her to stop. He seemed to have a way with *kinner*."

Aenti Ellen grinned. "Was he single?"

"How should I know?"

Her aunt gave her a look of disbelief. "Well, did he have a beard?"

"No, he didn't, but the man who was with him did. They were *bruders*."

"So, he was single."

Kira's cheeks felt warm as she shrugged. She stacked the yogurts beside the milk to avoid her aunt's curious expression. She couldn't bring herself to admit out loud that Jayden was attractive, and she'd found him charming. After all, they'd met in a grocery store and would probably never see each other again. "Not necessarily. He could have a girlfriend, but we didn't get that personal. We wound up standing in line at the cashier behind him and his brother, and Ruby talked their ears off. They both seemed to get a kick out of her. They were very friendly."

"Is that right?" Her aunt's pretty smile was wide. "It's a shame you didn't get more personal."

Kira ignored her aunt's comment. She hadn't come to Pennsylvania in search of a new boyfriend. As far as her heart was concerned, she wouldn't be ready to date again for a very long time. Philip had shattered her when he ended their engagement.

They had dated for a year, and when he proposed, they had planned for a future and hopefully a family together. Everything seemed perfect, but then he ended it, saying he wasn't ready to get married, wasn't ready for a family. Now she wasn't ready to open her heart again.

Besides, her family and her home were in Indiana, not here. It didn't make sense to start a relationship with a man whose life was in Pennsylvania.

"Since I found some *gut* meat prices, I was thinking I could make spaghetti and meatballs one night and meat loaf another night. I copied down a few of *mei mamm*'s recipes and brought them with me. She mentioned that she had her *mamm*'s favorite cookbook, and you liked some of the recipes in it."

Her aunt gave her a funny look.

"Why are you looking at me like that, *Aenti* Ellen?"

"Kira, I don't expect you to work the entire time you're here."

"But I came here to help you."

"You also need to have fun and be with young people your age." Her smile returned. "Maybe you'll meet someone special."

Kira frowned. "I'm not ready to risk my heart again."

"I know, sweetie, but you can't let what Philip did to you stop you from believing in love."

Kira's stomach churned at the mention of her ex-fiancé's name. "I appreciate your concern for me, but it's a little too soon for me to think about dating."

"I understand, but I want you to make *freinden* at church and go to youth group. You can't hide in my *haus* the entire time you're here, Kira. You're twenty-five. You need to be with *freinden* your age."

Kira pointed to the groceries. "Right now, I'd better get these put away."

Ignoring her aunt's sigh, she turned her attention to the remaining bags lining the kitchen counter and tried her best to evict thoughts of Philip and his betrayal from her mind.

Jayden jumped from the back seat of Jack Damon's Dodge later that evening. He yawned and stretched, certain that every muscle in his back ached after the long day he'd spent roofing an Amish farmhouse in New Holland.

Tyler plodded over and patted him on his back. "We made *gut* progress today. We'll finish up the barn tomorrow and be ready to start the big job over in Paradise Saturday."

"*Ya*, sounds good." Jayden grabbed his lunch cooler while Tyler and Jack began discussing their upcoming schedule.

When Jayden heard the storm door click shut on his father's house, he looked up just as *Dat* and Korey stepped out onto the porch, both smiling as Korey talked. The three Bontrager sons had inherited their father's height, but Jayden had often heard folks say that Korey most favored their father with his dark hair and eyes. Although *Dat*'s eyes and mouth were now lined with wrinkles, and his dark hair and beard were flecked with gray, Jayden could still spot the resemblance.

"Hey, Jay!" Korey jogged down the porch steps and over to him.

Jayden nodded. "Kore."

Korey continued to where Tyler stood with Jack and joined their conversation. Korey and Tyler traded a high five and soon they were swapping work stories and chuckling.

Jayden smiled as he joined his father on the porch. His two older brothers, who were twenty-seven and twenty-eight, were only sixteen months apart in age and used to always be at odds. Their constant bickering transformed into much deeper issues more than four years ago when Tyler fell in love with and eventually married Korey's ex-girlfriend, Michelle. Their rift drove Korey to Ohio, where he stayed for fourteen months.

Jayden was relieved that Korey had returned to Bird-in-Hand a changed man, and he not only worked out his issues with Tyler, but he also fell in love with Savannah.

And now Tyler and Korey were both married fathers and lived next door to each other on their father's land. They were brothers and the best of friends, and Jayden was grateful. He couldn't imagine his life without his brothers in it.

"It's so *gut* to see them laughing together." His father's smile was wide.

Jayden set his lunch cooler on a rocking chair. "I was just thinking the same thing."

"We'll see you tomorrow," Tyler told Jack before his driver returned to the driver's seat and started the truck.

Tyler and Korey started toward the path leading to their houses while the chattering diesel Dodge backed down the gravel driveway.

"Hey, *Dat*!" Tyler waved.

Dat called him over. "Hold on, you two. I have a quick question."

Jayden's two older brothers joined them on the porch.

"What's up, *Dat*?" Korey asked, rubbing his dark-brown beard.

Dat leaned on the porch railing behind him. "I forgot to mention earlier that I got a call from someone who needs an estimate. It's a *gut* size job. He wants his *haus*, barn, and business roofed."

"What kind of business?" Jayden asked.

"He builds sheds, and the business is located right on his property. He's over in Gordonville, close to Crystal's *bruder*'s farm." *Dat*'s gaze bounced between Tyler and Korey. "Any chance one of you could work in an estimate either tomorrow or Saturday? I really don't want to lose this job."

Tyler turned to Korey. "You're booked, right?"

"*Ya*, I am. We're working at an apartment complex, and I won't be done until the middle of next week. I could do the estimate, but I don't know when I could get to the job."

Tyler set his lunch cooler on the porch railing. "I can take care of the estimate on Saturday and start the job next week."

"Perfect," *Dat* said. "I'll call him back and let him know that you'll be there Saturday."

"We can handle the estimate in the morning on our way to the job site," Jayden added.

Tyler nodded. "*Gut* idea." Then he touched his flat abdomen.

"Well, I don't know about the rest of you, but I'm famished." He grinned. "And Michelle is back on her baking kick again. She's been making *kichlin* every day. I can't wait to see what she has for me today."

"Is that right?" Korey laughed. "She always spoils you with *kichlin* when she's expecting."

"That's the truth." Tyler picked up his cooler and then turned to Jayden and *Dat*. "*Gut nacht*."

Korey waved before following Tyler down the steps and toward the path leading to their houses. They walked side by side, talking and chuckling on their way home to their families. Jayden licked his lips and wondered if he'd ever have what his older brothers had built—a home and a family. He wasn't jealous of them, but sometimes he felt left out when they discussed shared experiences as husbands and fathers.

"I never get tired of seeing those two getting along." *Dat* looped his arm around Jayden's shoulder. "Hopefully soon you'll build a *haus* here and start a family."

Jayden snorted. "I don't think so. I'm only twenty-three."

Dat scoffed. "You never know what God has in store for you."

"I'm not in a hurry." Jayden shook his head. He dreamed of finding a loving relationship like his parents had enjoyed, and he would hold off as long as it took him to find it. He often recalled his parents chuckling in the kitchen and stealing kisses when they thought Jayden and his brothers weren't around. He could still hear his mother laughing while his father teased her. And Jayden hoped he could find a love like that someday too.

"Let's go eat some of Crystal's *appeditlich* stew." *Dat* steered Jayden toward the house.

Although Jayden would always miss his mother, who had

passed away nearly six years ago after a battle with cancer, he was happy his father had fallen in love and married Crystal four years ago. Crystal had been a blessing to not only his father but also to Jayden and his brothers. They were all thankful for the joy and love she had brought to their lives.

Jayden smiled. "Her stew is the best." He was grateful for his family.

Saturday morning Jack Damon nosed his large pickup truck into a space at the back of the parking lot in front of the Gordon-ville Sheds store. Jayden and Tyler climbed out of the truck and started across the parking lot. The early-September sun warmed Jayden's back as it shone in the bright blue sky. Birds sang in nearby trees while Jayden took in the line of sheds on display beside the building.

Tyler pushed open the door, and a bell rang, announcing their arrival. The smell of wood and stain swamped Jayden's nostrils as he followed Tyler into the front of the store, where they entered a small room containing a desk, a few chairs, and a long counter. Behind the counter a doorway led into the large work area, where hammers banged and loud voices spoke in Pennsylvania Dutch.

A young Amish man who looked to be in his early twenties came from the work area and met them at the counter. "*Gude mariye*. How may I help you?"

"Hi. I'm Tyler Bontrager, and this is *mei bruder* Jayden. We're here to talk to Stan Lapp about an estimate for his roof."

"I'll go get him."

"*Danki.*" Tyler leaned on the counter while the young man slipped back through the doorway.

A few moments later, an Amish man who looked to be in his mid- to late thirties came through the door. With dark hair and eyes, he was a few inches shorter than Tyler and Jayden and had a wide smile. "*Gude mariye.* I'm Stan Lapp." He held his hand out to Tyler. "You must be Tyler."

"I am, and this is *mei bruder* Jayden." Tyler motioned toward Jayden, who also shook Stan's hand.

"I've heard *gut* things about you from *mei fraa.* We used to go to church with your stepmom before she married your *dat* and moved to Bird-in-Hand," Stan said. "I appreciate you coming out today for an estimate. I've needed to get my barn roofed since that bad storm we had over the summer. The *haus* and the shop lost some shingles as well, so I'd like to get them done. I should have called you a while ago, but *mei fraa* just had our fourth *kind* last month." He chuckled. "Well, it's been busy."

Tyler held his hands up. "I understand. *Mei fraa* is expecting our second."

"Congratulations. *Kinner* are a wonderful gift from God." Stan rubbed his hands together. "Now that my niece is here helping us out, I feel like I can get a better handle on what needs to be done around here."

"We appreciate that you called us. We'll take care of the estimate and then come back in and talk to you."

"Perfect. *Mei fraa* is expecting you. Just knock on the back door and let her know that you're there."

"We'll be back soon," Tyler told Stan.

Jayden and Tyler returned to Jack's truck, and Jack drove down the winding gravel driveway that led to a two-story brick home with a small front porch. A large red barn sat beside it in front of a small pasture, where two horses basked in the bright morning sun. An elaborate wooden swing set complete with two swings, a fort, and a slide was located beside the porch.

Jack parked by the porch, and Jayden met Tyler beside the bed of the truck.

Tyler moved to the tailgate and dropped it open. "I'll pull out our supplies, and you can knock on the back door and let Stan's *fraa* know we're here."

"All right." Jayden jogged up the back steps and knocked on the door before rocking back on his heels and looking out toward the barn.

The door opened with a squeak, and Ruby, the little girl from the grocery store, grinned up at him.

Jayden huffed out a breath in surprise. "Ruby, right?"

"*Ya*, and you're Jayden," she announced.

Jayden's foolish heart betrayed him and actually skipped a beat as the pieces came together in his mind. If Ruby lived in this house, then Kira was there too. And that meant that Kira was Stan's niece.

He smiled. The Lord worked in mysterious ways.

Ruby turned and hollered, "Kira! Kira!" at what sounded like full volume.

A loud shushing sounded before Kira walked over holding a toddler in her arms. The little girl resembled Liesel, the fussy toddler who had sat in the grocery cart seat on Thursday, only younger. The sisters shared similar dark curls, button noses, and round faces.

Jayden took in Kira, looking beautiful in a red dress that complemented her dark eyes and hair. Her gorgeous face seemed to register the same surprise he felt. He opened his mouth to greet her, but he fell mute.

"Hi," she said, adjusting the toddler in her arms. "Didn't I meet you at the grocery store on Thursday?"

Jayden cleared his throat, hoping to find his voice. "*Y-ya.*"

"You're Jayden, right?"

She remembered his name! His heart did a silly little dance.

"*Ya*, and you're Kira. I didn't think I'd see you again." Jayden swallowed a groan as heat crawled up his neck. Why was he acting like a complete *dummkopp* in front of this *maedel*?

To his surprise, she graced him with a dazzling smile. "What are the chances? This is my *aenti's haus*. I'm visiting from Indiana and helping her with her *kinner*."

"I can tell you're not from here by your prayer *kapp*."

They stared at each other for a moment as an awkward silence filled the space between them.

Then Kira raised a dark eyebrow. "What brings you out here today?"

"Right, right." Jayden hoped she couldn't see the flush filling his cheeks. "*Mei bruder* and I are here to give your *onkel* an estimate to roof his house, barn, and store."

She craned her neck to glance past him. "So, you're the roofers. Apparently *mei aenti* is *freinden* with your *mamm*."

"*Ya*, my stepmother, Crystal."

"Oh, right. I'm sorry."

"It's okay."

She shifted the toddler in her arms, and the little girl whimpered before snuggling against her shoulder.

"Who's this little one?"

"Mimi." Kira angled her body so that the toddler faced Jayden.

21

"It's nice to meet you, Mimi."

The toddler sniffled and then turned to face Kira's neck.

Kira shook her head. "I'm sorry. She's not in the best mood this morning."

Jayden chuckled. "It's okay. My baby *schweschder*, Kristena, gets like that when it's nap time."

"*Ya*. She refused to go in for her nap, so I'm carrying her around until she falls asleep." Then she pointed her chin toward the kitchen behind her. "Would you like some *kaffi*? I just made a fresh pot."

"Oh, no *danki*. I don't want to impose."

"You're not imposing." Her smile was so pretty that for a moment he couldn't take his eyes off her.

"Jay?" Tyler suddenly shouted, breaking through Jayden's thoughts. "Is everything all right?"

Jayden took a step back and swiveled to face where Tyler had leaned their tallest ladder against the side of the house. He'd been so focused on Kira that he hadn't heard the rattle of the aluminum ladder when his brother had hoisted it from the truck rack.

"I'll be right there," he called to his older brother. Then he turned back to Kira. "I'd better get to work."

"Okay."

As Jayden hurried down the porch steps, he hoped Kira didn't think he was as awkward as he felt.

CHAPTER 3

JAYDEN TRIED HIS BEST TO CONCENTRATE WHILE HE HELPED Tyler measure the roof on the house and then the barn, but his mind kept replaying his awkward conversation with Kira. He'd never felt so tongue-tied around a pretty young woman before. Jayden wasn't a shy man, and he'd never had any trouble making friends. In fact, he always felt comfortable around people, even strangers. But when he was with Kira, he'd nearly forgotten how to speak. What was wrong with him?

He tried his best to put the conversation out of his mind as he followed his older brother down the tall ladder to the ground, where he closed the ladder and hoisted it onto his shoulder. Tyler picked up the front of the ladder, and they started toward the waiting pickup truck.

Tyler craned his neck over his shoulder. "*Was iss letz?*"

"Nothing. Why?"

Tyler studied him. "You're unusually quiet."

"I just don't have anything to say right now."

"Huh." Tyler looked unconvinced.

Jayden worked to keep his expression blank. He had no intentions of sharing his befuddled emotions with his older brother.

After this job, he probably wouldn't see Kira again. Besides, she was visiting from Indiana and would likely return to her hometown when her aunt no longer needed her help. For all Jayden knew, Kira had a boyfriend waiting at home for her, anyway.

When they reached the truck, Tyler hopped up into the bed and Jayden lifted the ladder as Tyler loaded it onto the rack.

The storm door creaked open, and Kira appeared on the porch carrying two Styrofoam cups. She navigated the stairs and then met them at the back of the truck. "I brought you each a cup of *kaffi*."

"*Danki*," Jayden told her as she handed him the cup.

Tyler sat down on the tailgate and held his hand out. "That's very kind of you."

"I assumed you'd like cream and sugar." Kira approached the side of the truck. "Would you like a cup too?" she asked their driver.

Jack nodded and then Kira turned back to Jayden. "I'm going to get one for your driver. Give me a minute." Then she dashed back into the house.

"*Gut kaffi*," Tyler said and then grinned at Jayden. "She's the *maedel* from the grocery store. What are the chances that we'd run into her again?"

Jayden sipped the coffee, careful to avoid his brother's knowing look. Surely Tyler sensed that Jayden had a crush on Kira, and he couldn't allow his brother to embarrass him in public—especially in front of Kira. "The *kaffi* is *gut*."

Kira returned with another cup and delivered it to their driver before joining Jayden and Tyler at the tailgate. "So, you're *bruders* and you run a roofing crew together."

Tyler nodded. "*Ya*, we are. I'm the oldest, and he's the baby *bruder*." Smirking, he reached out and patted Jayden's shoulder.

Jayden sighed, but Kira's laughter made him smile.

"And your stepmother is *gut freinden* with *mei aenti*," she said. "Apparently your stepmother used to attend church with *mei aenti* and *onkel*."

Tyler snapped his fingers. "That's right. I talked to *Dat* before we left for work this morning, and he said that Stan's *fraa* was *freinden* with Crystal."

Kira's dark eyes focused on Jayden's, and he felt tongue-tied once again. "Since *Aenti* Ellen and Crystal know each other, maybe I'll see you again."

Jayden cleared his throat in an attempt to rein in his frayed nerves. "That would be nice. *Danki* for the *kaffi*."

"*Gern gschehne.*"

"We'd better finish up this estimate and then get to our worksite." Tyler hopped down from the tailgate. "The *kaffi* is fantastic."

Kira's beautiful eyes met Jayden's once again. "I'm glad you like it. Have a *gut* day."

"You too," Jayden managed to say before he and Tyler returned to their seats in the truck to drive back to Kira's uncle's store.

Tyler swiveled around to peer at Jayden in the back seat. "So, you like Kira, huh?" His grin was wide.

"I didn't say that."

Tyler chuckled. "You didn't have to, Jay. It's obvious."

Jayden sighed and pinched the bridge of his nose.

After measuring the roof of the cinderblock building, Jayden and Tyler stowed the ladder and their supplies before Tyler completed his calculations and wrote up an estimate for Stan. Then they entered the store, and Tyler gave Stan the paperwork.

"This looks fair," Stan said while examining the document. "When can you start?"

"How does Wednesday sound?" Tyler asked.

"Perfect."

Stan held his hand out, and Tyler shook it.

"We'll see you Wednesday." Jayden also shook Stan's hand before he and Tyler headed back out to the truck.

"This will be a *gut* job," Tyler said as Jack steered the truck out of the parking lot and onto the highway. Then Tyler angled his body to face Jayden in the back seat. "How ironic that we ran into Kira again."

"*Ya*, definitely ironic." Jayden rubbed his hand over his clean-shaven jaw. Why did he have such a tough time talking to this *maedel*?

Tyler tilted his head. "You should tell her that you like her. You never know what the Lord has planned for you."

"I just met her, Ty. I think I need to get to know her before rushing into anything." Jayden drummed his fingers on his thigh and turned his attention toward the passing traffic. His heart lifted at the idea of talking to Kira again. Perhaps she would give him another cup of coffee on Wednesday, and he could find out more about her life in Indiana.

Kira stood on the porch and faced her uncle's store, where she spotted Jayden and Tyler measuring the roof. She folded her arms over her waist and considered how soft-spoken and humble Jayden appeared.

He seemed to be the complete opposite of Philip, who was larger than life, the loudest voice in their youth group, always trying to outdo anyone else's story.

But it wasn't fair of her to compare Jayden to her ex-fiancé.

Yet there was something intriguing about Jayden. Perhaps it was those bright hazel eyes. Or that smile. Or maybe it was his strong, chiseled jaw and those broad shoulders.

Not that she was even looking for a relationship.

The back door opened with a squeak, and *Aenti* Ellen appeared at her side. "I finally got Austin down for a nap, and Mimi and Liesel went in without any fussing too. Ruby said someone was here. I guess it was the roofers?"

"*Ya*, it was Jayden and Tyler."

"Crystal's stepsons." *Aenti* Ellen's smile was bright. "I don't see Crystal often anymore, but when I do, it's as if no time has passed."

Kira leaned back against the railing and faced her aunt. "What happened to their *mamm*?"

"*Ach*, so *bedauerlich*. She had cancer." *Aenti* Ellen shook her head and frowned.

Kira's heart clenched as she thought of Jayden and his siblings losing their mother. She couldn't imagine her sisters and herself facing life without their sweet mother. "I'm so sorry to hear that."

"*Ya*, I know. I think she passed away about two years before Crystal and Duane met."

"How did they meet?"

Aenti Ellen smiled. "Duane and his *sohns* fixed the roofs at Crystal's *bruder*'s farm. She lived with her *bruder* and his family before she married Duane. She shared that their relationship was complicated since his *sohns* weren't all supportive when they started dating. It was tough for them to see him find love again. At least, she said that two of his *sohns* struggled."

"Is that right?" Kira tried to put herself in Jayden's shoes and imagine one of her parents remarrying. The concept seemed too foreign. Had Jayden struggled with his father's relationship with Crystal?

"*Ya*, she shared that Tyler and Korey took a while to accept her."

"But Jayden didn't struggle?" Kira's mind latched on to that detail.

"No, I don't believe he did." *Aenti* Ellen shook her head. "Jayden was supportive from the beginning, but it was Korey who struggled the most. Duane was upset and wanted to confront Korey, but Crystal told Duane to just keep praying for Korey to soften his heart toward her. Eventually, he did accept her, and they have a very close relationship now."

Kira stared at her aunt. Jayden had accepted his father's relationship with Crystal sooner than his older brothers had. This fascinated her.

"Crystal and Duane overcame many obstacles. The Lord helped them find a way to make it work, and they are very *froh*. In fact, they have a two-year-old *dochder* together now."

"I'm so *froh* to hear that."

Aenti Ellen touched Kira's shoulder. "You'll have to meet Crystal sometime. You'd really like her."

Kira nodded. "That sounds fun."

"Well, I'd better get to my chores. Nap time never seems to last long enough."

As Kira followed her aunt into the house, she turned her attention to her chores too. But in the back of her mind, she continued to wonder about Jayden.

⸺⁓❦⁓⸺

Kira carried a coffee carafe into the Fisher family's barn Sunday afternoon. The barn was warm, and the aroma of animals, hay, and coffee permeated the air as she approached the line of tables where the men in her aunt's congregation had gathered to enjoy lunch after the service.

"*Kaffi?*" she asked the men sitting at the first table before she began filling their cups.

Then Kira moved down the line smiling at the men. Her first service in her aunt's church district hadn't been as nerve-racking as she'd imagined. Although she felt awkward sitting in the unmarried women's section among strangers, she appreciated the friendly smiles and nods from the young women surrounding her.

Kira had spent the service thinking of her parents, sisters, and friends in her home district, and she tried to keep her homesickness at bay. She missed sitting in the congregation with her younger sisters, Leah and Maribeth, and when she turned toward the married women's section, she almost expected to see her mother there, smiling at her.

Her homesickness had followed her around all week while she'd completed her chores at her aunt's house. This was the first time she'd ever been away from home. She missed singing with her sisters while they washed the dishes together and hung out laundry. She also missed talking to her older sister, Abigail, who had married and followed in her mother's footsteps to become a midwife. Both Abby and Kira had helped their mother deliver babies before *Mamm* decided to retire. Kira longed to talk to Abby and get caught up on how she was doing.

Kira kept herself busy in order to snuff out some of her yearning for home. When she plunged her heart into prayer, she felt some relief. It was almost like a warm hug from God.

Thank you, Lord.

Once her carafe was empty, Kira crossed the barn and stepped out into the warm afternoon air on her way back to the Fisher family's kitchen, where the women in the congregation were busy gathering the meal. Her aunt and other mothers fed the youngest children.

"Hi. You must be Kira."

Stopping in her tracks, Kira turned as a pretty young woman with gray eyes and light-brown hair stood behind her. She recognized her as one of the women who had smiled at her during the service. "*Ya,* I am."

"I'm Alaina Smoker." She held a coffee carafe in one hand and held out her other hand to Kira. "Your *aenti* has been so excited about your visit. It's nice to meet you."

Kira shook her hand. "*Danki.*"

"Are you going to youth group today?" Alaina seemed hopeful. "You can ride with *mei bruder* and me."

"Oh. I'll have to check with *mei aenti.* She might need my help with the *kinner.*" Kira couldn't imagine going to youth group without her sisters.

Alaina smiled. "Well, I hope you can join us. We're going to play volleyball at the Swarey farm. It will be so fun." She nodded toward the Fisher family's home. "Let's get more *kaffi.*"

Kira smiled as she ambled beside her new friend toward the kitchen.

⚜

Later, Kira picked up Mimi and took Liesel's hand as she walked with her aunt and Ruby toward her uncle's horse and buggy. Austin slept snuggled in *Aenti* Ellen's arms.

"I saw you eating lunch with Alaina Smoker and her *freinden*," *Aenti* Ellen said. "She's a sweet *maedel*."

"*Ya*, she is. And her *freinden* were very welcoming."

Aenti Ellen's smile was wide. "That makes me so *froh*. I wanted you to make some *gut freinden* while you're here."

"There they are," Kira said as *Onkel* Stan came around the back of the buggy, and Liesel squealed as she ran and leapt into his arms. He chuckled and kissed her head. "Hello, *mei liewe*." Then he gave his wife a warm smile. "Are we ready to head home?"

Aenti Ellen nodded. "*Ya*."

Onkel Stan loaded Liesel into the buggy and then took Mimi from Kira's arms.

"Kira!" Alaina called as she rushed over. She nodded a hello to Kira's aunt and uncle and then turned her attention back to Kira. "Are you coming with us to youth group? Nate and I can pick you up on our way."

"Oh." Kira met Alaina's eager expression. "I haven't had a chance to ask." She turned toward her aunt, who had taken a seat in the buggy with Austin on her lap. "Alaina invited me to join her at youth group, but I assumed you needed my help with the *kinner* today." Once again, she was hesitant to go to youth group

31

without her sisters and her friends. Would she fit in with a new youth group? She sucked in a deep breath. Would Pennsylvania ever feel like home without her precious family members?

Onkel Stan scoffed. "Am I invisible, Kira?" Then he grinned. "You need to have some fun."

"That's what I've been trying to tell her," *Aenti* Ellen agreed.

Kira turned toward Alaina. "It looks like I can go with you."

"Yay!" Alaina clapped her hands. "Nate and I will go home and get changed, and then we'll pick you up on our way."

Kira smiled. She was so grateful to have made a friend in her new church district.

CHAPTER 4

JAYDEN JUMPED UP AND SPIKED THE VOLLEYBALL OVER THE net later that afternoon. The ball sailed through the air, and although the members of the opposing team scrambled, it hit the ground.

"Yeah!" his best friend, Ben Ebersole, shouted before sharing a high five with Jayden. "Another game won, buddy." He pushed his hand through his dark-brown hair.

Jayden laughed. He was so grateful when Ben and his family had joined his church district last year. Jayden had felt a little lost when Korey married and stopped coming to youth group, but he and Ben had become fast friends, bonding over their enjoyment of volleyball and their hobby of woodworking.

"How about we take a break and get a drink?" Jayden asked Ben and the other members of their team, Ernest and Atlee.

When the three of them agreed, they shared high fives with the opposing team and then headed over to the snack table. Jayden waved to friends on his way to collect a cup of lemonade.

"Jayden!" Darla Kurtz called as she and her best friend, Lora Esch, hurried over to the table. "I saw you playing out there. That was some game."

Ben patted Jayden's shoulder. "He's a *gut* player."

Darla pushed the ties to her prayer covering off her shoulders, and her blue eyes seemed to shine. With their similar sky-blue eyes, hair the color of sunshine, and petite noses, she and Lora were often mistaken for sisters. "The four of us will have to play a game together. You, me, Lora, and Ben."

"*Ya*, that sounds *gut*." Ben turned to Lora, and they shared a smile.

As Jayden took another sip of lemonade, he suddenly had the feeling that Lora and Ben liked each other. Although the four of them often spent time together during youth gatherings, Jayden had only considered Darla and Lora to be two of his and Ben's many friends. Yet he now had the notion that perhaps Ben and Lora might want to become more than friends. This was an unexpected change, but he was happy for them.

Darla took another step closer to Jayden. "I brought peanut butter *kichlin* for dessert today. Aren't they your favorite?" Her pretty face seemed hopeful as she stared up at him.

"They are."

"Yay!" She clapped. "I'll be sure to save you a few."

"*Danki*." He finished his lemonade and then dropped the cup into the nearby trash can.

"How about we go play volleyball now?" Darla asked.

"*Ya*." Lora pointed to the net. "There's an empty court."

Ben finished his drink and pitched the cup into the trash can. "Let's go."

Lora beamed at him as they started toward the net together.

"Jayden?" Darla asked.

He spun toward her. "*Ya*?"

"Are you ready?"

"Sure." As he walked with her toward the net, he wondered what Kira was doing today. Was she also playing volleyball and talking with friends in her youth group? He hoped she was enjoying her Sunday. A thrill raced through him as he thought about seeing her again on Wednesday.

⌒⌒⌒◦◦○◦○◦◦⌒⌒⌒

Later that evening, Alaina's older brother, Nate, guided his horse down *Aenti* Ellen's gravel driveway toward her two-story brick home. Kira's hand fluttered to her mouth to stifle a yawn. She'd spent all afternoon playing volleyball with Alaina and her friends and then they had sung hymns into the night.

Her arms and legs were heavy with exhaustion, but her heart felt light. Spending the day with her new friends was good for her soul and helped keep her homesickness at bay. Still, thoughts of her sisters and her friends back home lingered in the back of her mind. Were her sisters missing her today too?

"Here we are," Nate announced as he halted the horse. With his light-brown hair and gray eyes, it was easy to see he and Alaina were siblings.

Kira scrambled out of the back of the buggy and then pulled her small flashlight from her pocket and flipped it on as she came around to the path leading to the porch. "*Danki* for the ride," she told Nate, and he nodded.

Alaina climbed out of the passenger seat and nearly knocked Kira off-balance as she pulled her in for a tight hug. "I'm so glad you joined us."

"I had fun."

"See you next week," Alaina told her before joining her brother in his buggy.

Kira waved and then started up the porch steps, the soft yellow beam from her flashlight guiding her way. When she spotted a light glowing in the kitchen, curiosity nipped at her. Since it was after ten in the evening, she hadn't imagined her aunt or uncle would wait up for her, especially since Austin woke them so early every morning.

After leaving her shoes in the mudroom, she stepped into the kitchen, where *Onkel* Stan sat at the table flipping through a tool catalog.

He peered up at her. "How was it?"

"*Gut.*" She sank down onto a chair across from him. "I thought you'd be asleep by now."

"Ellen and I wanted to make sure you made it home safely. She'd hoped to stay up for you, but she was too exhausted since she had a rough night with Austin last night."

Guilt weighed heavily on her back, and she pressed her lips into a flat line as she imagined her exhausted aunt trying to get through the day on so little sleep. She had come to Pennsylvania to help her aunt, not make friends. "I'm sorry. I should have been here to help with the *kinner.*"

"No, Kira. You were where you were supposed to be. You need to enjoy being young, and you deserve a break. Ellen tells me how hard you work around here all week, taking care of the *kinner* and doing more than your share of chores." He closed the catalog. "Now tell me. Did you make some *freinden*?"

"*Ya*, I did. Alaina is very sweet, and her *freinden* were funny. We had a lot of laughs while we played volleyball."

Kira ran her fingers over the tabletop and thought about

her younger sisters, Leah and Maribeth, once again. She missed laughing with them at youth gatherings, but if she'd stayed in Shipshewana, then she would have had to face Philip at their youth gatherings and possibly watch him flirt with other young women. The mental image caused her stomach to tie itself into a tight knot.

Onkel Stan tilted his head. "*Was iss letz?*"

"Nothing is wrong." She waved off her inner turmoil. "I'm looking forward to seeing Alaina next Sunday."

He shielded a yawn with his hand. "I'm glad to hear it. Well, we'd better head to bed. I'm sure Austin will ensure we're up before the rooster."

Kira chuckled. "*Gut nacht, Onkel* Stan."

While her uncle retreated to his bedroom on the far end of the first floor, Kira's flashlight guided her up the steep steps to the second floor, where two more bedrooms and a sewing room were located. She tiptoed to the first bedroom, opened the door, and peeked in to where Mimi and Liesel snored softly. Then she closed the door and peered into Ruby's room across the way and took in her soft snores.

Kira stepped into the sewing room at the end of the hallway, across from the bathroom. The large room contained two sewing machines, a desk, a single bed, and a dresser.

Thoughts of her sisters rolled through her mind as she readied for bed. Although her older sister, Abigail, had been married to Victor for three years, she and Kira had remained close. She would have to call her this week to check in and see how she was doing. Not only did she enjoy talking to Abby, but she loved hearing stories about the babies she had delivered in their community. Kira sighed. She missed helping her mother deliver babies, and she hoped to one day have an opportunity to work as a midwife again.

After removing her prayer covering and brushing out her waist-length dark hair, Kira pulled on her nightgown and climbed into the bed, settling under the sheet and quilt. She stared up at the ceiling through the dark and began her nightly prayers, asking God to protect her family. And then she waited for sleep to find her.

⁓⁓⁓

Jayden crouched on the roof of a toy store in Paradise Monday afternoon. He was grateful for the overcast day, which provided some relief from the hot sun. The sound of hammers banging echoed around him while he and his older brother worked together, and Roger and Dennis, the other members of their crew, worked on the far end of the strip mall's roof.

After hammering in another nail, Jayden sat back on his heels, lifted his straw hat, and pushed his hair back from his forehead. He took a sip from his cup of water and then waited for his older brother to stop hammering. "Hey, Ty."

"*Ya?*" Tyler looked up.

"How's Michelle feeling?"

Tyler's expression brightened. "She's ready to have this baby. We only have two more months before we'll be a family of four."

Jayden grinned. He was so proud of his older brothers, who were doting fathers and loving husbands.

"What's that smile for?"

"I'm just *froh* for you and Kore."

"Happy for us?" Tyler asked. "Why?"

"It makes me feel *gut* to know that *mei bruders* are settled."

"And what about you, Jay? Are you happy?"

Jayden ran his fingers over his hammer's wooden handle. "Sure I am."

"Are you dating?"

Jayden shook his head and took another sip of his water.

Tyler seemed to study him. "Why not?"

"I guess I haven't met the right *maedel* yet."

"What about Darla?"

"Darla?" Jayden scoffed. "We're *freinden*."

Tyler gave him a curious expression.

"We are," Jayden insisted. "I've known Darla and Lora since school, and we always got along. We started hanging out more when Ben joined our church district and youth group. I think Lora likes Ben."

"And Darla likes you."

Jayden hesitated. "Why would you say that?"

"It's obvious, Jay. She seems to seek you out at church. Even Michelle mentioned it to me yesterday."

Jayden frowned. "I have noticed that."

"And . . ." Tyler began.

"I don't like her that way."

"I understand. I felt the same way about Charity, but I didn't want to break her heart." Tyler picked up his hammer and a nail. "Don't worry about it. God has the perfect plan for you. You'll meet the right *maedel* when you least expect it." He lifted the hammer. "And what about Kira?"

"She's *schee* and seems sweet, but she's only here temporarily while she's helping out her *aenti* and *onkel*. Besides, I'm not in a rush. I enjoy my job and my *freinden*." *And I want to find a love like* Mamm *and* Dat *had.*

"*Gut*. Now get back to work." Tyler grinned.

"*Ya*, boss," Jayden teased.

Later, Jayden climbed down the ladder to find another box of nails. As he walked past the toy store's front window, he stopped and took in a wooden dollhouse in the center of a display surrounded by dolls, toy trucks, a scooter, a skateboard, and roller skates.

He rubbed his hand down his clean-shaven chin as he examined the dollhouse, taking in its basic shape and simple design. Then he studied the furniture, and an idea struck him. He could try to build dollhouses and furniture for his niece and sister. Although they were only two and a bit too young for the toys, he could start working on them now and have them ready when they were old enough for them.

"Hey, Jay!" Tyler called from atop the roof. "I thought you were grabbing us each a box of nails. Did you get lost?"

"Be right there, Ty." As he headed for the toolbox, Jayden felt a rush of excitement. He began to imagine putting the projects together in the woodworking shop that he shared with his father. He couldn't wait to get started.

Wednesday morning Kira rinsed another breakfast dish and set it on the drying rack. When she heard the clatter of an engine, she looked out the small window above the sink toward the driveway and spotted a gold pickup truck rumbling toward the house.

The truck parked near the porch and Jayden, Tyler, and two other Amish men climbed out. Joy flooded through her, and she silently chastised herself.

The truth was that she'd been looking forward to seeing Jayden again. And as much as she wanted to guard her heart, she still couldn't stop her curiosity about him, especially after learning how he had accepted Crystal into his family before his two older brothers had.

Aenti Ellen appeared, holding Austin on her shoulder. "The roofers are here."

"I see that." Kira set another dish in the drying rack.

Her aunt set the percolator on the stove. "I'll offer them some *kaffi*."

"You have your hands full. I'll make it." Kira started the percolator and then finished the dishes while the percolator hissed to life, and the delicious aroma of coffee wafted over the kitchen.

Onkel Stan hurried into the kitchen. "I'll see you all at lunchtime," he said before touching Mimi, Liesel, and Ruby on their heads as he walked by the table. Then he stopped and kissed *Aenti* Ellen's cheek and smiled down at Austin, who snored softly on her shoulder. "Have a *gut* morning," he called as he disappeared into the mudroom.

Kira returned to the kitchen window just as *Onkel* Stan jogged down the porch steps and shook Tyler's hand.

Tyler nodded while *Onkel* Stan spoke and then gestured around the property. Kira had the impression that Tyler was in charge of the roofing crew as he continued to talk while Jayden and the other two Amish men unloaded supplies from the back of the pickup truck. Jayden was the only member of the roofing crew who didn't have a beard, indicating he was the only bachelor.

"Are the men going to fix our roof today?" Ruby asked as she carried her empty plastic cup to the counter.

41

"They're going to get started today, but I think it will take a few days," *Aenti* Ellen said. Then she touched Kira's shoulder. "I'm going to say good morning to the men and find out how they like their *kaffi*."

Ruby lifted her chin. "I'll come and help."

Kira chuckled as her aunt and little cousin walked out the back door and then greeted Tyler, Jayden, and the other members of the roofing crew. Kira turned her attention to drying and stowing the dishes.

Behind her, Mimi and Liesel began singing and humming as they ate their pieces of toast. She finished the dishes and then retrieved Mimi from her highchair and helped Liesel down from her booster seat before settling them in the family room with their toys.

The back door opened and closed with a bang and Ruby scampered back into the kitchen. "They want sugar and creamer in their *kaffi*," she announced.

"Ruby!" *Aenti* Ellen called from behind her. "Don't run, sweetie. You might fall."

Ruby nodded, and her dark-brown braids bounced up and down. "*Ya, Mamm.* Can I help with the *kaffi*?"

"How about this, Ruby?" Kira bent down and touched Ruby's little nose. "I'll make the *kaffi*, and then we can carry it out while your *mamm* puts Austin in for a nap?"

Ruby clapped her hands. "Okay!"

Kira poured four Styrofoam cups of coffee and added cream and sugar, and then she held two up. "Now, Ruby, if you're going to help me carry these outside, then I need you to walk slowly, okay?"

"*Ya*, I will."

Kira gave her two cups and then picked up the other two before looking over at her aunt. "We'll be right back."

"Take your time," *Aenti* Ellen said.

Kira balanced two cups of coffee in her hands and pushed open the back door. She held the door open with her arm and looked down at Ruby, who gingerly stepped out onto the porch. Kira bit back a smile as Ruby absently stuck her tongue out, looking determined not to spill.

"You're doing a great job," Kira told her little cousin, who beamed up at her.

Ruby scampered to the end of the porch and then turned to where the men were setting up their ladders. "We have *kaffi!*" she cried, holding up her cups.

Kira couldn't stop her grin.

"*Danki!*" Tyler hurried over and took a cup. "*Gude mariye,*" he told Kira.

She smiled as the other two crew members followed, each nodding a greeting.

"Kira, this is Roger and Dennis," Tyler said.

Roger took a cup from Ruby and thanked her, and Kira gave a cup to Dennis.

Jayden gave Kira a warm smile as he came to the porch. "Another fantastic cup of *kaffi.*"

"I'm thrilled you like it," she told him as she handed him the cup.

Jayden took a long draw. "It hits the spot."

"My cousin makes the best *kaffi,*" Ruby said. "*Mei dat* said he secretly likes it better than *mei mamm*'s, but he doesn't want to hurt *mei mamm*'s feelings."

All of the men chuckled, and Kira and Jayden shared a grin. She was struck by how his hazel eyes lit up each time he smiled.

"We'd best get to work." Tyler lifted his cup as if to toast Kira and Ruby. "*Danki* again for the *kaffi.*"

Jayden rolled his eyes while still smiling. "Tyler likes to give orders."

Ruby scrunched her nose. "Is he your boss?"

"*Ya,* I am." Tyler wagged a finger at him. "And don't you forget it, Jay."

Jayden chuckled and took another sip. "I'd better do what my boss says."

"Just let me know if you need a refill," Kira told him. "I'll be inside doing my chores."

He seemed to study her for a moment, and her pulse leapt as her cheeks began to warm. "Have a *gut* morning, Kira."

"You too."

Kira and Ruby returned to the kitchen, and Ruby did a little dance.

"I didn't spill any *kaffi!*" she said.

"I'm so proud of you."

"Jayden and Tyler are nice," Ruby exclaimed before heading into the family room.

Kira lingered by the kitchen window and watched Jayden talk to Tyler before he picked up a hammer. She admired his handsome face and how gentle he seemed.

"*Ya,* they are nice," she whispered.

"Kira?" *Aenti* Ellen asked from behind her. "I'm running low on onesies. Would you mind doing a load of laundry for me?" She held up a basket full of clothes.

She turned to face her aunt. "I'll get right on it." Then she took the basket and started toward the utility room.

CHAPTER 5

JAYDEN SAT AT A PICNIC TABLE AT NOON AND UNWRAPPED HIS turkey sandwich. After a silent prayer, he picked up half and took a bite. The mid-September sun beat down on his shoulders while two squirrels chased each other up a nearby tree and colorful flowers in Ellen's garden danced in the afternoon breeze.

"Junior took his first steps yesterday." Roger beamed as he picked up his cup of water. "I was so grateful that he waited until I got home so I could see it."

Jayden smiled and once again wondered if he'd ever find his true love and start a family. He hoped God would guide him toward that life.

Dennis clapped from across the table. "That's wonderful!"

"*Ya*, it is. I still remember when little Connie took her first steps." Tyler shook his head. "There's nothing like that."

Jayden turned toward the porch, where Kira was hanging laundry on a line that stretched to a tall oak tree. She looked lovely clad in a gray dress and black apron. Her beauty and her tender smile had struck a chord in his heart again today. He'd been grateful that he'd been able to find his words and not stammered like a moron when she'd given him the cup of coffee.

The conversation drifting around him became background noise as he took another bite of sandwich while studying Kira. She lifted a onesie and hung it up before pushing the line out farther. Her motions were graceful as she continued her task. He took in her long neck, flawless ivory skin, and pink lips.

While his brother and coworkers continued discussing their children, he considered how patient Kira was with Ruby, Liesel, and Mimi. She was a natural with children. Kira's calmness seemed to mirror his own. While Jayden's older brothers would argue, he was the one who would calmly not take sides and try to convince them to work it out. It had always seemed like Jayden's duty to smooth over the conflict for their mother's sake. He could almost hear his mother's voice in his mind, begging him to keep the family together.

And for some strange reason, Jayden felt drawn to Kira's tranquility. Could she bring that same calmness into his life that he hoped he brought to his brothers'?

A sudden tornado of questions swirled in his mind as he watched Kira work. He longed to know everything about her and why she had chosen to come to Pennsylvania. And would she consider getting to know him?

"Jay?" Tyler's voice broke through his thoughts. "Are you okay?"

"*Ya.* Of course." Jayden met his brother's curious eyes across the table and worked to keep his own expression blank.

Tyler lifted a dark eyebrow before glancing toward the porch and then back at Jayden. Then curiosity lit his brother's hazel eyes.

Uh-oh. Jayden swallowed a groan. Tyler would tease him later about watching Kira.

"Tyler," Roger began, "are you ready to become a father of two?"

"I sure am." Tyler sat up taller.

Roger and Dennis shared a look and then chuckled.

Dennis picked up a chip. "You have no idea what you're in for."

While his coworkers continued to discuss their children, Jayden turned his focus back to the porch, where Ruby had joined Kira and began handing her clothes from the basket. Ruby spoke animatedly while they worked, and Kira gave her little cousin a warm expression as she spoke.

Soon the clothesline was full of the family's laundry. Then Kira followed Ruby into the house. A few moments later, Kira returned carrying a dollhouse, and Ruby tagged closely behind her holding a small doll. Kira set the dollhouse on a little table and then sank down onto a rocking chair while Ruby sat at the table and played with the toys.

Jayden finished eating his sandwich before enjoying a couple of Crystal's homemade chocolate chip cookies while he continued to watch Kira and Ruby. When Kira suddenly turned toward him, he stilled and held his breath, hoping she hadn't felt him staring. She smiled and waved, and he returned the gestures before huffing out a relieved breath.

"I suppose we need to get back to work." Roger gathered up his paper lunch bag and then climbed from the picnic bench.

Dennis stood. "We can't take too long of a break, or our boss will holler." He grinned at Tyler, who shook his head.

Dennis and Roger dropped their trash in a nearby can and then picked up their hammers and started up the ladder.

Jayden ate the last bite of cookie and then also collected his trash.

"Now it's completely obvious that you like Kira. So don't bother denying it."

"What?" Jayden's eyes snapped to his brother's.

Tyler snorted. "Oh, come on, Jay. Don't act like you have no idea what I'm talking about. We both know you haven't taken your eyes off her since she came outside."

Jayden frowned. He'd never hear the end of the teasing now.

"Hey." Tyler gave him a palms-up. "It's okay. She seems like a really sweet *maedel*."

"I don't really know her."

"Then you need to get to know her." Tyler waved him off. "Go talk to her."

Jayden leaned forward. "We're working."

Tyler shook his head as he pushed himself up from the bench.

"What does that look mean?"

"I know you guys like to taunt me about being rigid, but I'm not *that* strict. I just like to stick to a schedule. You can talk to her for a few minutes."

Jayden carried his trash to the can and dropped it in before gazing over to the porch, where Kira smiled down at Ruby as she continued to play with her dollhouse. "Fine," he told his older brother. "I'll talk to her later."

"*Gut.*" Tyler patted his shoulder. "Now, grab a box of nails and get up that ladder. Lunchtime is over." His eyes sparkled with mirth.

Jayden laughed. "*Ya,* boss."

⟶⸭⟵

Later that afternoon, Jayden climbed down the ladder and poured himself a cup of water from the large cooler Tyler had purchased the previous week. When he heard someone call his name, he spun toward the porch, where Ruby stood, waving.

"Jayden! Come here!" Ruby jumped up and down.

He tossed his cup into the trash can and then jogged to the porch and up the steps. "What's up?"

"Look at my dollhouse." The little girl made a sweeping gesture toward the wooden structure.

Jayden crouched down beside her. "Wow. It's amazing. Did your *dat* make it?" He ran his fingers over the smooth edges, taking in the two levels, four rooms, and staircase.

"Uh-huh. See, this is the kitchen." She pointed to the wooden table and chairs and cabinets. "And this is the bedroom." She picked up the wooden bed and handed it to him. "And here is the *schtupp*."

Jayden turned the wooden bed over in his hand and then gave it back to Ruby. "Very nice."

Then she held up her little doll. "This is Marie. She lives in the *haus*."

"It's nice to meet you, Marie."

Ruby snorted. "She's not real, Jayden. She's a doll."

Jayden shook his head and laughed.

Ruby set her doll in the kitchen.

"Did your *dat* make the furniture too?"

"Uh-huh," Ruby said. "He makes sheds, so he knows how to

make things with wood. I'm going to share my dollhouse with Mimi and Liesel when they get older. *Dat* says they're too young for it now because they'll try to eat the furniture."

Jayden leaned back on the railing. "Yeah, you don't want them to choke on it."

"Nope."

Jayden picked up the wooden sofa and then turned it over in his hand while trying to commit the design to memory. Once again, he imagined building a dollhouse for his baby sister and his niece. Surely, they would love a playset like this when they were closer to Ruby's age.

The back door opened with a squeak, and Kira joined them on the porch with a tray that held crackers and two cups. She blinked at Jayden and then smiled. "Hi."

"Hello." Jayden popped up to his full height.

Kira divided a curious look between Jayden and Ruby.

Ruby held up her doll. "I showed Jayden my dollhouse and told him *mei dat* made it for me."

"How nice." Kira set the tray down on the patio table beside her. "Would you like some crackers?" she asked Jayden.

He helped himself to a few. "*Danki.*"

Ruby took a cup of lemonade and a handful of crackers before thanking Kira and turning her attention back to her dollhouse.

"How's the roof coming along?" Kira picked up a cracker and popped it into her mouth.

"It's going well. We'll finish the *haus* up tomorrow morning and then start on the barn. We should have all three buildings done by the end of the day Friday."

"Oh." She nodded. "How far away do you live?"

"We're in Bird-in-Hand. It's only six or so miles from here."

She seemed to study him, and he felt as if he might get lost in her dark-chocolate-colored eyes. He wanted to ask her how long she planned to stay in Pennsylvania, but he was tongue-tied with his words stuck in his throat.

"Do you like my dollhouse, Jayden?" Ruby asked.

"I love it." Jayden stooped down to Ruby's level. "I think maybe I should make one for my baby sister and my niece."

Ruby's dark eyes widened. "Really?"

"*Ya.*"

"You work with wood?" Kira asked, her expression full of curiosity.

Jayden felt his expression become sheepish. "I'm not an expert, but I like to play around with it. It's sort of a hobby."

"Oh." She seemed to study him. "How old are your *schweschder* and niece?"

"My baby sister, Kristena, is two, and Tyler's *dochder* is two-and-a-half. His *fraa* is due with their second *boppli* in December."

"Really?" she smiled.

"*Ya.* My other *bruder,* Korey, has a *sohn.* His name is Ryan, and he's eighteen months old."

"He's the same age as Mimi," Kira said.

"That's right." Jayden took another cracker from the plate. "Do you have any siblings?"

"I have three *schweschdere,* two younger and one older."

Jayden hesitated for a moment, waiting for her to elaborate, but instead she held up her cup of lemonade.

"Would you like this?" she asked.

"Oh, no *danki.*" He glanced up toward the roof and spotted

Tyler watching him. "I'd better get back to work. I appreciate the snack." He finished the last cracker and then started for the stairs. "I'll see you later."

Ruby stood up and waved. "Bye, Jayden!"

He waved at them both and then jogged toward the ladder.

Kira slipped the chicken and rice casserole into the oven and then set the timer before opening the nearby cabinet and picking up a stack of dishes.

Aenti Ellen moved to the kitchen window. "Oh, it looks like they're heading home for the day. I wanted to send something home with Jayden for Crystal." She moved to the end of the counter, opened a drawer, and pulled out a notepad and pen. "Would you get that container of butter *kichlin* we baked the other day?"

"*Ya*, of course." Kira found the container in the cabinet.

Aenti Ellen finished writing the note and then set it on top of the container. "Please give this to Jayden and ask him to deliver it to Crystal, and I'll finish setting the table for you."

"Okay." Kira carried the container out to where Jayden, Tyler, Dennis, and Roger were loading supplies into the pickup truck.

When Jayden looked over at her, she beckoned him to meet her by the porch. He sauntered over to her, his expression warm, and happiness buzzed through her.

She held the container out to him. "*Mei aenti* asked me to give you this for Crystal."

"*Kichlin*?" he asked, and she nodded. "Did you make them?"

"I helped. They're butter *kichlin*."

"They sound *appeditlich. Danki.*"

"*Gern gschehne.*" She folded her arms over her waist. "I'll see you tomorrow."

"*Ya,* you will."

"*Gut nacht.*" She leaned on the railing as Jayden climbed into the back seat of the pickup truck with Roger and Dennis while Tyler sat in the front passenger seat.

When their driver steered the diesel truck toward the road, she waved. Kira couldn't wait to talk to Jayden tomorrow and learn more about his family as well as his woodworking hobby.

In fact, she longed to learn everything about him, even though she knew they'd never be more than friends.

CHAPTER 6

"Kira sent *kichlin* home with you, huh?" Tyler bumped his elbow against Jayden's arm as they walked up the driveway toward *Dat*'s house.

Jayden shook his head. "No, Ellen sent the *kichlin* for Crystal."

"Right . . ." Tyler snickered.

Jayden held up the note showing his older brother where Crystal's name was clearly written on the folded piece of paper. "See? The *kichlin* are for Crystal, not me."

When Tyler continued to smirk, Jayden worked to tamp down his irritation. "Why are you teasing me like I'm fifteen?"

"I'm sorry." Tyler's mirth faded as they stood at the path. "I'm just excited for you. I've never seen you this interested in a *maedel* before."

"I'm not interested."

Tyler scoffed. "You could have fooled me. You're never shy, and you seem so bashful with her. You're a different person around her than you are when you're with your *freinden*."

"I am?" Jayden asked and then he frowned. "Look, Ty, I don't even know her, so please stop making a big deal about this, okay?"

"*Ya, ya.* Calm down." Tyler gave Jayden's shoulder a light punch.

"I'll see you tomorrow. Say hello to Michelle and Connie for me."

"I will. *Gut nacht.*"

While Tyler continued down the path toward his house, Jayden jogged up the porch steps and into the house, where the delicious aroma of chili and corn bread billowed over his senses. He kicked off his boots and then entered the kitchen, where his baby sister sat at the table in her booster seat, waving.

"Jay!" she sang.

He kissed her strawberry-blond head. "*Wie geht's?*"

"I wuv you." Kristena rested her hands on his face, pulled him toward her, and kissed his cheek.

His heart melted for his baby sister. "I love you, too, Krissy."

She giggled and then took a bite of a cheese stick.

"How was your day?" his stepmother asked as she set dinner plates on the table.

"It was *gut.*" He held out the container of cookies. "Ellen sent you some *kichlin.*"

"*Kichlin! Kichlin!*" Kristena chanted.

Crystal shook her head. "You know you need to spell that word."

"Sorry." Jayden grimaced.

"*Kichlin,* Mama!" Kristena called.

Crystal opened the container. "Oh, butter *kichlin.* Ellen used to bring these as a treat when we had gatherings with other ladies from church." She held one out to Kristena. "Can you say please, Krissy?"

"Peeeeeeees." Kristena folded her hands as if saying a prayer, and Jayden couldn't stop his laugh.

Crystal handed her the cookie and touched her little nose. "Enjoy, *mei liewe*." Then she held a cookie out to Jayden. "Would you like one?"

"Won't it ruin my supper?" he teased.

She rolled her eyes. "Well, I'm going to eat one. Ellen's *kichlin* are the best, in my opinion. She's a much better baker than I am."

"I highly doubt that."

Crystal smiled. "You're sweet." She took a bite of a cookie and then set the container on the counter and opened the note.

Jayden crossed to the sink and scrubbed his hands before peeking into the large pot of chili. He inhaled the delicious scent, and his mouth watered as his stomach gurgled.

"Oh, how nice," Crystal exclaimed. "Ellen said she wants to come visit. It would be so fun to get caught up with *mei freind*. Since we're no longer in the same church district and we're busy with our families, we've lost touch."

Jayden leaned back against the counter and swiped a cookie from the container. "How did Ellen wind up here if she's from Indiana?"

"She came to visit cousins one summer, and then she met Stan and they fell in love. Since he ran a successful shed business here, she decided to stay."

Jayden considered this while he finished the cookie. "It had to have been difficult to decide to leave her family."

"*Ya*, it was. She's close to her siblings, but she prayed about it and felt God calling her to follow her heart." Crystal pulled utensils from the drawer and brought them to the table.

"*Kichlin!*" Kristena declared, holding her hands up in the air.

"Oh, *mei liewe*," Crystal sighed.

Jayden held his hand up. "It's my fault. I'm sorry."

"It's okay." Crystal began setting the table. "You can give her another one."

When Jayden brought the toddler a cookie, Kristena clapped. "Yay!" Then she took a bite.

Jayden and Crystal laughed.

Jayden chose three glasses from the cabinet and set them by the dinner plates. "Did you know Ellen's niece is staying with her for a while?"

Crystal spun to face him. "Oh *ya*? Which niece?"

"Kira."

"Ellen speaks very highly of her *bruderskinner*. I think Kira is one of her *schweschder* Celia's *kinner*."

"Do you know anything about her?" he hedged.

Crystal shrugged. "Only that Ellen is close with her *schweschder* Celia, so I assume she's close to her nieces as well. From what I remember, Celia has four girls."

Jayden nodded.

"I'll invite them over for lunch one day," Crystal said.

Just then a timer dinged.

"Oh! The corn bread." Crystal rushed to the oven. She grabbed a pot holder and pulled the pan from the oven, sending the delicious scent of corn bread throughout the kitchen.

Jayden brought a pitcher of water to the table and filled their glasses while Crystal flipped the corn bread onto a cooling rack.

A few minutes later, the back door opened and closed and *Dat* walked into the kitchen. "Hello!" he announced.

"*Dat! Dat!*" Kristena called from her booster seat while waving her arms in the air.

Dat grinned as he walked over and kissed Kristena's head. "How's my little munchkin?"

She reached for his face and then kissed his cheek. "I wuv you."

"Look at that." Crystal touched Jayden's shoulder. "She has you and your *dat* wrapped around her little finger."

"That's true." *Dat* laughed. "How was your day, *mei liewe*?" He kissed Crystal's cheek.

She beamed up at him. "*Gut.*"

"Supper smells fantastic." *Dat* scrubbed his hands at the kitchen sink.

Jayden brought the butter to the table while Crystal began filling bowls with chili. Soon they were seated at the table with bowls of chili and corn bread while Kristena ate another cookie and a piece of corn bread.

After a silent prayer, they began to dig into their delicious meal.

Dat looked over at Kristena, and his mouth lifted in a smile. "Is she eating *kichlin* for supper?"

"You need to spell that word," Jayden warned as he picked up his glass of water.

Dat's look bounced between Crystal and Jayden. "Am I missing something here?"

Crystal explained how Ellen had sent cookies and a note home with Jayden and then told *Dat* about how Kristena had yelled for a cookie.

Dat chuckled and then wiped his beard with a paper napkin. "Well, the *kichlin* sound *appeditlich*. I can't wait to have one." He ate another spoonful of chili. "Crystal, your chili is the best."

"I agree," Jayden said.

"*Danki.*" She stood and put a few spoonfuls into a small plastic bowl and then handed the bowl and spoon to Kristena. "Try this, sweetie."

Kristena smelled the bowl, looked up at Crystal, and then scooped a spoonful into her mouth. "Yum!" she exclaimed, and they all laughed.

"How's work going at Stan's *haus*, Jayden?" *Dat* asked.

"It's going well. We'll finish up the *haus* tomorrow and then take care of the barn. We'll have his shop done on Friday."

"*Gut*."

Jayden ate more chili and then buttered a piece of corn bread. "And how's your job going at that hotel?"

"Pretty well. It's a big job, so it will take the rest of the week."

Jayden and *Dat* continued to discuss work while they finished their meal. Then Crystal brewed coffee and brought out the rest of Ellen's cookies.

"Are you going to make those wooden trains to donate to the children's hospital again this year, *Dat*?" Jayden asked as he stirred cream and sugar into his coffee.

Dat picked up a cookie. "I was planning to since the *kinner* at the hospital always enjoy them. Did you want to help me?"

"I actually had an idea for gifts that I could make this year."

Crystal handed Kristena another cookie. "What's your idea?"

"I noticed dollhouses in the window at a toy store in the strip mall we worked on, and then today Ellen's *dochder* Ruby called me over to see her dollhouse that Stan had made for her." Jayden ran his fingers over his warm mug. "I might try to make a dollhouse for your nieces and then build them for Krissy and Connie when they get older."

Crystal's green eyes sparkled. "What a lovely idea, Jayden."

"I agree," *Dat* said. "The *kinner* would love dollhouses."

Jayden held his hand up. "I'm not sure I can do it, but I'd like to try. You've shown me how to build those trains, and I got the hang of it."

"You certainly did. In fact, your trains are much better than mine."

"No, they aren't better than yours." Jayden shook his head. "But I think I could handle a basic *haus* and easy furniture."

Dat lifted a cookie. "I believe you could, *sohn*."

"*Danki*. Could I work in your shop after I take care of the animals tonight?"

Dat gave a look of disbelief. "When have you ever had to ask to use my shop?" He ran his fingers over his mug of coffee. "Of course you can use it, and I might even join you out there tonight."

"Great." Excitement coursed through Jayden.

Dat picked up another cookie. "These really are *appeditlich*." Jayden nodded.

"I'll write Ellen a note to let her know we enjoyed them, and I'll make something for you to take to her tomorrow, Jayden," Crystal said.

When Jayden imagined Kira and her aunt working together in the kitchen baking the cookies, a smile curved his lips.

The following morning the sound of the diesel pickup truck filled the kitchen as Kira set pieces of toast and scrambled eggs in front of Mimi and Liesel.

After delivering Ruby's breakfast, Kira rushed to the window just as Jayden emerged from the back seat of the truck laughing at something Tyler said. She took in his handsome face and the way his intelligent hazel eyes sparkled when he smiled, and her heart gave a little kick. Then she dismissed her body's reaction to him and spun back to face the table.

Liesel held up her sippy cup. "More milk, peees."

"*Ya*, Liesel." Kira took her cup and poured milk into it.

Since her uncle had to rush to work early this morning to finish a big project, Kira had offered to feed the girls while *Aenti* Ellen took care of Austin.

She handed Ruby a cup of milk and then gave Liesel another piece of toast.

When a knock sounded at the back door, Kira scooted through the mudroom and pulled the door open. She found Jayden standing on the back porch, and her pulse picked up speed. He looked handsome clad in a green shirt that complemented his hazel eyes.

"*Gude mariye*," he said.

Kira pushed open the storm door. "Hi, Jayden. Would you like to come in?"

"That would be nice." His expression seemed bashful. He was adorable!

He followed her into the kitchen, where the girls continued to eat their breakfast.

"Hi, Jayden!" Ruby announced. "These are *mei schweschdere*, Mimi and Liesel."

The little girls waved.

"It's nice to see you again." Then he held a container out to Kira. "This is from Crystal. We enjoyed the treats that you sent home with me last night. She sent a note and something for you all as a thank-you."

He took a step closer to her, and she breathed in the aroma of soap mixed with a woodsy cologne or aftershave—and she felt a strange stirring in her chest. "I won't say what the treats are. I made that mistake last night, and then my little *schweschder* started yelling for them."

"You mean c-o-o-k-i-e-s," she spelled.

"*Ya.*" He chuckled. "That's exactly what I mean."

Their eyes locked, and when they shared a special smile, Kira was almost certain her breath paused. What was wrong with her? She felt as if she was developing a crush on Jayden Bontrager, and she had just met him.

"I was wondering if I could show Ruby something I made," he said, looking shy once again.

"Of course."

"*Danki.*" He moved to the table and then pulled something from his pocket. When he held it up, Kira realized it was a miniature chair carved out of wood. "I made this last night. I'm working on three other matching chairs and a kitchen table. What do you think?"

Ruby took it in her hand, and her dark eyes lit up. "Wow! Is this for me?"

"No, no, no." Kira shook her head as embarrassment covered her. "Jayden just wanted to show it to you and get your opinion on it, sweetie. It's not for you."

Jayden crouched down beside her. "How about this, Ruby? You keep the chair, and I'll finish the table and other chairs and bring them to you for your dollhouse."

"Really?" Ruby asked.

"Jayden, that's very kind, but you don't have to do that," Kira insisted.

Jayden stood up to his full height and shrugged. "I want to." When he smiled, Kira feared she might melt into a puddle. She felt an attraction toward this kind, thoughtful, and gentle man like something she'd never experienced. The attention and affection he showed for her cousin warmed her heart. He was different from all the young men she'd known in her former youth group, including Philip, who never showed any interest in small children. "Would you like some *kaffi*?" she managed to ask him.

"*Danki*, but I'd better get to work."

"*Ya*," she said as disappointment pinched her.

Jayden said goodbye to the girls and then looked over at Kira again, and his expression seemed hopeful. "I'll see you later?"

"I'd like that," she told him.

"*Danki*, Jayden!" Ruby called as he headed back outside.

Aenti Ellen walked into the kitchen and covered her mouth to shield a yawn. Her dark eyes were rimmed with shadows, evidence that she'd had a hard night with the newborn. "Austin is finally down for a nap. I thought he'd never fall asleep."

"I'm sorry you had such a bad night." Kira picked up the container. "Jayden brought this in. It's from Crystal."

Aenti Ellen took the container, and when she opened it, there was a note sitting on top of aluminum foil. She set the note on the counter and lifted the aluminum foil, revealing brownies. "Oh. My favorite. We'll save these for later."

Then she opened the note. "Crystal wants us all to come over for lunch sometime soon. She said she would like us to spend the afternoon with her and her daughters-in-law, Savannah and Michelle."

"That sounds like fun," Kira said.

"*Ya*, it does. I'll give her a call."

"*Mamm*," Ruby called. "Look at what Jayden made for me."

Aenti Ellen set the note on the counter and then slipped the top back onto the container of brownies before walking over to

Ruby. She took the little chair from her and turned it over in her hands. "Isn't this cute!"

"Jayden is making a dollhouse and furniture," Kira explained. "He asked Ruby for her opinion of the chair. He said he's going to make her a table and three more chairs to go with it."

Aenti Ellen smiled. "He's very talented." She handed the chair back to Ruby. "I hope you thanked him."

"I did." Ruby sat up taller.

"He seems like a very nice young man," *Aenti* Ellen said.

Kira nodded. "I agree."

"I want to make him something as a thank-you," Ruby said. "Maybe I'll draw him a picture."

Aenti Ellen tapped the table. "That's nice, but you need to finish your breakfast first."

Mimi arched her back before pushing her sippy cup off her highchair tray, sending it crashing down to the floor. Her lower lip began to tremble as her eyes filled with tears.

Kira hurried over and picked up the cup, thankful that it didn't break or leak. "It's all right, honey." She set the cup on the table. "No need to cry."

Mimi whimpered and rubbed her eyes.

Aenti Ellen sighed as she stood. "I'll take care of her."

"I can do it." Kira wet a rag and started to wipe Mimi's face. "Did you get a chance to eat breakfast?"

Kira nodded.

"Then I'll take over with the *kinner*, and you can go do something else." *Aenti* Ellen took the rag from her hand.

"I'll clean the bathrooms."

Her aunt raised a dark eyebrow. "Are you sure that's what you want to do today?"

"*Ya*, that's why you invited me out here, right? You needed someone to clean your bathrooms."

Her aunt laughed and tapped her shoulder. "You think you're funny, huh?"

"No, I think I'm hilarious," Kira quipped.

Her aunt touched her face. "Don't forget to give your *mamm* a call. I'm sure she's thinking of you."

"I will, *Aenti*." A wave of sadness overcame Kira as her mother's beautiful face flashed in her mind. She pushed the homesickness away as she headed to the utility room to gather up her cleaning supplies. She would keep busy in order to ignore how much she missed her parents and sisters. After all, she was there to help her aunt.

CHAPTER 7

LATER THAT MORNING, JAYDEN CROUCHED DOWN ON THE roof of Stan's barn while he and the rest of the crew worked to remove the old shingles. They had finished the house earlier and then started on the barn.

He looked out toward Stan's home and tried to imagine Kira inside doing her chores. She looked lovely today in a dark-green dress that complemented her dark eyes and hair. When he'd stood close to her, he was almost certain he'd caught a whiff of vanilla from her shampoo or possibly lotion. He'd been tempted to stay and talk to her when she'd offered him coffee, and he'd even fantasized about sitting in the kitchen with her all morning and asking her the questions that had haunted him. First and foremost—did she have a boyfriend waiting for her back in Indiana?

But Jayden had to evict all those thoughts from his mind. After all, Kira was most likely going to return to Indiana someday soon. Still, the idea of becoming her friend took hold of him, and he wanted to get to know her better. He just hoped she felt the same way about him.

Kira pushed the broom around the kitchen while humming softly to herself. She had spent the morning scrubbing the two bathrooms and then had swept and dusted the upstairs bedrooms. After feeding the children lunch, she had swept and dusted the family room while her aunt put Mimi, Liesel, and Austin in for their afternoon naps. Kira had then convinced her exhausted aunt to take a nap while she continued with the cleaning and tried to push thoughts of her sisters out of her mind.

Although she and her younger sisters bickered at times, they had always taken care of their chores together. She found herself wondering if Maribeth and Leah were busy sweeping and dusting at home. Were they singing together while they worked? Were they missing her as much as she missed them?

Kira swept the small pile of dust and dirt into a dustpan and dropped it into the trash can. Then she stowed the dustpan and broom and wiped down the counters and the kitchen table. She glanced at the clock on the wall and saw that it was almost three o'clock. She assumed the little ones and her aunt would awaken from their naps soon.

She moved to the sink and looked out the window toward the barn, where Jayden, Tyler, Dennis, and Roger were hammering new shingles onto the roof. She rested her elbow on the sink and her chin on her palm as she watched Jayden work for several moments. He lifted his straw hat and pushed his hand through his thick, sandy-blond hair.

"Kira?"

She jumped and spun to face Ruby standing by the kitchen table. "You startled me." She pushed her hand against her chest.

"I'm sorry." Ruby held up a picture she'd drawn with crayons. "I drew this for Jayden."

Kira smiled as she took in a farm scene, complete with a red barn, red house, and brown horses in a pasture. "Why, Ruby, that's beautiful. I think Jayden will love it."

"*Danki.*" Ruby studied her work. "Would you show me how to write 'Thank you, from Ruby' on it?"

"I'd be happy to. I just cleaned the table. Why don't you bring your crayons out here?"

Kira sat with Ruby at the table and helped her write a note before Ruby added a few stick figures and a dog to the picture.

Then Ruby stood. "I'm done. Can we take it to him now?"

"*Ya.*"

Kira held Ruby's hand as they walked down the path leading to the barn. The sun was bright, and the blue sky was dotted with big, puffy clouds. Birds sang in the trees, and a dog barked somewhere in the distance.

As they approached the barn, Kira spotted Jayden and Tyler standing by a water cooler and holding paper cups. Tyler turned toward her and waved and then said something to Jayden before patting his arm, tossing his cup into a trash can, and climbing up the ladder to the roof.

Jayden pivoted to face Kira and Ruby and smiled as they approached.

Ruby released Kira's hand and then took off running toward Jayden.

Kira quickened her steps. "Ruby! Slow down before you fall."

When Ruby reached Jayden, she held up her picture. "*Danki* for the chair. This is for you."

"Oh my goodness." Jayden leaned down and studied the picture. "This is fantastic." His eyes focused on hers. "You drew this all by yourself?"

Ruby's chest puffed out. "*Ya*, I did." Then she pointed to Kira. "But my cousin helped me write the words."

Jayden looked up at Kira and grinned before turning his focus back to the little girl. "I am impressed. You did a great job."

Ruby smiled and then pulled Jayden in for a hug. His expression lit up with elation as he hugged her back, and Kira's heart sang with admiration for this wonderful man.

Once again she was struck by how different Jayden was from Philip. She had dated Philip for a year, and while he'd always been respectful to her parents, she'd never witnessed him going out of his way to talk to her sisters. And Philip had never paid attention to any of the small children at church. In fact, once, when she held a toddler her mother had delivered, Philip had turned away and began talking to his friends. She used to imagine having a family with him, but now as she watched Jayden interact with Ruby, she felt as if Jayden would be a warmer, more attentive father than Philip ever could.

That thought took her by surprise and then settled deep in Kira's heart.

Ruby released him and grinned. "*Danki!*" Then she took off running toward the house, leaving Kira behind.

Jayden glanced at the picture and grinned at Kira. "I love this. I'm going to hang it on the refrigerator when I get home."

"She wanted to do something nice to thank you." She studied him for a moment. "How long have you been working with wood?"

He shrugged and set the drawing on the toolbox. "I think I was about Ruby's age when I first started. *Mei dat* makes wooden trains and donates them to children's charities every Christmas as sort of a ministry."

"Wow. That is such a special ministry," Kira said.

"*Danki. Mei dat* is pretty amazing. He said he made a train on a whim for Tyler when he was little, and Ty loved it. It's just a little engine pulling two cars. Not very fancy. He made one for Korey, and he enjoyed it too. So, according to *mei dat, mei mamm* thought it was so wonderful that she encouraged him to make more. He's been donating them to different Christmas toy drives since *mei bruders* were little."

"Your *dat* certainly is amazing." And now she knew from where he had inherited his kind heart and thoughtfulness. The more she found out about Jayden, the more fascinated she was with him, and the more she wanted to know about him. She couldn't remember a time when Philip had gushed about his father. Philip and his father were close, but she could feel how proud Jayden was of his father and it overwhelmed her.

Jayden's expression was unreadable as he paused for a moment. "And now you think I'm strange for wanting to make dollhouse furniture when I don't have any *kinner*."

"No. I think it's great that you want to make them for your niece and *schweschder* and also share them with my cousin."

"I was thinking that if they were *gut* enough, I could make a dollhouse and furniture for Crystal's nieces."

"I bet they would love that."

"Do you have any hobbies?" he asked, and he seemed to relax.

"I like to sew, but I haven't had time to since I came here. The *kinner* and my chores are keeping me busy, but I hope to at least help *mei aenti* with her sewing."

He sank down onto the edge of the table that held the water cooler and cups. "How long have you been here?"

"Two weeks."

"How long are you planning to stay?"

Kira shrugged. "I'm not sure yet. I told *mei aenti* I'll stay as long as she needs me."

"That's *gut*." He folded his arms across his wide chest. "Are you active in youth group?"

She laughed. "I've gone once."

Jayden opened his mouth to say something and then closed it as if he'd changed his mind.

Kira held her breath as curiosity gripped her.

"Well." He stood up and jammed his thumb toward the ladder. "I'd better get back to work before my boss yells at me."

"Does he yell a lot?"

"Oh yeah." He chuckled and then shook his head. "No, he doesn't, but Roger, Dennis, and I like to give him a hard time." Then he pointed to the drawing. "Please tell Ruby I love the picture."

"I will, and please tell Crystal thank you for the brownies and the note. *Mei aenti* said she'd love to get together."

"I will, and I'll do my best to bring Ruby the table and other chairs tomorrow."

"Great." Kira hesitated and then nodded. "All right."

Jayden smiled before climbing up the ladder toward the barn roof.

As Kira headed toward the house, she knew one thing for sure. She wanted to get to know Jayden Bontrager more than ever.

Jayden sat on a stool at his father's large worktable at the back of his cinderblock supply building later that evening. He had hurried to take care of the animals and then retreated to the workshop to start on the chairs and table for Ruby. Since he was certain he and his crew would finish the roofing job tomorrow, he was determined to keep his promise to Ruby and give her the completed table and chairs before they moved on to another worksite.

He was grateful he had kept the measurements for the first chair and also made a drawing before giving the chair to Ruby earlier that morning. He had managed to create two more chairs already, and he wasn't going to bed until he had the last chair and the table completed.

The door opened and *Dat* walked in carrying a lantern. He hopped up on a stool across from him. "What are you working on?"

"I made a chair last night, so I'm creating three more and then I'm going to build a table to go with them."

"Nice." *Dat* started pulling out tools and a piece of wood.

Jayden nodded toward a shelf lined with trains that were ready to go to a children's charity. "Are you going to build more trains?"

"*Ya*. It's nice to have company out here."

They worked in silence for several minutes. While Jayden continued to craft the last chair, his mind spun with thoughts of Kira. He had replayed their earlier conversation over and over in his mind, and he couldn't shake the feeling that they had a special connection, something more than just a budding friendship.

His mind had latched on to how attentive she'd seemed

while they talked, and he regretted not asking her if she had a boyfriend. But the question had seemed ridiculous since it didn't matter if she had a boyfriend or not since she wasn't planning to stay in Pennsylvania.

"Is something on your mind, Jayden?"

He looked up to find his father's brown eyes focused on him.

Jayden set the small chair down and took a deep breath. "When you first met Crystal, did you immediately feel a connection with her?"

Dat set his piece of sandpaper down. "I'm not sure. I think I felt our connection the more we talked and got to know each other."

"How did you know for sure that Crystal felt the same way about you that you felt about her?"

"That's an easy one, *sohn*. I asked her."

"You *asked* her?"

"Well, *ya*." *Dat* chuckled. "We had an honest conversation. I told her that I liked her, and I asked her if she would be interested in having dinner with me. She told me she liked me, too, and she wanted to have dinner." He shrugged. "We were just open with each other."

"Huh."

Silence fell between them again, and they each returned to their projects. *Dat*'s words echoed through Jayden's mind, but he couldn't imagine having the courage to tell Kira how he felt. What if she laughed in his face?

But what if she *didn't* laugh and instead told him that she cared for him? The idea gave his heart wings.

Jayden looked up at his father, who was busy sanding a piece of wood that would become a train's wheel. "How did you know that Crystal was the one you wanted to build a life with?"

Dat's expression brightened. "Jayden, have you met someone?"

"Sort of." Jayden swallowed.

"Who is it?"

"Her name is Kira, and she's Ellen and Stan's niece."

Dat grinned. "That's great. I'm so *froh* for you."

"Hold on." Jayden held up his hands. "Don't get your hopes up yet. Ty is pushing me to get to know her, but she's from Indiana. She's here helping her *aenti* and *onkel* for a short time, and she told me she plans to go home when her *aenti* doesn't need her anymore."

"But you care about her."

"*Ya*, that's true." Jayden kneaded the stubble on his chin. "I feel something for her that I've never felt before. She's easy to talk to, and she's funny. But she also has this calmness about her. I can't explain it, but I'm drawn to her." He paused and shook his head. "But I don't want to get my hopes up and then have her tell me that she's not interested since she's not staying here."

"Well, *sohn*, my advice to you is to be her *freind* and then see what happens. The Lord works in mysterious ways. If he led you and Kira to each other, then you might possibly find a way to make it work."

Jayden nodded. "*Danki, Dat*."

His father smiled and nodded toward the chairs. "You do *gut* work."

"Thanks."

⁓───⦂⊱⊰⦂───⁓

Jayden scrubbed his hands at the kitchen sink later that evening. He yawned as he dried them with a paper towel and then glanced at the clock. It had taken longer than he'd expected to finish the table and chairs, but he had done it. His father had come in earlier, saying that he was too old to stay up past his bedtime. Jayden was determined to finish his project, so he kept working after *Dat* left the shop.

He tossed the used paper towel into the trash can and then examined the finished table and chairs. He couldn't wait to give them to Ruby tomorrow.

When he heard soft footsteps, Jayden turned toward the doorway as Crystal walked in carrying a flashlight. "I thought you were in bed," he whispered.

"Krissy had a bad dream, so I stayed up with her for a while." She fetched a glass from the cabinet and filled it with water. "What are you doing up so late?" She took a long drink from the glass and then set it in the sink.

"I wanted to finish these for Ruby." He held up the table and chairs.

Crystal's green eyes widened as she took the table and one chair from his hands. "You made these?"

"*Ya.*" He shrugged.

"They are spectacular. I'm sure Ruby will love them."

"*Danki.*"

"I haven't seen Ruby in a long time. I can't wait to have Ellen, Kira, and the *kinner* over for lunch." Crystal handed the dollhouse furniture back to him. "Now, you need to get some sleep. It's late."

"I will. *Gut nacht.*" As Jayden climbed the stairs to his room with his flashlight guiding his way, he considered his father's advice. Perhaps he and Kira could somehow be friends, and possibly with the Lord's help, maybe even something more.

CHAPTER 8

KIRA CARRIED THE BROOM OUT ONTO THE PORCH THE FOL-lowing afternoon and tried to dismiss the disappointment that had hung over her all day like a dark cloud despite the bright, sunny sky. She leaned the broom against the porch railing and peered out in the direction of her uncle's store, where Jayden, his brother, Dennis, and Roger worked on the roof. With a heavy sigh, she hugged her arms to her middle.

She had expected Jayden to come and see her this morning to say hello and possibly give Ruby the furniture he'd promised to finish for her. But instead, she hadn't seen or heard from him, and she despised how much that hurt her heart. Kira was certain Jayden and the rest of the crew were busy working in order to meet their deadline. Most likely, they had another job lined up for tomorrow and they didn't have any time to spare. After all, they were hard-working men, and talking to Kira and her little cousin would be a secondary priority when there was a job to do.

Aside from that, a man as kind, thoughtful, and handsome as Jayden most likely had a girlfriend and didn't have any interest in getting to know Kira even as a friend. She had to let go of her childish crush on him and move on. She hadn't planned to stay in

Pennsylvania, so why would she want to set herself up for another heartbreak?

Kira huffed out a frustrated breath and then clasped the broom and began sweeping. If only her mother were here to listen to her share her disappointment. She sniffed as memories of her heart-to-heart talks with her mother filled her mind. Kira had always felt she could say anything to her mother, who would listen without judgment. Oh, how she missed her family!

When the storm door opened with a creak, Kira turned just as Ruby stuck her head out.

"Kira?"

"*Ya*, sweetie?"

"Would you help me carry my dollhouse outside so I can sit with you while you sweep?"

"Of course." Relief filtered through Kira. She was grateful for the company to help purge her sadness.

Kira followed Ruby to the family room and picked up the house while Ruby gathered up three of her little dolls. Then Ruby scampered ahead of her and held the storm door open while Kira delivered the dollhouse to the little table sitting at the far end of the porch.

Ruby settled herself in front of her house, and Kira returned to sweeping. She tried to dismiss all thoughts of her mother and Jayden from her mind while she worked. She breathed in the warm, early-fall air, enjoying the scents of honeysuckle and moist earth. She glanced across the field toward her uncle's barn, where two barn cats played in the tall grass.

After several minutes, Ruby suddenly jumped up from her seat, nearly knocking her dollhouse off its perch. "Jayden!" she shouted.

"Shh," Kira hissed. "Your *mamm* and siblings are taking a nap, Ruby."

Ruby pointed. "Look! There's Jayden."

Kira swiveled just as Jayden jogged up the path toward the porch carrying a small grocery bag. He wore a dark-blue shirt and gray trousers, and his eyes were bright. He blessed her with a warm smile, and her heart gave a little bump.

"Hi," he said as he came up the steps. "I've wanted to come over to see you." Kira was almost certain his cheeks flushed before he added, "I mean, I have something for Ruby."

"You do?" Ruby rushed over to him. "Is it my table?"

Kira shook her head. "Ruby, that's rude," she warned.

"It's okay." Jayden handed her the bag. "I hope you like it." He folded his hands as she opened the bag.

Ruby's mouth formed an *O* as she pulled out three small chairs and set them on the patio table. Then she held up a matching table. "They're *wunderbaar!*" She set the miniature table down and then wrapped her arms around Jayden's waist. "*Danki*, Jayden!"

"*Gern gschehne.*" Jayden patted Ruby's back, and his expression seemed to be full of admiration for Kira's little cousin. When he met Kira's stare, he smiled, and sweet adrenaline pumped through her veins.

Ruby pulled away and sat down in front of her dollhouse. "I'm going to put the table and chairs right here. Now my family has two places to sit and eat!" She set up the second table and chairs in the kitchen and then began moving her dolls around while they discussed the new kitchen set.

Jayden set the empty grocery bag on the patio table. "I'm sorry I didn't stop by this morning. Like I said, I wanted to come and see you both, but Tyler is a stickler when it comes to his schedule. We have another job lined up tomorrow in Ronks, and he was determined that we wouldn't fall behind today."

"I understand." Kira took a step toward him and lowered her voice. "*Danki* for being so nice to my cousin."

Jayden's expression seemed to become serious. "You don't need to thank me. I think the world of her—and also of you."

Kira's throat dried, and she had the sudden urge to ask if they could somehow keep in touch and get to know each other better.

She worked to find her words, but the storm door creaked open, and *Aenti* Ellen joined them on the porch. "Jayden. *Wie geht's?*"

"*Mamm!*" Ruby called. "Come and see the table and chairs Jayden made for me!"

Aenti Ellen scooted over to the dollhouse. "Oh my goodness. That is lovely, Ruby." She crossed the porch to stand beside Kira. "*Danki* for making the furniture for Ruby. That is so kind of you."

"It's my pleasure. In fact, it was *gut* practice for me," Jayden said.

Aenti Ellen snapped her fingers. "That reminds me. We really enjoyed the brownies. Please let Crystal know."

"I will, and she's excited to have you all over for lunch sometime soon."

"We can't wait." *Aenti* Ellen seemed to look between Jayden and Kira and then she nodded toward the back door. "I'm expecting Austin to wake up from his nap at any moment, and he'll be hungry. I hope we'll see you again soon, Jayden." She seemed to give Kira a curious look before slipping back into the house.

"I'd better get back to the shop before Tyler starts calling for me." Jayden adjusted his straw hat on his sandy-colored hair and then he hesitated.

Kira nodded. "*Ya,* of course." She searched for something to say aside from goodbye. But how could she tell him that she wanted to see him again without sounding forward—or even worse, desperate?

"My youth group often gets together with others in the area, so maybe I'll see you at a gathering sometime," he offered.

"*Ya*." She nodded. "Maybe." *Hopefully!*

He smiled. "Great." He held his hand out to her.

When she shook it, she didn't want to let go of his warm hand.

"Goodbye," he said, and then he turned toward Ruby. "Bye, Ruby."

She waved and grinned at him. "Bye, Jayden!"

Jayden smiled at Kira one last time and then jogged down the steps and toward the shop. Kira leaned on the railing and watched him go, and her heart began to sink. She hoped that she would see him again, but even if she did get a chance to, how would they sustain a friendship?

The storm door creaked open again and *Aenti* Ellen sidled up beside her at the railing.

Kira pivoted toward her aunt. "I thought you were going to check on Austin?"

"That was an excuse to give you and Jayden some privacy."

"Privacy?" Kira's voice nearly squeaked. "What does that mean?"

Aenti Ellen scoffed. "Please, Kira. It was obvious you and Jayden didn't want me butting into your conversation." She craned her neck over her shoulder to look at Ruby, who was happily playing with her dolls. Then she turned her dark-brown eyes back to Kira. "Now, tell me. What's going on between you two?"

"Nothing," Kira insisted.

Her aunt gave her a knowing look.

"I don't understand why you're acting as if I'm keeping secrets from you," Kira said, working to keep her voice low. "There's *nothing* at all going on between Jayden and me. I don't know him very well, and I don't know if he's even interested."

"But you *are* interested?"

Kira gave a little groan and rubbed her hand over her mouth. "I don't know. I mean, no, I'm not interested in dating. I'm only here to help you for as long as you need me, and then I plan to go back home to Indiana." She studied the toes of her black shoes.

"Please look at me," *Aenti* Ellen said.

Her aunt gave her a knowing expression. "Kira, you do realize that I was in the exact same situation that you're in right now. I know how you feel."

"You do?"

"Of course I do. I came here to visit cousins, and I met your *onkel* at a singing." She grinned. "It sounds *gegisch*, but I took one look at him, and I instantly felt something for him. Then we started talking, and it was as if we'd known each other our entire lives. And when it came time for me to go home, I had a choice to make. Your *onkel* told me that he loved me, and he wanted me to either stay or he wanted to come to Indiana with me."

Kira's hands began to shake when she considered what she would do if she had to face the choice of leaving her family behind in Indiana. She couldn't fathom not having her parents and sisters close by. "How did you manage to leave your family behind?"

"It wasn't an easy choice." She huffed out a breath. "I was torn, but I wanted to build a life and a family with Stan. Choosing to do that here made sense because he had already established his business."

Kira swallowed against her dry throat. The idea of never returning to her family made her nauseous. "I-I don't know if I could do that."

"But God could have other plans for you. I guess we'll just have to wait and see." *Aenti* Ellen patted Kira's back and then started for the door. "Who would like to help me make some *kichlin*?"

Ruby stood. "I would!"

"Let's go in the *haus*. You can leave your dollhouse here, and we'll come back for it." *Aenti* Ellen pushed Jayden's grocery bag into the pocket of her apron, opened the storm door, and then turned to Kira. "Are you going to join us?"

"*Ya*, I'll be there in a minute."

Her aunt smiled and then led Ruby into the house.

Kira looked out to where Jayden was perched back on the roof of the store and sighed. While she couldn't imagine leaving her family behind, she also felt her heart lift at the idea of Jayden Bontrager somehow being a part of her future.

Kira sat on a grassy hill beside Alaina the following Sunday afternoon. Since it was an off-Sunday without a church service, Alaina and her older brother, Nate, had picked her up and taken her to the Blank family's farm for the youth gathering.

She had enjoyed a few games of volleyball before she and Alaina took a seat together to relax and watch the others play. Kira ripped a piece of grass from the ground and wrapped it around her finger while she lost herself in thoughts of Jayden. He had seemed to hover at the back of her mind since their last conversation on her aunt's porch Friday afternoon.

She had hoped that today would be a combined youth group event, but it wasn't. And she longed to shove away this constant disappointment that clung to her like a second skin. Why was she allowing her silly crush on Jayden Bontrager to ruin her mood when this was a glorious Sunday that the Lord had made? She needed to enjoy her new friends and not dwell on how much she missed Jayden.

"I like Lewis." Alaina's announcement broke through Kira's mental tirade.

Kira's head popped up. "What did you say?"

Alaina frowned and rested her chin on her palm. "I said I like Lewis Hostetler, but I don't think he's even noticed I exist."

Kira couldn't stop her smile. Perhaps her friend was as pitifully heartsick as she was.

"Why are you smiling at me when I just shared my most embarrassing secret with you?" Although Alaina had raised one of her blond eyebrows, her lips were also twitching.

"I'm just surprised to hear your confession." Then Kira leaned over toward her friend and pointed toward the four volleyball games that were simultaneously going on below them. "Now, tell me which one is Lewis. I've met so many of your *freinden* that I can't keep all their names straight."

Alaina pointed toward the game at their far right. "He's in the front row of the team that's facing us. He has dark hair and *schee* sky-blue eyes. And he's just as tall as *mei bruder*." She frowned. "He's *gut freinden* with *mei bruder*, but he and I have never talked much."

"Have you always liked him?"

"*Ya*, I have."

"Have you told him?"

Alaina guffawed. "Of course not!"

Kira joined in, and she laughed harder when she realized that Alaina's giggle reminded her of her older sister Abby's unique laughter.

Alaina angled her body toward Kira. "Do you have a boyfriend back home in Indiana?"

"No, not anymore." Kira crisscrossed her legs and smoothed her burgundy dress over her lap.

"What happened?"

Kira pursed her lips and debated how much to share. "I was dating someone, but we broke up shortly before *mei aenti* invited me to come out here and help her."

"I'm sorry."

Kira shrugged as if Philip hadn't completely shattered her heart and her trust. "It's okay. I suppose it was better to find out now that he had changed his mind before . . . before we got too serious." She decided not to share that they had been engaged. Admitting those details felt too personal and too painful.

"*Ya*, I suppose that's true, but I'm certain it was difficult."

They both turned their attention to the volleyball game and then Kira took in Alaina's pretty profile once again.

"Why don't you try talking to Lewis when we eat supper?" she suggested. "I could go with you, and we could ask him something about volleyball."

"You're sweet, but it's okay. I'll just love him from afar until the Lord sees fit for me to get to know him."

"You're *gegisch*." Kira gave Alaina's arm a playful push. "Does your youth group sometimes get together with other youth groups?"

"*Ya*, all the time. Why?"

"I was just curious."

"I think we have a combined one coming up soon."

Hope lit in Kira's chest. "That's *gut*."

Alaina brushed a few pieces of grass off her lavender dress and black apron. "You mentioned you have three *schweschdere*."

Kira nodded.

"Have you spoken to them?"

"*Ya*, I called my family yesterday and talked to my youngest *schweschder*, Maribeth."

"How is everyone doing?"

"They're well." Kira ripped out another blade of grass and fiddled with it as she thought about how much she missed her family. "Maribeth and Leah have been busy with their chores and with youth group. Abby, our older *schweschder*, is married and works as a midwife. She delivered a couple of babies last week."

Alaina's expression brightened. "How exciting. I can't imagine what that's like. Have you ever helped deliver a baby?"

"*Ya*, I've assisted her and *mei mamm* many times. *Mei mamm* used to be a midwife too."

Alaina hugged her knees to her chest. "I'm sure you'll never forget that."

"No, I won't. I loved assisting her. In fact, someday, I hope to be married and also work as a midwife like *mei mamm*. There's nothing like witnessing the miracle of a baby coming into the world."

"Alaina! Kira!"

They both looked down toward the volleyball courts, where Nate stood with Lewis.

Nate beckoned them. "Come play with us."

"Here's your chance to talk to Lewis." Kira grinned as she stood and swiped her hands down her dress.

Alaina popped up and brushed her hands together. "Let's go!"

As they hurried down the hill, Kira's heart felt full. She was grateful for her new friends.

CHAPTER 9

JAYDEN STEPPED OUT OF THE KING FAMILY'S BARN AND INTO the cool mid-September evening later that night. With his flashlight beam pointed toward the ground, he lifted his eyes toward the stars sparkling in the clear, dark sky. He breathed in the aroma of a wood-burning fireplace somewhere in the distance.

He had enjoyed the off-Sunday without a service while he'd played volleyball and laughed with his friends before they'd spent the remainder of the night singing hymns. Throughout the day, he'd found himself wondering if Kira was also enjoying a day with her friends. And had she thought of him at all?

He snorted in spite of himself. He sounded like a lovesick teenager.

"Jayden! Jayden!"

He spun on his heel as Ben hurried over with Lora in tow, both of them grinning. "*Ya?*"

"We're heading out. You have a *gut* week." Ben shook Jayden's hand.

Jayden lifted an eyebrow. "You're giving Lora a ride?"

"*Ya*, I am." Ben touched Lora's shoulder. "We'll see you next Sunday."

How curious. So, Jayden's intuition had been right. Ben liked Lora, and it was obvious that Lora felt the same way. He was happy for his friends, who seemed to truly enjoy each other's company.

"Take care," Jayden told them before they took off toward the sea of buggies waiting in the King family's field.

Jayden nodded goodbyes as his friends walked past him on their way to find their horses and buggies. He started toward the barn for his horse and then stopped when he heard someone call his name.

"Jayden! Wait for me!" Darla hurried over to him. "I was afraid I'd missed you."

"I'm still here."

She grinned. "Oh *gut*. Ben is giving Lora a ride home."

"*Ya*, I know," he said.

Darla continued to smile at him, and he had the sneaking suspicion she was waiting for him to say something. They stood staring at each other, and he searched for a conversation starter.

"So," she finally began, "I need a ride."

"Oh. Okay."

She gave a laugh that seemed forced. "Will you give me a ride, please, Jayden?"

"*Ya*," he said, rubbing a spot on his cheek. "Of course." And just then, his oldest brother's words echoed in his mind:

Darla likes you . . . It's obvious, Jay. She seems to seek you out at church. Even Michelle mentioned it to me . . .

A strange feeling of foreboding overcame Jayden. He'd never refuse to give her or any other friend a ride home, but would Darla assume that he wanted to date her because he gave her a ride? He considered Darla a friend since they enjoyed each other's company during youth gatherings, and they often ran in the same circles of friends. In fact, he recalled when they were in school, and he helped her with her math problems. Still, he couldn't imagine asking her to be his girlfriend.

"*Danki!*" She looked relieved.

After Jayden had hitched his horse to his buggy, he waved goodbye to friends and then he and Darla set out on their journey home.

They rode in silence for several moments with only the sound of the clip-clop of horse hooves, the whirl of the buggy wheels, and the road noise from passing cars filling the space between them.

Jayden kneaded the back of his neck while wondering what on earth to discuss with Darla. He found it ironic that conversation seemed to flow between Kira and him, but here he was having a difficult time carrying on a conversation with Darla, whom he'd known for years.

"I had fun today," she finally said.

Jayden gave her a sideways glance and found her smiling at him. "I did too."

"I think Ben likes Lora."

"I do too."

"They would make a cute couple, right?" Darla gushed.

Jayden nodded.

"I had a feeling they would get together soon. It's so fun seeing our *freinden* become couples, isn't it?"

"Uh. *Ya*, I guess so."

"I noticed that Millie and Chad were talking a lot earlier too. I bet they'll be dating before long." Darla continued sharing her predictions about which of their friends would soon be dating, and her words became background noise to his thoughts.

Jayden halted the horse at a red light and tried to hide his frown. He had a feeling he was going to get every red light between the King family's farm and Darla's house, which would prolong this awkward conversation.

As he guided the horse through the intersection, his thoughts turned to Kira. He wondered if she was also on her way home. Had another man offered to give her a ride, or was she riding with a group of friends? He secretly hoped she was riding with friends, but it was none of his business. But then again, he felt such a close connection to Kira. She was easy to talk to, and he felt as if he could be himself around her. He recalled how he shared his idea to make dollhouse furniture, and she didn't think it was ridiculous. Instead, she encouraged him to give it a try. She seemed to understand him and support his new hobby, which warmed his soul.

"Don't you think so, Jayden?"

His eyes met Darla's hopeful expression, and he felt his cheeks begin to heat. "I'm sorry. What did you say?"

"I asked you if you thought our *freinden* would start marrying this season."

"Oh." Jayden was stumped by her question. "I really haven't thought about it."

Darla's expression become coy. "I have a feeling that we'll have some weddings soon. You just don't know what God has in store for our community."

"Right."

"Don't you want to get married and have a family like your *bruders*?"

"Sure." He shrugged. "Someday."

"I do. I want at least five *kinner*." Darla began talking on about what she would name her future children.

Jayden felt his posture begin to sag. This ride couldn't be over soon enough.

He was relieved when he spotted the sign for the road for Darla's father's dairy farm. By the time they reached the gravel driveway that led to her family's home, Darla had moved on to discussing her plans for the week and the cake she planned to bake for her grandmother's birthday.

Jayden halted the horse by her back porch and then plastered a smile on his face. "I hope you have a *gut* week, Darla."

"You too. *Danki* for the ride." She reached over and touched his hand before flipping on her flashlight, retrieving the container that had held her dessert, and then climbing out of the buggy and up the porch steps. She waved before disappearing into the large white farmhouse.

Jayden's thoughts were stuck on Darla and their tedious ride to her house when he exited his father's barn after stowing his horse and buggy. He strolled up the path to his house and spotted a light glowing in the kitchen window as he ascended the porch steps.

After leaving his light jacket and shoes in the mudroom, he moved to the kitchen, where *Dat* sat at the table with the glow of his lantern illuminating the room.

"Hi, *Dat*," he said. "You know that you don't have to wait up for me."

"I don't mind. How was your night?"

Jayden shrugged and then sank down onto a chair across

from him. He drew imaginary circles on the wooden tabletop while he continued to ponder his ride with Darla.

"Do you want to talk about it?"

Jayden slumped back in the chair. "I gave Darla Kurtz a ride home."

"Oh?" *Dat* seemed to wait for him to elaborate. When Jayden didn't, he added, "And how did that go?"

"It was . . . awkward. It's obvious that she likes me."

"But you don't like her," *Dat* finished.

"I like her, but not that way." Then he explained that Ben took Lora home. "I have a feeling Ben is going to ask Lora out, so that means Darla will expect me to ask her out."

"Maybe you need to have an honest conversation with Darla about your feelings for her."

Jayden grimaced. "I don't want to hurt her. We've been *freinden* for a long time."

"I understand that, but letting her think you care for her will hurt her feelings too."

Jayden groaned and rubbed his eyes. "Why does it have to be so complicated?"

"Life tends to be complicated, *sohn*." *Dat* chuckled.

Jayden shook his head. "We should get to bed. Tomorrow is Monday." He started to stand.

"Have you spoken to Kira?"

Jayden sank back down onto the chair. "Not since Friday."

"I'm certain you'll see her soon."

"Why do you say that?"

Dat shrugged. "It's just a feeling I have." He pushed back his chair and stood before picking up his lantern. "*Gut nacht.*"

Jayden started for the doorway. "Sleep well," he said as *Dat* headed down the hallway to the bedroom he shared with Crystal.

As Jayden climbed the stairs, memories of when his brothers lived at home floated through his mind. He missed those days when they would talk late at night. He even missed the times when Tyler and Korey would bicker, and Jayden would find himself stuck in the middle, trying to convince his brothers to forgive and appreciate each other. He always was the peacemaker, the one who reminded his brothers how important it was to be a family, just as he imagined *Mamm* would have wanted him to do.

Yet, as much as he missed the old days, he was grateful that both his brothers had decided to build homes on their father's land and raise their families there. Jayden cherished having his brothers close. He recalled *Mamm* telling him that keeping their family close was more important than anything, and he would never forget her words.

After changing for bed, Jayden slipped under the covers and rolled onto his side. He pushed away his confusion over Darla and allowed thoughts of Kira to fill his mind once again. He hoped *Dat* was right and he would see her soon.

And when Jayden did get a chance to see Kira, it would be a blessing.

❦

"Our driver will be here at eleven to pick us up and take us to Crystal's *haus* for lunch," *Aenti* Ellen said as she entered the kitchen Friday morning. "I have so much to do before we leave. When I spoke to Crystal yesterday, I told her I'd bring dessert." She set a pot on the stove and then took a box of oatmeal from the pantry.

Kira strapped Mimi into her highchair and then handed her a small container of Cheerios. "I can bake a cake for you. I saw a chocolate cake mix and a container of icing in the pantry. I'll start right after I finish the breakfast dishes, and it will be ready for when you leave."

"When I leave?" *Aenti* Ellen turned from where she stood at the counter stirring a pot of oatmeal. "You're coming, too, Kira."

"I can stay home with the *kinner* so you can enjoy time with your *freind*."

"Oh no, Kira," her aunt insisted. "You're coming, silly. This is *our* day out. Crystal and her stepsons' wives will be there too. All of the *kinner* will play together, and we'll enjoy time with Crystal, Michelle, and Savannah."

"Okay." Excitement skittered through Kira at the thought of seeing Jayden, but surely he'd be at work until after they left.

"I told Stan we'd be home in time to make supper. He told me to just take our time and enjoy it."

"Right. It will be fun."

After the breakfast dishes were washed and put away, Kira concentrated on baking the cake while her aunt took care of the children and then packed a diaper bag full of supplies for Austin, Mimi, and Liesel.

Kira had just finished icing the cake when she heard a van park outside the house.

"Oh dear!" *Aenti* Ellen called from the family room. "It's time to go already. Ruby, please get Liesel and Mimi for me. I'll gather up Austin."

Kira washed the knife and then snapped the cake topper in place. When she followed her aunt and the children out to the porch, she looked up at the gray sky and breathed in the scent of rain.

"Who's ready to visit our *freinden?" Aenti* Ellen asked as she loaded Mimi into a car seat.

Ruby bounced on her heels. "I am! I hope Jayden is there."

"I do too," Kira whispered before lifting Liesel into a car seat.

Kira sat in the back of the van with Ruby as the vehicle bumped up a gravel driveway that led to a modest, two-story brick home with a small front porch. Beyond it, she spotted a red barn, a white cinder-block building, and then a small pasture with two more two-story homes, which were white.

The van came to a stop, and almost immediately, the back door of the brick home burst open, and an attractive woman with red hair peeking out under her prayer covering hurried down the porch steps. Her pretty face lit up with a smile as she waited by the passenger door. With her flawless ivory skin and bright green eyes, she looked to be in her late thirties.

"Crystal!" *Aenti* Ellen called as she exited the van and embraced her friend. "It's been too long."

"I know! I miss seeing you at church. We live less than ten miles apart, but with our families and our chores, life has just gotten in the way of our friendship. I can't wait to see how your *kinner* have grown."

Aenti Ellen opened the back door. "This is Austin."

"Oh my goodness," Crystal gushed. "He is such a sweetheart."

"*Danki.*" *Aenti* Ellen lifted him into her arms. "And here are Liesel and Mimi."

Crystal shook her head. "They've gotten so big." She looked back at Ruby. "And look at you, Ruby. You're a young lady now."

"I am." Ruby touched Kira's shoulder. "This is my cousin Kira."

Kira waved. "Hi, Crystal. I've heard a lot about you."

"It's a pleasure to meet you, Kira. Please come in."

Kira followed Ruby out of the back seat and then lifted Liesel out of her seat and set her on the ground before retrieving Mimi. Then Kira picked up the chocolate cake and held it in one hand while balancing Mimi on her hip. While Liesel held on to her apron, Kira walked slowly into the house.

They entered the kitchen, where two young women who looked to be in their midtwenties stood at the counter. One had light-brown hair and bright blue eyes, and her distended abdomen gave the hint that she might be expecting soon. The other had dark hair and similarly bright blue eyes.

The sound of toddlers playing in a nearby room drifted into the kitchen.

"You must be Kira. I'm Michelle," said the woman who was expecting. Then she touched the other woman's shoulder. "This is my sister-in-law, Savannah."

"We're so excited to meet you." Savannah held her hand out to Kira, and Kira placed the cake saver on the counter in order to shake Savannah's hand.

When Mimi started to wiggle, Kira set her down on the floor.

Ruby waved. "I'm Ruby. I'm going to play with the *kinner.*" She took Mimi's hand in hers. "Come with me." Then she looked at Liesel. "Can Liesel play with us too?"

"Would you like to join them, Liesel?" Kira asked her little cousin.

Liesel nodded and then clapped. Ruby took her hand and then led both of her little sisters to the family room.

"Do you like egg salad or tuna fish?" Michelle asked.

Kira smiled. "I like both."

"Oh *gut*," Savannah said.

Then Kira pointed to the cake. "I baked a chocolate *kuche* this morning."

Michelle rested her hands on her protruding belly. "That sounds heavenly."

Crystal and *Aenti* Ellen walked into the kitchen, and Michelle and Savannah immediately gathered around *Aenti* Ellen to get a glimpse of sleeping baby Austin.

"Who is this?" Savannah asked.

Aenti Ellen beamed. "This is Austin. He's almost two months old now."

"He's so handsome," Michelle said. Then she grinned at Savannah. "You know, I think Tyler is hoping for a *bu*, but he hasn't admitted it to me. He says he'll be *froh* with whatever the Lord blesses us with this time, but I think he'd be thrilled with a *bu*."

Savannah laughed. "*Ya*, I believe Korey was happy that we had a *bu* first, but he said the same thing. We're hoping for more."

"When are you due, Michelle?" *Aenti* Ellen asked.

"At Christmastime."

"Oh, that's fantastic." *Aenti* Ellen smiled. "It will be here before you know it."

Crystal touched her abdomen, and *Aenti* Ellen's eyes widened.

"Are you expecting, Crystal?" *Aenti* Ellen asked.

Crystal nodded. "I'm due in February."

"I'm so excited, Crystal," Michelle exclaimed. "Krissy will love being a big *schweschder*."

Savannah laughed. "I wonder if it will be another girl. Wouldn't it be funny if all of Duane's future *kinner* are girls?"

Everyone laughed.

Kira ran her finger over the back of a kitchen chair while the women continued to talk about Crystal's news. Although she was excited to meet Jayden's family, she couldn't stop the feeling of being left out.

And deep in her heart, she wondered if she'd ever find a man who would love her enough to want to spend his life with her and build a family. She had once believed that she and Philip would have a future together—a home and a family. In fact, Philip had started to build her a house. But then he told her that he wasn't ready to get married, and when he broke up with her, her dream had died.

Kira's throat began to tighten, and she tried to swallow past the lump of grief swelling there. She couldn't allow herself to get emotional in front of her new friends.

She prayed that someday she'd be blessed with the happiness that these women clearly were enjoying. But jealousy was a sin, and she had no right to be jealous of these wonderful women.

Just then, Crystal touched Kira's shoulder, and when she smiled, Kira felt herself start to relax. "Are you okay?"

"*Ya*. Of course."

"*Gut*." Crystal moved to the counter and picked up a loaf of bread. "How about we have our lunch now?"

CHAPTER 10

KIRA TOOK ANOTHER BITE OF HER EGG SALAD SANDWICH while sitting at Crystal's kitchen table. *Aenti* Ellen and Crystal discussed friends from Crystal's former church district.

The children had eaten sandwiches and then returned to the family room to continue playing in their play yard with Kristena's toys, and the adults took turns checking on them. Austin had fallen asleep in his seat, which was on the floor beside Crystal. While Kira looked around the table, she wondered where Jayden sat for his meals. Was she possibly sitting in his usual chair?

Kira enjoyed getting to know Jayden's sisters-in-law, and she was tempted to ask them questions about him. She just had to find a way to ask the questions without giving away her curiosity.

"Do you have any siblings?" Michelle asked Kira before taking a bite of her tuna fish sandwich.

Kira wiped her mouth with a paper napkin. "*Ya.* I have one older *schweschder* and two younger *schweschdere.*"

"I have an older and a young *schweschder.*" Michelle smiled. "In fact, my parents and younger *schweschder* live at the farm next door."

"How about you, Savannah?" Kira asked.

"I have a younger *bruder* who lives in the western part of the state. His name is Toby, and he got married last year. *Mei dat* is remarried and lives out there too. I also have a half *bruder* and half *schweschder*, who are much younger. Korey and I try to visit them at least once a year."

"That's really nice." Kira picked up a chip from her plate as she considered how to ask about Jayden. "Are Tyler, Korey, and Jayden close?"

"Oh *ya*," Savannah said. "Very close."

"They used to not all be close, though." Michelle's expression became grim. "In fact, Korey and Tyler used to bicker all the time and then had a pretty terrible falling-out a couple of years ago."

Savannah picked up a chip. "Korey always says that Jayden is the glue that keeps the three of them together."

"Really?" Kira leaned forward. "What does that mean exactly?"

"Whenever Korey and Tyler would argue, Jayden would be the one who would convince them not to give up on each other. He always reminded them that they're family, and that their *mamm* would want them to be close," Savannah explained.

Michelle nodded. "That's right. Tyler said that Jayden never took sides. He always remained neutral and encouraged them to work out their issues and remain *bruders*."

"Wow." Kira sat back on the chair as she took in more intriguing information about Jayden. He truly was a special man.

"Do you like to cook?" Michelle asked.

Kira shrugged. "*Ya*, I do."

"We do too." Savannah pointed between them. "We're always swapping recipes, so you'll have to join us."

Warmth surged in her chest. "I'd love to do that."

"Great," Michelle said. "What are some of your favorites?"

Soon they were discussing recipes and then sharing when they hadn't turned out the way they'd planned. Kira and Michelle laughed while Savannah described a meat loaf that she'd left in too long and turned into a charred mess.

"Korey and I were newlyweds when that happened, and he didn't want to hurt my feelings," Savannah explained with a chuckle. "So he said he liked his meat loaf well done."

Kira and Michelle hooted while Savannah wiped her eyes.

"Did you make him eat it?" Kira asked.

Savannah held her hand up. "Would you believe he said he liked it?" She snorted and then laughed again.

"Oh look," Crystal called as she pointed at the window. "It's raining."

Kira angled her body to face the kitchen windows. Large, fat raindrops poured down from the sky, bouncing off the porch railing and drumming a steady cadence on the roof above them.

"That means the men will be home soon," Savannah said.

Kira's heart gave a kick at the thought of talking to Jayden again. It had been a week since she'd seen his handsome face, and she had missed him.

"What does your *dat* do, Kira?" Crystal asked.

Kira turned to face her. "He has a dairy farm."

"Oh, the work never ends at a dairy," Michelle said. "*Mei dat* has one next door."

Kira smiled at her. "That is true."

They spent the remainder of lunch talking about farms and then moving on to the weather. After they finished their sandwiches and chips, *Aenti* Ellen suggested they cut Kira's cake. Savannah started the percolator, and they ate pieces of chocolate cake and drank cups of coffee.

After a while, a pickup truck rumbled into the driveway and then the back door opened and closed before a tall man with dark-brown hair sprinkled with flecks of gray and a matching beard stepped into the kitchen.

"Hello there," he said. "Oh, look at that *kuche*. I hope you saved a piece for me."

Crystal laughed as she stood and touched his arm. "Of course we did. Duane, do you remember *mei freind* Ellen? And this is her niece, Kira."

"It's nice to see you, Ellen." Duane smiled and nodded at Kira. "It's great to meet you, Kira."

Kira couldn't help but notice that Jayden had his father's smile. "You too."

"Are the rest of the guys home yet?" he asked Crystal.

"No, not yet."

"They should be here soon. They know better than to try to work on a wet roof in the rain." He held his hands up. "Excuse me. I'm going to get changed out of these clothes. The rain caught my roofing crew and me off guard." Then he padded into the family room.

A little voice exclaimed, "*Dat! Dat!*"

Kira and the rest of the women chuckled in response.

After several minutes, Duane returned in dry clothes with little Kristena in his arms. He joined the rest of the ladies at the table with Kristena on his lap while they shared a piece of cake.

A second pickup truck parked in the driveway, and Savannah jumped up and rushed to the door before returning with a tall man, who shared the same dark hair and eyes as Duane.

Savannah rested her hand on the man's chest and said, "This is Korey. Korey, this is Ellen and her niece Kira."

Kira waved while *Aenti* Ellen said hello.

Korey scratched his cheek. "Is there any more of that *kuche* left?"

"*Ya*, of course." Savannah laughed.

While Savannah cut him a piece, Korey slipped into the utility room and returned with a couple of folding chairs. Then he squeezed in at the table between Savannah and Michelle. Soon he and his father were discussing work and how the weather would set them behind at least a day.

Kira was staring out the window at the pouring rain when the familiar gold Dodge diesel truck pulled into the driveway. She tried to ignore how her stomach flipped with the knowledge that Jayden was in that truck.

Michelle pushed back her chair and hefted herself up.

"Where are you going?" Korey turned toward her.

Michelle pointed to the window. "To tell Tyler to come in here for some *kuche*."

"Just relax," Korey said. "I'll go tell him."

Michelle seemed to breathe a sigh of relief. "*Danki*."

Korey smiled and then ambled through the doorway that led to the mudroom.

Kira brushed her hands down her red dress and black apron. She hoped she looked presentable for Jayden, and then she felt silly for even worrying about it. They were acquaintances and nothing more.

She turned back toward the window as Tyler and Jayden jumped out of the truck and then jogged through the rain and up the porch steps, where Korey met them. She heard muffled voices before heavy footsteps entered the house.

Korey and Tyler came into the kitchen first, chuckling on their way to the counter, where the cake sat. Tyler said hello to everyone and then turned to the cake.

"I hear there's *appeditlich kuche* here," Tyler said.

Michelle shot him a look. "And that's more important than greeting your *fraa*?"

"I'm sorry." Tyler feigned a frown, and chuckles broke out around the room as he closed the distance between himself and his wife and kissed her cheek. "Hi."

She touched his nose. "Hi. Now you may cut yourself a piece of *kuche* and bring me another one." She handed him her empty plate.

"*Ya*, dear."

While Tyler returned to the counter, Jayden appeared in the doorway. His navy-colored shirt was drenched, and his sandy-blond hair was soaked. He pushed his hair back from his bright eyes and smiled over at Kira, sending heat roaring through her veins. "Kira. Hi."

"You're drenched, *sohn*," Duane told Jayden. "I guess the rain caught you by surprise, too, huh?"

Jayden chuckled. "*Ya*. I was the only one up on the roof when the heavens opened."

"I told them I thought the rain was going to start any minute, but Jay insisted on finishing what he was doing," Tyler said as he cut two pieces of cake.

"Well, Ty," Korey began, while rubbing his dark beard, "I would imagine that he was anxious to get done since you're sort of, um, how shall I say it? You're a rather *demanding* boss?"

Tyler shook his head. "The stories about how rough I am as a boss aren't true, Kore."

"Hmm." Korey tapped his chin with feigned contemplation. "You seem to forget that I worked with you for a while."

"Ah. Well." A burst of laughter escaped from Tyler's lips, and everyone else joined in.

Jayden held his hands up. "I'm not going to get in the middle of this, but I am going to get changed." He met Kira's gaze. "I'll be right back." He shuffled through the doorway, where a chorus of little voices greeted him. "Hi, everyone. I have to run upstairs, but I promise I'll be right back." Then his heavy footsteps sounded as they ascended a staircase.

Tyler and Korey joined the group at the table, with Tyler squeezing in by Michelle, and Korey returning to sit beside Savannah.

Soon the group was laughing while the brothers and their father shared stories of their roofing job mishaps, and Kira couldn't stop her smile. She felt as if she were already part of their group, and that knowledge warmed her from her head to her toes.

After a few minutes, footfalls began descending the stairs, and Kira's heart did another somersault. She glanced around the table and tried to see where a chair for Jayden could squeeze in, but she didn't see how he might fit. She hoped that he would somehow find a way to sit by her, but it seemed unlikely.

Footsteps sounded in the family room, and then little voices greeted him.

"Jayden!" Ruby's volume sounded above the rest. "Jayden! Have you made more furniture?"

"*Ya*, I have."

"Can I see it?" Kira recognized the excitement in her cousin's voice.

Jayden returned to the kitchen with Ruby following at his

heels. He wore a tan shirt and black trousers, and his hair was still wet and pushed back from his handsome face.

"Ellen," he called. "Would it be all right if I took Ruby out to my woodshop to show her the doll furniture I'm working on?"

"*Ya*, of course," *Aenti* Ellen said.

Kira held her breath, hoping he would invite her too. When he turned toward her, she felt heat rise in her cheeks.

"Would you like to come, too, Kira?"

"I'd love to," she said, and adrenaline cascaded through her.

He smiled. "*Gut*."

Jayden found two large umbrellas in the mudroom before he stepped out onto the porch and opened them. He handed one to Kira and then held the second one over Ruby while he led them through the pouring rain to the cinderblock building.

He flipped on his flashlight and steered them past the tools and supplies to the back of the building and into the woodshop, where he turned on the four lanterns that helped illuminate the room. The rain continued to beat on the roof.

When he turned toward Kira, she shivered as she smiled at him.

"You're cold," he said.

She shook her head. "I'm fine."

He picked up a jacket he'd left in the shop a few weeks ago and held it out to her. "Would you like to wear this?"

"No, but *danki*." She rubbed her hands over the sleeves of her red dress, and he couldn't help but think that red was her color. She looked absolutely stunning, and for a moment, he couldn't tear his eyes away from her.

Ruby hurried over to the shelf of trains his father had built. "Look at these trains, Kira!"

"*Ach*, don't touch, Ruby." Kira hurried over to her. "Those aren't yours."

Jayden joined them by the shelf. "It's okay. These are the trains *mei dat* builds to give to children's charities at Christmastime."

"May I touch one?" Ruby asked.

Jayden nodded. "*Ya.* Just be careful, okay?"

"I will." Ruby picked up a train and ran her fingers over the engine and its two cars.

Kira touched it and then smiled. "It's wonderful. I'm sure the *kinner* love receiving them."

"*Ya*, they do." Jayden grinned. "He donates them anonymously, but he has received thank-you notes that the charities share with him. I know it warms his heart to hear that he brightened a child's day." Then he pointed to the tool bench where pieces of unfinished trains sat waiting to discover their purpose. "Those are the trains he's working on."

Kira lifted her chin. "Now show us your projects."

"All right." Jayden turned and gestured toward the worktable, where a half-finished dollhouse and random pieces of furniture sat. "I've been working on a *haus*. It's not done yet, and you can tell it's really plain. I've made a few pieces of furniture, too, but they're not spectacular."

Ruby rushed over to it. "This is neat, Jayden."

"It is." Kira ran her hand over the roof of the house and then touched the staircase leading from the first floor to the second.

When her gaze tangled with his, the warmth in her eyes stole his breath for a moment. "You are very talented, Jayden. You need to stop selling yourself short."

He nodded, unsure of what to say.

Kira pointed to the workbench behind her. "Are those your sketches?"

"*Ya.*" He beckoned her to follow him to the bench. "I sketch out what I want to build before I start. I have a couple of different designs for miniature dressers, a bunk bed, and cabinets."

Kira closed the distance between them, and he inhaled the scent of her flowery shampoo as she flipped through the drawings. "You have such a *gut* eye for this."

"*Danki.*"

Behind them, Ruby began talking softly to herself. When Jayden turned, he found her moving the furniture around and playing with a little doll that she must have hidden in her pocket.

Kira placed her hand on Jayden's arm, and he enjoyed the feel of her touch. "Is it okay that she's playing with the dollhouse?"

"Well, dollhouses are meant to be played with."

Kira grinned. "That's true."

Jayden moved two stools over to the workbench, and they each hopped up on one.

"How old are your *bruders*?" Kira asked.

"Ty is twenty-eight, and Kore is twenty-seven."

"Oh." Kira rested her hands on the workbench. "Savannah and Michelle told me that they used to bicker a lot, but they're close now."

"*Ya*, that's true. Kore and Ty used to not get along. It's a long story, but Kore left for a while and went to Ohio for fourteen months after they had a falling-out. Then he came back about three years ago, and they worked it out. They've been close ever since."

Kira seemed to give him a knowing look. "Savannah said that Korey calls you the glue that holds the family together."

He snorted. "I wouldn't go that far."

"What does that mean exactly?"

"Well, when *mei bruders* would argue, I would sort of act as their mediator and remind them that we all need to get along. I've always felt it was my role to keep the family together for *mei mamm*'s sake." He rubbed the back of his neck as memories of his sweet mother filled his mind. "*Mei dat* often tells me that I remind him of her. She was always the peacemaker, and I'm the same way."

"Wow." Kira's dark eyes seemed to sparkle. "Your family thinks very highly of you. Apparently, you're a big part of how they worked out their differences and how they're close now. You're pretty amazing."

Jayden suddenly felt itchy under her intense stare as well as unworthy of her praise. "I appreciate the compliments, but I haven't done much." He was certain he'd always fall short of his older brothers. He'd never be as confident as Tyler or as bold as Korey. After all, they both led their own roofing crews, and Jayden was still only Tyler's employee and wasn't sure if he'd ever want to lead his own crew.

"How old are you?" Kira suddenly asked.

He ran his finger along the edge of the workbench. "I'm twenty-three."

"Really?" She sat up straighter. "I thought you were older."

"How old did you think I am?"

"I thought you were twenty-five like I am."

Jayden felt his posture droop as reality hit him. He was two years younger than Kira. That meant there was no way she'd ever consider him as more than a friend. He'd never known a woman to date a younger man. Disappointment weighed heavily in the pit of his stomach.

"I noticed your *bruders* call you Jay," she continued, not seeming to notice his chagrin. "Do you prefer to be called Jay or Jayden?"

He shrugged. "I don't mind either as long as you call me," he joked, and when she laughed, he enjoyed the sweet sound. "Tell me about your *schweschdere*."

"Oh, okay. Let's see." She folded her arms over her waist. "Abby is twenty-eight, and she's been married to Vic for a few years now. She works as a midwife. Then Leah is twenty-two, and Maribeth is eighteen."

"Are you close?"

"*Ya*, very."

"You must miss them," Jayden said.

"*Ya*, I do. All the time." Her smile dimmed slightly, and she cleared her throat.

"Does Abby have any *kinner*?"

"No, not yet, but they're praying they'll be blessed soon." She rubbed the hem of her apron.

Jayden shifted on the stool. "How did Abby learn to be a midwife?"

"She learned from *mei mamm*. We used to go with her to her appointments, and we both assisted her with births."

"Wow." Jayden was fascinated. "That means you know how to deliver babies."

Kira nodded. "I'm a little rusty, but I could help in a pinch if I was needed. I miss delivering babies, and I'd love to get back to doing it again. There's nothing like witnessing the miracle of a life coming into the world." She rested her elbows on the workbench. "I haven't spoken to my family in about a week, so I plan to call them to check in tomorrow."

She turned toward the table, where Ruby continued to play, and Jayden studied Kira's beautiful profile. He had so many questions that his heart craved for her to answer. Did she have a boyfriend? Would she consider dating someone younger than she was? Would she stay in Pennsylvania?

A knock on the shop door drew Jayden's attention to the doorway where Korey stood.

CHAPTER 11

"Sorry to interrupt," Korey said while standing in the entrance to the woodshop. "Ellen's driver is here and she's ready to go home."

Kira hopped down from the stool. "Oh dear. I didn't realize what time it was." She walked over to Ruby. "We need to get going now."

Jayden took in his brother's curious expression and then quickly looked away. He was certain Korey would ask him questions later and most likely tease him just as Tyler had.

"Tell Jayden thanks for the tour of his shop," Kira instructed Ruby.

Ruby looked up at him. "*Danki*, Jayden!" Then she took off running past Korey and toward the other end of the supply building.

"Ruby!" Kira gave a frustrated sigh. "That girl is always running everywhere, and she's going to fall."

Korey pointed toward the doorway. "I'll get her." Then he disappeared.

Kira smiled. "I had a really nice time. Thank you for showing us your shop."

"You're welcome."

When they stepped back outside, Kira turned toward him. "I just realized that it stopped raining."

Jayden nodded as he breathed in the fresh scent of the earth after the rain. He turned toward the driveway, where the white van sat. Ellen was busy loading the children into their car seats while Crystal, Michelle, and Savannah stood nearby.

Disappointment pressed down on Jayden as he escorted Kira to the van. He wasn't ready for their time together to end.

When they reached the van, Kira turned toward him and held out her hand. "I hope to see you again soon."

Jayden took her hand, shook it, and then held on a few moments longer than necessary. "I hope so, too, Kira."

Ellen finished loading up Austin and set his diaper bag on the van's floor. Then she turned to Crystal and pulled her in for a hug. "Let's get together again soon."

Crystal agreed as Ellen climbed into the passenger seat.

"*Danki* for lunch," Kira told Crystal.

Jayden's stepmother pulled Kira in for a hug, and Kira's smile lit up her face. "I hope you'll come and visit again."

"I will." Kira shook hands with Michelle and Savannah before she also took a seat in the van. She turned toward the window and waved to Jayden as the van bumped down the gravel driveway toward the road.

"So, Jay," Korey began as the van disappeared from sight, "you and Kira seem to get along well."

Jayden faced his middle brother standing beside him. "*Ya.* And . . . ?"

"You tell me." Korey rubbed his beard.

Jayden heaved out a deep sigh. "Great. Now you're going to tease me like Ty does."

"What do you mean?"

Jayden folded his arms across his chest. "Ty has been giving me a hard time about Kira since we worked at her *onkel*'s house. There's nothing going on between us. I just like talking to her, and I think she likes talking to me."

"I'll say. You two were deep in a conversation when I came to the shop. That's why I had to knock on the door to get your attention."

Jayden nodded and waited for Korey to make a smart comment.

"I'm glad to see you getting to know a nice *maedel*. It's about time you started dating." Then Korey gave Jayden's shoulder a pat before he sauntered toward Savannah.

"*Mamm*," Ruby called to her mother from the back seat of the van. "You should have seen Jayden's woodshop. It was so neat. He's making a *schee* dollhouse with furniture."

Aenti Ellen craned her neck to face the back of the van. "That's really nice, Ruby."

Kira smiled as she settled in the seat beside Ruby. She had enjoyed her time with the Bontrager family. When she had first arrived, she felt out of place, but once Savannah and Michelle pulled her into a conversation about recipes, she felt herself relax and then realized she was laughing along with them while Savannah shared her cooking disasters.

But the true highlight of the visit had been having a chance to talk with Jayden. Her heart did a funny little flip as she recalled sitting with him at the worktable. If only they'd had more time together. She'd been disappointed when Korey had interrupted them and announced it was time to leave. She felt so comfortable talking with Jayden. In fact, he'd seemed more attentive than Philip. Although she and Philip had shared heart-to-heart conversations during the year they'd dated, at times she felt as if Philip wasn't truly listening to her. She would tell him what was on her mind, and he would nod or not respond. Yet Jayden seemed so in tune with her, and she could tell he was truly listening to her when his gorgeous hazel eyes were focused on her. She'd been shocked when he'd shared that he was two years younger than she was since he seemed so mature.

As she stared out the window at traffic passing them on the road, Kira once again wondered if he had a girlfriend. A young man as sweet and thoughtful as he was most likely had already won the heart of a young woman in his community. Kira, however, also had the feeling that Jayden had enjoyed talking to her as much as she had enjoyed talking with him. She just hoped that the Lord would allow their paths to cross again—and soon!

"Did you all have fun?" *Aenti* Ellen asked, turning to face Liesel and Mimi, who were both sound asleep in their car seats.

Kira leaned forward. "I'd say they had a fantastic time."

Aenti Ellen laughed, and Kira joined in.

When they arrived home, Kira helped Mimi and Liesel out of their seats and then picked up her cake saver, which was empty after each of the Bontrager men had helped themselves to a piece of cake.

Aenti Ellen paid the driver and then carried Austin up the back steps. "Would you please do me a favor, Kira?"

"Of course. What do you need?"

"Don't tell your *onkel* that we didn't save him a piece of chocolate *kuche*." Her aunt pointed to the empty cake saver. "He'll be very hurt if he finds out."

Kira chuckled. "The secret is safe with me. Before I start supper, I'll wash the cake saver and put it back in the cabinet."

"I knew I could count on you."

While her aunt took care of the children, Kira pulled out the sloppy joe and macaroni casserole she had put together the night before and then preheated the oven.

"Do you need any help?" Ruby asked as she scuttled into the kitchen.

Kira opened the utensil drawer. "How about you start setting the table for me?"

"Okay!" Ruby began pulling out utensils and then moved to the table and set them at each place.

Kira retrieved the plates from the cabinet and joined Ruby at the table, where they worked together. When the oven dinged, Kira put in the casserole and set the timer.

"*Danki* for your help," Kira told her little cousin. "You may go play until supper is ready."

Ruby ran off to the family room while Kira withdrew three glasses for her aunt, uncle, and herself and poured water into them. Then she picked up a plastic cup for Ruby and two sippy cups for Liesel and Mimi. She filled each of them with milk.

Aenti Ellen returned to the kitchen with Austin on her shoulder. "I changed Liesel and Mimi and then fed Austin. I'm hoping he'll sleep better tonight. I could really use a good night's sleep."

"Would you like me to handle his feeding in the middle of the night so you can sleep?"

Her aunt gave her a warm smile. "You're sweet, but that's not your job."

"I'd be happy to take him in my room for the night so that you can get some *gut* rest."

"*Danki* for offering, but I'll be fine."

"Well, then you need to nap tomorrow when he naps."

Her aunt sank down into a chair. "I will. Now tell me about your visit with Jayden."

"There's not much to tell." Kira sat down across from her. "He showed Ruby and me his woodshop, and we talked for a bit."

"What did you talk about?"

"He asked about my family, and I asked about his *bruders.* Savannah told me that Korey calls Jayden the glue that holds the family together, and I asked him about that. He said he's always been the peacemaker in the family, like his *mamm* was. He acted as if it wasn't a big deal, but I get the feeling he's very humble. He seems so thoughtful, kind, generous, and caring. He's very special."

Aenti Ellen gave her a knowing look. "You really care about him, don't you?"

"I do." Kira began folding a paper napkin into small squares. "I'm hoping that our paths will cross again."

Aenti Ellen smiled. "Like I said, the Lord works in mysterious ways. There's a possibility that you will see each other again."

Kira nodded, and she hoped her aunt was right.

The following morning, Kira sat in her uncle's office in his store and dialed her family's phone number. She leaned back on *Onkel*

Stan's desk chair and hoped that one of her family members was close to the phone shanty and would hear the phone ring.

After several rings, someone finally picked up. "Hello?" one of her sisters asked.

"Maribeth?" Kira asked, and her heart clenched when she heard her sister's sweet voice.

"Kira!" her sister yelled. "It's Leah. Hang on." Then she heard Leah yell, "Mari! It's Kira. Come here!"

"Kira! Hey. It's Mari. I'm here too."

Kira's eyes stung as she imagined her two younger sisters standing by the phone and sharing the receiver. "How are you doing?"

"Fine," Leah said. "We were just talking about you. How are things in Pennsylvania?"

"They're *gut*. I'm having a lot of fun. Ruby is such a hoot. I wish you were here to see her. And Liesel and Mimi have gotten so big. Austin is still tiny, and he keeps *Aenti* Ellen up at night. She tries to nap during the day when he's napping." Kira talked on about their little cousins while her sisters listened.

"Oh *gut*," Leah said. "I'm going to run into the *haus* to get *Mamm*. I'll be back."

"Mari, tell me how *Mamm* and Abby are."

"Oh, they're just fine. Abby was here yesterday. She was nearby delivering a baby and then stopped by to say hello on her way home. She looked really tired but *gut*. She asked about you too."

"And *Dat*?"

"He's the same. He's so busy with the farm, but he's doing well. He ran to town with our driver for supplies, but he'll be back soon," Maribeth said. "Oh, here are *Mamm* and Leah."

Kira heard rustling.

"Hi, Kira. I'm back," Leah said. "*Mamm* is here too. She said I can talk before she does. Have you gone to youth group and made some *freinden*?"

Kira rocked back in her uncle's chair. "*Ya*, I have. What's new with youth group there?"

"Oh, Kira, so much! Let's see." Leah paused. "Well, Lena is dating Ervan."

"We saw that coming, right?" Kira laughed.

Leah snorted. "I know."

"Who else?" Kira relaxed while her sister listed off more couples who had either started dating or broken up. When Leah ran out of information, Kira said, "Any other news?"

"Uh. Well . . ."

Kira could tell by her sister's voice that she was hedging. "Leah, what is it?"

"Nothing, nothing."

"Leah Joy, tell me," Kira insisted.

"Oh, Kira. I don't want to hurt you."

Kira cradled the receiver between her ear and her shoulder and ran her finger over the edge of the desk as her stomach tightened with worry. "Leah, now you have to tell me. What's going on?"

"Philip has been going to youth group."

Kira stilled at the sound of her ex-fiancé's name. "What do you mean?" she finally asked.

"He's been participating."

"Is he seeing anyone?"

"Um . . ."

Kira's stomach dropped. "Leah . . . Please tell me."

"He's been spending a lot of time with Yvonne Coblentz."

"But she's been dating Hans Stutzman for months."

"They broke up."

A vision of Yvonne Coblentz hijacked Kira's mind, and bile rose in her throat. Yvonne was beautiful with sunshine-colored hair, gorgeous green eyes, a perfect nose, and ivory skin. She was tall, most likely close to five-foot-nine, and she'd always turned the heads of all the young men in their community. So, of course, Philip would want to date her.

And that was when Kira realized the truth. Philip broke up with her because he said he wasn't ready to get married, but instead, he didn't want to marry Kira. Perhaps he had dated her because he was just biding his time until someone better became available. Maybe he thought Kira was fun to be around and he toyed with the idea of marrying her, but he never was going to, which was why he finally broke up with her.

"Kira?" Leah called her name. "Are you all right?"

"*Ya*, I'm fine," Kira said quickly, her voice trembling. "Is *Mamm* still there?"

"Here she is," Leah said.

"Kira. Sweetheart, how are you?" *Mamm's* voice was warm and comforting, and the sound caused Kira's eyes to burn as more homesickness grabbed her by her throat.

"*Mamm*," she managed to say, but her voice sounded thin and reedy. "I miss you."

"We miss you too. Tell me everything."

Kira sniffed and then shared stories about her time with her aunt and her cousins. *Mamm* laughed as she talked about Ruby's antics, and she asked for details about the little ones and their schedules. Kira asked about the farm, and *Mamm* shared how busy *Dat* was with the cows.

"Kira, I'm sure Leah upset you with the news about Philip," *Mamm* said when they finished discussing the news from the farm. "I didn't want her to tell you. You don't need to concern yourself with what he's doing. He broke your heart, and he shouldn't be in your thoughts."

"Right." Kira sniffed.

"*Ach*, Kira. Tell me you're okay."

"I will be, *Mamm*." Kira swiped a tissue from a box on her uncle's desk and wiped her eyes and nose. "It was just a shock to hear that he's moved on already."

"I know it hurts, *mei liewe*, but I believe God has the perfect man in mind for you. Who knows, you might have already met him, and you just don't know it yet."

A vision of Jayden filtered through Kira's mind, and then she pushed it away. How could Jayden be her future when she wasn't planning to stay in Pennsylvania permanently? She couldn't fathom leaving her family behind in Indiana. In fact, the idea made her feel as if her heart would break.

"Kira, I had my heart broken before I met your *dat*. I dated a man whom I was sure I was going to marry. I was convinced I was in love with him, and I thought he loved me too. One evening he came to visit me, and I was certain that he was going to ask *mei dat*'s permission and then propose to me."

"What happened?" Kira sank back on the chair, riveted by her mother's story.

Mamm sighed. "Well, instead of proposing to me, he told me that he'd met someone else, and he needed to break up with me."

"*Ach* no!"

"*Ya*, that's what happened. I was crushed. I cried for days. That following Sunday, I went to youth group, and a couple of young men from a nearby community were there. One of them was your *dat*."

Kira smiled. "Really?"

"*Ya*. He asked me if he could give me a ride home. We sat in the driveway in his buggy and talked for more than an hour. Then he came to visit me during the week. Six months later, we were engaged. We were married that following spring, and about a year later, Abby arrived."

Kira sighed. "Wow."

"You may feel like all is lost right now, but I promise you that God has someone special in store for you. You can't give up hope just yet. You keep on praying."

"*Ya, Mamm*."

"Well, I need to get back to my chores, and I'm certain Ellen has plenty for you to do. Call again soon, okay?"

"I will, *Mamm*."

"*Ich liebe dich*, Kira."

"I love you too. Please give my love to *Dat*, Abby, Leah, and Maribeth."

"I will."

Kira hung up the phone and then hurried back to the house. As she started mopping the kitchen, she tried to put Philip and beautiful Yvonne out of her mind, but they loitered in the back of her thoughts.

She took a deep breath and sent a prayer to God:

Please God, give me peace and lead me to the path you've chosen for me.

CHAPTER 12

THE FOLLOWING MORNING, KIRA CARRIED MIMI TOWARD THE Stoltzfoos family's house while she walked beside her aunt. She balanced Mimi on her hip and covered her mouth with her hand to shield a yawn.

She'd spent most of the night tossing and turning while trying to come to grips with the news her sister had shared. Her heart still ached with the knowledge that Philip had already moved on and was dating someone else.

"Are you feeling *krank*, Kira?" *Aenti* Ellen asked, slowing her gait to walk beside her. She cradled Austin in her arms while giving Kira a concerned expression.

Onkel Stan and Ruby continued on in front of them while her uncle rested Liesel on his shoulder.

Kira had considered telling her aunt about Philip, but she'd decided against it, not wanting to give a voice to her heartache. "I didn't sleep well last night. I think I might skip the youth gathering today and come home with you to rest while the *kinner* nap."

"I'm sorry you didn't sleep well, but are you sure you want to miss time with your *freinden*?"

"I think I need a nap more than time with *freinden*." The idea of watching all the happy couples at the youth gathering made her stomach sour.

Her aunt continued to look concerned, but she nodded. "Okay."

When they reached the spot where the young women stood together, Kira set Liesel on the ground, and *Aenti* Ellen took her hand before leading her toward the Stoltzfoos family's kitchen where the married women visited together before the service began.

Kira straightened her pink dress and white apron and then went to stand beside Alaina, who was talking with a group of friends. After nodding hellos, she worked to keep her expression interested while Cecily talked on and on about her week working in her parents' store.

After several minutes, Kira glanced around, taking in a group of young men standing by the barn. She wondered if Philip was on his way to church right now. During the service, would he watch Yvonne and think about how lovely she looked today?

She sucked in a breath, trying in vain to erase all thoughts of Philip from her mind. *Stop torturing yourself!*

"Kira?"

She turned as Alaina took a step closer to her. "*Ya?*"

"Is everything all right?"

"I didn't sleep well last night. I'm tired." It wasn't a lie.

Alaina frowned. "I'm sorry to hear that." Then she smiled. "We'll have fun with our *freinden* after church, and that will help energize you."

"I don't know . . . I was thinking about going home and taking a nap this afternoon."

"Oh no. You can't go home. We're going to meet two other

youth groups this afternoon. It's going to be very fun." Then her smile widened. "And I'm wondering if Lewis might ask to give me a ride since we talked last Sunday." She touched Kira's shoulder. "And I have you to thank for that. You're the reason why we started talking."

Kira shrugged. "I'm glad I could help, but I really didn't do anything."

"You encouraged me, and now I'm going to encourage you to not go home today and miss youth group." Alaina glanced behind Kira and then looped her arm around Kira's shoulders. "It's time for church."

Kira smiled as Alaina guided her toward the barn. She was grateful for her friend.

"If you come to youth group today, there's a possibility you might meet a nice and handsome young man who will lift your mood," Alaina told Kira after lunch while they stood outside the barn.

"I'm not interested in dating."

Alaina blinked. "How could you say that?"

"Because I'm not planning to stay in Pennsylvania. I'm going to go home to my family after *mei aenti* no longer needs me."

"Well then," Alaina began, "you can just come and meet new people and have a *gut* time. If you're really tired, then Nate can bring you home early."

Kira considered this.

Alaina folded her hands as if praying and then bit her lower lip. "Please, Kira? Please say you'll come."

"Fine." Kira huffed out a breath, and Alaina clapped. "I just need to go home to change and pick up the peanut butter brownies I baked yesterday."

"Yay!" Alaina said, and Kira laughed.

***

"*Danki* for giving me a ride to youth group today." Darla gazed over at Jayden as they rode in his buggy. "I'm so excited to see my cousin. She's a member of the youth group we're meeting today."

Jayden smiled over at Darla.

"I've been excited about this youth gathering all week. I haven't seen my cousin in a while. It's going to be great. I can't wait for you to meet her. You're going to love her." As Darla talked on about her cousin, Jayden snuck another peek over at her. She looked pretty in a blue dress, and her expression seemed to glow. He could feel her enthusiasm coming off her in waves.

But even more than that, he could feel how much she liked him and how she wanted to be more than friends with him, and he knew that she cared for him. But he couldn't make himself feel the same way about her.

He considered his father's advice about being honest with Darla, but he couldn't imagine hurting her feelings. After all, they'd been friends for years, and he didn't want to risk losing her friendship. At the same time, however, he didn't want to lead her on.

He pressed his lips together as confusion rushed over him. How could he keep her friendship and not hurt her? It seemed impossible.

"My cousin lives over in Gordonville. I used to see her more often when we were little, but now that we're older, we're just so busy with chores, you know? Today will be a special treat," she continued.

Jayden turned toward her once again. "Gordonville, huh?"

"*Ya*, that's right."

"Interesting," he said, while wondering if Darla's cousin knew Kira.

Darla chuckled. "Why is that interesting?"

"No reason." He shrugged. "Tell me more about your cousin."

Darla brightened. "I just adore her. She's so sweet and funny. When we get together, we never run out of things to talk about."

Jayden settled back on the seat while Darla continued to ramble on, and he wondered if Kira would also be attending a youth gathering today.

"Kira, this is Shane Bender," Alaina said while they stood near the volleyball games at the Yoders' farm later that afternoon. "He's *gut freinden* with Nate and Lewis."

After changing clothes and retrieving the container of peanut butter brownies she had baked yesterday, Kira had climbed into Nate's buggy and ridden with Nate and Alaina to the youth gathering.

And now as she took in Alaina's megawatt smile, she realized what Alaina had meant when she said Kira might meet a nice and handsome young man who would brighten her mood today. Apparently, Alaina had been planning to set Kira up with Lewis's friend Shane.

Kira tried to hold back her frown. She should have stayed home this afternoon and taken that nap she'd craved.

Shane lifted his straw hat and raked his hand through his thick, curly, dark hair. "Hi, Kira." His voice rumbled low, and his Adam's apple bobbed as his lips turned up in a nervous smile. "It's nice to meet you."

"Hi, Shane." Kira tried to smile, but it felt more like a grimace.

When he held his hand out, she gave it a quick shake and then longed to run and hide. She wasn't in the mood to be set up with any man, even one as handsome as Shane with his strong jaw and dark-brown eyes. She knew her friend meant well, but her heart had been too battered and bruised by Philip. The only man she could imagine spending time with today was Jayden, and he was nowhere to be seen. Why hadn't she stayed home?

Kira and Shane stared at each other for a moment, and Kira tried to think of something to say to him.

"I hear you're from Indiana," Shane said.

Kira nodded. "*Ya*, that's true. I'm here helping *mei aenti*. She just had her fourth baby."

"Wow."

"Uh-huh." She rubbed the bridge of her nose. "So, what do you do?"

Shane's dark eyes flickered down toward his shoes and then back up to her eyes. "*Mei dat* breeds, trains, and sells horses."

"That sounds really interesting."

"It is."

Alaina stood behind Shane and winked at Kira before turning toward Lewis and saying something to him.

Shane touched his straw hat again. Was he nervous? "Would

you like to play volleyball?" He jammed his thumb in the direction of the games behind them. "We could join a team."

"Oh, I don't—" Kira began.

"Alaina! Alaina!" A pretty young woman rushed over shouting before she threw her arms around Alaina's shoulders. "It's so *gut* to see you, cousin!"

Alaina pulled the petite and pretty blonde in for a hug. "Darla! It's been too long. How are you?"

"I'm great. I was so excited when I heard that we were going to combine our youth groups today." She pointed to a blonde standing beside her. "You remember Lora."

"I do." Alaina rested her arm on her cousin's shoulder and angled her toward Kira. "Darla and Lora, this is *mei freind* Kira. She's from Indiana and staying with her *aenti*." Then she made a sweeping gesture between them.

Darla and Lora said hello to Kira.

Then Darla turned back to Alaina. "So, how are *Aenti* and *Onkel*? Is Nate here today?"

Kira turned to her right, and when she saw Jayden talking to a young man with dark hair and eyes, her heart thudded in her chest. Jayden looked so handsome wearing a tan shirt, and his bright hazel eyes seemed to shine in the afternoon sun.

He turned, and when his eyes focused on her, his handsome face lit up with a bright smile.

"Kira!" Jayden closed the distance between them and shook her hand. "Darla told me we had a gathering today with her cousin's youth group in Gordonville, but I had no idea you'd be here."

Kira felt her smile wobble as she glanced between Jayden and Darla. Were they a couple?

"This is Ben." Jayden introduced the young man standing beside him.

Kira shook Ben's hand. "Hi."

"How's Ruby doing?" Jayden asked.

"She's fine. How's your hobby going? Have you made more furniture?"

Jayden rubbed his hands together. "I have. Would you believe I figured out how to create a grandfather clock?"

"You have?"

"*Ya*. I'm going to paint the numbers on it." He chuckled. "I'm becoming a little too obsessed with this project."

"I think it's great. I'd love to see it."

Jayden's eyes shifted to focus beside Kira, and his smile dimmed for a moment before he focused on Kira once again.

When Kira turned, she found Darla watching them with something that looked like suspicion in her expression.

Kira took a step away from Jayden, and her stomach clenched. Her intuition was right that a man as kind, thoughtful, and handsome as Jayden would have a girlfriend. It made perfect sense, and in some ways it was a relief that he wasn't single. After all, Kira wasn't planning to stay in Pennsylvania, and she felt such a strange connection with him. Now she wouldn't have to worry about losing him when she went home since he was already someone else's boyfriend.

Darla's smile seemed manufactured and didn't quite meet her blue eyes. "How do you know each other?"

"Ty and I worked at her *onkel*'s *haus*, and her *aenti* is *freinden* with Crystal," Jayden explained.

"How nice." Darla's tone sounded too sugary sweet as she seemed to study Kira. "So you know Alaina and Jayden. What a happy coincidence."

Jayden stuck his hands in his pockets. "*Ya.*" His smile waned and then flattened.

Kira shifted her weight on her feet. She could nearly cut the tension with a knife, and it was obvious her presence was only making it awkward for Jayden. The last thing she wanted to do was to get in the way of his relationship with Darla.

She met Shane's sheepish look and smiled. "Shane, did you still want to play volleyball?"

Shane brightened. "*Ya,* let's go."

"Excuse me," Kira told Jayden and Darla. "Maybe we can play volleyball together."

Something unreadable flashed over Jayden's face before he lifted his lips in a half-smile. "*Ya,* that would be fun."

"Great." As Kira walked with Shane toward the volleyball games, she craned her neck over her shoulder and spotted Jayden watching her with a strange expression.

When Darla smiled sweetly at Jayden and began speaking to him, Kira tried to dismiss the disappointment coursing through her veins. Then she reminded herself that it was better this way since she planned to go home soon, and this wasn't her community.

Still, deep down, there was a part of her that wanted to have Jayden in her life as more than a friend. She just had to find a way to convince her heart to let go of that silly idea.

CHAPTER 13

LATER THAT AFTERNOON, KIRA JUMPED UP TO SPIKE THE BALL, and when she missed it, she bent at the waist and dissolved in giggles.

"Do they play volleyball differently in Indiana?" Jayden teased from the other side of the net. His eyes sparkled with mirth. "Here in Pennsylvania, we actually try to *hit* the ball."

Kira shook her head while attempting to get her laughter under control. "Don't use me as an example of how we play in Indiana. I'm not a very *gut* player."

"That's *gut* to know," Shane quipped from beside her.

Kira laughed as she tossed the ball over to Jayden. "Here you go."

She and Shane had played two games before Jayden, Darla, Ben, and Lora joined their opposing team. Although she'd noticed Darla shooting her dirty looks in her peripheral vision, Kira had enjoyed the games, especially since she had a chance to see agile Jayden in action, leaping and spiking the ball over the net. And she blamed her poor performance on the fact that she couldn't take her eyes off him.

"How about we take a break?" Shane suggested.

Kira swiped the back of her hand across her brow. "I could use a drink."

They all retreated to the snack table, where they each took a cup of lemonade. Nate walked over to Shane and Ben, and soon they were talking about work. Lora and Darla joined Alaina and a few of her friends.

"Did you call your family yesterday like you planned?"

Kira turned as Jayden came to stand beside her. She was speechless for a moment, surprised he'd remembered that she'd mentioned calling her family when they spoke on Friday. "*Ya*, I spoke to them yesterday."

"How are your folks?" He took another step toward her.

"They're doing fine. *Mei mamm* said *mei dat* is staying busy running his dairy farm."

"And your *schweschdere*?" His expression was warm and open, and possibly even curious. "Has Abby been delivering babies?"

"*Ya*, she has. *Mei mamm* said she stopped by after a birth the other day."

"How are Leah and Maribeth?"

He recalled her sisters' names! Kira couldn't stop her smile as warmth curled in her chest. "They're fine." She ran her fingers over her cup of lemonade as the news Leah had shared echoed through her mind, and she felt her lips press down in a frown.

Jayden tilted his head. "Is something wrong?"

Kira shook her head and took a sip of lemonade.

He seemed to study her, and she felt something inside of her break apart as the truth crowded her throat, the words crying for escape.

"*Mei schweschder* told me some things about my ex-fiancé that upset me."

Jayden's jaw almost became unhinged, it dropped so far. "Your ex-fiancé?"

"*Ya*, that's right," Kira began. "Leah told me that he—"

"Jayden! There you are!" Darla interrupted them. She smiled at Jayden before spearing Kira with a sharp look. "Did Jayden tell you that we've known each other since school? In fact, he helped me with my math problems. I had so much trouble with math back then. We always played together during recess too. He would push me on the swing when we were small. I'm so grateful that I've always been able to rely on Jayden." She turned toward him and fluttered her eyelashes as her sugary-sweet smile returned. "Would you like to play more volleyball?"

Kira's insides coiled. As much as she longed to confide in Jayden and share her heartache, she was aware of Darla's hold over him. She gave them a little wave. "I'll see you later."

She was almost certain Jayden looked disappointed as she moved to join Shane, Lewis, and Alaina.

"Kira!" Alaina announced. "We were just talking about forming another volleyball team. Would you like to join us?"

"Sure," Kira said.

Shane smiled at her. "*Gut.*"

Jayden's mind whirled as Kira walked over to where her friends stood. Kira had been engaged. She had left an ex-fiancé in Indiana. This news nearly rocked him to his core as questions seized his mind. From the sadness he found in her beautiful eyes, he surmised that the man had hurt her. Why had they broken up? Perhaps the breakup hadn't been Kira's idea. Jayden yearned to know more about what had happened.

"Jayden, are you listening to me?"

"Huh?" He faced Darla, who watched him with a mixture of annoyance and hurt lining her pretty face.

As irritated as he was with her for her constant interruptions during his conversations with Kira, he couldn't bear the thought of hurting her feelings. After all, they'd been friends since they were children. "I'm sorry, Darla. What did you say?"

Darla's sunny expression was back. "Alaina told me in confidence that she thinks Lewis is going to ask her to ride home with him. She really likes him, and he seems like a kind and caring man. His father owns a construction company. They build barns." She tapped his arm. "Alaina told me that she set Kira up with Shane. She's such a wonderful matchmaker. Don't they make a cute couple?"

Jayden nodded and turned toward where Kira stood with Alaina, Lewis, and Shane. When Kira smiled at Shane, jealousy nearly devoured him from the inside out. "What do you know about Shane?" The question jumped from his lips before he could stop it.

Darla turned toward where Kira walked beside Shane toward the volleyball games. "Alaina said he's *gut freinden* with Lewis. His family breeds, trains, and sells horses."

Jayden frowned. Shane's family bred, trained, and sold horses, which meant they were financially comfortable—*very* comfortable. And Shane looked to be at least twenty-five. No wonder Kira was interested in him. Jayden could never compete with him.

He tried to swallow back the sudden wave of chagrin that threatened to drown him.

"Hey, Jay!" Ben called as he and Lora walked over to them.

Ben looped his arm around Jayden's shoulder. "Are you ready to beat another team?"

Jayden nodded and pasted a smile on his face. "Sure."

"Let's go." Lora clapped her hands.

While Jayden walked beside Darla, he turned toward where Kira laughed with Shane on the volleyball court, and more despondence moved through him. It appeared he'd never have a chance to be more than Kira's friend, but for some strange reason, his heart refused to let go of that hope.

Later that evening, Jayden stepped out of the Yoder family's barn and into the cool late-September evening air. The dark sky above him was dotted with gray clouds as the aroma of earth and animals hovered around him. His friends shook hands as they said goodbye and headed toward the barn to collect their horses and leave for home.

Jayden had enjoyed playing volleyball, eating supper, and then playing more volleyball with his friends. He'd worked hard to keep his jealousy at bay while he witnessed Kira spending time with Shane. He was grateful each time she'd blessed him with one of her stunning smiles, but he longed to talk to her and not watch her from afar.

He bit back a groan as he acknowledged how he seemed like a lovesick teenager with a crush. Still, he couldn't deny how he cared for Kira. If only things were different . . .

While he sang hymns with the youth group, Jayden had snuck glances over at Kira, and more questions about her ex-fiancé taunted his mind. He kept wondering why her relationship with the man had ended. What had happened between them? Who had decided to call off their wedding? He wanted to get Kira alone and find out the details, but it wasn't his place to pry, especially if she was dating Shane.

Ben appeared at Jayden's side and smacked his shoulder. "Lora said that Alaina wanted to talk to us before we left tonight. Come with me."

Jayden and Ben headed over to where Alaina, Lewis, Shane, Darla, Kira, and Lora stood together with their faces illuminated by their flashlights.

Alaina turned toward Jayden. "Jayden, I think Darla mentioned that you're a roofer. Is that right?"

Darla gave Jayden a bashful smile.

"*Ya*, that's true. Why?" Jayden asked.

"I have an idea I wanted to share with all you." Alaina glanced around the group of friends. "There's a widow in my community who needs work done on her *haus*. She's a very sweet older woman, and she never had *kinner* of her own. I know she doesn't want to burden anyone and ask for help, but I feel called to give her a hand. If you're interested, maybe Darla, Lora, Kira, and I could clean while the guys fix her roof. What do you think?"

Darla beamed. "Oh, I love this idea!"

"I do too," Kira said. "I'll ask *mei aenti* if she's okay with letting me help."

"Sounds *gut* to me," Lewis said, and Shane nodded.

"*Ya*, let's do it," Ben said.

When Ben turned toward Lora, she smiled. "I'll be there."

Darla grabbed Jayden's arm. "What do you think?"

"I have a feeling *mei bruder* Ty would agree to letting me

donate time to fix the roof. I'll talk to *mei dat* about donating supplies as well." Jayden's eyes locked on Kira's, and her smile warmed his blood.

Alaina clapped her hands. "*Wunderbaar!* I'll put a plan together, and we can see about helping her later this week."

Lewis rubbed the back of his neck as if he were gathering his words, or possibly his courage, and then touched Alaina's arm. "Alaina, would you like to ride home with me?"

Alaina's gray eyes widened, and she smiled. "*Ya*, I'd love to."

"Great." Lewis blew out a breath.

Alaina snuck a glance at Kira, and the two women seemed to share a look.

Lewis glanced around at the rest of the group. "See you next week."

Courage trickled through Jayden, and he took a step toward Kira, determined to ask if she wanted a ride home. If he could get her alone, he could find out what happened with her ex-fiancé and also ask her if she cared for Shane.

But before Jayden could get to her, Shane touched her arm.

"Kira, would you like a ride home?" Shane asked her.

Kira swallowed and then smiled. "*Ya*, that would be nice. *Danki*."

Jayden turned his attention to Darla beside him. "Would you like a ride?"

"Of course I would." Darla rested her hand on his arm. Then she looked around at their group of friends. "*Gut nacht*."

As each of them responded, Jayden cast his eyes toward Kira once again. She gave him a tentative smile before walking with Shane toward the barn.

Jayden heaved out a deep breath. It was probably for the

best that Kira was seeing Shane. But somehow, he would have to convince his breaking heart.

⁓⁓⊱❦⊰⁓⁓

Kira set her empty container on her lap and stared out the window at the passing traffic while Shane guided his horse down the road. She moved her fingers over the corners of her plastic container while she considered how the day had gone.

While she'd enjoyed time with her new friends, she still struggled to accept the surprising news that Jayden had a girlfriend. She longed to extinguish the sadness and disappointment that had gripped her the moment she'd realized he was in a relationship with Darla, even though it shouldn't have surprised her. After all, as kind, sweet, and special as Jayden was, it only made sense that one of the young women in his community would have jumped at the chance to date him.

Still, she had held on to a tiny shred of hope that they could have gotten to know each other better and possibly dated.

But why would she want to date someone after the way Philip had broken her heart? She had dated him for a year and had been certain that they would build a life together before he'd told her he wasn't ready to get married. How could she trust her instincts again when she'd been so wrong about Philip? And, besides that, she wasn't planning to stay in Pennsylvania, which meant the idea of dating was preposterous!

"I think Alaina's idea for helping a widow in her community is really nice," Shane said. "I don't have much roofing experience, but I'm a fast learner."

She turned toward Shane, and he gave her a sheepish smile.

"Are you okay?" he asked.

"*Ya*, I'm fine. I'm just tired."

Silence expanded in the buggy, and she took in the rhythmic sounds of the horse's hooves and the buggy wheels. She continued to ponder Jayden and how easy conversation seemed to flow between them. When she had sat with him in his woodworking shop, they had seemed to never run out of words, but now as she rode in the buggy with Shane, she found herself trying to think of something to say.

"Do you like Pennsylvania?"

She met his eager expression and nodded. "I do. Everyone has been so kind and welcoming, and I'm having fun getting to know my little cousins."

"Tell me about your cousins."

Kira spent the remainder of the ride sharing stories of her cousins' antics while Shane laughed along with her stories. Soon they reached her aunt and uncle's house, and he halted the horse by the porch.

Shane angled his body toward her as she picked up her flashlight and empty container. "I really enjoyed talking with you today."

"I had fun too." Kira considered her earlier suspicion. "I was wondering . . . Did Alaina arrange for us to meet today?"

He chuckled. "She did."

"I had a feeling that she was part of it."

"Is that all right?" He looked hopeful.

"*Ya*, of course it is." She flipped on her flashlight and pushed opened the buggy door before glancing up toward the house, where she found a warm yellow light glowing in the kitchen window.

"I have a question for you now." Shane hesitated and licked his lips. "I would like to see you again, if that's all right with you."

Kira paused while considering how to respond to his request. While she had enjoyed Shane's company, she didn't feel a connection to him. At the same time, she liked him as a friend, but only as a friend. She didn't want to hurt his feelings, but she also didn't want to lead him on and risk breaking his heart. She never wanted to break someone's heart the way Philip had broken hers.

"I like you Shane, but I need to be honest," she began. "I recently got out of a relationship. What I need right now is a *freind*."

He smiled, but she didn't miss the disappointment in his dark eyes. "I appreciate your honesty, Kira, and I would be honored to be your *freind*. I hope to see you when we help the widow work on her *haus*."

"I do too." Kira hopped out of the buggy and waved before heading inside, where she found her aunt sitting at the kitchen table. "*Aenti* Ellen. Why are you still up?"

Her aunt placed her hand over her mouth to cover a yawn. "It was apparent that you really didn't want to go today, so I wanted to make sure you were okay."

"Oh." Kira sat down across from her and placed her empty container on the table. "I'm sorry I worried you. Everything went fine."

Aenti Ellen examined Kira's features. "Kira, you're like a *dochder*, or even a *schweschder* to me. You can tell me anything."

"I know."

"What was bothering you earlier?"

"I was just feeling a little homesick." It wasn't a lie. Kira did miss her parents, her sisters, and her friends. Yet she also wasn't ready to admit to her aunt the heartbreaking news that Philip had moved on and decided to date again.

"I'm sorry." Her aunt paused for a moment. "If you feel it's time for you to go home—"

"No, no, no," Kira interrupted her aunt. "I didn't mean to make you feel bad or make you think I want to go home. I just need sleep. I promise I'll be better tomorrow."

Her aunt nodded. "Okay."

"Alaina suggested that a group of us get together to help a widow in our community who needs some work done on her *haus*. Would it be okay if I participated?"

"Of course it would. What a wonderful idea."

"I thought so too. Jayden is going to see if he can coordinate the roofing."

Her aunt looked surprised. "You saw Jayden today?"

"*Ya.* Our youth groups got together today. I was surprised when I saw him." Kira pressed her lips together. "I think he has a girlfriend." Then she shared how Darla had made it obvious that she wasn't pleased whenever Kira spoke to him and how she shared how long they've known each other.

Her aunt frowned and touched Kira's hand. "I know you like him. Are you upset?"

"I'm disappointed, but I'm not surprised. I thought a man as kind as he is would have someone special." Her shoulders sagged. "It's okay. I plan to go home at some point, so why would I want to get attached to someone who lives here?"

Her aunt gave her a knowing smile. "Sometimes you meet someone when you least expect it. When I came here, I never thought I'd wind up staying either."

"I know." Kira moved her fingers over the smooth tabletop.

"Alaina tried to set me up with one of Lewis's *freinden*. His name is Shane, and he gave me a ride home. He's very nice, but I told him I only want to be *freinden*. He seemed to understand."

"I think making *freinden* is a *gut* plan."

"You look tired. You should get some sleep."

"*Ya*, you're right." Her aunt yawned again and then stood. "Austin will be awake early again tomorrow."

Kira popped up, hurried around the table, and wrapped her arms around her aunt. "I'm sorry you felt like you had to wait up for me."

"Don't be *gegisch*." *Aenti* Ellen patted her back. "I'm glad we had a chance to talk. Now get some sleep."

"You too."

While her aunt carried her lantern to her downstairs bedroom, Kira tiptoed upstairs and changed into her nightgown. Then she climbed into bed. As she snuggled under her sheets and quilt, her thoughts turned to her sisters. She hoped they had enjoyed the day with their youth group. She missed laughing and playing volleyball with them, but when she recalled what Leah had shared, she slammed her eyes shut. She couldn't imagine attending the youth gathering and watching Philip flirting with beautiful Yvonne.

Kira shifted onto her side and considered her surprising day. She recalled how sweet and kind Shane had been while she also tried to dismiss her thoughts of Jayden and Darla. She was certain Jayden was a wonderful boyfriend to Darla. Surely, he treated her with respect and made her deliriously happy.

Moving onto her back, Kira heaved out a heavy sigh. She had to find a way to remove her feelings for Jayden from her heart and instead concentrate on enjoying her time with her aunt, uncle, and cousins. But she would need the Lord's help to make that happen. Closing her eyes, she began to pray:

Lord, thank you for the wonderful friends I've made here in Pennsylvania. Please guide my heart and help me focus on being a good helper to Aunt Ellen. Please rid my heart of my confusing feelings for Jayden and help me heal after learning that Philip has moved on.

CHAPTER 14

THE DELICIOUS SMELL OF EGGS, BACON, TOAST, AND COFFEE washed over Jayden as he jogged down the stairs and into the kitchen the following morning. Kristena sat in her highchair and hummed while picking up Cheerios, holding them up in the air, and then popping them into her mouth.

"Jay! Jay!" Kristena called.

Grinning, Jayden leaned down and kissed her strawberry-blond hair. "*Gude mariye, mei liewe.*" He turned to greet his step-mother and then stopped short when he found Crystal standing at the counter, cradling her abdomen with her arms.

His eyes moved from her distended abdomen to her face, and he opened and then closed his mouth.

Crystal leaned back against the counter. "*Gude mariye,* Jayden."

"Hi, Crystal." He wanted to ask her if she was expecting, but the awkward question sat on the tip of his tongue.

As if she could read his mind, she nodded. "*Ya,* I am expecting."

"Wow!" Jayden gushed. "When are you due?"

"February."

"That's fantastic." He clapped his hands together.

"I wasn't sure if your *dat* had told you yet. I told Savannah and Michelle last week. I'm sorry you didn't know."

Jayden shook his head. "It's okay. I'm really excited."

"We are too." Then her expression became serious. "You've always been the most understanding and mature, and I'm grateful to have you as a stepson."

Jayden nodded, feeling unworthy of her compliments. And then another thought hit him—Could he possibly ever be good enough for Kira?

Crystal pointed to the table, where a platter of scrambled eggs, bacon, and toast sat. "Please have a seat. Everything is ready."

Jayden sat in his usual spot at the kitchen table. "*Danki*."

"*Gude mariye!*" *Dat* sang as he stepped into the kitchen.

Kristena threw her arms up into the air and squealed. "*Dat! Dat!*"

He chuckled before kissing her head. Then he turned and kissed Crystal's cheek. "How is everyone today?"

"I'm *froh*. I just heard the *gut* news." Jayden scooped a small pile of scrambled eggs onto this plate.

Dat took a seat beside Kristena's highchair and then looked between Jayden and Crystal before understanding flashed in his brown eyes. "Oh!" He seemed to share a special smile with Crystal before turning his attention back to Jayden. His expression seemed to glow. "I'm so glad you know now."

Crystal joined them at the table, and after filling their plates, they bowed their heads in silent prayer and then began to eat.

"How was the youth gathering yesterday?" Crystal asked.

Jayden swallowed a bite of toast and then wiped his mouth with a paper napkin. "It was *gut*. Kira was there."

"Really?" *Dat*'s eyes lit with curiosity.

Crystal lifted her mug of coffee. "I didn't realize it was going to be a combined gathering."

"I was surprised to see her there," Jayden said. "One of her *freinden* suggested that a group of us get together to help a widow in their community." He explained Alaina's idea of fixing her roof and doing other chores for her. "Do you think it would be okay if I took a day off to roof her *haus*?"

Dat picked up a piece of bacon. "It's a fantastic idea. Helping someone in need is exactly what we strive to do in our community."

"*Danki*." Jayden ate another bite of toast. "But you know how Ty is about his schedule. I'm not sure if he'll agree to give me the day off."

Dat chuckled. "I hope your *bruder* will respect your wanting to help someone in need. In fact, we could talk about donating some of the supplies if her bishop isn't able to help pay for them through their community fund."

"Great." Jayden's happiness billowed through him at the thought of not only helping someone, but also having the opportunity to see Kira once again.

At lunchtime, Jayden sat across from Tyler at a bench and unwrapped his sandwich. He and the rest of the crew had been busy working at a motel all morning, and since they were working on different sides of the roof, Jayden hadn't had a chance to discuss the community project with Tyler.

Jayden pulled out a small resealable bag of chips and opened it. "There's something I wanted to discuss with you. We didn't get to talk about it in the truck this morning since you wanted to talk about our upcoming schedule."

"What is it?" Tyler picked up his ham and cheese sandwich and took a bite.

"A group of *mei freinden* want to get together for sort of a community project." Jayden explained how they were going to help a widow fix her roof and also handle other chores around her *haus*. "I really want to participate, but since you're my boss, I figured I'd better discuss it with you."

Tyler rubbed his dark-brown beard. "It's a great cause, but how many days do you expect to be gone?"

"Maybe one."

"I suppose I can try to live without you for one day." Tyler picked up his cup of water.

"Thanks, boss."

Tyler chuckled.

"Looks like we'll finish this one up today," Dennis said.

Roger held up a pretzel. "What's next on the schedule?"

Jayden looked down at his turkey and cheese sandwich while Tyler began discussing their future projects. Soon he lost himself in thoughts of Kira.

He had stayed awake for a while last night wondering about Kira and Shane. He'd been so surprised when he saw her with him, but the more he considered it, the more it made sense. Kira was two years older than Jayden, and Shane definitely looked as if he was at least twenty-five. Surely Kira was interested in an older, more successful man than Jayden. For all Jayden knew, Shane might already have his own home and could offer Kira so much more than Jayden ever could.

Jayden looked up at his older brother and considered what Tyler had—a home, a wife who adored him, a beautiful daughter, and another child on the way. Tyler had it all, and Jayden was happy for him and also happy for Korey, who had a similar life. And the more Jayden thought about it, the more he realized he wanted a life like theirs.

Tyler ate a bite of his sandwich. Then he looked at Jayden and arched an eyebrow. "You okay?"

"*Ya.*" Jayden continued eating while considering asking his brother for advice about Kira, but he shooed away that thought. If Kira was happy with Shane, then he was happy for her.

He would do his best to be her friend and hoped that it would be enough to satisfy his heart.

Kira sat at the sewing machine Wednesday afternoon and stitched the hem of a little blue dress she had made for Mimi. She smiled as she held the dress up and turned it over in her hands. She enjoyed sewing and the time it gave her to not only be creative, but also to lose herself in her thoughts of home and talk to God.

The door opened with a quiet creak and Alaina stepped in.

"Hi," Kira said. "What's new?"

Alaina hurried over and sank down on the edge of Kira's bed. "I was hoping you would have time to talk."

"*Ya,* of course. The *kinner* are in for their naps, so I was just doing some sewing."

"I have news." Alaina reached out and touched Kira's hand. "When Lewis brought me home Sunday night, he asked if he could see *mei dat*." She rubbed her hands together. "He talked to *mei dat* and then he asked me to be his girlfriend."

"How exciting!" Kira leaned over and gave her friend a hug.

"*Danki.*" Then Alaina gave her a knowing look. "And how's Shane doing?"

Kira wagged a finger at her. "Shane admitted that you had planned to set me up with him."

Alaina shrugged. "Maybe."

"Why didn't you just tell me?"

"Because that would have ruined the surprise."

Kira shook her head.

"How did it go?"

"He's very nice, but I told him that I'd like to just be *freinden.*"

Alaina leaned forward. "He's perfect for you, Kira. Why would you only want to be *freinden*?"

Kira moved her finger over the edge of the sewing table as the truth bubbled up in her throat. "I got out of a relationship shortly before I came here, and I'm not ready to risk my heart yet."

"I understand, and I'm sorry for meddling."

"It's okay. Shane understands that I'd like to just be *freinden.*" Kira brightened. "Do you have an update on when we can help the widow?"

"Yes! So, Fern Lambert doesn't have any *bruders*, and she never had any *kinner*. Her husband passed away about a year ago. I spoke to the bishop, and he loved the idea of us helping her. He said that the community fund can contribute for any costs, so then we're only donating our time. I thought we could work at her *haus* on Saturday."

Kira clapped. "Oh, this is fantastic."

"I spoke to Darla earlier today, and she said she spoke to

Jayden, and he and his *bruder* are going to stop by Fern's *haus* after work to measure the roof and then get the supplies."

Kira's stomach dipped at the mention of Jayden's name. "That's . . . that's great."

"We're all set then. Lewis is going to talk to Shane, and Darla will tell Lora. Of course, Lora will tell Ben since they're dating. And we'll all be there to help Fern and have fun!"

"*Gut.*" Kira folded her hands in her lap as the question that had been haunting her floated through her mind. "How long have Jayden and Darla been dating?"

Alaina scoffed. "They're not dating yet."

"Not yet?" A pang rippled in Kira's chest.

"She's had a crush on him for years, but he hasn't asked her out. I bet it will be soon."

"Really?" Kira asked with surprise.

Alaina waved her off. "All Darla ever talks about is Jayden. They've been *freinden* since they went to school together, and she's always secretly liked him. I think she should just tell him how she feels, but she's holding on to the hope that he'll realize how *gut* they'd be together and then ask her out. I guess we'll see."

"*Ya.*" Kira swallowed. Alaina had confirmed what she'd already believed—that Jayden and Darla were destined to be a couple.

"I'm going to go to the grocery store to buy the ingredients to make Fern a casserole."

"That's a *gut* idea." Kira stood. "Let's share our plans with *Aenti* Ellen."

Kira and Alaina found *Aenti* Ellen in the kitchen flipping through a cookbook. She smiled at them. "What are you two up to?"

"We were talking about going to help Fern Lambert on Saturday. Would that be okay?" Kira asked.

"I think it's a lovely idea. I'm certain Fern will enjoy both the help and the company."

"*Danki.*" Kira turned to Alaina. "I think we'll have fun helping Fern."

Alaina pulled a piece of paper out of her apron pocket. "Lewis told me that Shane forgot to give you his number Sunday night. He wrote down Shane's number so you can call him and ask him to pick you up on Saturday."

"I could just walk. Fern's *haus* isn't too far from here." Kira shrugged.

"But won't you have cleaning supplies to carry?" Alaina asked.

"Oh *ya.*" Kira turned toward her aunt. "I was going to ask if I could make a casserole or bring a few groceries for her."

Aenti Ellen rested her hands on the cookbook. "That would be fine, but I think you might want to call Shane for a ride if you have several things to carry."

"Okay. I will." Kira took the number from Alaina.

"I should get home," Alaina said. "It was *gut* seeing you, Ellen."

Aenti Ellen smiled. "You too."

Kira walked Alaina out to where her driver waited in a burgundy van. She told her friend goodbye and then hurried down the path toward her uncle's store to call Shane and ask him for a ride. Her heart gave a little bump at the thought of seeing Jayden again soon.

CHAPTER 15

TYLER'S DRIVER NOSED HIS DODGE PICKUP TRUCK INTO THE driveway at Fern Lambert's small, one-story brick house Saturday morning. Jayden climbed out of the back seat and met Tyler at the back of the truck.

"*Danki* for dropping me off today," Jayden told Tyler as they began unloading supplies and tools for Fern's roof.

Tyler lifted one side of the ladder. "I don't mind. I appreciate that her bishop is going to use their community fund to cover the supplies."

"*Dat* said that too." Jayden took the other end of the ladder, and they carried it to the side of the house. Then they unloaded tools and the rest of the supplies Jayden would need to repair her roof. They had stopped by Thursday evening to measure, and Jayden and Tyler had made sure to introduce themselves before they ventured up on her roof.

The front door opened, and Fern hobbled out onto the small porch. She was a petite woman with gray hair peeking out of her prayer covering, bright brown eyes, and glasses, and Jayden guessed she looked to be in her early- to mid-seventies. Her smile was nearly as bright as the late-September sun shining down from the clear, blue sky.

"Jayden! Tyler! *Gude mariye!*" She waved. "It's *gut* to see you again."

"Hi there," Tyler called. "I have to get to another job, but I just helped unload the supplies. If I get done early enough, I'll be back to help."

"You be safe now, young man," she told Tyler.

He chuckled. "I will, Fern." Then he turned to Jayden. "I'll see you later."

"All right." Jayden waved as Tyler returned to the truck, and then his driver backed down the gravel driveway toward the street.

Once the truck was gone, Jayden sauntered up to the porch, where Fern leaned against the railing. "How are you doing this morning?" he asked.

"Just fine. And you?"

"I'm great. I'm going to get up on your roof and start removing the old shingles. You'll hear a lot of noise up there, but I promise it's just fine."

"I hope you're not going to be working alone." Then she looked past him. "Oh, here comes a buggy. That must be a couple of your *freinden* here to help."

Jayden spun as Ben's horse trotted up the driveway. Ben halted the horse in front of Fern's house before he and Lora jumped out. Then Lora helped Darla out of the back of the buggy.

"I'm Ben, and this is Lora and Darla." Ben waved to Fern. "Would it be all right if I release my horse in your pasture?" He pointed to the small pasture beside a red barn.

"Of course," Fern told him.

Darla gave Jayden a bright smile. "Hi, Jayden!"

"*Gude mariye*," he told her.

Lora collected a disposable casserole dish while Darla carried a large basket that looked as if it was full of supplies. Then both women joined Fern on the porch.

"We made you a cheesy chicken and broccoli casserole," Lora said.

Darla held up her basket. "And we brought plenty of cleaning supplies."

"Why, isn't that the sweetest? Let's go inside." Fern pointed toward the front door and then gave Jayden a stern expression. "You and your *freind* be careful on my roof. I don't want to have to call the rescue squad for you."

Jayden held his hands up. "I will, but I promise you I've been on a roof more times than I can count."

"That might be true, but there's always a first time to fall."

Darla wagged a finger at him. "Listen to Fern, Jayden."

Jayden bit back his annoyance at Darla's familiarity with him. "*Ya.* I will." He gathered up tools and then climbed up onto the roof while Ben unhitched his horse and led it into the pasture.

Soon Ben was up on the roof helping Jayden rip off the shingles. "What's going on between you and Darla?"

"There's nothing going on between us. You'd know if there was." Jayden turned toward him. "Why?"

Ben shook his head and sat back on his heels. "She's talking like you two are dating, but you haven't said anything to me about it. That's why I was confused."

"We're not dating. I've given her a ride home from youth group, but I haven't asked her out." He blew out a frustrated sigh.

"I know she likes me, but I don't want to hurt her. She's always been *mei freind,* and that's all I can ever see her as."

"You need to tell her how you feel."

"I know. I kept hoping that she'd get the hint if I didn't ask her out, but it's obvious that I need to be honest with her and let her down easy. I don't want to lead her on because that will hurt as much as telling her the truth. I'll tell her that I only want to be *freinden* when the time is right." Jayden swiped the back of his hands across his brow. "How are you and Lora?"

"We're great. I really like her."

"That's *gut.*"

They returned to their work, and a few minutes later, another horse and buggy appeared in the driveway as Alaina and Lewis arrived. While Alaina walked into the house carrying a disposable casserole pan, along with a large picnic basket, Lewis took care of his horse and then waved before climbing the ladder.

"I'm here to learn how to roof," Lewis said before joining Jayden and Ben.

"Great," Jayden said. "It's not that hard." He explained how to remove the old shingles and then they all set to work.

After several minutes, Jayden looked out toward the road, hoping to see another buggy or car arrive. All week he had looked forward to seeing Kira. Disappointment wrapped around his chest as he worried she wouldn't come. While he was grateful to have the opportunity to help Fern, he also hoped to spend more time with Kira.

"Shane should be here soon, and we'll have more help," Lewis said. "He had to pick up Kira on his way."

Jayden gritted his teeth as jealousy spiked through him. Then he silently reminded himself to let it go. Kira wasn't planning to stay in the community, and he would be blessed to be her friend.

"Here's Shane," Lewis announced a few minutes later. "He was probably just running late."

A horse pulled a buggy up to the house, and Kira climbed out. She looked pretty in a blue dress. Jayden sat back on his heels as she lifted a casserole dish and a basket from the buggy floor and balanced them on one arm. She said something to Shane and then laughed, and Jayden bit back more envy.

Then she tented her free hand over her eyes before peering up toward the roof. When her gaze collided with Jayden's, she smiled and waved. He felt a warm, prickly sensation in his chest as he waved back before she disappeared on the porch and then into the house.

Shane took care of his horse and buggy and then joined Jayden and the other men on the roof. "Put me to work," he said rubbing his hands together.

———————

Kira entered the house, where Alaina and Darla stood in the kitchen.

Alaina turned. "Kira! You made it." She rushed over and hugged Kira with such a force that Kira nearly dropped her broccoli and wild rice casserole. Then she took Kira's free arm and steered her over to where an older woman with gray hair, intelligent brown eyes, and glasses sat in a chair. "Fern, this is Kira. She's Ellen Lapp's niece."

"Hi," Kira said, shaking her hand. "I've seen you at church."

Fern's smile widened. "*Ya,* I remember you. You're from Indiana, right?"

"I am. I brought you a broccoli and wild rice casserole." Kira held up the disposable casserole dish.

Fern chuckled. "You *maed* are spoiling me. *Danki* so much."

"We're *froh* to help you." Kira turned to Alaina. "So, what's the plan?"

Alaina made a sweeping gesture toward the kitchen. "Darla is cleaning the kitchen, and I'm going to start on the bathroom. Lora is working on her laundry."

"I can start sweeping the floor then." Kira turned toward the kitchen, and Darla gave her a half-smile before dipping her chin and focusing her attention on the counter she wiped.

As she crossed to the kitchen, Kira tried to hide her frown. She couldn't comprehend why Darla would give her the cold shoulder when it was clear Darla was the one who had a chance to become Jayden's girlfriend. She set her casserole in the refrigerator and placed her basket of cleaning supplies on the floor before spinning toward the utility closet. "Is there a broom in there that I could use?"

"*Ya.*" Alaina opened the closet and handed her a broom. Then she pointed toward a short hallway. "I'll be working in the bathroom if you need me."

Kira moved to a small dining room and began sweeping. While she worked, she listened to the muffled voices of the men working on the roof above her while hammers pounded and their footsteps sounded. She imagined Jayden working with the three other men, and her heart fluttered.

She finished sweeping the dining room and brushed the small pile of dirt into a dustpan before depositing it into the kitchen trash can. Then she moved on to a small sewing room containing a sewing table, a couple of dressers, and two chairs. She began sweeping while she considered her ride over with Shane. He had been pleasant while they made small talk about their week and the weather. She had a feeling that Shane still liked her, and she was grateful that he seemed to be trying to be friends.

After she finished working in the sewing room, Kira moved on to Fern's bedroom. She made her bed and then began sweeping. The sound of Jayden's voice in the house sent a tremor through her like an earthquake. She continued sweeping as heavy footsteps sounded in the hallway.

Kira suddenly felt as if someone was watching her, and when she looked up, she found Jayden lingering in the doorway. He looked handsome clad in a gray shirt and dark trousers. She smiled as he lifted his straw hat and pushed his hand through his sandy-blond hair.

"How was your week?" he asked.

Kira leaned on the broom. "*Gut*. Busy. How was yours?"

"The same." He glanced down the hallway and then toward her again before shifting his weight on his feet. Was he nervous?

"How's your dollhouse project going?"

His expression brightened. "I finished the grandfather clock and started on a set of end tables."

"Is that right?"

Jayden lifted a finger. "Each one has a drawer. They are more complicated than you might think."

"Oh, I'm sure they are." She chuckled.

He laughed, and she relished the sound.

"Jayden?"

He looked down the hallway, and his smile seemed to dim slightly. "Hi, Darla."

"I thought I heard your voice." Footfalls sounded and then Darla sidled up to him. "How are things going on the roof?"

"They're going well. I just came in for a glass of water." He licked his lips.

"Oh, I must have missed you. I was in the utility room checking on Lora to see if she needed help with Fern's laundry." Darla glanced over at Kira and speared her with a glower before returning her attention to Jayden. "I'm going to help Lora hang out the laundry. Would you walk me out?"

Kira swallowed back her irritation. She was so tired of Darla's interference in her conversations with Jayden as well as her dirty looks.

Jayden nodded. "Sure." He gave Kira an apologetic look. "I'll see you later."

"*Ya*," Kira told him as he and Darla walked away. She huffed out a sigh and then returned to sweeping.

⁓⁓⁓◦⊙◦⁓⁓⁓

After a short break for a lunch of sandwiches and chips, which Alaina had brought, Jayden, Ben, Lewis, and Shane returned to the roof to continue hammering in the new shingles. The sound of their hammers echoed around them as they all worked. Time seemed to move quickly as the new shingles began to cover the roof, and Jayden silently admired their progress.

While the afternoon wore on, Jayden considered Ben's advice about telling Darla how he truly felt about her. He knew that he needed to initiate that honest conversation, but he dreaded hurting her feelings. Yet, at the same time, Darla had consistently interrupted his conversations with Kira. If he was honest with her, then he might be able to talk to Kira without Darla's intrusion.

"Are you two in the same church district?"

Ben's question broke through Jayden's mental tirade. He looked up as Ben pointed between Lewis and Shane.

"We're not in the same church district, but we went to school together," Lewis explained.

Shane nodded. "*Ya*, we met twenty years ago in first grade, and we've been *freinden* ever since."

Jayden looked down and started hammering as frustration boiled under his skin. His intuition had been right. Shane was twenty-seven and had a successful business. It was no wonder Kira liked him. He was kidding himself thinking he could compete with a man like Shane.

Besides, all he and Kira ever talked about was his stupid, immature hobby of creating dollhouse furniture. Humiliation rained down on him as he hammered in another shingle.

"Ben," Lora called from the porch. "You asked me to let you know when it was almost three. It's two forty-five."

"Thanks! I'll be right down." Ben stood. "*Mei dat* needs my help with a few projects. I told him I'd be back while there was still some daylight."

Shane stood. "I'm sorry, but I have to get home to help with chores too."

"I do too," Lewis added.

Jayden waved them off. "It's fine. I can finish if you need to go."

Shane, Lewis, and Ben descended the ladder and then disappeared into the house. Jayden kept working and hoped that Kira didn't have to leave early too. He wanted to finish their conversation from earlier and ask her if he could give her a ride home.

Kira finished dusting Fern's rooms and walked into the kitchen just as Shane, Lewis, and Ben walked into the house. She peeked past them for Jayden but didn't see him. Then a hammer sounded above her, and she imagined him on the roof working alone.

Lewis's eyes met Alaina's. "I need to get going. I promised *mei dat* I'd help with chores. Do you want a ride?"

"*Ya.* That would be nice." Alaina began gathering up her things.

Lora touched Ben's arm. "Are you heading out with me?"

"*Ya,* I am."

"Okay." Lora also looked around for her purse and tote bag and then turned to Darla. "Would you like a ride?"

Darla looked at the clock above the sink. "Oh dear. It's almost three. Is Jayden leaving?"

"No. He said he was going to stay and finish the roof." Ben shook his head. "I think Ty is picking him up after he finishes a job. They'll need to take all the supplies and the ladder in the pickup truck."

Darla looked disappointed as her lips pressed down in a frown. "Oh. I promised *mei mamm* I'd help make supper, so I'd better go with you."

Shane nodded at Kira. "Are you ready to go?"

Kira glanced around at her friends. Everyone was leaving—except for Jayden. Here was her chance to talk to him without

Darla's rude interruptions! She met Shane's eager expression. "I'll stay. I can walk home, but *danki* for the offer."

"Oh, okay." His smile flattened. "Do you need a ride to youth group tomorrow?"

"*Ya, danki.*"

Shane's expression brightened once again. "Perfect. I'll see you then."

Kira said goodbye to her friends, and they each shook Fern's hand as she thanked them before they left.

After her friends were gone, the sound of Jayden's hammer reverberated through Fern's little house. Kira turned to Fern. "I don't mean to poke my nose in your business, but I noticed a couple of dresses on your sewing table. Do they need mending?"

Fern's expression brightened. "They do."

"Would you like me to mend them for you?"

Fern patted the empty wing chair beside hers. "Only if you sit here and talk to me while you sew."

Kira smiled at her new friend. "I'd love to."

CHAPTER 16

KIRA PICKED UP THE TWO DRESSES AND TWO APRONS THAT she'd found on the sewing table, along with a small sewing basket. Then she took a seat beside Fern and began mending the light-blue dress.

"Kira, I have a question for you." Fern leaned toward her. "Is Shane your boyfriend?" Her voice took on a conspiratorial tone as if they were two friends sharing gossip or secrets.

Kira shook her head. "No, he's not."

"Well, dear, in case you haven't noticed, he's sweet on you."

Kira chuckled. "*Ya*, I have noticed. He took me home from the youth gathering Sunday night, and he asked me if he could see me. I told him that I'm only interested in being *freinden*."

"Ah. You don't like him that way, I suppose."

"I'm just not looking for a boyfriend right now."

"Why?"

Kira took in the older woman's warm expression, and she felt as if she could trust her. For some reason, she felt a connection to this woman, as if she could be her surrogate grandmother. "I recently had my heart broken."

Fern reached over and touched her hand. "Sweetie, I remember how that feels, but then I met my Hiram, and the Lord healed my heart."

"Tell me about Hiram."

Fern settled back in the chair and lifted her chin toward the ceiling as if her memories were projected there. "I had been dating Elijah, and he decided that he wasn't ready for a serious relationship."

"*Ach*. I'm so sorry." Kira shook her head. It was as if Fern was sharing her own story.

"*Danki*," Fern said. "But I promise this will have a *froh* ending. Elijah broke up with me, and I was devastated. I felt as if I was floating through life with no purpose. I kept praying and asking God to help heal my broken heart. I was ready to give up on love, but one Sunday *mei schweschder* Gladys told me to stop feeling sorry for myself and stop moping. She insisted I go to youth group with her, and Hiram was there."

Kira looked up from her mending. "And . . . ? What happened?"

"Well, he was the most handsome young man I'd ever seen."

Kira grinned.

"He had the bluest eyes that reminded me of the summer sky, and dark-brown hair. And he was tall and had broad shoulders. I felt my heart come to life when I saw him. I wanted to meet him, but I was afraid of being too forward. Then he came over and introduced himself to me. At the end of the night, he asked if he could take me home. Then he asked *mei dat*'s permission to date me. Six months later, we were married."

Kira sighed. "What a lovely story."

"*Danki*. We had our ups and downs like all couples. The Lord never blessed us with *kinner*, but we had *bruderskinner* to love. But what was important is that our marriage was like a sturdy house.

We had a good foundation and a good roof, and my husband became my heart's shelter, if that makes sense."

Kira nodded. "*Ya*, it does."

"I just wish we'd had more time. But we were married for forty-four years. The Lord gave us many happy memories."

Outside, the ladder rattled as if Jayden was climbing down it.

"I'm so glad you had that time together," Kira said.

Heavy footsteps sounded on the porch steps and then the door burst open, revealing Jayden cradling his left hand. Blood was splattered on his gray shirt. His expression was embarrassed. "Do you possibly have a bandage?"

"Jayden!" Kira gasped and jumped into action, taking his arm and steering him to the kitchen sink. "Let me see the wound."

He winced as he opened his hand, revealing a deep gash.

Fern joined them in the kitchen. "I'll fetch the first-aid kit and some salve."

"What did you do?" Kira asked as she began to clean out the wound.

Jayden shook his head. "I picked up a piece of rotten wood, and it slipped and cut my hand. I guess I was trying to work too fast."

Kira took his hand, and warmth danced up her arm as she held it under the water.

Jayden slammed his eyes closed and hissed as the water hit his wound.

"I'm sorry," she whispered as he grimaced.

His eyes blinked open, and he gave her a hesitant smile. "It's okay."

She began to wash the gash out with soap, and his hazel eyes fixed on hers. A chill moved through her as he watched her.

"I feel like such a *dummkopp*," he groaned. "I can't imagine what *mei bruders* will say when they see my bandage."

"Accidents happen. I'm sure they've gotten hurt on the job too."

He sighed. "I suppose so."

"I brought the peroxide, bandages, and salve," Fern said as she appeared behind them and set the supplies on the counter. Then she returned to her chair in the family room.

"*Danki*," Kira and Jayden said at the same time. Then they looked at each other and laughed.

After she turned off the water, Kira opened the bottle of peroxide and poured it over his hand. Jayden closed his eyes and hissed again.

"I'm sorry," she said.

Jayden gave her a shy expression. "Promise me you won't tell anyone what a klutz I am."

She clucked her tongue. "Jayden, you're not a klutz at all. I once tripped and fell with a carrot cake in my arms, and what a mess that was. You should have seen my dress and apron." Kira dried his hand, covered the gash with salve, and then wrapped it in a bandage. "There you go."

"*Danki*." He opened and closed his hand. "It's a *gut* thing it's my left hand or I wouldn't be able to work." Then he leveled his gaze with hers. "Why are you still here?"

"I wanted to do some mending for Fern." Kira closed the bottle of peroxide and then the salve.

"That's kind of you." His gorgeous eyes seemed to search hers, and every cell in her body sizzled to life. "Is Shane coming back to get you?"

Kira shook her head. "It's not a far walk. I told *mei aenti* I'd be home by six."

"Ty should be here soon, and we can give you a ride." Was he hopeful that she'd say yes?

"Okay." She closed the first-aid kit and tried to hide her excitement at the idea of riding home with him.

"Great." Jayden pushed off the counter, and they walked out to the family room together. "The roof is done. I'm going to start cleaning up."

"Do you need help?"

"No, but thank you." Jayden nodded at Fern. "*Danki* for the first-aid supplies."

Fern wagged a finger at him. "I told you to be careful, young man."

"*Ya*, you did." He grinned. "I'll try harder."

"You'd better," she ordered.

Jayden disappeared out the front door.

Kira took a seat beside Fern, and the older woman grinned at her. "So, tell me more about Hiram."

"Do you want to talk to me about Jayden?" Fern's expression was eager.

"Nope." Kira returned to her sewing and tried to calm her racing heart as she recalled how she'd enjoyed holding Jayden's hand. "I want to hear about when you and Hiram first started dating."

"All right," Fern said before launching into a story about her first dates with him.

Jayden's heart raced as he started picking up his tools and setting them in the toolbox. He felt as if he were walking on a cloud as he recalled how it had felt when Kira held his hand. Despite the throbbing pain his wound had caused, he'd longed for Kira to hold his hand all night. The feel of her warm skin against his was almost too much.

He had never before felt such a rush of emotion, and he hoped she had felt it too. If she had, however, she'd hidden it well as she'd cleaned and bandaged his wound. She'd seemed completely unaffected, but he'd also noticed how her eyes had locked on his when he spoke. At the same time, he wondered if he had imagined her interest since he'd gotten the impression she was dating Shane.

Jayden considered this as he gathered up the old shingles. But if she was dating Shane, then would she have agreed to ride home with Jayden? It was only a ride. It wasn't a date. He was reading too much into this.

Then he groaned. Jayden was going to drive himself crazy with all of his confusing feelings for Kira.

Jayden had almost finished cleaning up when the gold Dodge pickup truck rumbled up the driveway.

As soon as it came to a stop, Tyler jumped out. "I'm sorry for being so late. Our job went longer than we expected. We ran into a few issues that slowed us down, but we got it fixed." He stopped talking as his eyes focused on Jayden's left hand. "What happened to you?"

"Rotten piece of wood."

"Ouch. Are you all right?"

"*Ya.*"

Tyler clucked his tongue. "You need to be more careful."

"*Ya,* I've gotten that same piece of advice a couple of times today." Jayden jammed his thumb toward the house. "Kira is still here. Is it all right if we give her a ride home?"

Tyler's lips formed a smile.

"Please, Ty," Jayden pleaded with him, "don't start teasing me, all right? It's just a ride home, and I think she has a boyfriend."

Tyler frowned. "I'm sorry. And *ya*, of course we can give her a ride. Let's get this picked up, and then we'll head out."

Working together, they loaded up the ladder, supplies, tools, old shingles, and trash.

When they finished, Tyler pointed to the roof. "You did a *gut* job."

"*Danki*." Jayden stood up taller. This was the first time he'd managed a job, and he appreciated the praise. He followed Tyler up the porch steps and into the house, where Fern sat in her chair, and Kira worked in the kitchen, setting the table.

The delicious smell of chicken overwhelmed Jayden, making his stomach growl.

Tyler patted his flat abdomen. "What's for supper?"

"Kira made me a casserole," Fern said. "She's warming it up."

Admiration rose up in Jayden for the sweet *maedel*. "That's very kind." He was almost certain Kira blushed as she collected her basket. "We finished the roof for you, and it's all cleaned up."

"*Danki*," Fern said. "I'm so grateful for all of you. I can't thank you enough."

Kira crossed the room to Fern and bent to embrace her. "I really enjoyed our visit. I'd love to come see you and bring you groceries if you'd like."

Fern took Kira's hand in hers. "That would be such a blessing to me, sweet Kira."

"Me too," Kira said. "I'll see you soon, Fern. I left the phone number to *mei onkel*'s shop on the counter by the stove. Please call there and leave me a message if you need anything."

They all waved goodbye to Fern, and then Jayden held the door open for Kira as she walked out onto the porch and down the steps to the truck.

Jayden opened the back door of the truck for her, and she climbed in before he jogged around the truck and hopped in beside her.

Tyler took his usual spot in the front seat beside his driver, Jack, who started the truck and backed down the driveway.

"Are you planning to go to your youth group tomorrow?" Jayden asked as the truck drove down the street.

Kira turned to face him. "*Ya*, I am. Shane is going to pick me up."

Jayden tried to mask his frown at the mention of Shane.

"Alaina told me that she has ideas for more community service projects." She paused. "Do you think you might come and help too?"

Jayden shrugged. "*Ya*, as long as my boss will let me."

Tyler swiveled in his seat and shot Jayden a glare.

Kira grinned. "Oh, that's right. I forgot your boss is strict."

"The strictest." Jayden pointed toward Tyler.

Kira laughed, and he loved the sound. "How's your wound feeling?" Her smile faded, and she reached over and touched his hand.

"It's all right," he managed to say. Heat sparked on his skin where her fingers brushed his. Her gentle touch felt like a balm to his throbbing gash.

"You need to be more careful, Jayden."

Tyler turned around once again. "I said the same thing."

"It's good advice." She nodded.

Jayden sighed and shook his head, and Kira laughed again.

Disappointment trickled over Jayden when the diesel truck motored down the gravel driveway leading to her aunt's house. The truck came to a stop, and he jumped out before walking her up the path to the porch.

When they reached the back door, she pivoted to face him and held her hand out. He shook it and then held on to her hand a few moments longer than necessary.

"*Danki* for the ride," she said. "I hope to see you soon."

Jayden smiled. "I hope to see you too." Then he jogged down the steps and returned to his seat in the truck.

Kira stood on the porch and waved as the truck drove away.

"Are you going to visit Kira?" Tyler asked Jayden while they carried their tools and supplies to the cinderblock building on their father's property after they had arrived home.

"No. Why?" Jayden set the toolbox down and faced his brother.

"Because it's so obvious you two like each other."

Jayden scoffed. "I already told you that I think she's dating someone else."

"Who?"

Jayden explained who Shane was and how she had ridden home from the youth gathering with him on Sunday and then rode to Fern's house with him again today. "He's twenty-seven, and his *dat* raises, trains, and sells horses."

"So?" Tyler shrugged.

"So?" Jayden exclaimed. "He's much more her type than I am. He's older and surely more financially comfortable than I am."

171

"But she rode home with *you*." Tyler poked Jayden in the chest.

Jayden shook his head. His older brother was missing the point. He picked up the toolbox and started toward the supply building.

"Hold on, Jay." Tyler raced after him and took his arm, stopping him. "Why are you doubting yourself?"

"Because I'm only twenty-three. There's money in horses that we don't have in roofing, Tyler. How can I possibly compete with a man of that caliber?"

"Have you told her how you feel?"

"No, of course not. Why would I?" Jayden scoffed.

"You encouraged me with Michelle. You need to take your own advice."

Jayden stared at his brother. Perhaps Tyler had a point.

CHAPTER 17

KIRA HELD A DISPOSABLE CASSEROLE DISH ON HER LAP WHILE she rode beside Shane in the buggy. She gazed out the passenger side window, taking in the colorful leaves on the trees and the yellow grass in the nearby pastures. The late-October Saturday morning air held a chill and smelled of wet hay.

She turned toward Shane and took in his handsome profile as she considered the past three weeks. It had been three weeks since she'd last seen Jayden. It had been three weeks since she'd bandaged his hand and then ridden home with him after they left Fern's house. Kira had hoped that she and Jayden had bonded that day. At least, she'd felt as if they had become closer friends, and she'd hoped that he would come to visit her. But that would have meant that he wanted to be more than friends, and she was still convinced that Darla had a hold over him.

During the past three weeks, she had ridden to and from the youth gatherings with Shane, and he seemed content to remain her friend without the promise of more. She was grateful for his easy friendship, and she was certain it was best to keep Jayden at a distance. But deep in her heart, she still hoped for more with Jayden.

"You're quiet this morning," Shane said, giving her a sideways glance. "Is everything okay?"

Kira smiled at him. "*Ya*, of course. I'm excited to help another member of our community. Did Lewis tell you anything about Omar Weaver?"

"Darla told Alaina that he's a member of her church district. He's in his early seventies and has never been married. He cared for his sister, who was ill, and she passed away a few months ago. So, he's alone now."

"*Ach*, that's so *bedauerlich*. I'm glad we're going to help him."

"*Ya*. Alaina mentioned that Omar hasn't done much maintenance on his *haus*, so we're going to fix his fence. Jayden and Ben have already picked up the lumber and the paint. Darla and Lora are bringing lunch for everyone too."

Kira's heart gave a little bump at the thought of seeing Jayden today. Maybe they would have a chance to talk without Darla's intrusion, but she doubted it. That thought sat heavy on her heart.

"How are your little cousins?" Shane asked.

Kira turned toward him again and smiled. "Oh, they're keeping me busy for sure."

She spent the remainder of the ride discussing her cousins while Shane chuckled.

When they arrived at Omar's driveway, Shane guided the horse down a long, winding gravel driveway that led to a two-story white house with two red barns. Kira looked out toward the pasture, where Jayden, Ben, and Lewis worked replacing rotten pickets. Five horses stood nearby, nibbling on the yellow grass.

An older man with graying hair and a short, gray beard sat on the porch and rocked back and forth on a rocking chair. Although Omar hadn't married, he had grown a beard. Most Amish bachelors would grow a beard when they reached the age of fifty in order to keep with the community's tradition.

Shane halted the horse and then smiled over at Kira. "I'll take care of the horse and buggy and then join the guys in the pasture."

"See you at lunch." Kira pushed the buggy door open and climbed out before buttoning her black sweater and then gathering up her tote bag and casserole dish. She gazed out toward the pasture, and Jayden waved, sending her pulse into a wild flurry. She lifted a hand in a wave and then climbed the porch steps. "Hi. I'm Kira. You must be Omar."

The older man popped up from the chair and opened the storm door for her. "I am. I appreciate you young folks taking time out of your busy day to help me out."

"We're glad to help someone in need."

He shook his head. "It was just *mei schweschder*, Stella, and me here, and I sort of let the place go when she passed away a few months ago."

"I'm very sorry for your loss, and *mei freinden* and I are going to do our best to get the *haus* back in order for you." She held up the casserole dish. "I made you a hamburger pie casserole that you can warm up for supper one night."

"How kind of you, Kira."

"I hope you enjoy it. I taped a piece of paper to the aluminum foil with instructions for how to heat it." Stepping into the house, she passed through a small family room and into the kitchen, where Alaina was scrubbing the sink.

"Hi, Kira!" Alaina removed her blue rubber gloves and pushed the ties to her prayer covering over her shoulders.

"Let me know how I can help." Kira slipped the casserole into the refrigerator.

"Lora and Darla are cleaning the upstairs, and I'm working on the kitchen."

Alaina looked past Kira to where Omar stood. "Didn't you mention that you have some clothes that need to be mended?"

Omar nodded. "*Ya*, there's a pile in the downstairs bedroom. Stella's sewing basket is on the floor in the closet." He pointed toward a hallway. "I moved into Stella's bedroom after she passed away so that I don't have to go upstairs if I don't need to. I didn't bother moving the sewing machine upstairs, so it's there for you to use. Of course, that's if you don't mind sewing. I'd appreciate the help."

"Oh, I love to sew. It's no bother at all," Kira said.

Alaina smiled. "You're the only one of us who likes to sew. That's why I thought you could get started on that while Lora, Darla, and I handle the cleaning and laundry."

"Perfect." Kira padded to the large bedroom at the end of the hallway. She found the pile of clothes on top of a small sewing table and then located the sewing basket in the closet.

Then she sat down at the table and fished through the basket for a needle and thread. Her eyes wandered to the window beyond the desk, and she peered out over to where Jayden worked on the fence. He said something to Ben and then they both laughed. She smiled as she imagined the sound of his laughter. She couldn't wait to have the chance to talk to him. She just hoped he would want to talk to her too.

Turning her attention from her crush on Jayden, Kira unfolded a pair of gray trousers and found where the seam had come undone on one of the legs. Then she threaded the sewing machine and began to sew.

Thoughts of her parents and her sisters swirled through her

mind while she worked, and she swallowed back that familiar homesickness. She wondered what her family members were busy doing today. And were they thinking of her?

With a sigh, she turned her attention to her task at hand.

⁓⁓⁓☙❧⁓⁓⁓

"It's lunchtime."

Looking up from the sewing machine, Kira turned toward the doorway where Lora stood. "Is it really?"

"*Ya*, it is." Lora beckoned Kira to follow her. "*Kumm*. Darla and I brought food for lunch."

Kira nodded. "I'll be right there. I just need to finish fixing a shirt." She had been so wrapped up in her thoughts of her family while sewing that she hadn't even noticed the sound of the voices down the hallway in the kitchen.

She mended the sleeve and then scooted out of the bedroom to the dining room, where her friends were gathered around a rectangular table set with lunch meat, cheese, rolls, condiments, and bags of chips. Omar and her friends were squeezed in around the worn wooden table.

When Kira found the only empty chair between Jayden and Alaina, her hands trembled. She finally had her chance to talk to Jayden. Her eyes found Darla perched on the chair on the other side of him, and her hope deflated like a balloon. Most likely Darla would capture his attention and keep it throughout lunch.

As if reading her thoughts, Darla's pretty blue eyes focused on Kira, and her lips formed a manufactured smile. "Hi, Kira. I heard you were here helping, but I hadn't seen you. I was starting to wonder if that was a rumor."

"I was mending Omar's clothes in the downstairs bedroom."

"Oh. How nice."

Jayden swiveled on the chair, and his handsome face lit up with a smile. "Kira! Have a seat beside me."

Darla frowned and then turned away.

Kira slipped into the chair beside Jayden, and when their legs brushed, heat shimmied up her leg. She snuck a glance at him and found him staring down at his plate. Had he felt that too?

After bowing their heads in silent prayer, conversations broke out around the table while they began building their sandwiches. At the far end of the table, Shane and Lewis talked with Omar about their progress fixing the fence. Next to them, Ben and Lora discussed their plans for the following week, and Alaina and Darla talked about their favorite meals.

"Are you having fun sewing?" Jayden asked.

Kira's head popped up, and she turned to where he watched her, his hazel eyes glittering in the afternoon sunlight pouring in through the nearby windows. "*Ya*, I am."

"*Mei mamm* liked to sew." He added mayonnaise and mustard to his ham and cheese sandwich. "She liked to quilt too. Do you quilt?"

Kira bit back her surprise. He was opening up about his mother, and for a moment, she was speechless. "I'm not an expert quilter, but I have made a few quilts."

"I have a feeling you're a very *gut* quilter, but you don't like to brag." He cut his sandwich in half.

She smiled. "Actually, I'm being honest about my quilting."

Curiosity swelled inside her. She yearned to keep him talking about his mother. "What was your *mamm's* name?"

"Connie. Ty named his *dochder* after her." He took a bite of his sandwich.

"How lovely that Tyler named his *dochder* Connie. I imagine it means a lot to you, Korey, and your *dat*."

Jayden swallowed and wiped his mouth. "It does. Who taught you how to sew?"

"*Mei mamm* and *mei mammi*." Kira piled turkey and cheese on her roll. "Do you have a special quilt your *mamm* made for you?"

"I do. I keep it on my bed. I have a smaller one that was mine when I was little that I've kept in case I have *kinner* someday."

"That's special."

"Are you close to your *mammi*?"

Kira added mustard to her sandwich and then cut it in half. "I was. She passed away last year."

"I'm so sorry." He shifted to face her. "You must miss her."

When their eyes locked, she felt something unspoken pass between them. Something warm and comfortable. Did he feel that too?

"I do, and I'm sure you miss your *mamm*."

Jayden huffed out a breath. "*Ya*, I do. Sometimes I expect to find her humming in the kitchen while cooking. I can still remember her laugh. Other times I forget her voice or what she looked like." He shook his head. "Grief is a funny thing. It's always changing and morphing."

"That is very true." A beat of silence passed between them, and she felt the need to lighten the conversation. "I'm going to assume you finished those end tables and moved on to something even more challenging."

He chuckled. "Would you believe I'm working on creating a bookshelf now?"

"Is it more challenging than the end tables?"

"No, actually, the end tables were much more difficult." Jayden lifted his sandwich. "This dollhouse furniture hobby is more complicated than I ever imagined."

Kira picked up a chip. "I'm sure you're better at it than you admit."

He shrugged.

"How's your hand doing, by the way?" she asked.

He held up his left palm. "It has healed up quite nicely."

"I'm glad to hear that."

Darla turned toward Jayden. "Did you hear what Alaina said, Jayden?"

Tension built in Kira's neck as Jayden focused on Darla beside him.

"No, I didn't hear it," he told Darla. "What did she say?"

Darla's smile brightened. "Alaina said that after we finish our chores inside the house, we should come out and help you all paint the fence."

"That's a great idea," Ben said from across the table. "The painting will go much faster if we have more help."

Lora swirled a chip in the air. "Many hands make light work."

"I really appreciate your help," Omar said. "I've wanted to fix that fence for a long time, but Stella required a lot of care."

"How long have you lived here?" Lora asked.

Omar picked up his roast beef sandwich. "My parents built

this home many years ago. Stella and I were raised here, and then I inherited it. I did a little bit of work here and there. *Mei dat* ran a small dairy farm, but I decided to go into construction instead of farming."

Kira relaxed while Omar talked on about his home and his family. When she felt Jayden looking at her, she sneaked a peek and found him smiling in her direction. She returned the smile, and happiness exploded through her.

After finishing their sandwiches and enjoying brownies for dessert, Jayden and the rest of his friends began cleaning up their dishes. He piled his used napkin and utensils on the plate and then reached for the mustard just as Kira moved to grab it. Their hands collided, and when his fingers brushed hers, a shock wave of heat moved up his hand to his arm.

Kira's cheeks flushed bright pink as she pulled her hand back and gave a nervous laugh. "I'm sorry."

"No, no. It's my fault." He picked up the mustard and the mayonnaise. "I'll carry it to the kitchen."

"*Danki.*"

Jayden followed her into the kitchen, where he set his utensils on the counter, along with the condiments, and then dropped his paper plate and cup into the trash.

Kira stood at the sink and began to fill one side with soapy water. She craned her neck over her shoulder and smiled, and for a moment he couldn't take his eyes off her. She was beautiful in her royal-blue dress and black apron.

A hand on his shoulder startled Jayden. "Are you ready to conquer that fence?" Ben asked. "It's time to start painting."

"*Ya*." Jayden smiled, and Ben furrowed his brow in question. Ignoring him, Jayden looked at Kira. "See you soon."

She nodded just as Ben nudged Jayden toward the door.

Jayden walked with him.

"What's going on between you and Kira?" Ben asked as they walked to the back porch where the paint and brushes sat waiting to be used.

Jayden shrugged. "Nothing. Why?" He poured some of the white paint into two smaller containers before replacing the lid on the gallon.

"You two seemed awfully comfortable chatting during lunch. You looked completely engrossed in each other."

"We're *freinden*."

Ben scoffed. "You could have fooled me." He seemed to study Jayden. "Is Kira the reason you're not interested in Darla?"

"What? No." Jayden shook his head. "I've always only considered Darla a *freind*. The way I feel about Kira has nothing to do with that."

"You're telling me that you do care about Kira."

Jayden sighed. "*Ya*, I do, but I think it may be one-sided. I think she's seeing Shane."

"From the way she looks at you, I think she's more interested in you than Shane. I didn't notice her look at Shane once during lunch."

"Really?" Jayden asked.

"*Ya*, really." Ben nodded. "I haven't gotten the impression that she's dating Shane."

"But he always gives her a ride."

"That doesn't mean they're dating. You give Darla rides all the time, but you're not dating. Besides, from what I've noticed, you and Kira seem to gravitate to each other."

Jayden looked toward the side of the house just as Lewis and Shane started toward them. "I think we need to talk about this later." He handed one of the small containers of paint to Ben and then chose a brush.

"I think you need to talk to Kira and ask her about Shane."

Jayden picked up a brush and his container of paint and then they started toward the pasture fence. "It's obvious Shane likes Kira, so I'd rather not discuss it now."

"Fine, but she likes you, Jay. If you pay attention, you'll see."

Ben's words settled over Jayden while he tried to focus on painting the pickets. He worked in silence, moving down the pasture fence while Ben worked the other way, and Shane and Lewis painted on the opposite side.

After what felt like an hour or so, he heard soft footsteps padding up to him.

"Would you like some help?"

Jayden tented his hand above his eyes before looking up at Kira peering down at him. "Sure."

"I've done a little bit of painting, but I'm not an expert." She held up a brush.

He looked past her and spotted Lora helping Ben and Alaina working near Lewis. He didn't see any sign of Darla.

"Are you looking for someone?" she asked, following his gaze.

"No." He stood up straight. "I was wondering if the other *maed* had come out with you."

Kira's eyes narrowed and then returned to normal. "Darla is still inside mopping the upstairs bathrooms, but she'll be out soon."

"Oh, I wasn't looking for her," Jayden said quickly. "I was just wondering if everyone had come out with you."

She nodded, but her smile didn't quite reach her eyes. She couldn't feel threatened by Darla, could she?

"I need to get some more paint and then we can get to work," Jayden said.

"Okay."

Jayden hoofed it over to the porch and poured paint into two small containers before returning to where Kira stood. He handed her one of the containers. "Here's your paint."

"Okay." She held up her brush. "Do you want to give me a lesson?"

"Sure." Jayden walked over to a nearby post and began painting it.

Kira stood close by him, and a gentle breeze brought the vanilla scent of her shampoo or maybe her lotion to his nose, sending a flash of heat through him. "I need to just use long strokes, right?"

"*Ya.*" He looked over at her. "Honestly, no matter how you paint it, the fence will end up looking better than how it looks now."

She laughed. "That is true." She pointed to the next picket. "Is it okay if I work beside you?"

"I'd like that very much."

Her smile widened and then she began painting the picket.

They worked side by side in silence for several moments.

"I've visited Fern once a week since we helped out at her house," she said. "She's doing really well."

Jayden pivoted toward her. "You've been visiting her?"

"*Ya.* I bring her groceries and I stay to talk to her for a while. She's a really sweet lady."

Jayden's heart swelled with admiration for Kira's kindness. "That's really thoughtful of you."

She shrugged. "I enjoy her." She brushed more paint onto the picket. "Omar seems like a nice man too. Maybe you can keep in contact with him. I'm sure he'd like the company. He nearly broke my heart when he shared how lonely he is."

"*Ya,* you're right. We need to do a better job of taking care of each other."

"That's true, but it's not about work, though. When you get to know Omar, I'm sure he'll become your *freind* just as Fern has become mine." She took a step back and pointed her brush at the picket. "How am I doing?"

Jayden couldn't take his eyes off Kira. "You're doing great."

CHAPTER 18

LATER THAT AFTERNOON, KIRA RINSED HER PAINTBRUSH IN the sink in Omar's kitchen. She and Jayden had talked about their families while they worked their way around the pasture, meeting up with where Shane painted.

Kira had enjoyed listening while Jayden had shared stories about his older brothers' adventures when they were children. He also talked about his mother, sharing how she never seemed to lose her temper, even when Jayden and his brothers came home covered in mud or drenched from falling into a creek while fishing. Kira had soaked up the stories, trying her best to memorize the details about Jayden's precious family.

When it was her turn, she also discussed her best memories of her sisters and told him about her parents. Soon they were done painting, and the time seemed to fly by too quickly.

After her brush was clean, she moved on to rinse the remainder of the brushes while the men loaded up the supplies in Ben's buggy and the women picked up around the house.

"I really appreciate all of your hard work today," Omar said behind her. "This has really been a treat, and *mei haus* and property haven't looked this *gut* in years."

"We enjoyed our time here," Jayden said.

Kira twisted and found Jayden standing in the doorway of the kitchen while he spoke to Omar. She turned and finished washing the brushes and wrapped them in paper towels.

"*Danki* for cleaning those," Jayden said, close to her ear.

She jumped with a start, spinning toward him. Then she pressed her hand to her chest while working to catch her breath.

His eyes crinkled at the corners, and his lips quirked. "I'm sorry for startling you."

"The way you're working to hide your grin tells me that you're really not."

He laughed and held his hands up, palms facing her. "You caught me. No, I'm really not."

She shook her head and then handed him the paintbrushes. "I suppose these are yours?"

"*Ya*, they are."

She gathered up her tote bag from the counter and then looked over at Omar. "I enjoyed meeting you."

"*Danki* for all of your help today." Omar shook her hand.

"*Gern gschehne.*" She turned toward Jayden. "Would you walk me out?"

His face brightened. "I'd love to." He nodded at Omar. "I'll see you at church."

"Give my regards to your *dat* and your *bruders*, Jayden," the older man said.

"I will. *Danki*, Omar." Then Jayden pushed open the storm door and held it for Kira. "After you."

Kira moved to the porch and looked out to where their friends were gathered around the buggies, which had already been hitched to their horses. Disappointment rained down on her. The day had gone by too quickly.

"I hope you have a *gut* week," Jayden told her as he came to stand beside her. "Maybe I'll see you at a youth gathering sometime soon."

Kira smiled at him. "I would really like that."

"I would too."

Silence fell between them, and she had the sudden urge to tell him that she'd like to see him sometime, and she longed to invite him over for supper so that they could talk on her aunt's porch in private after the meal. Courage bubbled up inside her, and she opened her mouth to speak.

"Kira!" Shane called, cutting off her words. "Are you ready to go?"

She pressed her lips together and then looked out to where Shane stood by his buggy. "*Ya*. I'll be right there." Then she faced Jayden and took in his frown. "I'm sorry, but I have to go."

Jayden held his empty hand out to her, and she allowed him to shake hers. Then he held on to her hand a moment longer and ran his thumb over her knuckles. His soft touch sent a thrill racing through her veins. "I'll see you soon, Kira."

"I hope so," she told him before she took off toward Shane's buggy.

<hr />

The following Thursday, Kira and Ruby walked up the path leading to Fern's house. Kira balanced a disposable casserole dish in her hands and a tote bag on her shoulder while Ruby carried the two aprons that Kira had sewn for Fern. The sky above them was bright blue, and a crisp, late-October breeze snuck in through Kira's black sweater and caused her to shiver as they climbed her front steps.

"I can't wait to give Fern the aprons," Ruby said. "And I'm going to draw her a picture while you talk to her."

Kira smiled down at her sweet cousin. "I think she will be excited to see you, and she'll love the picture you make for her." She knocked on the door and then peered out toward her uncle's driver waiting for them in his white van.

The door opened, and Fern greeted Kira and Ruby with a bright smile. "What a nice surprise!"

"We brought you presents." Ruby held the aprons up to Fern. "Kira made you these aprons and a casserole."

"These are lovely." Fern took the black aprons and held them up. "Please come in." She opened the door wide and beckoned for Kira and Ruby to join her in the house.

Kira and Ruby followed Fern to her kitchen.

"We're on our way to the store, and we wanted to drop off a few things," Kira said. "I made you a Philly cheesesteak casserole."

"You are too generous, Kira."

"We like visiting you," Ruby announced before taking the tote bag from Kira. "I'm going to draw you a picture." Then she sat down at the table and began coloring with her crayons.

Kira opened the refrigerator and slipped the casserole dish inside. "I put a note with instructions on the foil."

"*Danki.* Please sit with me."

Kira sat beside Ruby and across from Fern at the table. "Do you need any groceries from the store?"

"Oh, no *danki.* My niece Lucy dropped off eggs, bread, and

milk earlier today." Fern's dark eyes focused on Ruby, and her lips formed a wistful smile. "You know that Hiram and I didn't have any *kinner*. I love spending time with little ones, and I often wonder what it would have been like to have *kinner*. I suppose Hiram and I could have had *grosskinner* by now as well."

Fern seemed to have a faraway look in her dark eyes. "I never thought I'd be alone at the age of seventy-one. I imagined that Hiram and I would keep each other company well into our nineties, but I suppose the Lord's plan for us isn't always what we imagine for ourselves. However, I am grateful for the years we had together."

Kira's heart squeezed for the older woman. "I'm sorry, Fern."

"Oh, don't be. The Lord has blessed me with wonderful new *freinden*, including you and sweet Ruby. You both and my niece Lucy help keep the loneliness at bay." Then Fern looked down at the aprons in her hands. "These are lovely. *Danki* so much."

"*Gern gschehne.* You know I love to sew, and you've been on my mind. How are you doing?"

"I'm fine." Fern leaned forward and lifted a gray eyebrow. "Have you seen Jayden?"

Ruby looked up from coloring a flower that resembled a bright pink daisy. "Jayden is *mei freind*."

Fern grinned. "Is that right?"

"Uh-huh." Ruby nodded and then returned to coloring, adding orange to the daisy's petals.

Fern lifted her eyes to meet Kira's. "Have you seen him?"

"*Ya*, we helped out a man in Bird-in-Hand on Saturday, and he was there."

"And . . . ?" Fern set the aprons down beside her and then tapped the table. "I want details."

Kira laughed. "There aren't any details. We talked, and it was fun."

"Oh *ya*?" Fern waggled her gray eyebrows. "I think you and Jayden would make a nice couple. You know, I was a bit of a matchmaker in my day. I actually introduced *mei schweschder* Gladys to her husband." She held up a finger. "I detected something special between you and Jayden. I have an eye for this sort of thing, and I predict that you and Jayden will date sometime soon."

Kira felt her cheeks heat as she stole a glance at Ruby and then turned back to Fern. "I'm not so sure how long I'll be in Pennsylvania, so I don't know if that will happen."

"I want you to stay here forever, Kira." Ruby's head popped up, her dark eyes wide. "Promise you'll stay."

Kira patted Ruby's head. "We'll see, okay?"

Ruby nodded and then returned to coloring her picture, adding stick figures beside the colorful flowers.

"Kira, you need to tell Jayden how you feel about him." Fern tapped the table again. "That will encourage him to be honest with you too."

"I don't know if I could do that," Kira said.

"Why not? Honesty is always the best policy."

Kira considered this, and something that felt like excitement enveloped her. What if she told Jayden that she liked him?

But what about Darla?

"There!" Ruby set her red crayon back in the box. "I finished it." She handed the picture to Fern. "This is you, me, Kira, and Jayden walking in *mei mamm*'s garden."

Fern clucked her tongue. "It's beautiful, Ruby. *Danki* so much."

Ruby popped up from her chair, trotted around the table, and hugged Fern. "*Gern gschehne.*"

Fern beamed as she patted Ruby's back.

Kira peeked up at the clock above Fern's sink. "We'd better get to the store. We'll come and visit you again soon."

"I can't wait," Fern said.

Later that morning, Kira pushed the loaded grocery cart across the busy parking lot while Ruby guided the front of the cart. Kira stopped when they reached her uncle's driver's white van, then pulled open the back door and started lifting bags.

"I'll help!" Ruby yanked a bag containing a gallon of milk and groaned as she lifted it up with all her might.

Kira tried to hide her amusement. "*Danki.* You are so strong, Ruby." She placed the container of milk into one of the coolers she had loaded into the van in case their errands ran longer than expected.

"*Ya,* I am. Here's another one." Ruby handed Kira another bag.

Soon all the perishable groceries were deposited in the coolers and the other bags were stacked beside them. As Kira closed the van's doors, she was almost certain she heard someone call her name.

"Jayden!" Ruby grabbed the sleeve of Kira's sweater and yanked it. "Kira, it's Jayden."

Kira turned just as Jayden loped over to them. Her heart gave a kick as she took in his smile. "Jayden. Hi."

Ruby rushed over to him and wrapped her arms around his waist. "I've missed you." She lifted her chin and grinned up at him.

"I've missed you too." Jayden rubbed her back and then grinned down at her as he touched her nose.

Affection swirled in Kira's chest at the sweet scene between her cousin and the man for whom she cared.

Jayden then turned his electric smile to Kira. "Hi."

"What are you doing here?" Kira asked.

"Ty sent me for supplies." He pointed toward a diner across the parking lot. "Is there any chance you and Ruby could join me for a quick lunch? My treat." His expression seemed hopeful.

Ruby folded her hands as if saying a prayer and then bounced on the balls of her feet. "Please, Kira? Please?"

"Well, our groceries are safely stored in coolers." Kira looked toward the front of the van. "Let me just ask our driver." She walked up to the driver's side of the van, where Dottie Stafford sat.

Dottie lowered the window. "Are you ready to go?"

"I was actually wondering if it would be okay if Ruby and I met a friend for lunch. We were going to walk to the diner across the parking lot. Would that impact your schedule too much?"

"Oh, that's fine." Dottie peered in her side mirror where Jayden stood talking to Ruby. Then she smiled at Kira. "Go and enjoy. I can run a quick errand and then I'll meet you here."

Kira nodded. "Thank you." She spun to face Jayden, who grinned down at Ruby while she talked on about going to visit Fern and the picture she had drawn for her. Suddenly, Fern's advice echoed in her mind:

Kira, you need to tell Jayden how you feel about him. That will encourage him to be honest with you too.

Butterflies flapped in her stomach, and her hands began to tremble as she imagined confessing to Jayden the truth about how she felt about him.

But after Philip had crushed her heart, was Kira strong enough to risk it again?

Jayden looked over at her. "You ready?"

"*Ya.*" She sucked in a breath and tried to calm her quavering hands. "I think so."

Jayden sat across from Kira and Ruby at the diner and worked to contain his excitement. He'd been so surprised when he spotted them across the parking lot on his way to the hardware store. He'd done a double take, convinced he'd imagined Kira since he'd been thinking about her since Saturday. And now as she sat across from him clad in a purple dress, he had a difficult time taking his eyes off her.

"What are you going to order?" Kira's gorgeous dark-chocolate-colored eyes met his over her menu.

Jayden rubbed a spot on his chin. He'd been so immersed in his thoughts of her that he hadn't even noticed the selections on the menu. "The BLT sounds good. It's been a while since I've had one."

Ruby looked up from the children's menu, which she'd been busy coloring with the crayons that had accompanied it. "What's a TLB?"

Kira shared a smile with Jayden and then turned to her little cousin. "It's a BLT. It stands for bacon, lettuce, and tomato sandwich."

"Oh." Ruby looked up at her. "I want one."

Kira's brow furrowed. "I thought you didn't like tomatoes."

"I'll just take them off the sandwich."

Kira looked as if she were working hard to hold back a smile. She pointed to the children's menu. "Why don't you get chicken fingers and fries? You always like those."

"Okay." Ruby shrugged.

A young woman with bright red hair, a diamond stud in her nostril, and round purple glasses appeared at their table. Her name tag said "Brenda." She held up a notepad and pen. "Hello. What can I get you?"

"I'd like chicken fingers and fries, please," Ruby said before returning to her coloring.

"Sounds good." Brenda wrote down her order and then focused on Kira. "And you, ma'am?"

Kira perused the menu and then looked up. "I'll have a BLT and chips, please."

"I'll have the same," Jayden said as he handed the server his menu.

The young woman took Kira's menu and then nodded. "Great."

After she left, Jayden and Kira met each other's gazes and then both started to speak at once.

Kira laughed and shook her head. "I'm sorry. Go ahead."

"No. You first." He held his hand out to her.

"Okay." She paused for a beat and something imperceptible flashed over her pretty face. "How's Darla?" Her words were soft and halting as if she dreaded the response.

CHAPTER 19

Jayden stared across the table at Kira as she watched him with a hesitant expression. Confusion rained down on him. "How's Darla?" he repeated her question.

Kira nodded.

"I guess she's okay. I haven't seen her since youth group on Sunday." He rested his hands on the table. "Why are you asking about her?"

"When did you and Darla start dating?"

"Dating?" He leaned forward and scoffed. "I'm not dating Darla or anyone else."

Her eyes widened, and her expression relaxed. "You're not?"

"No, I'm not. Why did you think I was dating her?" He tilted his head.

Kira moved the tip of her finger along the edge of the table. "She's very possessive of you."

He heaved out a deep sigh. "She is. We've been *freinden* since we were in school. I haven't wanted to break her heart and tell her that it will never happen between us, but I need to."

"That's sweet that you don't want to hurt her."

He studied her expression. "What about you and Shane?"

"He told me that he wants to see me, but I explained to him I only want to be *freinden*. He's been very understanding and respectful, but we're not dating."

Relief filtered through Jayden, and he couldn't stop his smile. "Really?"

She nodded and then her lips tipped up in a dazzling smile.

Ruby looked up from her drawing. "Have you made more dollhouse furniture, Jayden?"

"*Ya*, I have."

"Like what?" Ruby's dark eyes sparkled with interest.

"Let's see." Jayden began counting off the pieces of dollhouse furniture he had been working on, and soon the server approached their table with their meals.

Brenda placed the meals in front of them and then headed to another table.

After bowing their heads in silent prayer, Jayden, Kira, and Ruby began eating their lunch.

Kira suddenly looked over at Jayden. "I have an idea."

"What's your idea?" Jayden picked up a chip.

"I mentioned to you that I've been visiting Fern once a week," she said, and Jayden nodded. "Last week when I stopped by, Fern admitted to me that she's lonely. Today she was so thrilled to see us, and I felt bad about leaving. While we were talking today, she mentioned to me that she was a matchmaker, and she introduced her *schweschder* to her husband."

Jayden grinned. "Really?"

"*Ya*, and that got me thinking. What if we were matchmakers for Fern?"

"What do you mean?" Jayden popped a chip into his mouth and swallowed it.

Excitement danced in her eyes. "Omar is lonely, and he's never been married, and Fern lost her husband. What if we introduced them?"

Jayden grinned. "Kira, that's brilliant."

"Do you think so?" She leaned forward, took his hand in hers, and gave it a gentle squeeze.

Jayden threaded his fingers with hers. "*Ya*, I do think it's a great idea."

Kira looked down at their hands, and her cheeks flushed bright pink before she released his hand and rested her hands by her plate. She picked up a potato chip. "I'll have to come up with an excuse to get Fern and Omar together."

They were silent for several moments while they ate, and the question he'd longed to ask her bubbled up in his mind. He glanced over at Ruby, who was engrossed in eating her chicken fingers and coloring her kids' menu.

Jayden turned back to Kira. "I've wanted to ask you something."

"What is it?"

Jayden hesitated. "When we were at that youth group gathering together, you said something to me that I've wondered about. I don't know if it's appropriate to ask you."

"Go ahead and ask me. I trust you, Jayden."

These words hit him square in his chest and gave him the courage to push on. "You mentioned that you had an ex-fiancé."

Kira frowned and nodded. "*Ya*, I did."

"May I ask what happened?"

Kira swallowed another bite of her sandwich. "His name is Philip. We were supposed to get marred in November." She shook her head and looked down at her plate. "He changed his mind, and he called it off."

Stunned, Jayden opened and closed his mouth, unable to gather his words for a moment. "Why would he do that?"

"He said he wasn't ready to be a husband and make that commitment." She shrugged. "I thought we were fine, but looking back, the signs were there. He seemed distant all of a sudden. He stopped opening up to me and he stopped discussing the future. I would talk to him, and he would remain silent. He became someone I didn't know."

"I'm sorry."

"Thanks." She sighed. "We had plans to build a *haus* and start a family, but I guess I wasn't enough for him."

"Why would you blame yourself, Kira?"

She pressed her lips together. "*Mei schweschder* told me that he's been talking to another *maedel* at youth group. He's already moved on, so that tells me that I was the problem."

He shook his head as frustration toward a man he didn't know bubbled up inside him. "Kira, that only means that he's the one with the problem. He's *narrisch* if he thinks you're not enough for him. You got it all wrong. You deserve someone who will cherish you, Kira. He wasn't the one for you."

"*Danki*." She clutched her glass of water and took a drink. "Shortly after Philip broke up with me, *mei aenti* invited me to come here and help her with the *kinner*. I saw it as a way to get away from my community and try to heal my broken heart. I'm sure *mei mamm* called *Aenti* Ellen and asked her to invite me since I was so devastated."

She set her glass down. "*Mei aenti* has told me more than once that she doesn't want me to work the entire time I'm here. I need to concentrate on making *freinden*. She says I need to heal my heart and not let what Philip did to me allow me to give up on love. But I just don't . . ." Her words trailed off as she stared down at her half-eaten sandwich and shook her head.

"But you don't what?" Jayden leaned forward as curiosity overtook him. "What is it, Kira?"

When she met his gaze, a frown had pressed her lips into a flat line. "Philip broke my heart and my trust. As much as I want to believe in love, I'm afraid to trust again. I feel as if I need to put a cover over my heart." Then she seemed to shake off the thought as she peeked over at Ruby, who hummed while coloring the children's menu. "But while I'm here in Pennsylvania I really just want to concentrate on my family. A relationship would complicate things."

"I understand." But even as he said the words, disappointment nearly shredded Jayden. Although he'd been elated to find out Kira wasn't dating Shane, his heart sank at her admission that she wasn't ready for another relationship. Still, being her friend and her confidante would be a blessing.

But then a surge of courage overtook Jayden, and he reached across the table to take her hands in his. "I'm sorry he hurt you. In my humble opinion, he made a grave mistake when he pushed you away and told you he wasn't ready to get married. And your *aenti* is right, you shouldn't allow Philip to destroy your faith in love or your dreams. But you also don't need to rush into another relationship. And, as I said earlier, you deserve a man who will love and cherish you for the rest of your life."

She threaded her fingers with his. Her pretty face lit up with a gorgeous smile, and he was mesmerized by how effortlessly beautiful she was. "*Danki*, Jayden. I'm so glad I met you."

"I feel the same way." His body warmed at her words as their gazes locked.

"Do you need anything else?"

Jayden's head popped up as the server divided a look between him and Kira. He released Kira's hands and sat back in the seat. "No, I think we're ready for the check."

"Great." Brenda handed him the check. "I can take it whenever you're ready. Thank you!" Then she flounced off to another table.

Jayden pulled his wallet from the back pocket of his trousers as Kira reached for her purse. "My treat, remember?" Jayden said with a wide grin. "*Danki* for having lunch with me." After choosing a few bills, he set them on top of the check.

"*Danki*," Kira said as she gave him a shy smile.

"It was fun." Ruby pushed her menu over to Jayden. "This is for you."

Jayden's heart expanded as he took in the colorful drawing of food peppered with flowers, stick figures, the sun, and trees. "It's beautiful, Ruby."

The little girl beamed.

He turned toward Kira and found her watching him with an intensity in her eyes that caused his breath to pause. But she'd made it clear that she wasn't interested in dating. Still, he yearned to be her boyfriend, and he was determined to find a way to convince her to give him a chance. He would show her how wonderful she was and how she deserved to be treated. And then maybe, just maybe, she would allow him to be her boyfriend.

"I suppose we should go," Kira said. "I need to put the groceries away and then start on my chores."

Jayden carefully folded the picture and placed it into his pocket before scooting out of the booth. "I'd better get back to the worksite before Tyler thinks I ran away with the supply money."

Ruby slipped the crayons into her apron pocket and then

climbed out of the booth before turning to Kira. "This has been a super fun day, and it's only lunchtime."

Kira chuckled. "*Ya*, Ruby. It sure has."

Jayden couldn't agree more.

Kira walked between Jayden and Ruby as they crossed the parking lot. Her heart felt light after unloading her burdens during lunch. She silently marveled at how easy it was for her to share her heartbreak with Jayden. He'd been sympathetic and supportive, and she felt so comfortable with him. He was such a special man. If only things were different and she were planning to stay in Pennsylvania, then she could possibly pursue a relationship with him.

"I hope you enjoy the rest of your day," Jayden said when they reached the van.

Ruby hugged his waist and then looked up at him. "Bye, Jayden."

"Goodbye, Ruby." He patted his pocket, where he had stored her drawing. "*Danki* for the lovely picture."

Ruby scampered toward the van. "*Gern gschehne!*" she called over her shoulder before yanking open the back door and jumping into the seat.

"*Danki* for lunch." Kira held her hand out to Jayden.

As he shook it, she relished the feel of his warm skin against hers. "I enjoyed having a chance to talk with you."

"I hope we can do this again soon."

Jayden nodded. "I do too. Keep me posted on your plan to

get Omar and Fern together. I think it will be a blessing to both of them."

"I'll let you know. Please tell your family hello for me." Kira took a step away from him.

"I will."

Kira took a spot in the front passenger seat of the van. After buckling her seat belt, she waved to Jayden as Dottie drove away.

"How was the grocery store?" *Aenti* Ellen asked Kira and Ruby as they carried in a load of bags.

Ruby set a bag of crackers on the table. "It was fun. We had lunch with Jayden."

"Is that right?" *Aenti* Ellen grinned at Kira before she began placing the boxes of crackers in the pantry.

Kira explained how Jayden had seen them in the parking lot and then invited them to join him at the nearby diner. "We had a nice time." She set a box of eggs in the refrigerator and then picked up a gallon of milk.

"*Gut.* I'm glad you saw him." *Aenti* Ellen retrieved two boxes of cereal. "I was thinking that it's been too long since we've seen Crystal, Michelle, and Savannah. Why don't we invite them to come for lunch tomorrow? I had promised to have them over, and it would be fun to get the *kinner* together and have some adult company."

Excitement filtered through Kira. "*Ya,* I would love that. I'll look through your cookbooks and find something fun to make for lunch."

Ruby took off toward the family room. "I'm going to draw more pictures!"

"Shh," *Aenti* Ellen told her. "Your siblings are sleeping." Then she touched Kira's arm. "Tell me everything about your lunch with Jayden."

Kira frowned. "There's nothing exciting to tell." She turned her attention toward a grocery bag containing lunch meat and opened the refrigerator.

"Oh, no you don't, Kira. You're not going to get away with avoiding my question. I know you like him. Did he tell you that he likes you? Is he going to come and visit you?"

Kira sighed, and her lips turned down. "I told him what happened with Philip."

"And . . . ?"

"And he was very supportive and sympathetic."

Aenti Ellen clapped her hands. "That's great."

"But I also told him that I'm not looking for a relationship, and I'm not ready to trust again."

Her aunt's expression clouded with a frown. "Oh."

"He's a sweet, kind, and thoughtful man, but I'm not ready to date."

Her aunt's smile returned, and she shrugged. "Well, you never know what the Lord has in mind for you."

Kira slipped the lunch meat into the drawer in the refrigerator and then withdrew another bag while her aunt's words settled over her. She smiled as she considered her easy and fun conversation with Jayden. She felt as if she could be herself with him—completely open and honest. The warmth in his hazel eyes while she spoke not only relaxed her but also felt like a warm hug.

While she stowed more groceries, Kira tried to imagine what

it would be like to date Jayden, but it seemed like an impossible dream. As much as she liked him, she couldn't imagine giving up her family for him. The thought of not returning to Indiana to be with her family made her heart feel heavy.

If only she and Jayden could be more than friends, but it would never work out between them. All she could pray for was a special friendship with him.

Still, as she set a container of butter and a block of cheese into the refrigerator, a tiny glimmer of hope took hold of her heart. Perhaps her aunt was right. After all, the Lord worked in mysterious ways.

CHAPTER 20

"Kira, this beef enchilada casserole is *appeditlich*," Savannah said the following afternoon.

Michelle lifted her spoon. "I agree. I would love your recipe."

"Absolutely," Crystal agreed. "I think Duane would enjoy this very much."

Kira smiled as she glanced around the table at her new friends. She was so delighted that Crystal, Michelle, and Savannah had come for lunch. After the little ones ate a lunch of grilled cheese, they went into the family room to have fun in a play yard while Austin napped in his bassinet. Once they were settled, Kira served the beef enchilada casserole, and the women ate their lunch while getting caught up on the latest news. They each took turns checking on the children.

"Jayden mentioned that he had lunch with you and Ruby yesterday, Kira," Crystal said as she lifted her glass of water. "What a wonderful coincidence that you ran into each other by the grocery store."

Kira's heart kicked at Jayden's name. He had talked to Crystal about Kira? Her hands began to tremble as she felt all the eyes around the table focus on her.

Savannah's and Michelle's eyes glittered with curiosity.

Kira held her breath, hoping her cheeks wouldn't flame. "*Ya*, it was a fun coincidence."

"He said he had a nice time, and Ruby drew him a picture," Crystal continued. "He just thinks the world of Ruby."

Kira smiled. "Ruby feels the same way." *And I think the world of him too.*

Her aunt gave her a warm smile.

"You know," Savannah began, "Jayden isn't dating anyone. Do you have a boyfriend back home?"

Kira blinked, surprised by Savannah's outspokenness.

Michelle swatted Savannah's arm. "You don't beat around the bush, do you?"

"You know I like to get to the heart of things." Savannah shrugged. "Why not say what you mean and mean what you say?"

Michelle shook her head as she met Kira's gaze. "You don't need to answer that question. It's very personal."

"I don't mind. I trust you all." Kira cleared her throat as heat climbed her neck. But despite her nerves, she longed to share the truth with her new friends. "I was engaged, but he broke up with me. We were supposed to marry in November." She shared the story of her relationship with Philip while Savannah, Michelle, and Crystal listened. "So, no, I don't have a boyfriend back home."

Crystal leaned over and rubbed Kira's shoulder. "I'm sorry he hurt you. He clearly wasn't the right man for you, but God will lead you to your perfect match."

"I'm sorry too." Michelle leaned over and touched Kira's hand.

Savannah shook her head. "He was a *dummkopp* to break your heart."

Kira sighed. "*Danki. Mei schweschder* Leah told me that he's seeing someone."

"What?" *Aenti* Ellen asked. "You never told me that."

"He's been spending time with a *schee maedel* in our youth group." Kira moved her fork over her plate.

"Don't let that bother you," Savannah insisted. "He made the mistake by breaking up with you, and he'll regret it. Mark my word."

Michelle's smile was sweet. "Savannah is right."

"I appreciate that." Kira smiled.

Savannah held up a finger. "You and Jayden seem to like each other. Since you're both single . . ." She let her words trail off.

Michelle shook her head. "You never cease to surprise me with your boldness, Savannah," she said with a laugh. Then she looked at Kira. "Do you like Jayden?"

Savannah gave Michelle a light tap. "See? You wanted to know too."

Everyone chuckled.

"I do like Jayden," Kira began, "but I'm not ready to get into another relationship quite yet."

Crystal rubbed Kira's arm. "She's still nursing a broken heart. I understand that."

Kira smiled at Crystal.

Silence hovered over the kitchen for a few moments, and Kira let their comforting words settle over her. She was grateful to have Jayden's family in her life.

"Jayden mentioned that you and your *freinden* have been helping older folks in our community. How are those projects going, Kira?" Michelle asked as she rested her hand on her protruding abdomen.

"They're going well, and I actually have an idea for something else we can do." Kira explained how they had worked at Omar Weaver's home and then told them about Fern. "They both mentioned to me that they're lonely, and then yesterday Fern said she'd been a matchmaker for her *schweschder* and her husband. I was thinking that maybe I should introduce Omar and Fern. Omar has never been married since he took care of his *schweschder,* who was gravely *krank.* Perhaps Omar and Fern could become *freinden.*"

Savannah grinned and lifted her fork. "Or more than *freinden.*"

"Exactly," Kira agreed with a chuckle.

Aenti Ellen clapped her hands. "What a marvelous idea."

"*Danki,* but I haven't figured out how to get them together." Kira forked another bite of casserole.

Crystal snapped her fingers. "I have the perfect idea." She tapped the table. "Duane's birthday is next Saturday. Why don't you invite them to come to a little party? He's turning fifty-one. He insisted that we didn't make a big deal about turning fifty last year, but he hasn't mentioned not wanting a party this year. How's that for an excuse to have a big party?"

"That's brilliant, Crystal," Michelle said as everyone chuckled.

Excitement hummed through Kira. "I love it. What can I bring?"

"How about we make a list? Do you have a notepad, Kira?" Savannah asked.

Kira found a notepad and pencil and then began a list of what they'd need for a party.

Crystal smiled. "I'll make Duane a chocolate cake."

"I can put together a couple of pans of lasagna," Michelle offered.

Savannah forked more casserole. "I'll bring garlic bread and salad."

"Kira and I can bring appetizers," *Aenti* Ellen said. "Maybe a vegetable tray as well as cheese and crackers."

Crystal rubbed her hands together. "This is going to be so fun."

Kira looked up at her friends. "I think this is the perfect plan. I'll invite Fern, and I'll talk to Alaina about inviting Omar. She can reach out to her cousin." She couldn't imagine being so forward as to call Jayden. She would talk to Alaina at youth group and ask her to pass Omar's invitation on to Darla, who would then invite him.

After they finished lunch, they sat in the family room and drank tea and ate cookies while the children played.

Later, *Aenti* Ellen and Kira walked Crystal, Michelle, Savannah, and the children out to their van, where they said goodbye.

Crystal hugged *Aenti* Ellen. "*Danki* for a lovely lunch."

"*Gern gschehne.* We'll see you next Saturday," *Aenti* Ellen told Crystal.

Then Crystal pulled Kira in for a warm hug. "Let your heart heal," she whispered, "but be careful not to miss the signs when you find your true love. I met Duane when I least expected it, and the same could happen to you."

"*Danki,*" Kira whispered, and her heart felt full as she smiled up at Crystal.

After Crystal climbed into the van, the driver started the engine.

As the van drove away, *Aenti* Ellen turned to Kira. "Next Saturday will be fantastic."

"I can't wait to see how Fern and Omar react when they meet each other." Something warm and fuzzy fluttered in Kira's stomach. Not only would she be able to introduce Fern and Omar, but she would also have an excuse to see Jayden. Even though she wasn't sure she was ready to risk her heart again, she couldn't deny the invisible magnet she felt pulling her toward him. While her head kept telling her not to date anyone, her heart craved

Jayden, and she had a feeling that her heart might be the one to win her internal struggle.

Later that evening, Jayden sat on a stool in the woodshop and stained a miniature sofa. He breathed in the sweet aroma of the stain mixed with wood while working by the warm yellow light of the lanterns glowing on the table and workbench.

Tyler, Jayden, and the crew had finished up a roofing job at a quilt shop in Bird-in-Hand, and they would start another job tomorrow. The day had flown by quickly, but his thoughts had been stuck with Kira.

Throughout the day, he'd contemplated their conversation during lunch yesterday, and he found himself trying to make a plan that would convince her to trust him with her heart.

He frowned as he recalled the anguish flickering on her beautiful face while she discussed Philip. He would never understand how that man could have broken his engagement with her. Was the man *narrisch*?

Jayden finished staining the sofa and set it aside to dry. Then he picked up the bunk beds he had created earlier in the week and began staining them.

The door squeaked open, and Korey joined him in the shop. Jayden nodded a hello as his middle brother stepped inside.

"*Dat* said you were out here." Korey perched on the stool beside him. He glanced around the shop and then studied the two dollhouses sitting on the shelf beside the worktable. Running his finger over the roof of each house, he gave a low whistle. "You've built two dollhouses, and they're nearly completely furnished. I had no idea you had such talent when it comes to woodworking."

Jayden snorted. "Gee, thanks, Kore."

"I didn't mean it as an insult." Korey held his hands up as he snickered. "I'm just saying that you're talented. You're like *Dat* when it comes to woodworking."

Jayden sat up a little taller, surprised by the compliment. "*Danki.* What's up?"

"Savannah told me that Crystal is planning a surprise birthday party for *Dat* next Saturday since he wouldn't let her give him one last year."

"That will be fun." Jayden continued staining the bunk beds.

Korey rubbed his dark-brown beard. "*Ya,* I was surprised when Savannah told me that the party was prompted by your *freind* Kira."

Jayden stilled and looked over at his brother. "What do you mean?"

"Apparently, Kira wants to introduce Omar Weaver to a widow you helped over in Gordonville. She said she needed a reason to get them together, so Crystal suggested the birthday party."

Jayden nodded. "I had lunch with Kira and one of her cousins yesterday, and she mentioned that she wanted to get them together. That's a *gut* idea."

"I agree." Korey seemed to ponder something. "So, you had lunch with Kira. Are you seeing her now?"

Jayden huffed out a deep breath. "No, no, I'm not."

"Have you told her that you care about her?"

Jayden set his paintbrush down and considered how much to share with his brother. "No, I haven't."

"Why not?"

"It's complicated."

"You like her, and it seemed obvious to me when she was here that she likes you." Korey lifted his hands, palms up. "How can that be complicated?"

"She made it clear she's not interested in a relationship. She recently went through a breakup, and she came to Pennsylvania for a new start."

Korey smiled. "And God could have inspired her to come here to meet you."

"I doubt it," Jay scoffed.

"Why would you say that?"

"Because she's twenty-five, and I'm twenty-three. I haven't ever been in a relationship, and I have nothing to offer her. Why would she be interested in me?"

Korey shook his head. "Jay, you're an amazing man. You're the most intuitive, kind, and thoughtful man I know. No matter what went on between Ty and me, you were always there encouraging us to work it out. You never took sides. You were always focused on keeping our family together. Kira would be blessed to have you in her life. You should tell her how you feel."

"But she's already said she isn't looking for love."

"Then be the *freind* she needs and leave the rest to God."

Jayden considered this. "*Ya*, I plan to do that."

"*Gut.*" Korey patted Jayden's shoulder and then slid off the stool. "Don't stay out here too late."

"I won't."

Korey walked over to the door and then stopped. "What are you planning to do with the dollhouses?"

"I was thinking that they would be a good Christmas gift for Crystal's nieces."

Korey nodded. "You definitely should give them to someone special." He tapped the doorjamb. "See you later."

As Korey walked away, Jayden considered his brother's advice. He opened his heart to God.

Lord, please help me be the friend that Kira needs.

Then he returned to working on the bunk beds.

"This is the most delicious chicken salad I have ever had, Kira," Fern said Tuesday afternoon. "I'm so grateful that you came to see me today."

Kira smiled as she sat across from Fern at her kitchen table. She and Ruby had come over to visit Fern and help with chores. While Ruby swept the porch, Kira washed and hung out Fern's laundry. Then they sat down to enjoy the lunch that Kira had brought to share.

Kira considered the other reason why she had come to visit today. On Sunday, she and her friends had firmed up the plans for inviting Fern and Omar to Duane's surprise party. Now she just had to convince Fern to come. "Fern, do you have plans on Saturday?"

"No, I don't believe I do. Why do you ask?"

"Kira wants to invite you to a party on Saturday." Ruby popped a chip in her mouth and then smiled up at Fern.

Fern chuckled. "You're having a party on Saturday?"

"*Ya*, we're invited to a party, and we'd like you to come. It's our *freind* Duane's fifty-first birthday. His *fraa* wanted to give him a party last year, and he refused. So, she decided she's going to have the party this year," Kira explained, then held her breath as Fern seemed to consider the invitation.

"Oh." Fern frowned. "It's very kind of you to invite me, but I don't know your *freind*. I think I'd feel very awkward."

Kira shook her head. "You wouldn't feel awkward. You know *mei freinden*, and they'll all be there." Then she counted her friends off on her fingers. "Alaina, Lewis, Ben, Lora, Darla, Shane, and Jayden. Plus, *mei aenti, onkel*, and cousins will be there, and we'd love for you to join us."

"*Ya*, we would." Ruby nodded with such conviction that her dark-brown braids bounced off her shoulders.

Fern shook her head. "Oh, I don't know . . ." She picked up her napkin and began to fold it in her hand. "I really enjoy being at home, and I don't want to be a burden to anyone."

"You have to come," Ruby insisted. "Pleeeeease, Fern? Pleeease?"

Fern laughed. "Well, if you insist, Ruby, then I will."

"Yay!" Ruby clapped her hands, while Kira and Fern laughed.

"Perfect," Kira said as excitement expanded inside her. "*Mei freinden* will give you a ride to the party. Shane is going to ask his driver to bring you, Lewis, and Alaina. I'm going to ride with my family, and we will see you there."

"Do I need to bring anything?" Fern asked.

"No, we've already planned the meal," Kira said. "All you need to bring is yourself and a smile."

Fern chuckled again.

Kira beamed. The plan was coming together perfectly.

CHAPTER 21

JAYDEN STEPPED INTO THE KITCHEN WEDNESDAY EVENING and breathed in the delicious aroma of fried chicken. "Hello," he told Crystal as she set a stack of dishes on the table. Just as he turned, his little sister came running toward him with her hands raised in the air.

"Jay! Jay! Jay!" she exclaimed as he scooped her up into his arms. She wrapped her arms around his neck and kissed his cheek.

Joy expanded in his chest as he hugged her close. "How are you today, Krissy?"

"*Gut!*" she called before patting his cheek.

Crystal smiled over at them as she set the table. "I wanted to tell you about Saturday before your *dat* gets home. You know we're planning something for your *dat*, right?"

"*Ya*, Korey told me." Jayden leaned against the counter while he continued to hold his sister.

"*Gut.* I haven't had a chance to talk to you alone. I spoke to Ellen, and everyone is coming, including Fern. Kira told her that Shane is going to pick up Fern, Alaina, and Lewis on his way here. Also, Darla called me today and confirmed that Omar is coming." Her expression brightened. "I think it's going to be perfect."

Jayden's heart hammered at the thought of seeing Kira again. "*Wunderbaar.*"

"Savannah and Michelle are going to tell your *bruders* that you need to be home by five on Saturday." Crystal crossed to the counter and collected three glasses. "We're having a special supper, and I'm making your *dat*'s favorite *kuche.*"

Kristena raised her hands up in the air once again. "*Kuche!* *Kuche!*"

Jayden laughed and then kissed her little cheek.

"Now we just have to keep this all a secret." Crystal glanced at the doorway leading to the mudroom and then back at Jayden. "Hopefully, we'll manage to do that."

Jayden nodded. "I'm sure we will." Saturday couldn't come soon enough.

⁂

Kira swept the downstairs bathroom Thursday morning. She tried to keep her mind engrossed in her work, but her eyes kept defying her and locking on her aunt's calendar hanging on the wall.

Her stomach twisted as it focused on the date—the first Thursday in November. It was the date Kira was supposed to be married. Today she and Leah were supposed to don their peacock-colored dresses and stand with Philip and his brother while Kira and Philip were married.

All of their plans whipped through her mind and battered her like waves hitting the shoreline while she moved the broom across the floor. They were planning the reception in her father's largest barn, and hundreds of members of their community would have come. They would have served baked chicken for the wedding dinner and plenty of cakes and pastries for dessert. Philip was building a house on his father's land for her.

Had he finished the house? Would he propose to Yvonne and then move into the home with her?

Kira slammed her eyes shut and kneaded her fingers on her forehead.

Stop torturing yourself!

"*Was iss letz?*" her aunt's voice sounded from behind her. "Do you have a headache?"

Kira spun toward *Aenti* Ellen standing in the doorway leading to the family room with a concerned expression on her face.

Gripping the broom, Kira forced a smile. "I'm fine. I was just lost in thought."

Her aunt nodded slowly. "Are you sure?"

"*Ya.* Of course." Kira pushed the broom again.

Her aunt closed the distance between them and placed her hand on Kira's shoulder. "I know what today is, Kira." She paused. "If you want to talk, I'm here to listen anytime."

"I appreciate that, but I'm fine." When *Aenti* Ellen looked unconvinced, she took her aunt's hand in hers. "I promise you I'll be okay."

Her aunt hesitated and then nodded before continuing to the counter. "I need to get ready for lunch. Your *onkel* will be here soon. Mimi and Liesel are in the play yard, Ruby is coloring at the coffee table, and Austin is napping."

Kira finished sweeping and then discarded the pile of dirt into the trash can. After washing her hands, she began to set the table. Her aunt carried over packages of lunch meat and cheese, along with a loaf of bread, condiments, and a bag of chips.

Soon the table was set, and Kira fastened Mimi in her high-chair before placing Liesel on her booster seat. Ruby took her seat, and they were ready for lunch by the time *Onkel* Stan walked into the kitchen.

"Hello!" He kissed each of his daughters and then Ellen before sitting down in his usual spot at the head of the table. They all bowed their heads in silent prayer and then he looked around the table. "How's your day going?"

Aenti Ellen smiled. "Just fine. I've been doing some cleaning."

"I helped *Mamm* dust and then I drew a few pictures," Ruby announced.

Onkel Stan turned his attention to Kira. "Your *mamm* called. She asked me to tell you to call her."

Kira pressed her lips together. She was certain she knew why her mother had called. Surely *Mamm* remembered what day it was. Her grief began to bubble up again as she thought of her parents and her sisters. She longed to be with them today and drown her sadness in their sympathy and support.

"*Danki*," Kira managed to say. "I'll call her after lunch."

"Is everything all right, Kira?" *Onkel* Stan asked while he added ham to his sandwich.

"*Ya*, of course. I'm just tired."

Aenti Ellen seemed to give him a look. "How's your day going, Stan?"

"Busy. We've gotten a few orders this morning that will keep us busy, which is *gut* since November is here. You know work seems to slow down in the colder months," he said before continuing on about his workload.

November is here.

Kira's uncle's words echoed in her mind. Today was the day

Kira was supposed to have changed her name as well as her mailing address. But she was still Kira Detweiler, and although her address had changed, it wasn't permanent.

"Don't forget we have a party to go to on Saturday." *Aenti* Ellen's words broke through Kira's thoughts.

"Party! Party!" Liesel chanted while Mimi clapped and laughed.

Onkel Stan chuckled before he leaned over and touched Liesel's cheek. "That's right."

"Kira," *Aenti* Ellen began, "we have to get those appetizers together, and we need to find a gift for Duane."

"*Ya*, I know. I'll go to the store tomorrow." Kira turned her attention to the party. At least she would see Jayden on Saturday, and she was certain he would warm her soul.

After helping her aunt clean up the lunch dishes, Kira carried Mimi and held Liesel's hand while they climbed the stairs to their second-floor bedroom. She set each of them into their cribs and then sang to them until they fell asleep for their afternoon nap.

Then she hurried down the driveway to her uncle's shop and waved hello to his coworkers on her way to his office. She sat in his desk chair and then dialed the number for her parents' phone shanty. After several rings, her mother finally answered.

"Hi, *Mamm*," Kira said. "*Onkel* Stan said you left a message for me to call you."

"Kira! How are you?"

Kira sniffed. Her mother's voice helped to soothe her battered soul. "I'm fine. How is everyone there?"

"We're *gut*. Busy as usual."

"That's great." Kira wound the phone cord around her finger.

"So," *Mamm* began and then she hesitated.

Kira held her breath, and when her mother didn't continue, worry began to prick at her neck. "*Was iss letz, Mamm?*"

"I'm concerned about you, Kira. I know what today is. Or, actually, what today was supposed to be." *Mamm* paused again. "How are you *really* doing?"

"I truly am fine. I'm staying busy today. I've been cleaning, and we're going to a birthday party on Saturday. I'm bringing appetizers. I'll also need to figure out what to get for a gift."

"That sounds fun. Whose party is it?"

Kira explained who Duane was and how she planned to introduce Fern to Omar at the party.

"Oh, that is delightful! How nice of you to play matchmaker for the older folks. I'm sure they will be thrilled to meet each other."

"I hope so." Kira rested her elbow on the desk and her chin on her palm.

"You've always had a kind and loving heart."

Kira frowned. "But it wasn't enough for Philip." When her mother was silent, Kira sat up straight. "What's on your mind, *Mamm*? You don't normally hold back."

Mamm sighed. "I wasn't going to tell you, but Philip was here yesterday."

Kira opened her mouth and then closed it as confusion stole her words.

"Kira? Are you there?"

"*Y-ya*, I am." Kira cleared her throat. "What did he want?"

"He asked about you, and he wanted to know if you were okay."

"What did you tell him?" Kira's body began to quiver with a tangle of emotions—anger, confusion, frustration, and grief.

"I told him that you're having a wonderful time with your cousins in Pennsylvania and that I didn't know when you were planning to come back."

"And what did he say?" Kira bit her fingernail as she awaited her mother's response.

"He asked for your address and phone number."

"Why?"

"He says he wants to talk."

Kira slumped back on the chair as her body continued to shake. "Why would he want to talk now?" Her voice sounded thick and reedy. "What is left to say?"

"I'm sorry, *mei liewe*. I shouldn't have told you. I didn't want to hurt you, and that's exactly what I did."

"No, it's all right. I'm glad you told me." Kira needed to change the subject. She'd already spent too much of her energy today thinking about Philip. "How's Abby?"

"Oh, she's doing well. She called yesterday, and she's delivered a few babies this week."

Kira relaxed while her mother talked on about Abby's deliveries. She was relieved to have something else to think about.

"Oh, here come your *schweschdere*," *Mamm* said. "I'll put them on."

Kira perked up when Leah took the phone and shared the latest news from their youth group. Maribeth also joined in, and the three of them chatted about friends in their community. Then Kira's mother came back on the line.

"We should let you go," *Mamm* said. "I need to put together a shopping list and then head to the grocery store."

"Please give my love to *Dat*," Kira said.

"Of course I will. *Ich liebe dich*."

"I love you, too, *Mamm*. I'll talk to you soon." Kira hung up the phone and then stared at the receiver as she reflected on the news her mother had told her. Why would Philip want to contact her after he told her it was over between them? And why was he even thinking about Kira if he was seeing Yvonne? None of it made sense.

Pushing herself up from the chair, Kira exited the office and then ambled toward the front of the shop.

"Is everything all right?" *Onkel* Stan asked as he traipsed toward her.

Kira forced her lips to curve into a smile. "*Ya*, everything is fine. *Danki* for allowing me to use your phone."

"Anytime." He patted her shoulder. "I'll see you at suppertime."

As Kira headed back toward the house, she tried to push away all her thoughts of Philip, but questions continued to bounce like fireflies in her head. She couldn't stop wondering if Philip would contact her. And what would she say to him if he did?

"Lord, guide my heart and give me strength," Kira whispered as she climbed the back porch steps and headed into the house.

Crystal stood in the middle of the kitchen Saturday evening. "The food is out, and the cake is iced." She wrung her hands together. "I think we're ready."

Jayden breathed in the delicious aroma of Michelle's lasagna and Savannah's garlic bread. "Everything is perfect, Crystal."

"*Ya*, it is." Savannah touched Crystal's shoulder. "You can relax."

Michelle stood in the doorway to the family room while the children played in the play yard behind her. "Duane is going to be so surprised."

"I just hope everyone is here on time." Crystal peeked out the window.

"Tyler and Korey should be here soon," Savannah said. "They just ran home to shower and get changed."

Just then a van rumbled into the driveway. The passenger door opened, and Stan appeared.

"Kira is here," Jayden said before he hurried through the mudroom, out into the early-November crisp air, and down the porch steps. He reached the path as Kira climbed out of the back seat. She looked stunning in a red dress that was the perfect complement to her dark hair and eyes.

Kira smiled. "Hi, Jayden."

"May I carry something?" he offered.

"That would be helpful." She reached into the back of the van and emerged with two large serving dishes. "Would you please take these for me?"

Jayden took the dishes. "Of course."

"*Danki*," Kira said.

Ruby launched herself from the van and hugged Jayden's waist. "Jayden!"

"Hi, Ruby," he said before greeting her parents and siblings.

Then he led them all into his house, where they said hello to his stepmother and sisters-in-law. Soon his brothers joined them and then another van arrived with Shane, Fern, Alaina, and Lewis. And the van carrying Darla, Lora, Ben, and Omar appeared in the driveway a few minutes later.

Soon they were all gathered in the family room just as *Dat* walked into the kitchen.

"Duane!" Crystal said. "How was your day?"

"*Gut.*"

"Would you go into the *schtupp* for me?" Crystal asked. "I think I left my sweater in there, and I'm cold."

"Sure."

Just as *Dat* walked into the family room, everyone yelled, "Surprise!"

Dat reared back, glanced around the room, and then chortled. "What on earth?" He turned toward the doorway, where Crystal stood beaming. "Did you plan a surprise party for me?"

"*Ya*, I guess I did." Crystal smiled. "Happy birthday, Duane."

Everyone began singing the birthday song, and *Dat* smiled.

"*Danki*," he said when they finished, and everyone clapped.

Crystal held her hands up. "Michelle made some *appeditlich* lasagna. Let's eat."

CHAPTER 22

WHILE CRYSTAL AND JAYDEN'S SISTERS-IN-LAW HEADED INTO the kitchen, Jayden watched Kira approach Fern.

"I'd like for you to meet someone, Fern," Kira said before taking Fern's arm and leading her over to Omar. "Fern, this is Omar Weaver. He lives here in Bird-in-Hand. Omar, this is Fern. She lives in Gordonville."

Jayden smiled as the older man and woman shook hands and began to talk. Kira turned to face Jayden and winked, and he smiled at her before following her into the kitchen, where his sisters-in-law distributed plates of lasagna, salad, and garlic bread. The children sat nearby in highchairs while eating rolls.

He and Kira each grabbed a plate before heading to one of the tables. He took a seat at the table between his brothers and across from Kira. Jayden had set up two extra tables with chairs in order to make room for their company. Kira's aunt and uncle sat at a table, along with their children. Shane, Lewis, Alaina, Ben, and Lora were beside them at the other table.

When Jayden peered down at the end of his table, he found Omar and Fern engrossed in a conversation. Fern laughed while Omar shared a story about his teenage years.

"I think they like each other," Kira said.

Jayden looked over at her. "I do too."

Darla sank down in the chair beside Kira. "Hi, Kira," she said before focusing her blue eyes on Jayden. "How was your week, Jayden?"

"*Gut.* Busy," Jayden replied before looking back at Kira. She was so beautiful that he couldn't keep his eyes off her.

Darla cut up her lasagna and then took a bite. "Oh, this is superb." She turned to Michelle beside her. "You make fantastic lasagna."

Michelle smiled and they began discussing lasagna recipes.

Kira leaned forward. "It's so *gut* to see you, Jayden."

"You too," he told her. "I'm so relieved that the plan came together so perfectly."

Kira looked toward the far end of the table, where *Dat* and Crystal talked and laughed. "Your *dat* seems so *froh.*"

"*Ya.*" Jayden lifted his glass of water. He was so grateful for his family and his wonderful friends.

After supper, Kira helped the women carry the dishes to the counter. Then she began washing the dishes while Jayden's sisters-in-law dried them. Jayden gathered up the leftovers and stored them in containers.

When he scanned the family room, he spotted Fern and Omar sitting on the sofa together while they continued to talk. Happiness surged through him. It seemed that Kira's plan had already paid off and a friendship had been formed.

A hand on his shoulder surprised him, and Jayden turned toward Kira.

"I'm sorry!" She held her hand up. "I didn't mean to scare you."

Jayden chuckled. "From what I remember, you owe me."

She chuckled. "I think Omar and Fern have already hit it off." She nodded toward the sofa.

"I do too."

Kira brushed her hands down her black apron. "Savannah said we should let our food settle before we have cake."

"Oh." An idea lit up in Jayden's mind. "Would you like to go for a walk?"

Kira smiled. "I'd love to."

"Great." Jayden's heartbeat sputtered.

After pulling on their coats, Jayden pushed open the back door, and Kira stepped out onto the porch. He pulled his flashlight from his pocket, and they started down the porch steps into the cool evening. Above them, the sun had started to set, sending brilliant hues of orange, red, and yellow chasing one another across the sky.

Their shoes crunched on the rock path as they ambled toward the pasture. The air was crisp and held the hint of wet earth.

"How was your week?" he asked, breaking the amiable silence between them.

She huffed out a breath and shook her head.

He stopped walking and faced her. "Is something wrong?"

"No. It was just a tough week." She licked her lips and then peered out toward the pasture. "I was supposed to be married on Thursday."

Jayden frowned. "I'm sorry." He paused. "Are you okay?"

"*Ya.*" Kira began walking again, and he fell into step beside her. "I spoke to *mei mamm* on Thursday, and she said that Philip had stopped by to see her. He asked about me, and he asked for my contact information. I asked why, and apparently, he wants to talk to me."

Worry threaded through Jayden. "Do you want to talk to him?"

"I don't think there's anything left to say." Kira stopped and leaned on the pasture fence. "After all, he said he wasn't ready to get married and spend the rest of his life with me. He told me that it was over."

"What if he wants you back?" Jayden asked while working to keep the panic out of his voice. "What would you do?" Dread pooled in his gut as he awaited her response.

Kira rubbed her eyes and then turned toward a line of trees at the back of his father's property. "I've been contemplating that, and he's already hurt me once. Why would I want to put myself through that again?"

Jayden blew out a relieved sigh as they both trained their eyes toward the back of the pasture. He suddenly felt the overwhelming need to follow Korey's advice and tell Kira how he felt about her.

He covered her hand with his. When she smiled up at him, he took a deep breath.

"I like you, Kira."

Her smile widened. "I like you too."

"I mean I *really* like you." His voice trembled.

"I really like you, too, Jayden," Kira said. "I've liked you since the day we met."

"I know you're not looking for a relationship now, and I'm younger than you . . ."

Her brow puckered. "Why would age matter?" she asked.

Jayden blinked, shocked by her comment.

"But the truth is that I'm not ready for another relationship, and I'm not planning to stay in Pennsylvania. But if I were, you would be my first choice."

Jayden nodded as a mixture of happiness and disappointment warred in his stomach.

Kira threaded her fingers with his and gave his hand a squeeze. "I'm so glad I met you, Jayden. You're a blessing to me."

Happiness ignited in his chest. "You're a blessing to me."

They stared at each other for a few moments, and then she released his hand.

"How are your dollhouse projects going?"

Jayden nodded toward his father's shop. "Why don't I show you?"

Kira followed Jayden into the woodshop, where he flipped on the lanterns throughout the room. When her eyes found two dollhouses sitting on a shelf, she gasped as she rushed over to them. She ran her finger over their smooth roofs and then examined the intricate furniture sitting in each room.

When she turned toward Jayden, she found him watching her with a simmering stare. Heat rushed through her veins as she considered his declaration of his feelings for her outside.

Jayden was just so special. If only things were different and she planned to stay in Pennsylvania . . .

"You think the dollhouses are ridiculous," he deadpanned. "Just admit it, Kira."

She held her hands up. "No, no, no! They are spectacular." She pointed to the first house. "I can't get over the furniture. The detail you put into the grandfather clock and the dressers is incredible. These are just beautiful. You should sell them."

"No." He scoffed. "They're not that *gut*."

"But they are. You're just too modest."

He shook his head and sat on a stool.

She studied him for a moment as questions whirled in her mind.

Jayden crossed his arms over his wide chest. "Why are you looking at me as if you're trying to figure out a puzzle?"

"Have you dated much?"

He ran a finger over the edge of the workbench. "Why do you want to know?"

"Because I'm nosy." She hopped up on the stool beside him.

He pursed his lips. "I haven't dated at all."

"You haven't?"

"Why are you surprised?"

"Because you're so kind, sweet, and handsome. You seem to always think about others before you think about yourself. You've gone out of your way for Ruby and for your *bruders*. You always put your family first. It's obvious to me that you'd make a *wunderbaar* boyfriend."

His smile widened as heat crawled up her neck. Why had she admitted that aloud?

"What about you?" he asked. "How much have you dated?"

Kira frowned. "Philip was my second boyfriend."

"I'm sorry you had a bad experience."

"*Danki.*"

He took her hand in his, and her skin warmed at his touch. "You deserve to be treated with respect, Kira. You deserve a man who won't give up on you, or hurt you, or make you feel bad." His voice sounded gruff, and his eyes were intense. "You deserve someone who will love you for the rest of his life. Don't ever forget that."

Kira's body trembled as she held his hand. She felt her feelings for this man expand and morph into something even more intense and meaningful.

The door to the shop opened, and Darla walked in.

Kira felt her back stiffen. She released Jayden's hand as Darla glanced around and settled her eyes on Jayden.

"Korey said you'd probably be in here," Darla said. "Crystal wanted me to let you know that we're going to cut the *kuche* now." Before they could answer, she crossed the room and stood in front of the dollhouses. "What are these?"

Jayden hopped off the stool and joined Darla by the dollhouses. "I made them."

"You did?" Darla spun toward him, her pretty face full of surprise. "I had no idea you liked to work with wood."

Jayden shrugged. "It's sort of a hobby." Then he explained how he had replaced a roof at a toy store and was inspired to try to build dollhouses. "I was thinking of giving them to Crystal's nieces for Christmas. I'll eventually make one for my niece and my *schweschder* when they're old enough."

"Wow." Darla picked up a wooden sofa and touched it.

Kira couldn't stop her frown. Would Darla ever stop flirting with Jayden? Didn't she realize how desperate she seemed?

Darla pointed to the wooden trains on a far shelf. "Are these the trains your *dat* makes for the children's charities?"

"*Ya*, they are."

Darla glided over to the trains. "They're lovely."

Jayden gave Kira an apologetic expression and then turned back to Darla. "We'd better get inside before they cut the *kuche*."

Kira followed Darla to the door, and while Jayden flipped off the lanterns, Darla shot her any icy glare. Kira sighed as irritation gripped her. Darla needed to grow up and let go of her animosity toward her.

Jayden closed the shop and led them back into the house, where Kira and the rest of the guests and Duane's family sang the birthday song to him again before Kira helped distribute pieces of the moist chocolate cake.

Michelle brewed coffee, and Kira handed out cups. Then she helped herself to a piece of cake and a cup of coffee. When she walked into the family room, she found Omar and Fern still sitting on the sofa and talking while they each ate a piece of cake. Her heart warmed as she took in the happiness on Fern's face. She sent up a silent prayer, asking God to initiate a special friendship between Omar and Fern.

Then Kira looked around the room and found Michelle and Savannah sitting on chairs near where the children played in the play yards. Kira took a seat in the empty chair near them.

"Kira," Savannah said. "I'm so glad you joined us."

Michelle swallowed a piece of cake. "I am too." She leaned over toward her. "I saw you and Jayden go outside together. Did you have a nice talk?"

"We did." Kira sipped her coffee. "We went for a walk and then we sat in his workshop and talked."

Savannah nudged Kira with her elbow. "And . . . ?"

"And that's it. We just talked."

Savannah snorted. "Come on now. Tell us the truth."

"He told me that he really likes me, and I told him that I really like him too." Kira sighed. "But I'm still not ready to date yet."

Michelle nodded. "I understand."

"How are you feeling?" Kira asked.

Michelle touched her distended abdomen. "I am so ready for this baby to come. Only one more month."

"You say that now, but you should enjoy sleep while you can." Savannah twirled her fork in the air. "Those sleepless nights will be here before you know it."

Michelle pointed to little Connie. "I haven't slept since she was born. Nothing will change."

They all laughed.

"Oh, I heard from *mei bruder*, Toby, today," Savannah announced. "He's going to be a *dat*. I can't believe it."

Michelle grinned. "Oh, that is the best news. Did you talk to your *dat* too?"

"Oh *ya*. He's doing well, and his *fraa* is too. It seems like everyone is having babies. I hope Korey and I are blessed with more."

While Savannah talked on about hoping for more children, Kira glanced across the room to where Jayden sat talking with his brothers, Shane, Alaina, and Lewis. Jayden's gaze collided with Kira's, and when he smiled, she once again considered how he'd admitted that he cared for her.

Her heart took on wings, but she knew that they could never be more than friends. It would never work since she wasn't ready to share her heart, and she knew she wasn't going to stay in Pennsylvania. Still, that didn't change the fact that she not only cared for Jayden, but she admired him. She was certain to the depth of her bones that Jayden would cherish her and treat her with respect and kindness if she gave him a chance to date her. He would never break her heart the way that Philip had.

When Jayden turned back toward his friends, Kira's eyes moved to where Ben and Lora stood in the corner, standing close together while they talked. She took in the love in their eyes for each other, and her heart yearned for that kind of relationship.

But it wasn't meant to be, and Kira needed to find a way to convince her heart that there was no future for her and Jayden— no matter how much that truth hurt.

"We had such a lovely time," Ellen told Crystal later that evening. "*Danki* so much for inviting us."

Crystal embraced her. "I'm so glad you could all come. Duane was so surprised, and he's loved every minute of the party."

Stan shook Jayden's hand. "It was nice seeing you and your family."

"*Danki* for coming," Jayden told him.

The evening had flown by much too quickly for Jayden. It seemed as if they had just started eating the cake, and then the cake and coffee were gone and the children had started to get grumpy. Both Tyler and Korey had gathered up their little ones and said good night to everyone before they left with their wives.

"Jay! Jay!" Kristena whined as she held on to his trouser leg and sniffed.

Jayden lifted her into his arms, and she stuck her thumb in her mouth before resting her cheek on his shoulder. "You're tired, little one."

"No," she protested.

He snickered and then turned, surprised to find Kira watching him. "I didn't know you were standing there."

"We're getting ready to leave. I wanted to be sure I said goodbye to you." Kira reached up and touched Kristena's back. "It was nice seeing you, Krissy."

His baby sister sniffled and closed her eyes.

Kira grinned up at him.

Jayden mouthed, "Tired," and Kira nodded.

Jayden held his hand out to her, and she shook it. Then, to his surprise, Kira pulled him toward her for a hug, wrapping her arms around both Kristena and his waist.

"Jayden," Kira whispered, "I'm glad you're *mei freind*."

Jayden closed his eyes and breathed in her flowery scent. Although he longed to be more than her friend, he was grateful to have her in his life. "I am too."

Then Kira stood on her tiptoes and kissed Kristena's cheek. "*Gut nacht*," she said before touching Jayden's hand and then heading through the door to the kitchen.

"I hope to see you soon," Jayden called after her as she left. Then he heaved out a happy sigh.

<hr />

Kira pulled on her coat and then picked up Liesel before traipsing out the back door to where her aunt and uncle were loading the children into the van.

When she felt a hand on her shoulder, she spun to face Fern.

The older woman smiled as she shook a finger at her. "You brought me here to meet Omar, didn't you?"

"Maybe?" Kira shrugged.

Fern laughed. "Well, thank you. He's going to call me."

"Oh, that's fantastic!" Kira gave a little squeal. "I'm so happy for you."

Fern hugged her. "You get home safely, and I will see you soon."

Kira waved goodbye to Shane, Lewis, and Alaina and then joined Ruby in the back of the van.

Her aunt and uncle also buckled in and then the van started down the driveway toward the road. Almost instantly, the children were asleep in their car seats.

Aenti Ellen swiveled in her seat to face Kira. "Omar and Fern seemed to hit it off."

"*Ya*, they did. Fern told me that he's going to call her."

Aenti Ellen grinned. "You're a *gut* matchmaker, Kira."

With a happy sigh, Kira settled back in the seat. She wrapped her arms around her waist as she recalled the hug she'd shared with Jayden before she left. She'd like more hugs like that soon. And then a thought occurred to her: Which would be worse, never having Jayden hug her again . . . or not having her mother's warm hugs each night?

The question sat heavily on her heart, and her eyes suddenly stung as she considered leaving Jayden behind when she returned home to Indiana.

<hr />

Jayden padded out to the kitchen while Kristena snored softly on his shoulder. When he found Darla standing by the sink, he stopped. She set a platter on the drying rack and then faced him.

"Darla," he said. "I didn't realize you were still here."

She dried her hands with a paper towel. "Ben just went to call his driver to see if he's on his way."

"Oh." Jayden nodded, not knowing what else to say.

A serious expression flashed over her face. "Are you and Kira dating?"

"No." Jayden rubbed Kristena's back. "We're not dating. We're just *gut freinden*."

Darla seemed to consider this. "It's obvious that you two like each other."

"We do." He hesitated as he took in her red-rimmed eyes and her quivering lip. "I'm sorry, Darla. I know you care about me. You're important to me. We've been *freinden* for a long time."

She looked stricken. "I care about you, Jayden. I've always cared for you. But you don't care for me that way, do you?" Her face crumpled.

He shook his head. "I'm sorry, but I don't. But you are a very special *freind* to me."

She sniffed and wiped her eyes. Tension seemed to hover between them like a dense fog.

"Darla, please believe me when I tell you that I never meant to hurt you."

She cleared her throat and gave him a watery smile. "You and Kira make a nice couple. I wish you well."

"*Danki*, but we're not dating." He hesitated as the truth took hold of him. "But I do care about her."

They studied each other, and guilt washed over him.

After a few moments, Lora appeared in the kitchen. "Our ride is here, Darla." Then she nodded at Jayden. "*Gut nacht*."

Jayden waved at them both as they walked outside. Then he huffed out a deep breath. He'd finally told Darla how he felt. It had been more difficult than he'd imagined, but he was relieved that she finally knew the truth.

A few moments later, heavy footsteps sounded on the porch and then the back door opened and clicked shut before Korey rushed into the kitchen. "Ryan forgot his pacifier, and he's not *froh*."

"I think I saw it in the *schtupp*." Jayden leaned back on the counter and continued to rub Kristena's back.

Korey disappeared into the family room and then reappeared holding up the pacifier. "Found it. Thanks." He touched Kristena's back and kissed her head before meeting Jayden's eyes again. "I saw you and Kira went outside for a walk. Did you tell her how you feel?"

"I did, but it didn't go the way I'd planned. She said she's only looking for a *freind* right now." Jayden worked to keep his expression even despite his disappointment.

Korey smiled. "Don't give up, Jay. Keep the faith, and don't doubt God." Then he headed for the door. "See you tomorrow."

Jayden waved as his brother left.

CHAPTER 23

KIRA HELD A GROCERY BAG WHILE RUBY KNOCKED ON FERN'S door on a Tuesday afternoon two weeks later. The mid-November sky was dotted with puffy clouds as a cool breeze lifted the ties to her prayer covering and caused her to shiver. She turned toward the yard as two squirrels ran by chattering, leaves crunching under their feet.

The door opened, and Fern clapped her hands. "Kira! Ruby! Come in."

"We brought you some groceries," Kira told her as she and Ruby followed her into the family room, where Omar sat on a wing chair holding a cup of coffee. "Omar. *Wie geht's?*" she asked with surprise.

The older man smiled. "It's great to see you, Kira. Hello, Ruby."

"You are too kind to bring me groceries." Fern continued to the kitchen, where Kira set the bags.

Kira pulled out a half-gallon of milk, a dozen eggs, and a loaf of bread. "I went to the store for *mei aenti*, so I thought I'd get you a few essentials." She set the milk and eggs in the refrigerator.

Then Kira turned toward the family room, where Ruby stood in front of Omar and shared a story about how she had helped her father sweep his shop. The older man looked on with a smile as his eyes twinkled with interest.

Kira swiveled toward Fern. "Omar seems to be enjoying himself."

"He is the kindest man I've known since Hiram." Fern took Kira's hand in hers. "I can't thank you enough for introducing us. He called me the Monday after the party, and we talked on the phone for a few hours. Then he came to visit me. He's so sweet. I'm so *froh*."

Kira patted her hand. "I'm thrilled to hear this, Fern. When you mentioned you were a matchmaker for your *schweschder*, the idea of introducing you to Omar took hold of me. I'm grateful it worked out."

"You're a blessing, Kira." Fern hugged her. "Now, tell me about Jayden."

"There's really nothing to tell. We've decided to be *freinden*."

Fern gave her a look of disbelief. "Who decided that?"

"I did." Kira looked down at the worn gray linoleum floor. "I'm not ready to risk my heart, and I'm not planning to stay in Pennsylvania."

Fern gave her a wistful smile. "Don't let your insecurities dictate your happiness. God will lead you to the person you're meant to love. Be sure to be listening so you don't miss his guidance."

Kira nodded as Fern's words soaked through her. Then she smiled. "I'd better get back home."

Kira and Ruby said goodbye to Fern and Omar and then hurried back to the van. While the van rumbled down the gravel driveway toward the road, her mind spun with confusion while she considered Fern's advice.

She couldn't help but wonder if God had led her to Jayden. But if that were true, then how could she overcome her broken heart to allow Jayden in? And how could she consider leaving her family in Indiana to start a life with him?

She closed her eyes and opened her heart to God:

Lord, please guide my heart and show me the path you have chosen for me.

Jayden squatted on a large farmhouse roof Thursday morning. He looked out across the Johnson family's farm and then turned toward where Tyler, Dennis, and Roger worked, hammering in shingles.

"Did you hear that Elias Miller's barn burned down Sunday night?" Dennis asked as he sat back on his heels.

Jayden swiped his hand over his forehead. "No, I didn't."

"*Mei dat* told me last night," Dennis said.

Roger shook his head. "That's terrible."

"Is everyone okay?" Tyler asked.

"They managed to get their animals out, but the barn burned to the ground." Dennis set his hammer down. "*Mei dat* said there's going to be a barn raising on Saturday. They're working to get the land cleared and all the materials delivered by the end of the day tomorrow."

Jayden sat down and crossed his legs. "Is there any chance we could help?"

Ty rubbed his beard. "We should have this job finished up tomorrow and we're scheduled to start the next one on Monday." He shrugged. "Sure. We haven't helped with a barn raising in a while."

"I'm sure the Miller family will appreciate all the help they can get," Roger said.

"I agree," Jayden said. It had been two weeks since he'd seen Kira, and he missed her. He had been looking for an excuse to go see her and now he had it. He turned toward his brother. "That would be a great community service project for us to participate in. I have a feeling *mei freinden* would like to join in."

"I'm sure they would," Tyler agreed.

Then an idea took hold of Jayden. "Can we make a stop on the way home?"

"*Ya*, no problem."

Jayden rubbed his hands down his thighs. He had contemplated his conversation with Kira the night of his father's party over and over again and how she had said that she wasn't ready for a relationship. Still, he couldn't stop wondering if he asked her to be his girlfriend if she would see how serious he was about her. He had told her that he cared for her, but he hadn't found the courage to ask her if she would give him a chance to prove to her how much he cared.

His throat dried as an idea filled his mind. Perhaps if he convinced her to date him, she would realize he wasn't like Philip at all. She'd already told him that she liked him, but if she just gave him a chance, he'd prove to her that he would treat her the way she deserved to be treated.

"Jay? Are you all right?" Tyler asked.

"*Ya*, I am." Jayden stood as a surge of courage overwhelmed him. "Could I borrow your work phone for a few minutes?"

Tyler's eyes squinted with confusion before he pulled his cell phone from the back pocket of his trousers. "*Ya*. Who do you need to call?"

"I promise I'll explain it later." Jayden pocketed the phone and then climbed down the ladder. Then with his hands trembling, he dialed the number for Kira's uncle's shop.

"Gordonville Sheds. This is Stan," her uncle said.

"Stan, hi. This is Jayden Bontrager." He hoped his voice wasn't quivering as much as his hands were as he leaned back against the side of the house.

"Jayden! What can I do for you?"

Clearing his throat, Jayden lifted his straw hat with his free hand and swiped his palm over his sweaty brow. "Stan, I was hoping to talk to you for a moment. I don't know if you're aware that I've become *gut freinden* with Kira."

"Ellen has mentioned it to me."

"Your niece means a lot to me, and the truth is that I care for her." Jayden rubbed his eyes and took a deep breath. "What I'm trying to say is that I'd like to ask her if she'd consider being my girlfriend, and I'd like your blessing."

"You know, Ellen mentioned to me that she thought this day might come soon."

Jayden swallowed against the ball of nerves expanding in his throat.

"We both think the world of you, and since Kira is living with us, I feel it's my place to give you our permission to date her. So yes, you have our blessing."

Jayden blew out the puff of air that he hadn't realized he'd been holding. "Thank you, Stan."

"You're welcome. I'm sure I'll see you soon."

Excitement bubbled up in Jayden's chest as he disconnected the call. He had Stan's permission, but now he had to find the perfect moment to ask Kira. He prayed that she would just give him a chance to prove that he would never break her heart.

Kira set the last bowl of stew on the table just as a knock sounded on the back door later that evening. She scooted through the mudroom and opened the back door.

When she found Jayden standing on the porch, her heart gave a kick. "Jayden. Hi."

"I'm sorry for just stopping by," he said.

Kira looked past him to where the gold diesel Dodge pickup truck waited for him, humming in the driveway. "It's no problem. You're welcome here anytime. Please come in."

"Oh no." He held his hand up. "I don't want to impose. Ty and I were on our way home from a job, and I wanted to ask you if you were interested in going to a barn raising on Saturday." He explained how the Miller family's barn had burned down in Bird-in-Hand. "Ty, Dennis, Roger, and I plan to go, and I thought it might be a fun community service project for us and our *freinden.*"

Kira's heart lifted. "I'd love to. Come inside, and I'll ask *mei aenti.*"

They entered the kitchen, where Kira's family sat at the table.

"Jayden!" Ruby called. "Hi!"

He waved before greeting Kira's family. "I'm sorry for just stopping by. I wanted to invite Kira to come to a barn raising with me on Saturday."

"Would it be all right if I went, *Aenti*?" Kira asked.

"Of course, Kira," her aunt said. "We'll make some food that you can bring to share."

Kira clasped her hands together. "*Danki.*"

"Why don't you join us for supper, Jayden?" *Onkel* Stan asked from the far end of the table.

Kira turned to face Jayden. "That's a great idea. I made plenty of stew and biscuits."

"Oh, no *danki*," he said. "Ty needs to get home."

Aenti Ellen frowned. "Can't you ask your driver to come back for you later?"

Jayden rubbed his chin as if considering the suggestion. "Well, that is a great idea." He jammed his thumb toward the door behind him. "I guess I could ask him."

"Yay!" Ruby said.

Jayden excused himself and then hurried outside. While he spoke to his driver, Kira set a place for him between her and Ruby. The sound of the truck backing out of the driveway was music to Kira's ears as Jayden joined them in the kitchen after hanging his coat and hat in the mudroom.

"*Danki* for the invitation," Jayden said while he scrubbed his hands at the kitchen sink. Then he took a seat beside Kira.

After a silent prayer, they all began eating their stew and buttering their biscuits.

"Where have you been working this week, Jayden?" *Onkel* Stan asked before taking a bite of stew.

Jayden set his spoon down beside his bowl. "We're reroofing a large *haus* and five barns at a farm out in Gap."

"Wow. That's a big job. How do you like roofing?"

"I enjoy being outside and working with *mei bruder*."

Kira smiled as Jayden continued to discuss work with her *onkel*. While she ate, she took in his handsome profile, silently admiring his clean-shaven, chiseled jaw, along with his high cheekbones and those gorgeous hazel eyes. But it wasn't just his good looks that she found attractive.

She was also drawn to how kind, generous, and thoughtful

Jayden was. He was so different from any man she'd ever met. While Philip had always seemed to focus on what he wanted and what was convenient for him, Jayden worried about how he could help others. He had the most generous heart she'd ever known.

When she felt someone watching her, Kira looked across the table and found her aunt smiling at her. As her cheeks began to heat, Kira turned her attention toward her stew.

Jayden and *Onkel* Stan discussed their work while they finished supper. When their bowls were empty, Kira and her aunt served coffee and brownies they had baked earlier.

"Everything was fantastic," Jayden said. "I can't thank you enough."

Kira picked up their mugs and carried them to the counter. "I'm glad you enjoyed it."

"Why don't you and Jayden sit on the porch and talk until his driver arrives, Kira," *Aenti* Ellen said as she gathered up their dishes.

Kira leaned against the counter. "I'll help you with the dishes first."

Then Kira watched a look pass between her aunt and uncle, and *Onkel* Stan stood.

"Go enjoy your company." *Onkel* Stan gathered up the utensils. "I'll take care of the dishes while your *aenti* bathes the *kinner.*"

Kira met Jayden's curious expression. "Would you like to take a cup of cocoa out to the porch?"

"*Ya*, that sounds nice." Jayden's warm expression sent a shock wave of excitement down to her toes.

Kira brewed two cups of hot cocoa before they pulled on their coats and took their seats in rocking chairs on the porch. She looked out over her uncle's property toward the barn and shivered before taking a sip of hot cocoa.

"Are you cold?" Jayden asked.

She shook her head. "I'm fine. The cocoa is warming me up."

"I'll let Ben know about Saturday, if you want to tell Alaina," Jayden offered.

"*Ya*, that sounds *gut*. *Danki* for writing down the Miller family's address. I'm sure Alaina will spread the word, and everyone will come and help."

A comfortable silence filled the air between them, and she settled back in the chair before pushing it into motion. She turned toward him and found him watching her. "I saw Fern on Tuesday."

"How is she?"

"She's great. Omar was there visiting her."

Jayden angled his body toward her. "He was?"

"*Ya*." Kira couldn't stop her grin. "I got the impression that they really like each other a lot."

Jayden chuckled. "I told you that your plan was brilliant."

Kira sipped her cocoa.

"I finally told Darla that I'm not interested in dating her." Jayden ran his finger over the arm of the wooden rocker.

"What?" Kira almost spilled her cocoa as she shifted to face him. "When did this happen?"

"The night of *mei dat*'s party." He explained that after Kira and her family had left, he carried Kristena out to the kitchen, where Darla was. "She asked about you and me and wanted to know if we're dating. I said we weren't, but she said it was obvious we cared for each other."

Kira nodded as her throat dried. "What else did she say?"

"She looked like she was going to cry. I told her that I know she cares for me, and I'll always care for her as a *freind*. And I said I was sorry for hurting her." Jayden sighed. "It nearly broke my heart to make her cry, but I had to be honest with her."

Kira reached for his hand. "You're such a wonderful man, Jayden."

Just then, the headlights from Jayden's driver's Dodge pickup truck flashed across the porch as the truck rumbled up the driveway. Disappointment threatened to crowd out her happiness. Why did their wonderful visit have to come to an end so quickly?

The truck came to a stop at the top of the driveway, and the headlights flipped off as the engine died.

Jayden set his mug on the table beside his chair and then touched his hand to Kira's cheek. The contact of his skin against hers nearly stole her breath. "As I've already told you, I really like you, Kira. I would be honored to be your boyfriend. I called your *onkel* at his shop earlier today, and he gave me permission to ask you."

"I really would like you to," she whispered, "but I'm not sure I'm going to stay here. I don't want to start a relationship with you and then have to face going home and leaving you behind."

His fingers moved gingerly over her cheek. "I understand, but I want you to know I'm serious about you and ready for a commitment." Then he leaned forward, and his lips brushed her cheek with a nearly featherlike touch that sent her blood thrumming through her veins. "I'll see you Saturday, Kira."

Her body shivered and her heart took on wings as Jayden loped down the porch steps and climbed into the truck.

As she watched the truck motor down the driveaway, Kira pressed her hand to her cheek where his lips had been, and she sucked in a breath as the truth took hold of her—she was falling in love with Jayden Bontrager.

Midmorning on Saturday, Kira carried two disposable serving trays into the Miller family's kitchen, where a buzz of conversations hovered over her as Amish women worked, preparing food.

Alaina rushed over and gave her a hug. "I'm so glad you're here."

"I brought chicken salad, rolls, and chocolate chip *kichlin*." Kira glanced around. "Are Lora and Darla here?"

Alaina pointed toward the counter. "*Ya*, they're making iced tea and lemonade." Then she took a step toward her. "I wanted to ask you something before Darla comes over here. Are you dating Jayden?"

"No." Kira set her serving trays on the table.

Alaina gave her a suspicious look. "Darla told me that Jayden said you care about each other."

"We like each other, but we're not dating." Kira recalled the kiss Jayden had given her on Thursday night and her pulse zoomed.

"Why aren't you dating if you care about each other?"

Kira frowned. "My family is back in Indiana, and I'm not ready to leave them. So, even though I really do care for Jayden, it doesn't make sense to date and then have to break up. I think that would be more painful than not dating him at all."

Alaina studied her, and Kira longed to read her friend's thoughts.

"Just say what you're thinking, Alaina."

Alaina glanced across the kitchen and then back at Kira. "I know my cousin cares about Jayden, but when I see you with him, it's obvious that you two are crazy about each other. I get the feeling that you would be great together, and if I'm completely honest, I'd love to see you stay in Pennsylvania."

"*Danki.*" Kira touched her arm. "That's really sweet."

A middle-aged woman with blond hair, glasses, and a pretty smile approached them. "Hi. I'm Lizzie Miller."

"Lizzie, this is Kira Detweiler," Alaina introduced her.

Kira shook Lizzie's hand. "It's nice to meet you."

"I'm so grateful that you've come out to help us today." Lizzie sniffed. "My husband and I are overwhelmed at how the community has come together for us."

Kira smiled. "That's what we do for one another."

"The tables are set up," an older woman called from across the kitchen. "We can carry our food outside now."

Kira clutched her serving platters and then followed the line of women out the door to where the folding tables were set up to serve the noon meal.

After setting her dishes down, she shivered as she tented her hand over her eyes and peered out to where the barn had begun to take shape. While dozens of Amish men worked hammering boards for the walls, another dozen or so were busy working on the new roof.

Kira spotted Tyler and Korey and then found Jayden nearby. She smiled as she tried to imagine Jayden as her boyfriend. But what kind of future could they possibly have if she wasn't going to stay in Pennsylvania?

CHAPTER 24

JAYDEN CROUCHED ON THE ROOF OF THE BARN AND GLANCED out to where the women were busy setting up tables of food. "Looks like it's almost lunchtime," he called to his brothers working nearby.

"Oh, thank goodness." Korey stood and patted his flat abdomen. "My stomach has been growling for what feels like hours. I'm starved."

Tyler snickered and rubbed his nose. "You're always hungry, Kore. But that explains the growling I heard earlier."

Jayden shook his head and glimpsed out toward the Millers' house. While he had witnessed Ben, Shane, and Lewis hammering sheets of wood for the barn walls, and he had seen Lora, Darla, and Alaina carrying food out to the tables, he hadn't seen Kira. He tried to ignore the disappointment that had followed him around all morning while he looked for her.

He'd worried that he'd been too forward when he kissed her Thursday night, but she had seemed to like it. Still, it was presumptuous of him to assume she'd accept a kiss from him after she'd made it clear that she didn't want to date him. At the same time, he couldn't stop himself when the urge to brush his lips over her cheek engulfed him. He just prayed he hadn't lost her friendship forever.

"Do you have any nails, Jay?" Korey's question broke through Jayden's thoughts.

Jayden's eyes snapped to his. "Nails?" he asked. Then he picked up his box. "I'm out."

"I have some," Tyler said. "Take some of mine."

Jayden jumped up to his feet. "I'll get a few more boxes. I wanted to get a drink anyway." *And also look for Kira.* He started for the ladder. "I'll be right back."

"All right," Korey called. "Don't get lost down there."

Jayden snickered as he mounted the ladder. He took a few steps and then his foot suddenly lost traction and missed a rung.

He gasped and tried to right himself, but he felt off-balance.

His sweaty hand slipped off the ladder, and when he tried to catch himself, he felt his body go weightless and then start to fall.

He tumbled to the ground with a whoosh before crashing down on his back and his right arm with a loud thud.

Pain like fire shot through his right arm as all the air escaped his lungs. He slammed his eyes shut as he worked to catch his breath while his head throbbed.

The fire in his arm blazed, and his heart hammered in his chest. All of his muscles felt as if they had been forced through a meat grinder. His body was cemented to the cold ground, and he couldn't move.

"Jay! Jayden!" Korey shouted, his voice full of panic.

"Someone call nine-one-one!" Tyler hollered. "*Dummle! Now!*"

Conversations hummed around him as Jayden worked to settle his heart and catch his breath. Why couldn't he breathe?

Why couldn't he move?

What had happened to him?

"It's all right, Jayden," a masculine voice close to his ear told him. "Don't try to move."

Jayden worked to suck in air, but he couldn't. He closed his eyes and prayed for God to stop his pain.

"Kira! Kira!" Alaina cried as her feet pounded into the kitchen.

Spinning to face her, Kira's heart dropped when she saw the alarm on her friend's face. *"Was iss letz?"*

"Kumm! Dummle!" Alaina's gray eyes were wide. "You need to come with me."

"Why?" Kira asked as worry threaded through her.

Alaina swallowed and looked toward the door and then back at her. "It's Jayden. He fell off a ladder. An ambulance is on its way."

Kira's knees wobbled, and she gripped the edge of the table to steady herself as cool and clammy dread spread through her. "He-he fell? Is he . . ."

"He's awake and talking." Alaina came to stand beside her and held on to her arm. "One of the Amish men here today is an EMT, and he's with him now. I'll walk with you, okay?"

Kira's stomach twisted, and her heart began to thump as she allowed Alaina to steer her back outside into the cold and across the field to where a group of men stood in a circle.

As they approached the group, she spotted Tyler and Korey crouched next to Jayden while he lay sprawled on the ground with his right arm at an odd angle. Kira's breath came in short bursts while an Amish man bent over Jayden and talked to him in a soft, calming voice. A crowd of Amish men were gathered nearby like bees in search of honey.

With her eyes burning with tears, Kira held on to Alaina's arm and took a quaky breath. *Lord, protect Jayden. Heal his injuries. I can't imagine losing him. He means too much to me. Please, Lord.*

"Can you move your toes?" the man asked Jayden.

Jayden gave an almost imperceptible nod before his lips moved. "*Ya.*" His tone sounded soft and weak.

"Where do you feel the most pain?"

"My head and my right arm." Jayden's voice was a raspy whisper.

"Okay." The man divided a look between Korey and Tyler. "We shouldn't move him. The ambulance will be here soon."

As if on cue, a siren wailed in the distance and then drew closer and closer. The crowd backed up as the ambulance came to a stop, and the EMTs jumped out. The Amish man who had been talking to Jayden trotted over to the EMTs and looked as if he were giving them an update.

"I'll ride in the ambulance with him," Tyler told Korey. "You call *Dat* and meet us at the hospital."

Korey nodded and then turned, and his dark eyes found Kira's. He jogged over to her. "I'm going to call my driver and get a ride to the hospital. Would you like to come with me?"

"*Ya.*" Kira sniffed. "*Danki.*"

Korey's expression was warm. "He's going to be okay."

"I hope so." She sniffed again as tears spilled from her eyes and poured down her cheeks.

Kira sat in the waiting room at the hospital later that afternoon. She tried to flip through a magazine, but her mind was spinning too fast to comprehend the words in the articles. She kept envisioning Jayden sprawled on the ground with his arm lying at an odd angle. Watching the EMTs load him up onto a stretcher and take him away in an ambulance had almost been too much for her to bear.

The ride to the hospital had seemed to take days while she had sat in the back seat of Korey's driver's four-door pickup truck, biting her nails and praying for Jayden. Korey's leg had bounced up and down the entire ride while he had stared out the windshield.

When they arrived at the hospital, she and Korey had nearly run into the Emergency entrance and found Tyler waiting for them. He explained that Jayden had been taken back immediately, and he was instructed to stay in the waiting area.

Now they sat together in a far corner, waiting for news. Kira had worked to keep her emotions in check, and occasionally, one of Jayden's brothers would give her a hopeful smile. She had appreciated that Korey had invited her to join them at the hospital, which had led her to wonder if Jayden had talked to his brothers about her. Joy blossomed inside her at the idea of Jayden sharing his feelings for her with his family.

Her lips quaked again. *Lord, heal Jayden. Please. I can't imagine losing him!*

The doors opened with a whoosh, and Duane hurried in. His dark eyes were wide, and a deep frown lined his face as he scanned the waiting area.

"*Dat!*" Tyler called. "Over here!"

Duane weaved through the sea of chairs until he came to them. "Have you heard anything?"

"No," Tyler said. "But he was awake and talking in the ambulance. He said his worst pain is his head and his right arm."

Korey gave a solemn nod. "I have a feeling his arm may be broken."

"*Ach*." Duane dropped into a seat across from them and rubbed his beard. "Well, he will be blessed if that is his worst injury. I thank God he's awake."

Kira sniffed and wiped her eyes.

Tyler yanked a handful of tissues from a box beside him on a small end table. Then he gave them to Kira. "He will be grateful that you're here."

"That's true," Korey said, and then he paused for a moment. "He may be angry that I'm saying this, but he cares for you. If he hasn't told you yet, then you should know."

She wiped her eyes and then her nose. "I care for him too. I don't know what I would do if something happened to him." She tossed the tissues into a nearby trash can. "*Danki* for inviting me to come with you."

A young woman with auburn hair, glasses, and a white coat came to stand in the middle of the waiting area. "Is the family of Jayden Bontrager here?"

"*Ya*, we are." Duane stood. "I'm his father, and these are his brothers."

"I'm Dr. Armstrong," she said. "Would you please come with me?"

Duane turned to Kira. "Did you want to come with us?"

Nodding, she stood.

They followed the doctor into a small conference room located beside the waiting area.

"How is Jayden, Doctor?" Duane asked after they all had taken seats around the table.

"He's stable," she said. "He fractured his right arm, and he has a concussion. We're prepping him for surgery on his arm now."

Kira swallowed back more tears.

"Will he be able to come home today?" Tyler asked.

The doctor shook her head. "I'd like to keep him overnight for observation due to his concussion, but most likely he'll go home tomorrow." She gave them a warm smile. "I expect him to make a full recovery, but he'll have a cast for about eight weeks until his arm heals."

Kira felt the tension in her back release slightly as Jayden's brothers both seemed to expel relieved breaths.

"Thank you, Doctor," Duane said.

Dr. Armstrong stood. "You can all have a seat in the waiting area, and one of the nurses will come and get you when Jayden is ready for company."

They followed her out to the waiting area, where the doctor waved before disappearing through the emergency room doors.

Kira turned to Duane. "I need to call *mei onkel* and tell him where I am."

"Of course. Let Stan know that we'll give you a ride home," Duane said.

"*Danki.*" Kira made her way to the desk, where a young man with thick dark eyebrows and a thin face looked up at her. "Could I please use your phone for a few minutes?"

The young man hesitated and then gave a curt nod before lifting the desk phone and placing it on the counter.

Kira dialed the store and then held her breath while the line rang.

"Gordonville Sheds. This is Stan," her uncle said.

"*Onkel* Stan. This is Kira." Her words came out in a huff. "I'm at the hospital. Jayden fell off a ladder, and he's going to have surgery."

"*Ach*. No!"

Kira explained his injuries and how she had ridden to the hospital with Korey and his driver. "I want to stay to make sure he's okay. I'm hoping I can see him before I come home."

"*Ya*, I understand. Please give him and his family our regards. I'll let Ellen know where you are."

"*Danki*," she said. "I'll see you when I get home."

Kira hung up the phone and then thanked the man at the desk before returning to sit with Duane, Tyler, and Korey.

As she looked out toward a television displaying a news program, she sucked in a deep breath and began praying for Jayden once again.

Jayden stared up at the fluorescent lights buzzing above him. For a moment he had no idea where he was.

And then the memory came back in a flash. He'd been on top of the Millers' barn with his brothers. Korey had asked for nails, and Jayden had offered to get them. He'd been on the ladder and then he'd been on the ground before an ambulance had taken him to the hospital and he'd been prepped for surgery.

Jayden groaned. The pain behind his eyes and the fire in his right arm had both transformed to a dull throb while a haze had overtaken his mind.

He glanced around the hospital room and frowned. This was not how he had imagined today going. Instead, he had expected to enjoy a day with his friends while helping an Amish family rebuild their barn. He'd never in his wildest dreams envisioned himself trapped in a hospital bed with a roaring headache and a cast on his right arm.

The door to his room opened, and his father and two brothers filed in.

"Hi," Jayden croaked, his voice sounding strange.

Dat clucked his tongue as he came to the side of his bed. "How are you feeling, *sohn?*"

"Like a *dummkopp*." Jayden pushed a button on a remote, and the bed raised him up so that he was in a less painful and awkward position.

Korey smirked as he stood at the end of the bed. "Well, you are a *dummkopp*, little *bruder.*"

"You know, Jay," Tyler began, "if you wanted to take some time off work, all you had to do was ask me. You didn't have to fling yourself off a ladder and nearly scare us all to death."

Jayden sighed.

Dat sank down onto a nearby chair. "Please don't scare us like this again, okay?"

"I wasn't planning on doing it today," Jayden told him.

Tyler took a seat on the opposite side of the bed from their father. "How many years have you been climbing ladders, Jay?"

Jayden glowered at his older brother. "Since I was about seven, I would imagine."

"Don't fall again," Tyler said.

Korey snorted. "You weren't the one who saw it happen, Ty. It was the most horrible scene I've witnessed. I thought you were..." He swallowed, and his Adam's apple bounced up and down.

"I'm sorry." Jayden pressed his lips together.

"That's enough," *Dat* said. "We've made our point about how much he scared us. Did the doctor tell you that you have to stay overnight for observation?"

Jayden nodded.

Tyler rested his right ankle on his left knee. "Michelle, Savannah, and Crystal all send their love. They're concerned about you."

"*Danki,*" Jayden said.

Korey seemed to share a look with their father before he turned his attention back to Jayden. "There's someone here who is also very worried about you."

"Who?" Jayden asked.

Dat stood. "I'll be right back."

"Who's here?" Jayden asked. He longed for his thoughts to not be so fuzzy. How long would the haze from the painkillers last?

Korey tapped the edge of the bed and grinned. "You'll see."

The door to the room opened, and Kira walked in. Her beautiful dark eyes were red-rimmed and puffy as if she'd been crying. She clutched her black coat to her middle while her pink lips turned up in a weak smile.

"Kira." He breathed her name as his eyes focused on her cheek and the memory of the brief kiss he'd given her only a few days ago.

She sniffed and then crossed to the side of his bed. "How are you, Jayden?"

Tyler stood and then nodded toward Korey. "We'll let you two have some privacy." He walked over to Korey and gave his shoulder a pat. "Let's go find the cafeteria."

"Right." Korey winked at Jayden and then turned toward Kira. "Would you like something to eat?"

She shrugged. "Sure."

"We'll see what they have and bring you something back," *Dat* told her.

Then the three of them filed out the door, closing it behind them.

Kira pulled a chair over beside the bed and sat down before unzipping and removing her coat.

For a moment, he stared at her and tried to gather his thoughts. Earlier in the day he had been convinced that she was angry with him and hadn't come to the barn raising, but now she was sitting beside him looking as if she'd cried for him.

"I was so scared something had happened to you." Her voice was hoarse. "I can't imagine losing you."

"You're not angry with me?" His question leapt from his lips without any forethought.

Her laugh sounded ironic. "Why would I be angry with you?"

"Because I kissed you after you made it clear you didn't want to date me. I had no right to do that, and I'm sorry, Kira."

She took his hand in hers. "Jayden, I was never angry with you. I was pleasantly surprised that you kissed me, but you didn't offend me."

"I'm so relieved to hear you say that." He entwined his fingers with hers. "I'm sorry for scaring you. I never imagined I would fall off a ladder. I feel like a complete *dummkopp*."

She gripped his hand a little tighter as if she were holding on for dear life and then she sniffed. "I was so worried that you wouldn't be able to walk. I'm sorry that you broke your arm, but I'm so grateful that your injuries weren't worse."

"I'm just glad you're here."

They continued to hold hands while a comfortable silence fell between them. He yawned and longed for the haze to leave his mind.

"Talk to me," he said.

Her brow furrowed. "About what?"

"About anything," he said. "I just want to listen to your voice. Tell me about your *dat*'s farm."

She chuckled. "Okay. Well, *mei dat* runs a dairy farm that has been in my family for generations."

Jayden felt his body relax while he listened to the beautiful lilt of her voice. She discussed her father's cows and his land and then described her house.

After a while, the door opened, and his father and brothers returned. Kira released his hand and sat back on the chair as the three men walked into the room.

Dat held up a disposable container and a bottle of water. "I got you a ham sandwich and some chips. There wasn't a big variety there."

"That's perfect. *Danki*." Kira opened the container and held up half of the sandwich toward Jayden. "Would you like some?"

Jayden shook his head. "No *danki*."

Kira ate the sandwich and chips while Korey and Tyler entertained them with stories about their children.

Soon more than an hour had passed, and *Dat* pointed to the phone beside Jayden. "I'd better call for a ride. It's getting late."

Jayden yawned. "*Ya*, it is."

After *Dat* called his driver, he stood. "I'll be back tomorrow to see you, *sohn*. Have a restful night." *Dat* shook Jayden's left hand.

"I guess you're going to have to get a sub for me for a while, Ty," Jayden told his oldest brother.

Tyler snorted. "Like I said, Jay, this is one way to get out of working, huh?"

"Well, I always said you weren't the easiest to work for, Ty," Korey joked.

Tyler shook his head and then gave Jayden a pointed look. "You get better. We expect to see you at home tomorrow."

"I hope so," Jayden told him.

Korey touched Jayden's hand. "Be *gut*. See you at home."

"Tell everyone I miss them," Jayden called as his brothers walked out to the hallway.

Dat smiled at Kira. "Take your time. We'll be in the waiting room." Then he left the room, closing the door behind him.

"I'd like to come visit you when you're back home." Kira took Jayden's hand in hers once again.

Jayden gave her hand a gentle squeeze. "I'd like that."

Then she bent down and brushed her lips over his cheek. He leaned into the contact and closed his eyes, soaking in the feel of her soft lips against his skin.

"Please take *gut* care of yourself, Jayden," she told him as she pulled on her coat. "I'll see you soon."

Jayden smiled as she walked to the door.

<hr />

Kira found her aunt sitting at the kitchen table when she arrived home. The house was quiet, and a single lantern on the table cast a warm yellow glow over the room. Kira assumed that the children had gone to bed at least an hour ago.

"How's Jayden?" *Aenti* Ellen asked as Kira sat down across from her.

Kira blew out a deep breath. "He's going to be okay. The doctor is supposed to release him tomorrow." She shook her head as all of the emotions of the day bubbled up inside her. "I'm so sorry for being late. I know that I came here to help you with the *kinner*, and there are chores that you need me to do. I didn't expect to be gone this long."

"Don't apologize. I didn't only invite you here to help me out. I invited you here to help you heal your broken heart. Your *mamm* called me and told me how devastated you were after Philip broke your engagement, and I felt led to help you. I'm glad you met Jayden. And you're not a prisoner here. I want you to have fun with folks your age. I'm just sorry that you had such a stressful day and spent most of it at the hospital."

"*Danki* for understanding," Kira said. "I had to go to the hospital to make sure he was okay. I was grateful Korey invited me to go with them."

"I know how much Jayden means to you, and I'm glad you went with him." *Aenti* Ellen reached across the table and touched Kira's arm.

"When Alaina told me that he had fallen off the ladder and the rescue squad was on the way, I was so afraid I'd lost him forever." Kira rested her elbow on the table and her chin in her palm. "He's told me twice that he cares for me, and both times I told him that I couldn't date him. Now I regret ever saying that because ..." Her words trailed off.

"Because of what, Kira? Please tell me what's weighing on your heart, *mei liewe*."

Kira sniffed and stared up at the ceiling as she tried to gather her thoughts. Then she darted a glance toward her aunt. "I regret not agreeing to date him, because the truth is that I'm falling in love with him, *Aenti*."

"Oh, Kira." Her aunt stood, scooted around the table, sat beside her, and pulled her in for a warm hug. "Let the Lord guide your heart and leave your fears behind. Allow yourself to see where this love leads you."

Kira rested her cheek on her aunt's shoulder and sniffed. "I will." Then she closed her eyes and once again prayed.

Lord, please heal Jayden. Also, please guide me to the path you've chosen for me. My heart is open, and if it's your will, I'll allow myself to love again.

CHAPTER 25

"*Danki* for bringing such a delicious lunch over," Crystal told Kira the following Wednesday afternoon. "I haven't had potato soup and baloney sandwiches in a long time. And your peanut butter *kichlin* were fantastic."

Kira smiled as she sat beside Ruby and across from Jayden at Crystal's table. "I'm glad you enjoyed it."

"The food was amazing, but, honestly, Kira, I'm just glad you're here," Jayden told her. He smiled, but the happiness didn't quite reach his eyes. Instead, he looked tired or possibly even sad.

Ruby turned toward Crystal. "Would it be okay if I played with Krissy?"

"Play!" Kristena held her hands up and then smacked her highchair.

Crystal chuckled as she stood. "I think she'd like that very much." She wiped Kristena's face and hands and then lifted her out of the chair and onto the floor.

Ruby climbed off her chair and took Kristena's hand before leading her into the family room.

Then Crystal began gathering up their dishes and carrying

them to the sink. Kira couldn't help but notice that Crystal's abdomen was more distended than the last time she'd seen her. It was obvious that she was now six months along and her due date was coming quickly.

"How is Michelle doing?" Kira poured the leftover soup into a container.

Crystal smiled over at her. "She's been cleaning constantly, so Tyler thinks it's a sign that she's going to go into labor soon."

"So exciting." Kira set the utensils and glasses in the soapy water and then began drying the dishes Crystal had washed.

Kira and Crystal worked together while Ruby and Kristena played in the room next door.

"I feel so useless," Jayden suddenly announced before groaning. "I can't work. I can't do much in the kitchen since I can't let my cast get wet. I can't work in my shop without struggling. I can't write my name since I'm right-handed. Just brushing my hair and brushing my teeth are chores. And shaving is nearly impossible." His light eyebrows drew together as he scowled. "I struggle to pick up Krissy when she asks me to."

Kira spun to face him, and her heart sank when she found his left elbow resting on the table and his head in his hand. "Jayden, you have to be patient and allow your arm to heal."

"If I hadn't been so careless, this never would have happened."

"It was an accident," Kira insisted.

Crystal gave her stepson a knowing expression. "Kira is right, Jayden. You need to give yourself some grace. No one thinks you deliberately fell off that ladder. Just give your body time to heal."

"The Lord protected you," Kira added. "It could have been so much worse."

He sighed. "I know, and I'm grateful."

They were silent for several moments while Kira continued drying the dishes and setting them in the cabinets.

"Are you ready for Thanksgiving tomorrow?" Crystal asked Kira.

"*Ya*, we're ready. I'll be up early tomorrow to get the turkey in the oven," Kira said before they began discussing the food she planned to make, what Savannah and Michelle planned to contribute to the meal, and their plans for the day.

Once the dishes were done, Crystal started toward the family room. "I'll sit with the *kinner* while you visit."

Kira took a seat beside Jayden and reached for his left hand. "I don't want to ever hear you say that you're useless, Jayden. You're not useless. You're just healing."

"I know." He sagged in his seat. "I'm sorry. I'm just frustrated. I watch *mei dat* and *mei bruders* go to work every day, and I feel like a lazy bum staying home and doing nothing."

"Are you still sore?" she asked him.

He shrugged. "My bruises are a little better." Then he nodded toward the porch. "Let's go outside so we can talk in private."

Kira helped Jayden pull on his coat before she slid into hers. Then they sat together on the glider, and she rested her head on his left shoulder. She felt his body relax as he pushed the glider into motion and threaded his fingers with hers.

"I'm glad you're here." His voice sounded husky next to her ear and sent a shiver dancing down her spine.

Kira smiled and her heart bumped against her rib cage as she recalled the thoughts that had gripped her since the accident. "Jayden, there's something I've been thinking about."

"*Ya*?"

A rush of heat saturated her body. "I knew that I cared about you, but your accident helped me get a new perspective on things."

"What do you mean?" His brow pinched as he swiveled to face her.

She took a deep breath. Then her throat closed, but her heart opened. "Jayden," she began, her words quaking, "I'd be honored if you would be my boyfriend."

"Do you mean that, Kira?" His expression lit up.

She held her hand up to caution him. "*Ya*, I mean it, but I want to make something clear. I need to take it slow since I'm still not sure what my future is going to bring. I don't know how long I'm staying here, but I know one thing for sure."

"And what is that?"

"I know to the very depth of my heart that I care for you, Jayden." She cupped her hand to his cheek. "I care for you very much."

Jayden's eyes seemed to smolder, and then he leaned forward and touched her cheek before he brushed his lips over hers.

Heat roared through her veins as she lost herself in the feel of his lips caressing hers. She wrapped her arms around his neck and pulled him close. Jayden deepened the kiss, and she lost track of everything as the world around them fell away. Her fingers moved to the nape of his neck, and she ran her fingertips through his soft hair.

When he broke the kiss, she held on to his broad shoulders, working to slow her heartbeat to a normal rate.

The kiss had been nothing like she ever experienced with Philip. In fact, at that moment she realized that the way she felt about Philip was nothing compared to the love she already had for Jayden.

He angled his body back toward the porch steps and stretched his left arm behind her on the swing. His thumb swept along her shoulder, sending goose bumps cascading down her back. Kira scooted closer to him and rested her head on his shoulder while she worked to calm her racing heart.

They relaxed in the swing in silence for what felt like a long time. Then he turned toward her. "*Danki*, Kira."

"For what?"

He smiled. "For giving me a chance. I won't let you down." Then he leaned over and kissed her again, and she melted against him.

A knock sounded, and Jayden hurried to the back door on Sunday afternoon. He pulled the door open, and when he found Kira standing on the porch holding a plastic container, he smiled. "Hi."

"May I come in?" She lifted the container. "I brought *kichlin*."

Jayden leaned on the door and grinned. "Since you brought *kichlin*, I have to let you in." He made a sweeping gesture, and she chuckled as she walked past him.

"Why didn't you go to youth group?" he asked as he followed her into the kitchen.

Kira set her container on the table and removed her coat before hanging it on the back of a chair. "I wanted to come and see you. I asked *Onkel* Stan if I could take his horse and buggy since we had an off-Sunday without a service, and he and *Aenti* Ellen wanted to stay home today. So, here I am. Is that okay?"

"Of course it is." His heart leapt as he studied his beautiful girlfriend.

His girlfriend.

He had tried to get used to thinking of Kira as his girlfriend since Wednesday, and it still felt like a foreign concept, even though it made him so happy. And he had relived their kisses over and over again in his mind. He couldn't wait to taste her lips again.

Loud voices sounded from the family room, and Kira's eyes focused on the doorway. "Do you have company?"

"*Ya, mei bruders* and their families since it's an off-Sunday."

Just then Crystal walked into the kitchen. "Kira. I was wondering who was at the door. I'm so glad you're here. Join us in the *schtupp*."

"*Danki*." Kira met Jayden's eyes, and he held his hand out to her. She took it, and he guided her into the room, where his brothers sat with their wives while the children played on the floor.

Everyone greeted Kira, and he towed her over to the sofa, where they sat together.

Kira turned toward Michelle, who sat on a chair beside Tyler. "How are you feeling?"

"I told Tyler I'm convinced this baby will be here within the next week." Michelle rested her hands on her large belly.

"Are you going to deliver at home or at the hospital?"

Michelle smoothed her hands over her apron. "I have a midwife that I really like who will deliver at *mei haus*."

"*Mei schweschder* is a midwife. *Mei mamm* used to be, and *mei schweschder* and I assisted her with many births."

Michelle's eyes widened. "I didn't know that."

"Did you say your *schweschder* is a midwife?" Savannah moved her chair closer and joined their conversation.

"*Ya*. Abby is still delivering babies."

Jayden smiled while Kira continued to talk about her sister while his sisters-in-law listened with rapt attention. He looked around the room at his brothers and then took in his sister, niece, and nephew playing together, and his heart felt happy. He suddenly realized that he wanted what his brothers had—a wife, a home, and a family—and he wanted those things with Kira.

But it seemed ridiculous to feel this certain about Kira when they hadn't been dating a week. Still, the seed was planted in his heart, and he couldn't deny those feelings. He just had to pray that she would choose to stay in Pennsylvania.

And then another idea hit him. What if he offered to move to Indiana with her? The thought nearly took his breath away when he considered leaving his precious family. Yet the idea latched on to his mind. He cared so deeply for Kira that he would consider following her to Indiana. Then he would have to find a new job and join a new church district. But if he did those things, he would still have a chance to build a life with her, and he could visit his family once a year.

Jayden let that notion settle over him, and although he would miss his family, he would still have a chance to build the life he dreamed of. He would have a chance to have the things his brothers had, and he wanted that so badly he could taste it.

Jayden and Kira spent the afternoon visiting with his family. He enjoyed watching how Kira interacted with his stepmother and sisters-in-law. It seemed as if she were already part of his family while she shared stories about her life in Indiana and laughed with them.

Later they drank cups of coffee and ate her cookies before he walked her outside and they stood by her uncle's horse and buggy.

Above them, the sun began to set, sending a beautiful rainbow of colors bursting across the sky. The air was cold, and the aroma of moist earth and animals drifted over them.

"I'm so glad you came by today," he told her.

Kira grinned. "Well, since my boyfriend isn't going to come and visit me, I thought I should come and see him."

Jayden frowned and pointed to his cast. "I could come and see you, but I haven't tried guiding a horse with one hand yet."

"I'm only teasing you, Jayden." She set her empty container inside the buggy and then turned toward him. "I missed you."

"I like it when you call me your boyfriend." He touched her shoulder.

"Well, you are my boyfriend, aren't you?"

Jayden took a step toward her. "*Ya*, I am." He used his left arm to pull her to him and then brushed his lips over hers. The contact made him feel as if all the cells in his body were lit on fire and he was dissolving into a puddle.

When he broke the kiss, she rested her hands on his shoulders as if to steady herself. "Be safe on your way home," he told her.

"I will," she told him. "I'll come back to see you soon."

Jayden stood by the porch steps while Kira climbed into the buggy and then guided the horse down the driveway toward the street. He waited on the bottom step until her flashing taillights disappeared into the darkening evening light.

Kira's mind spun as she guided the horse toward her aunt's house. She kept reliving how her knees had nearly given way when Jayden had kissed her. His touch had made her dizzy, and she had to hold on to his broad shoulders in order to prevent herself from losing her balance. She had never felt so light-headed after a kiss.

She had also enjoyed every minute with his family. Although Kira had liked Philip's family, they had never made her feel as comfortable as Jayden's family did. She felt as if his sisters-in-law were already her sisters, while Crystal and Duane treated Kira like one of their own. She had relished her time so much that the afternoon had flown by too quickly.

While her uncle's horse's hooves echoed in the buggy, she considered her relationship with Jayden. She was certain she loved him, and she felt closer to him every time they spoke. But now she felt herself at a crossroads. If she wanted to plan a future with Jayden, then she had to decide where she belonged. Did she belong in Indiana or Pennsylvania? Her heart began to break when she considered leaving her family behind, but the thought of leaving Jayden behind caused her just as much pain.

The question taunted her during the remainder of her ride home. When she reached the back porch, she spotted a lantern glowing by the swing. She halted the horse just as a tall figure descended the porch steps.

"Kira?" her uncle called. "Would you like help with the horse?"

"That would be nice." She climbed out of the buggy and walked with him as they led the horse to the barn.

Onkel Stan set his lantern on a barrel and then began unhitching the horse. "How was your visit?"

"It was *gut*." She told him how she spent time with Jayden and his family and they enjoyed the cookies she'd made.

Her uncle smiled. "That sounds nice."

"*Ya.*" She sighed.

He finished unhitching the horse and then led it to the stall. When he returned, *Onkel* Stan seemed to study her. "Is something bothering you, Kira?"

"Have you ever felt as if you were standing at a crossroads, and the next decision you made would change the rest of your life?"

Her uncle folded his arms over his coat. "Well, I suppose I felt that way when I proposed to your *aenti*. What is making you feel this way?"

"Jayden and I are dating, and I care for him."

Her uncle smiled. "I had wondered if he'd asked you since he called me at the shop and asked my permission. Rather than call your *dat*, I granted him permission on behalf of the family. You and Jayden seem to like each other very much. What has you so upset?"

"I had originally hesitated saying yes to dating him. I'm not sure how our relationship will work since his life is here, and mine is in Indiana. But after his accident, I realized how much I care for him, and I told him that I wanted to date him. Now I'm not sure what our future will look like if we continue seeing each other."

Onkel Stan leaned back against the barn wall. "I think where you might build your future is a decision you and Jayden would talk through if you decided to plan a life together. Right now, you should enjoy getting to know each other and see where God might lead you. Does that make sense?"

She nodded but anxiety still tightened her chest.

He stood and brushed his hands down his trousers. "It's late and it's cold out here. We should get inside."

Kira helped him stow the buggy and then they walked toward the house together. After saying good night, she hurried up to her room, where she changed for bed.

As she crawled under the covers, she considered her uncle's wise words. Then she closed her eyes and asked God to lead her heart.

CHAPTER 26

JAYDEN WALKED OUT TOWARD THE BARN ON WEDNESDAY, A WEEK and a half later. It was the first Wednesday in December, and the air held the hint of snow. He shivered as his boots crunched on the cold ground, and when he thought he heard someone yell, he stilled.

He turned toward his brothers' houses, and when he saw Michelle standing in the doorway to her house, he took off running toward her.

"Jayden!" Michelle hollered. "Jayden!"

"*Ya?*" he called as he approached the porch.

She leaned against the doorframe and sucked in a breath while holding her stomach.

Jayden walked up a step and then stopped while worry and fear crashed over him. "Michelle?"

Savannah's door flew open, and she hurried out to her porch. "Michelle?" she asked. "Is it time?"

"*Ya,*" Michelle managed to say. "I need help. The pain started right after Tyler left for work, and now the contractions are coming closer together. Would you please call the midwife?"

Jayden nodded. "*Ya,* of course. The number is by the phone, and I'll call Tyler."

"I'll come and help you," Savannah said.

"But the *kinner*," Michelle said. "Connie is in for a nap, and she'll wake up soon." She closed her eyes and sucked in another breath.

Savannah looked toward *Dat's* house and then at Jayden. "Could I bring the *kinner* over to your *dat's* house?"

"*Ya*, of course. I'll watch them, and Crystal can come and help you."

Michelle sucked in a deep breath and then pointed toward the barn. "Go call Tyler and the midwife. Please, Jayden. We'll figure out the *kinner* later."

Jayden jogged toward the barn and found the number for the midwife. After leaving her a message on her voice mail, he dialed Tyler's cell phone.

"This is Tyler," he answered on the second ring.

"Ty, it's Jayden. You need to come home. Michelle is in labor."

"She is?" Tyler's excitement rang through the phone. "Oh my goodness. I'll be there as soon as I can. Did you call the midwife?"

"*Ya*, I left her a message, and she'll hopefully be here soon." Jayden smiled.

"Great. See you soon."

Jayden disconnected and then checked the voice mail. Using his left hand, he slowly wrote down a few messages from potential customers looking for roofing estimates. When he came to a message from Kira, the sound of her voice warmed up his insides.

"Hi, this message is for Jayden. This is Kira. I wanted to let you know that I plan to stop by on Wednesday and bring lunch. See you then. Goodbye."

Happiness flittered through Jayden. He had seen her on Sunday when she came by after church instead of going to youth group. They had enjoyed a pleasant visit with his family and then sat on the porch and kissed before she left. He smiled as excitement sizzled through him at the thought of his lips touching hers. He could definitely enjoy another one of those kisses.

Then he shook himself. He needed to help his sister-in-law and not stand around fantasizing about his girlfriend. Jayden pocketed the messages for his father and then double-timed it into the house.

After hanging up his coat and hat, he left the messages for his father on the counter and then moved to the family room, where Crystal sat on the sofa while Connie, Kristena, and Ryan played in the play yard.

Crystal pushed herself up from the sofa when Jayden walked in. "Did you reach the midwife?"

"I left her a message, asking her to come right away." He sat down on a chair across from her. "You can go help Michelle and Savannah, and I'll stay with the *kinner.*"

Crystal rested her hands on her distended belly. "I'm not sure I'll be much help."

"You could calm Michelle until the midwife gets here."

"*Ya*, I suppose I could. Are you sure you'll be okay?"

"*Ya*, I will." He held up his good arm. "I've figured out a way to pick them up with one arm. I can handle it."

Crystal walked over to the play yard, leaned down, and kissed each of the children. "You all be *gut* for Jayden." Then she started toward the door. "I'll be back soon to check on them."

"We'll be fine." Jayden sat back on the chair and sent up a silent prayer:

Lord, please protect Michelle and help her have a smooth delivery. Please bring her baby safely into this world.

Then he looked toward the window and hoped Kira would arrive soon.

Kira shivered as she knocked on Jayden's door a couple of hours later. She balanced her tote bag on her shoulder and her serving dish in her hands. Excitement bubbled up inside her when she heard footfalls coming from inside the house.

The door opened, and Jayden held his good arm out to her. "Hi. Let me take that for you."

"*Danki.*" She stepped into the house and hung up her coat. "It's cold out today. December is here."

"*Ya*, it is. Michelle is in labor."

Kira gasped. "She is?"

He explained how Michelle had yelled to him for help this morning and how he had called the midwife and his brother.

"Crystal and Savannah are over there with her now. The midwife and Tyler arrived a little while ago. I'm here with the *kinner*." He pointed toward the family room. "I'm so glad you're here." He kissed her cheek, and she relished the feel of his touch.

"I am too." She picked up the serving dish. "I brought some leftover meat loaf from last night. I thought we could make meat loaf sandwiches for lunch."

He touched her hand. "That sounds great."

She set the serving dish in the refrigerator and then they walked into the family room, where the children played in the play yard.

When Kristena saw Kira, she brightened and held her arms up. "Kiwa!" she exclaimed.

"Hi, sweetie." Kira hoisted her up and balanced the toddler on her hip.

Kristena touched her face and then rested her cheek on her shoulder.

Kira bounced her on her hip and then spun to face Jayden. He leaned on the doorway and smiled at her, and something in his expression sent a shock wave of warmth through her. Suddenly, her uncle's advice echoed through her mind:

I think where you might build your future is a decision you and Jayden would make together if you decided to plan a life together. Right now, you should enjoy getting to know each other and see where God might lead you.

Her heart seemed to stutter as she imagined a life with Jayden—a home, a family, a future.

But why would she think about all those things when they'd only been dating for a week and a half?

"Jayden?" Crystal appeared behind him in the kitchen. "Oh, hi, Kira."

Kristena sat up and started wiggling in Kira's arms. "Mama! Mama!"

"Shh. It's all right." Crystal crossed to Kira and took her daughter into her arms and then sat down on one of the wing chairs.

Kira pushed the ribbons from her prayer covering off her shoulders as she sat on the chair beside her. "How is Michelle doing?"

"It's going very slowly. Savannah and I were sitting in the family room in case they needed us, but the midwife said it's going to be some time. I decided it was better if I came back here." Crystal rubbed Kristena's back while her daughter rested her head on her shoulder.

Kira looked over at Jayden, who continued to stand by the doorway. "Maybe it's best if I go home."

"Oh, don't be *gegisch*, Kira," Crystal said, touching her shoulder. "You're part of our family, and you're welcome to stay and visit with us for as long as you'd like. Savannah is going to take care of some chores and then come over."

Kira nodded, her heart warming at Crystal's insistence that she was part of the family. "Okay. I can warm up lunch if you'd like."

After Kira, Jayden, and Crystal ate meat loaf sandwiches, Kira helped feed the children grilled cheese. Then she and Jayden played with the children while Crystal took care of some chores. Later, Savannah joined them, and they visited in the kitchen while the children napped.

After a couple of hours, Kira called her driver and then she and Jayden waited on the porch for him to arrive.

"I had a nice time today," Kira told Jayden while he held her hand.

He touched her cheek. "I did too."

Kira looked down toward Tyler and Michelle's house. "I can't stop thinking about Michelle."

Jayden frowned. "I know. I keep praying that everything is going well."

"Would you please let me know when the baby is born? Maybe just leave me a message?"

"*Ya*, of course." Leaning over, he brushed his lips over hers, sending her stomach into a wild swirl. "I can't wait to see you again. I miss you already, Kira."

She smiled. "I miss you, too, Jayden."

Her driver's van bumped up the driveway, and she stood and picked up her empty container and her tote bag.

Jayden walked her down to the van and then he kissed her cheek.

She smiled up at him and touched his shoulder. "I'll see you soon, Jayden."

"I can't wait."

Kira climbed into the van and waved as the van drove away.

Later that night, Jayden and *Dat* walked into Tyler's family room. Jayden's heart felt as if it might melt as he witnessed his older brother smile down at the tiny baby in his arms. Michelle's parents, Elaine and Simon, sat on the sofa talking to Korey.

"*Dat*. Jay." Tyler walked over to them and angled the tiny baby toward them. "This is Tyler Junior. We're going to call him T. J."

Dat's dark eyes watered as he took in his newest grandchild. "Oh, Tyler. He's perfect."

"Isn't he?" Tyler beamed. Then he looked up at Jayden. "Would you like to hold him?"

Jayden hesitated. "Oh, I don't—"

"Go ahead," Tyler said. "If you sit, you can balance him on your lap and hold him with your *gut* arm."

Jayden nodded despite his hesitation.

"Hey, Jay," Korey called from the sofa. "Wash your hands before you touch the newborn."

Jayden shot his middle brother a look. "I know that, Kore, but thanks for the reminder."

Elaine and Simon chuckled.

After carefully scrubbing his hands in the kitchen sink, Jayden returned to the family room. Then he sat on an armchair, and Tyler positioned the infant on Jayden's lap.

Jayden stared down at his newborn nephew, taking in his shock of dark hair, his tiny nose, tiny chin, and tiny ears. He breathed in his warm smell of baby lotion and silently marveled at how extraordinary God was. Life was truly a miracle.

"I think you might be holding one of your own someday soon, Jay," Tyler quipped.

Jayden remained silent as he recalled how that same thought had flickered through his mind earlier in the day when he'd witnessed Kira snuggling Kristena in her arms. He'd felt overwhelmed as he watched his girlfriend interact with his baby sister, and he found himself wondering if Kira would ever consider him as her life partner.

If Jayden were to propose to her, would she give him a chance to be her husband and build a life with her? Would she want to have children with him? Those questions had echoed through his mind while they played with the children after lunch.

Jayden was aware that he was jumping ahead since he and Kira were still getting to know each other, but he couldn't stop those dreams from taking hold of him.

"Could I have a turn?"

Jayden looked up at his father. "*Ya*, of course."

"I washed my hands." *Dat* held up his palms and grinned.

Dat gently lifted the baby and smiled down at his newborn grandson.

"It's so nice to meet you, T. J.," *Dat* said. "Welcome to the Bontrager family."

Jayden shared a smile with Tyler while *Dat* continued to talk to the baby, sharing stories about Tyler's childhood.

Soon T. J. started to cry, and Tyler took him back into his arms. "I'm sorry, but I'm going to have to take him to his *mamm*."

"It's fine," *Dat* said. "We just wanted to stop by. We'll head back to the *haus* now."

Jayden patted Tyler's arm. "*Gut nacht.*"

Then Jayden and *Dat* said good night to Korey as well as Michelle's parents before they headed back out into the cold December night air.

"Tyler has himself a handsome little *sohn*," *Dat* said as they started up the path with their flashlights guiding their way.

Jayden nodded. "He does. I'm so *froh* for him and Michelle."

"I am too." *Dat* glanced over at Jayden. "How are you and Kira doing?"

"We're fine. She wants to take it slow, which I think is a *gut* idea. I just don't know what will happen if we decide to talk about a future. I don't know if she'd stay here or if I would go to Indiana with her."

Jayden said the words and then hesitated, hoping that the idea of his possibly moving away wouldn't break his father's heart. Their family had endured so much when they lost their mother, and then when Korey chose to go to Ohio for fourteen months after he and Tyler had their falling-out.

Dat nodded slowly. "I guess it is a possibility that you might go to Indiana with her if you decide to build a life together. We would miss you."

"I don't know if I'd go. Right now, I'm just hoping we can work it out somehow. I really care for her."

Dat rested his hand on Jayden's shoulder. "I can tell that you do, and I believe she cares for you too. I think you should take it slow and keep praying about it. The Lord will lead you."

"*Danki, Dat.*"

CHAPTER 27

"CAN I GIVE THE GIFT TO MICHELLE?" RUBY ASKED WHILE SHE stood beside Kira on Jayden's porch on Friday, a week and a half later. She lifted the shopping bag that held a pack of wipes, newborn diapers, and a blue blanket that Kira had made.

Kira smiled down at her while balancing a container of lemon bars. "*Ya*, you can give it to her. That's a heavy bag. You're very strong since you can carry it."

Her little cousin beamed before knocking on the door.

A moment later, footsteps sounded and then Crystal opened the door. "*Wie geht's?*"

"We have a gift for Michelle and baby T. J." Ruby held up the bag.

"Isn't that nice of you." Crystal turned to Kira. "Jayden went to the store. He insisted that he was tired of hanging around the *haus*, so he took my shopping list and called our driver."

"Oh," Kira said. "I hope the shopping is going well for him."

Crystal leaned on the door. "I have Krissy in for a nap right now, so I can't leave the *haus*. But you can go on down to Michelle's. Stop by here after your visit."

"Okay!" Ruby hefted the bag and started down the steps.

Kira and Crystal shared a smile.

"I don't mean to overstep, but I was so thrilled to hear that you and Jayden are dating."

Kira's smile widened. "*Danki.*"

"Jayden has shared that's he's very content as well." Crystal reached out and touched Kira's arm. "If you ever want to talk, don't forget I'm always here, okay?"

"*Danki.*" Kira gestured toward the steps. "I'd better catch up with Ruby."

Crystal chuckled. "*Ya*, you'd better."

Kira hurried after her little cousin and then fell into step with her.

"I can't wait to meet the baby," Ruby said while they walked through the cold mid-December afternoon.

The sky was gray, and the trees were bare without their leaves.

When they reached Michelle's house, Ruby scampered up to the door and knocked before bouncing on the balls of her feet.

After a few moments, the door opened, and Michelle peeked out. "Ruby! Kira!" She opened the door wide. "Oh, it's so nice to have some company."

"We brought you and baby T. J. presents." Ruby hoisted the bag in the air.

Michelle bent down and hugged her. "Oh, *danki*, Ruby." Then she took the bag. "Please come in."

Kira followed Michelle and Ruby into the family room, where Connie sat on the floor playing with a doll, and T. J. slept in a bassinet. Kira couldn't help but think that Connie looked like a miniature version of her mother with her sandy-brown hair and bright blue eyes. T. J. already resembled his father with his head of dark hair.

Ruby greeted Connie and then took off her coat before she hurried over to the bassinet.

"Don't touch him," Kira warned as she hung her coat and Ruby's on hooks by the door.

Ruby turned toward her. "I'm just looking." Then she sat down beside Connie and began discussing her doll with her.

"Ruby and I made lemon bars last night." Kira held out the container.

"You are so kind." Michelle started toward the kitchen. "Would you like some *kaffi* or tea?"

Kira followed her. "You should sit. If you point me in the direction, I can make it."

"Why don't we both make it?" Michelle offered.

Kira walked with her to the kitchen, and while Kira filled the kettle, Michelle brought out a container of tea bags.

"How are you feeling?" Kira asked.

"I'm tired, but I'm fine. T. J. is a *gut* baby. He's eating well. We're just not getting much sleep, but Tyler has been a great help to me."

Kira smiled. "I'm glad to hear it. Would you like me to do any chores for you while I'm here?"

"Oh, no *danki*. Savannah and Crystal have been helping me. I'd love for you to just visit with me."

"That would be wonderful."

Michelle pulled out two mugs, along with sweetener and milk. When the kettle began to whistle, Kira poured the water into the mugs before they steeped the tea bags and then added sweetener and milk.

Then they returned to the family room with their tea, along with plates and napkins, and sat on chairs near the bassinet.

"Open your presents," Ruby told her.

Michelle smiled. "Okay." She pulled out the diapers and wipes and set them on the coffee table. "*Danki*."

"There's something else in there. Kira made it." Ruby pulled out the baby-blue blanket. "Isn't it *schee*?"

Michelle clucked her tongue as she ran her fingers over the soft fleece blanket with satin trim. "You made this?"

"*Ya*." Kira shrugged.

Michelle folded it in her lap. "You are very talented."

"She loves to sew," Ruby announced. "She's made dresses for *mei schweschdere* and me. She makes the best dresses."

Kira chuckled and shook her head.

Then Ruby pointed to the container. "May I please have a lemon bar?"

Kira handed her a plate and napkin and then Ruby chose a lemon bar. She sat on the floor and shared it with Connie.

Michelle settled back in her chair and then sipped her tea. "How are you and Jayden doing?"

"We're doing fine." Kira moved her fingers over her warm mug.

Michelle gave a knowing smile. "Tyler mentioned that Jayden seems really *froh* with you. Tyler said that if he asks about you, Jayden always smiles."

Kira nodded shyly.

They both were silent for a few moments while Ruby and Connie continued to play with Connie's baby doll.

"Whenever I feed T. J., Connie gives her doll a bottle." Michelle chuckled. "She's the little mama."

"That's sweet."

Michelle took another sip of tea. "I can't believe Christmas is less than two weeks away. It will be the new year before we know it."

Kira felt a tug at her heart. She would be away from her family on Christmas. She felt her lips press down into a frown.

"Are you all right, Kira?"

When she turned, Kira found Michelle watching her with a concerned expression. "I just feel so torn."

"About what?"

Kira bit her lower lip while she gathered her thoughts. "I care deeply for Jayden, but I miss my family. I don't know how we can make it work unless one of us gives up our family for the other. But if I give up my family for Jayden and stay here, I think I'll always have a hole in my heart."

Michelle took a deep breath and pressed her lips together.

Kira immediately regretted her words. She shook her head as guilt nearly drowned her. "I'm sorry, Michelle. I shouldn't have said that aloud. Please don't repeat what I said to anyone."

"It's okay." Michelle smiled. "I won't tell anyone what you said—not even Tyler. I wasn't judging you, and I'm sorry if I gave you that impression. I was just thinking about what you said. You're in a tough situation. You've fallen in love while you were visiting family in another state."

"I never said I was in love."

Michelle tilted her head. "Aren't you, Kira?"

"*Ya*, I am." Kira sighed. "But he hasn't told me he loves me yet."

"I'm certain that he will. Tyler has even mentioned that he sees love in his *bruder*'s eyes when you're together."

Kira's heart thudded at her words. "He has?"

"*Ya*, he has. I believe that one of you will have to make a sacrifice in order for you to plan a future, but if your relationship is blessed by God, I don't think it will feel like a sacrifice. Instead, I think it will feel like a compromise, and you will still be able to visit your families. If he moves to Indiana with you, then you can come visit us or we'll come to you. And if you stay here, then you and your family will do the same. But if God has chosen Jayden for you, then I believe you will build a *froh* life together, and your families will still be part of that life."

Kira nodded slowly as she took in Michelle's words. "*Danki.*"

Just then T. J. began to stir.

Michelle set her cup of tea down and picked him up. "I'm going to change his diaper. I'll be right back." She padded down a nearby hallway and disappeared.

Kira chose a lemon bar and took a bite while she mulled over Michelle's words.

A few minutes later, Michelle returned carrying a bottle and T. J. bundled up in a blanket. "Would you like to feed him, Kira?"

"Oh, I'd love to." Kira sat back in the chair.

And as Michelle handed her the newborn, Kira began to imagine what a life with Jayden might be like. While she fed the baby a bottle, she felt the pull of having her own family and working as a midwife. Could she possibly have that life with Jayden?

<hr />

Crystal met Jayden at the back porch when their driver parked the van in the driveway.

Jayden climbed out and trotted to the back of the van. "I got everything on the list at Savannah's aunt and uncle's store."

"Let me help you," Crystal said as she took a few of the shopping bags.

Jayden grabbed three and they climbed the back steps.

"Kira is here," Crystal said. "She and Ruby are visiting Michelle."

Jayden looked at her with surprise. "I didn't know she was coming today."

"She brought gifts for Michelle. I told her that you were at the store. You should go see her."

"I'll help you put the groceries away first."

Crystal held the door open, and Jayden passed through. "Don't be *gegisch*. Let's carry in the bags and then you go see your girlfriend."

After Jayden helped carry in all the bags and then paid the driver, he hurried down the path to Tyler's house. After knocking, he pushed open the door and then stepped into the family room, where Kira sat on an armchair feeding T. J. a bottle. She looked beautiful in a hunter-green dress. When she turned toward him, a lovely smile lit up her face, and her dark eyes seemed to sparkle.

"Jayden!" Ruby called.

"Hi, Ruby," he said before Connie rushed over to him and hugged his legs. "Hello, sweet Connie."

Kira smiled at him. "I heard you went to the grocery store this morning."

"Did you really go shopping?" Michelle grinned.

"I was determined to get out of the *haus*," he said, and they all laughed. "It just took a little longer than usual to load up the groceries." He took a seat beside Kira and peered down at T. J. "He's eating well."

Michelle chuckled. "Oh *ya*. He's a *gut* eater."

"Baby," Connie said while holding up her baby doll and a bottle.

Kira beamed down at the little girl before turning her attention back to Jayden's nephew. Then she looked up at Jayden, and the softness in her eyes took his breath away.

At that moment, Jayden felt compelled to tell Kira that he loved her, and he wanted to plan a future with her. But it wasn't the right time. Those were words that were meant to be shared in private, not in a room full of other people.

"I think he looks just like Tyler, and Connie looks just like Michelle," Kira said.

Michelle laughed. "It's funny because *mei schweschder* Jorie thinks that T. J. looks like me, and Connie looks like Tyler, only with my hair and eyes. *Mei mamm* says that everyone sees something different."

"They're both perfect, Michelle," Kira told her. "You and Tyler are very blessed."

"*Danki*, Kira." Michelle placed her hand on her mouth to shield a yawn.

Then Kira looked concerned. "Maybe we should go and let you and the *kinner* rest." She handed the baby back to Michelle.

"Did you want to hold your nephew before you go, Jayden?" Michelle offered.

Jayden shook his head. "Oh no. I can hold him another time."

Kira cleaned up the mugs and then helped Ruby with her coat. After buttoning her own coat, she turned to Michelle. "Would you like me to leave the lemon bars?"

"You brought lemon bars?" Jayden asked.

Michelle nodded toward the container. "You can take them, Jayden."

"*Danki*," Jayden said as he gathered up the lemon bars. Then he hugged Connie and said goodbye before he, Kira, and Ruby headed back out into the cold.

Kira took the container from Jayden as they walked down the porch steps.

"*Danki* for coming," Michelle called as they started down the path.

Ruby skipped ahead of them, and Jayden threaded his fingers with Kira's.

"I wasn't expecting to see you today," he told her.

Kira looked up at him. "I thought I'd surprise you."

"You know, I'll have this off in a month." Jayden held up his cast. "That means I'll be back to work. I can't wait."

"You mean you don't like hanging around the house and going grocery shopping?"

He stopped and smiled down at her. "I do like getting to spend time with you." He released her hand and brushed his fingers down her cheek. Once again, he felt moved to tell her that he loved her. His heart began to pound as he imagined saying those sacred words aloud. Would Kira say them back to him and mean them?

"Look at the cat, Kira!" Ruby yelled.

Kira spun toward where Ruby pointed toward a large, orange barn cat before it leapt and sprinted after a squirrel. "That's a big one, Ruby." She faced Jayden and took his hand before tugging him toward her. "Let's get back into the warmth. It's cold out here."

"*Mei dat* wants to deliver his trains to the children's hospital tomorrow. I know it's last minute, but I was planning to call you and ask you to join us. Would you like to come?"

Kira's expression brightened. "Yes! We can invite our *freinden*. I'll call Alaina, and you can call Ben. How does that sound?"

"Perfect," he said.

"Can I come?" Ruby asked.

Kira nodded as she touched one of Ruby's long braids. "Of course, *mei liewe.*"

As Jayden, Kira, and Ruby climbed the back porch steps, Jayden looked toward his brothers' homes and tried to imagine building his own home close to theirs. Would Kira ever want to live here on his father's land with him?

Deep in his heart, he prayed she would say yes.

CHAPTER 28

THE FOLLOWING AFTERNOON, KIRA AND JAYDEN SAT AT A table in a diner surrounded by their friends, along with Ruby and Duane.

That morning they had delivered the trains to the children's hospital, and the hospital community relations representative had been delighted with Duane's craftsmanship. The woman promised that the trains would be cherished by the special patients who received them on Christmas.

After they left the hospital, Duane had suggested that they go to lunch together. Now Kira sat between Jayden and Alaina and looked across the table, where Shane and Darla whispered while Lewis shared a story about working in his father's hardware store. When Darla smiled up at Shane, Kira's heart felt light. She was happy to see that Shane and Darla had struck up a friendship and possibly more.

"Are you okay?" Jayden whispered in Kira's ear. His warm words sent a tingle trilling down her back.

Kira touched his hand under the table. "*Ya*, I'm fine."

"So, Jay," Ben called from where he sat with Lora. "When are you going to actually go back to work?"

Lewis laughed. "Haven't you had that cast on for six months now?" he teased.

"That's not funny." Alaina thumped Lewis on the arm, and he jumped with a start. "You shouldn't make fun of someone's injury."

Jayden's lips twitched and he swallowed, looking as if he was trying not to laugh. "I'll actually get this off in a month, and I can't wait to get back to work. Hanging around the *haus* is rather dull."

"But he has been a great help to his stepmother," Duane added. "There are a few chores he can do, and he's also gotten very astute at grocery shopping."

Jayden sighed. "*Danki, Dat.*"

The server arrived with their meals, and soon they were eating and sharing stories.

"Are you ready for Christmas, Kira?" Lora asked.

Kira swallowed a bite of her grilled chicken sandwich. "I'm still working on some gifts, and I need to make cards to send to *freinden* back home."

"I'll help you make cards," Ruby said from the other side of Jayden.

Kira smiled at her cousin. "I would love to have your help." Then she looked over at Lora. "Are you ready?"

"Oh no. I have plenty to do. Christmas has snuck up on me."

Kira and her friends discussed their Christmas plans while they finished their lunch. Then they headed back out to Duane's driver's van. Jayden and Kira held hands as they walked through the parking lot. She shivered in the breeze and looked up at the gray sky. The air seemed to hold the promise of snow.

"What are your plans when you get home?" Jayden asked after they had taken their seats in the van.

Kira turned toward him. "I'm actually working on a couple of surprises for you."

"What are the surprises?" he leaned closer and whispered. "I promise I won't tell."

His nearness sent a shivery wave over her skin, and she had to work to keep her voice even. "I'm not going to tell you."

He frowned.

Ruby laughed from beside him. "You're *gegisch*, Jayden."

"Am I?" he asked before tickling her.

Kira laughed, enjoying the affection between her boyfriend and her cousin. She cherished seeing how easily Jayden interacted with children. He truly had a gift, and he blessed all of the children in his life.

Alaina turned around to face Kira, and they shared a smile. Then Kira settled back in the seat. She was so happy to have her wonderful boyfriend and friends.

Jayden sat on a stool in the woodshop later that evening. He frowned as he looked down at the workbench. He had ideas for what he wanted to create, but working with the cast made it nearly impossible.

The door opened, and *Dat* joined him in the shop. "What are you building?"

"Not much." Jayden sighed. "I wanted to make something for Kira for Christmas, but my hands aren't cooperating."

Dat hopped up on the stool beside him. "What if I helped?"

"You want to help me?"

Dat lifted a dark brow. "Why wouldn't I?" He pointed to the empty shelves where the trains had once sat, waiting to serve their purpose. "My trains are gone, and now I need a new project. I'd love to help you."

"*Danki.*" Jayden shared his idea and then he found a few pieces of wood. Soon they were working together.

"Your new sibling will be here in less than two months," *Dat* said while they worked.

"You must be excited."

"I am." His father beamed. "I never imagined I'd have five *kinner*. I'm blessed beyond measure with my family."

They worked in silence for a few moments while they sanded pieces of wood.

"You and Kira seem very *froh*," *Dat* said.

"We are." Jayden hesitated. "I want to tell her that I love her, but every time I feel like we have the perfect moment, my courage dissolves."

Dat gave a knowing smile. "When you give her this special gift, I think you'll have your perfect moment."

"That would be wonderful."

Dat bumped his shoulder against Jayden. "I think you will, and I have a feeling God has a very special plan for you and Kira."

"I hope so," Jayden said.

"*Frehlicher Grischtdaag!*" Kira exclaimed as she opened the door and found Jayden standing on her porch on Christmas Eve, a week later.

Jayden took a step toward her and kissed her cheek, sending

happiness curling through her. "And Merry Christmas to you, too, Kira."

"Come in." She pushed the door open wide, and a blast of cold afternoon air tickled her nose.

He followed her into the kitchen, and she had hot cocoa and Christmas sugar cookies waiting for him. A murmur of conversations floated in from the family room, where her aunt and uncle sat reading and the children played.

"Everything smells *appeditlich.*"

He set a bag on the table and then pulled off his coat and hung it on the back of the chair.

Kira's stomach flip-flopped as she held up a bag for him. "This is for you."

"*Danki.*" He handed her his bag. "And this is for you."

She thanked him and then opened the bag and pulled out a beautiful wooden trinket box with her initials—KSD—carved in the top and surrounded by a heart.

"Jayden. This is gorgeous." She opened the top and moved her fingers over the smooth cedar while breathing in the sweet aroma. Then she found an inscription on the back—*Always, Jayden.* "You made this. It's spectacular."

He nodded, and his expression seemed sheepish. "I was able to use my hand a little bit, and *mei dat* helped with some of it. He had to assist with the inscriptions. But I designed it. I also called your uncle, and he told me that your middle name is Suzanne."

"I love it." She kissed his cheek. "Thank you so much. I will treasure it always."

Jayden beamed.

"Open your gift now." She pointed to the bag.

Jayden pulled out the two light-green shirts she had sewn for him, along with a matching green hat and scarf.

"I thought that the green would look so nice with your *schee* eyes." She pointed to the shirts. "I made the shirts, but I bought the hat and scarf." She laughed.

"*Danki*. I love them." He kissed her cheek, and she leaned into his touch.

Then they sat down and ate cookies and drank cocoa while they talked about their week.

Later Kira carried their mugs to the sink and began to wash them.

"Have you spoken to Fern?" Jayden asked as he sidled up to her at the counter.

"I was actually thinking about going to visit her today."

"Why don't we bring her some Christmas *kichlin* and check on her?"

"Now?"

Jayden grinned. "*Ya*. Now. I'll hitch up my horse and buggy, and we can go wish her a Merry Christmas."

"I'll let *mei aenti* and *onkel* know we're going."

Jayden kissed her lips, and Kira drank him in before he shifted away. Then he pulled on his coat, new hat, and new scarf before hurrying out the back door.

"*Frehlicher Grischtdaag!*" Kira and Jayden exclaimed when Fern opened her door.

Fern laughed and pulled them both in for a hug. "Merry Christmas."

Kira held up a container. "We brought Christmas *kichlin*."

"Did you say Christmas *kichlin*?" Omar called from behind Fern.

Jayden and Kira chuckled as they walked into the house.

"Merry Christmas, Omar," Jayden said before shaking his hand.

The older man examined Jayden's cast. "What happened to you, *sohn*?"

"I took a tumble off a ladder, but I'm doing much better. I'll have this cast off soon." Jayden shucked his coat and sat across from Omar. "How are you doing?"

Kira hung her coat on a peg on the wall while the men began discussing the latest news.

"Come and help me make hot cocoa to go with your *kichlin*, Kira," Fern said.

Kira followed Fern into the kitchen and set the container of cookies on the counter. "How is your Christmas Eve going?"

"It's fantastic." Fern took Kira's hands in hers. "Omar asked me to marry him."

Kira gasped. "He did?"

"*Ya!*" the older woman exclaimed. "We're getting married in a month, and he's going to move in here with me. I'm so excited. I can't thank you enough for introducing us. I haven't been this *froh* in a very long time, and I owe it all to you, sweet Kira." Fern pulled Kira in for another tight hug.

Kira patted Fern's back as her head spun. Fern and Omar were getting married! It all seemed so sudden, but Fern was clearly happy. "I'm thrilled for you."

"We're going to talk to our bishops the day after Christmas and then we'll have a small ceremony here since it's my second marriage. I would like for you and your *freinden* to come. After all, you all brought us together. You blessed us beyond measure, and I'm so very thankful for each of you." Fern filled the kettle and set it on the burner. Then she turned toward Kira again. "You'll come, right?"

"*Ya*, of course. I'll talk to Alaina, and we can each bring a dish to share. It will be a special day."

After the kettle whistled, Kira stirred hot cocoa mix into four mugs and then carried them out to the family room on a tray. Fern delivered the cookies, and the two couples sat down together. They talked and laughed and then sang a few Christmas carols.

"*Danki* for coming to visit us," Fern said as Jayden and Kira pulled on their coats later that evening.

Kira hugged Fern. "Merry Christmas, Fern. We will see you soon."

"It was *gut* to see you, Jayden," Omar said as he shook Jayden's hand. "You be careful on those ladders."

Jayden laughed. "I will, Omar." Then he shook Fern's hand.

"You take *gut* care of Kira," Fern said softly.

Jayden peeked over at Kira and found her talking to Omar. "I plan to if she'll let me."

"I think she will, *sohn*. She thinks the world of you."

Jayden nodded and hoped Fern was right.

He and Kira waved to the older couple before they headed

out into the cold, late-December evening air and took their seats in his buggy.

Using his left hand, Jayden flipped the reins and guided the horse down the road toward Kira's uncle's house.

"That was fun." Kira touched Jayden's arm. "*Danki* for taking me to see Fern." Then she turned toward him. "I've been meaning to ask you about your dollhouses. Have you decided what you're going to do with them?"

"I'm going to give them to Crystal's nieces for Christmas."

"They will love them, Jayden."

"*Danki.*" He gave her a sideways glance. "What do you think about Fern and Omar getting engaged?"

"I was honestly surprised."

"Surprised?" Jayden felt his eyebrows rise. "You had told me that they seemed *froh* when you visited Fern. Why are you surprised?"

Kira gave him a palms-up. "They haven't been dating very long, and now they're going to get married. Don't you think it's soon?"

"But they're *froh*. Isn't that what matters?"

"Sure, but they're going to make a commitment before God to spend the rest of their lives together. Do they know each other well enough to do that?"

Jayden was flummoxed as he stole another glance at his girlfriend.

"Why are you looking at me like I'm *narrisch*?" she asked, her voice sounding a trace defensive.

"I don't think you're crazy, but I'm just surprised. I thought you'd consider Omar's proposal romantic instead of too soon."

Kira frowned. "It *is* romantic. I just assumed they'd date longer since they've barely been together two months. That's all."

Jayden pressed his lips together as doubt spun in his chest. He had planned to tell Kira that he loved her today, but now he felt as if that declaration might not go as well as he had hoped. He feared that instead of repeating those words to him, she might say that it was premature.

For a moment he wondered if he and Kira could have a future if she believed there was a timeline for love. Was he kidding himself when he imagined a home and a family with her? Or had her broken heart changed her opinion about what would be an appropriate time for a proposal?

He cleared his throat and racked his brain for something to say that would change the subject. "Have you heard from your family?"

"I'm planning to call them the day after Christmas. I'm hoping that my Christmas package arrived in time."

Jayden forced his lips into a smile. "What did you send them?"

"I made some pretty pot holders for Abby, along with some matching dishcloths and tea towels."

While Kira talked on about the gifts she had created for her family, Jayden tried to fight back the sudden feeling of foreboding that began to creep into his chest. But he couldn't stop the sinking feeling that Kira was going to break his heart and then return to Indiana without him.

CHAPTER 29

"You got a package, Kira," *Aenti* Ellen called.

Kira hurried into the kitchen, where a large cardboard box addressed to her sat on the table. It was the day after Christmas, and her youngest cousins had all gone in for their afternoon naps.

Ruby stood on her tiptoes and examined the large box. "What is it?"

"It looks like it's from *mei mamm* and *dat*," Kira told her.

Ruby scrunched her little nose. "What are you waiting for? Open it!"

Kira chuckled before finding a pair of scissors and slicing the package tape. When she opened the box, she found a Christmas card addressed to her and signed by her parents and sisters. She pulled out the gifts they had sent to her—a pink scarf with matching mittens from Leah, a stationery set featuring flowers and scripture verses from Maribeth, a sweater and fuzzy socks from her parents, and a couple of books from Abby and her husband. She also found a few toys and sugary treats for Ruby, Liesel, and Mimi.

"How nice," *Aenti* Ellen said after Kira had opened everything.

Kira nodded and her throat suddenly felt thick as homesickness overtook her. She worked to keep a smile on her face despite her heart squeezing for her family. "I need to call *mei mamm* and thank her."

"The *kinner* are going to sleep for a while. Why don't you go to your *onkel's* shop and call her now?"

"That's a *gut* idea." Kira put on her heaviest coat and her new scarf and mittens from her sister and then pushed her feet into her boots before heading out into the cold December air. Her boots crunched along the worn path to the shop.

Since the store was closed for the holiday, she used the key to enter the shop, and with the help of a flashlight, she found her way to her uncle's office, where she turned on the propane lamp and took a seat in the chair before dialing the number for her parents' phone shanty. After a few rings, her mother answered. Kira was grateful that their phone shanty was close to the house so that her mother seemed to always hear it. Her father had located it there for when her mother worked as a midwife and had to respond to calls quickly.

"*Mamm!*" Kira called into the phone. "Merry Christmas. *Danki* for my package."

"I was hoping you received it on time. We received yours as well. *Danki* for the lovely pot holders and apron. Your *schweschdere* love the tablecloths and doilies you made for their hope chests. And your *dat* really likes his blue shirt."

Kira nodded and tried to fight the homesickness that swelled inside of her at the sound of her mother's sweet voice. "I'm so glad you all like everything."

"Do you have snow in Pennsylvania?"

"No, not yet. How about you?"

"Oh *ya*." *Mamm* chuckled. "We have plenty. The little *kinner* at the next farm have been outside playing in it. We can hear the joyful sounds of their laughter."

Kira imagined her father's barns covered in snow. She'd always considered it a beautiful and peaceful scene.

"How was your Christmas?"

"It was *gut*." Kira shared how Jayden had visited and they went to see Fern and heard the exciting news.

"Oh my goodness. Fern and Omar are getting married, and you introduced them. That shows how God has worked in your life, Kira. That is such a blessing."

"*Ya*, it is."

"Did you and Jayden exchange gifts?"

Kira sank back in the chair. "*Ya*, he made me a trinket box with my initials carved in it, and I gave him two shirts that I made him, along with a hat and scarf."

"That's so nice." *Mamm* paused. "Have you received any other packages from Indiana?"

"No. Why?" Kira asked.

"No reason," *Mamm* said, her voice sounding a bit too sunny. "How is little Austin doing? I bet he's gotten so big since when you first arrived."

Kira sat forward in the chair. "Wait, *Mamm*. I received Abby's gifts in the package you sent. Who else would plan to send me a package from home?"

"I shouldn't have said anything to you." *Mamm* sighed. "Philip talked to me at church last week, and he said he was planning to write you a letter."

Kira's stomach twisted as bile rose in her throat. "Why would he write me?"

"He told me that he wants to apologize to you. No, he said he *needs* to apologize."

Kira closed her eyes as they started to sting with her frustrated tears. "There's no need for him to apologize. It's our way to forgive, and I've already forgiven him."

"That's true, but I suppose he has something he needs to say to you."

Kira shook her head. "I hope he doesn't write me."

"Well, if he does, you can just read his letter and then let it go. Or pray about it and see if you feel led to write back to him," her mother said.

Kira shook her head. Her mother made it sound so easy when her feelings toward Philip were a tangled mess.

"Oh! Here come your *schweschdere*," *Mamm* said. "Leah! Maribeth! Kira is on the phone."

As Kira turned her thoughts toward her sisters, she tried to release the frustration and confusion that began to build in her chest for Philip.

Lord, please guide and heal my heart.

━━━━⬥❈⬥━━━━

Jayden stood in Fern's family room a month later and glanced around at his friends. It was the last Thursday in January, and Omar and Fern had been married earlier in the day. Conversations buzzed around the room while Jayden's friends ate the delicious dishes that the women had brought to share.

Glancing across the room, he focused on Kira. She smiled while Alaina and Lora talked to her. She looked more beautiful than usual wearing a butter-colored dress. Her dark eyes sparkled as she laughed at something Alaina said.

And then it struck him that perhaps she wasn't more beautiful today. Instead, he was seeing her in a new light.

During the past month he'd felt himself fall more and more in love with her, but he still hadn't shared his feelings for fear that she might tell him it was too soon for them to declare their love for each other.

Still, during the wedding, he couldn't take his eyes off Kira, and he couldn't dismiss the feeling that he and Kira were supposed to be together. In fact, he was almost certain that their relationship had been blessed by God.

If only Jayden could find the courage to tell her how he felt.

"Why so glum?" Ben appeared beside Jayden and patted his shoulder.

Jayden held up his cup of punch in his right hand. "I'm not glum. I'm celebrating."

"Are you celebrating that your cast is gone and you're back to work?" Ben pointed to Jayden's right arm.

Jayden grinned. "*Ya*, I am. Not working was torture."

Ben chuckled.

"I have an announcement," Lewis suddenly called. "Everyone, I have something I want to say."

All of the conversations ceased as everyone turned their attention to Lewis in the center of the room. Lewis reached for Alaina's hand, and she gave him a sweet smile as he pulled her against his side.

Lewis held up his cup of punch while still holding on to his girlfriend's hand. "Alaina and I want to wish Omar and Fern a long and *froh* life together."

Everyone else held up their cups.

"We are so blessed to be a part of your life, Omar and Fern, and we're grateful that you invited us to spend this special day with you," Lewis said. "We wish you God's blessing upon your marriage."

He lowered his cup and then looked at Alaina. "Also, you two have inspired us to follow in your footsteps. I received Alaina's *daed*'s permission a few days ago, and I've asked Alaina to marry me. We've decided to get married in March."

A collective gasp and a few squeals sounded around the room.

Alaina blushed and looked down at her pink dress and white apron.

Lewis turned toward the older couple again. "*Danki*, Omar and Fern, for your inspiration, and I pray that Alaina and I will find the happiness that you two have."

A chorus of claps sounded, and then conversations wafted over Jayden again.

"Wow," Ben said.

Lora took Ben's hand in hers. "Isn't that wonderful? Alaina and Lewis are going to be married!"

When Jayden felt a hand on his shoulder, he turned to find Kira. He set his empty cup on the coffee table. "What do you think of that announcement?" he asked her.

Kira looked to her left and right before holding on to Jayden's left arm and guiding him into the hallway that led back to Fern's bedrooms. A feeling of foreboding twisted up his insides when she frowned.

"I'm stunned, actually."

Jayden pressed his lips together. "Why are you stunned?"

"They've only been dating four months, Jayden," she spoke in a hushed tone. "Don't you think it's—"

"Too soon," he finished her sentence.

When she nodded, he tried to stop the disappointment crowding his gut. Then her expression relaxed. "It's not that I'm against marriage. I want to get married and have a family, too, but I don't think it's something that should be rushed. Marriage is a commitment before God, and it's not to be taken lightly."

"I don't think Omar or Fern or even Lewis or Alaina take it lightly, Kira." He threaded his fingers with hers, grateful to have the use of both of his hands. "I think they all believe God has led them to each other and that it's his plan for them to build their lives together."

Kira blinked rapidly with tears. "But what if they're moving too fast?" Her voice quavered. "What if Lewis changes his mind and breaks sweet Alaina's heart?"

Ah, there it was. This wasn't about Lewis or Alaina. And it wasn't about Omar or Fern. It was about Philip and what he'd done to Kira.

Jayden released one of Kira's hands and rested his palm on her cheek. "Just because Philip changed his mind doesn't mean Lewis will." He licked his lips and gathered up his courage from the depth of his soul. "And that doesn't mean that I will change my mind about you either, Kira, because I care for you that deeply."

Kira drew in a quaky breath as she stared at him.

"I hope and pray that you believe in me the way that Alaina believes in Lewis."

Tears trailed down Kira's pink cheeks. "I don't know if I can. It's too soon." Her voice shook, and the sound nearly broke his heart.

Jayden pulled her into his arms and held her close while she rested her cheek on his shoulder. "Then I'll wait for you."

He closed his eyes while she cried, and he sent a silent prayer up to God:

Please, Lord, help me prove to Kira that I will always love her and cherish her no matter what.

⁂

Kira held on to Jayden while tears poured from her eyes. She had to get ahold of herself.

When her tears finally stopped, she stepped out of Jayden's arms and whispered "Excuse me" before she ran and hid in Fern's bathroom.

After wiping her eyes and blowing her nose, she splashed cold water on her face. She contemplated her conversation with Jayden, and it had been clear that Jayden cared so much for her that he would wait for her. He had almost told her that he loved her, and while Kira was certain she loved him, she wasn't certain she was ready to commit her life to him and leave her family behind.

Help me, Lord.

A knock sounded on the bathroom door.

"I'm almost done." Kira checked her reflection before brushing her hands down her dress and apron.

Then she lifted her chin and pulled the door open.

Darla gave Kira a worried expression. "Are you okay?"

"*Ya*, of course." Kira forced her lips into a smile. "How are you and Shane doing?"

Darla's smile was wide. "We're doing great." Then she leaned forward and lowered her voice. "In fact, I'm hoping that maybe we'll be the next couple engaged."

"I'm so happy for you both," Kira said, and she was. Then she scooted past Darla. "I'll see you later."

She made her way out to the family room, where a crowd had gathered around Alaina and Lewis while they congratulated them.

When Jayden gave her a worried expression, she smiled at him and then forced herself to keep smiling for the remainder of the wedding celebration.

"How was the wedding?" *Aenti* Ellen asked as Kira joined her in the family room later that evening. The house was quiet, and Kira assumed her uncle and cousins were already in bed for the night.

Kira took a seat across from her on the sofa. "It was very nice." She moved her fingertip over the seam on the cushion. "Alaina and Lewis announced their engagement. They're getting married in March."

"Are you happy for them?"

Kira's chin lifted, and she met her aunt's unreadable expression. "*Ya*, of course I am."

"Then what's bothering you?"

Kira took a deep breath and then unloaded all her confusing feelings. "Fern is married and now Alaina is engaged. When Jayden told me that he was excited for them, I told him I felt like it was too soon for them to be married or engaged. Jayden said he thinks it's romantic. He doesn't understand my point of view, and when I told him I was worried Lewis might change his mind, he told me he won't change his mind about me because he cares about me so deeply."

She sniffed as her eyes misted over with tears. "And he said he would wait for me."

"Kira, why does his commitment to you make you sad?"

"Because I'm not sure I can make the same commitment to him."

"Do you not love him?"

Kira's tears poured down her cheeks, making her soul bleed. She pulled a handful of tissues from a box on the end table and wiped her eyes. "I do love him, but I'm not ready to trust him with my heart completely."

"Is it because of what Philip did to you?"

Kira nodded since her words were stuck in her throat. Her grief and sorrow weighed her down.

Aenti Ellen crossed to the sofa and sat beside her. "Kira, no one is forcing you to get married. If you're not ready, then it's okay. You're right that marriage is a big commitment and shouldn't be taken lightly. Marriage is wonderful, but it's also difficult. It's a lot of work, and it's a commitment for life. If you're not sure about Jayden, then don't force yourself into a situation where you feel like you have to marry him."

"It's not that, *Aenti*." Kira took a deep breath. "I do love him, and I feel as if he might be the one God has chosen for me. I'm just afraid of getting hurt, but I also don't want to lose my family."

Her aunt tilted her head. "Why would you lose your family?"

"I love it here, and I love being with you, *Onkel* Stan, and the *kinner*, but I'm not sure I want to stay here for the rest of my life. I miss my parents and *mei schweschdere*. I don't have the heart to ask Jayden to leave his family since I know how close they are. They're everything to him. So that's why I feel stuck." She studied the seam on the edge of the sofa arm. "Why would God lead me to someone who would have to give up everything for me? Why would God want me to give up everything for him? It's confusing." She mopped more tears from her face with another handful of tissues and then she turned toward her aunt once again.

To her surprise, her aunt smiled. "You do realize I faced the same decision, right?"

Kira nodded.

"I gave up my family for Stan."

"How did you do it?"

Aenti Ellen huffed out a breath. "It wasn't easy. I still miss my siblings and my parents, but I realized that my love for Stan was more important than seeing my family every other week at church." She held her hand up as if to correct herself. "It's not that it was more important, but it was bigger than that. I found a way to keep my family close but still build a life with Stan."

She touched Kira's shoulder. "I still have my family in my life. I talk to my siblings and parents, and when I have time, I write them letters. But the love that Stan and I have with our *kinner* is the most important love in my life. There's room in my heart for my entire family, but Stan and the *kinner* have the biggest part of my heart."

Kira nodded.

"You have to decide where you want to plant your heart and your life. Pray about it, and if you want to talk to me, you can anytime."

Kira hugged her aunt close and opened her heart to God:

Please, Lord, guide my heart toward the path you've chosen for me.

Jayden sat at his worktable later that night and dropped his head into his hands. He couldn't stop recalling how Kira had cried to him when they talked about Alaina and Lewis. He couldn't stop the sinking feeling that he was losing her, and that reality crushed his heart.

He looked across the table and an idea took form in his mind. He was going to build her something that would prove how much he loved her.

Pulling out a notepad, he began to sketch out the idea for the project. Once it was drawn out in front of him, he smiled. Then he began to gather the wood.

While he worked, he opened his heart to God:

Lord, please help me prove to Kira how much I love her and that I will never, no matter what, give up her or our relationship. Help me find the words to prove to her that I will love her and cherish her for the rest of my life.

Then Jayden set to work.

CHAPTER 30

RAIN BEAT A STEADY CADENCE ON THE ROOF ABOVE KIRA
Saturday afternoon while she sat in her uncle's office and dialed
her parents' phone number. She wound the cord around her finger while the phone rang.

"Hello?" one of her sisters asked.

"Leah? Mari?" Kira asked. "It's Kira."

"It's Leah. We were just talking about you. Abby is here, and
she has big news. Hang on, and I'll go get her."

Kira glanced around her uncle's desk, taking in his store's shed
catalogs while she waited for her older sister to come to the phone.
Her mind spun with questions while she waited to hear the news.

"Kira!" Abby exclaimed, sounding breathless over the phone.

"What's your news, Abby?"

"Kira, I can't believe it. It finally happened. I'm expecting."

Kira's mouth fell open. "You are?"

"*Ya.* I'm due in August. Vic and I have been praying so hard
and for so long, and the Lord has finally blessed us." Her sister's
words sounded thick. "Oh, Kira, I want you to be part of this. Do
you think you'll be home by August?"

Kira winced as confusion ached through her. "I-I don't know."

"Say that you will. Surely *Aenti* Ellen can find a *maedel* to help her so that you can come back home. I want my baby to know my family. It's really important to me. And maybe you and *Mamm* can help me deliver."

Kira swallowed.

"I miss you so much," Abby continued. "It's just not the same without you here. Leah, Maribeth, and I were just saying that."

"I miss you too," Kira whispered as her throat began to thicken.

"I'm sure *Aenti* Ellen would understand if you told her that you needed to come home in July. You could always go back to Pennsylvania and visit her in the fall."

Kira thought about leaving Jayden, and her heart started to fracture. The rain began pounding harder on the roof above her, and her head started to spin.

She felt as if that crossroads was now directly in front of her—would she choose her family or Jayden? She was certain her heart would be torn in two with this decision!

Help me, God.

"Oh, *Mamm* is here," Abby said. "She wants to talk to you. Call me, okay? Let me know what *Aenti* Ellen says."

"I will," she managed to say, her voice thick.

Rustling sounded over the phone and Kira flopped back onto the chair. She rubbed her hand over her face.

"Hi, Kira," *Mamm* said. "I sent your *schweschdere* into the *haus.*" Then she sighed. "I told Abby not to pressure you and she did exactly that."

Kira sniffed, determined to keep her tears at bay.

"Are you okay?"

Kira cleared her throat. "*Ya*, I am."

"I hope she didn't make you feel bad."

Kira shook her head, hoping to dislodge her confusion. "She just drove home the problem I've been wrestling with—Do I belong here or back home?"

"*Mei liewe*, that is a decision that only you can make. If you feel the Lord calling you to stay in Pennsylvania, then you should stay. Only you can make that determination. We will support you and love you, no matter what you decide."

Kira nodded and sniffed. "I care for Jayden, but I'm afraid of how I feel about him. I'm afraid to give my heart completely to him."

"Like I said, Kira, let God guide your heart."

Kira asked about her father, and her mother shared news about their friends at church before they hung up.

Then Kira pushed open the front door of the store, opened her large umbrella, and started back toward the house. She stopped at the mailbox for the stack of mail.

When she reached the house, Kira closed the umbrella and hung up her coat before kicking off her boots in the mudroom. She hugged the stack of mail to her chest as she breathed in the warm air in the kitchen.

Dropping the mail on the table, Kira sifted through it, hoping to find a letter from one of her friends or her sisters. When she spotted familiar, slanted penmanship, her breath stilled. Then she read her name and her stomach turned and dropped.

Kira sank onto a chair and read the return address: *Philip Troyer.*

She set the envelope aside and considered tossing it into the trash. But then her curiosity took hold of her and she picked it up. She moved her fingers over it and imagined Philip sitting at the desk in his room while writing to her.

Kira closed her eyes and took a deep, shuddering breath. Then with her hands trembling, she opened the envelope and began to read:

Dear Kira,

I convinced your mother to give me your address nearly two months ago. And for two months, I've tried to figure out what I would say if I wrote you. I've prayed about it, and I finally decided to just start writing.

My thoughts are a jumbled mess. You don't owe me anything. The truth is, I owe you everything. But right now, I just want to ask you to read this letter with an open mind. That's all I can ask of you.

I've wanted to apologize to you for a long time. When we broke up, I was confused. I felt as if I was standing on the top of a mountain getting ready to jump into the rest of my life. When I proposed to you, I was certain that I wanted to marry you and build a life with you. It felt like the natural progression of our relationship since we had dated for a year. Many of our friends had gotten engaged, so it felt as if it was what we were supposed to do.

But when the reality of that decision hit me, I wasn't sure I was ready for the pressure of being in charge of a family. I was afraid. No, I was a coward, and I recognize that now.

When I heard that you'd left to go to Pennsylvania to help your aunt with her children, I was stunned. First, I was shocked, but then I was sad. And I acknowledge how selfish that is, Kira. I told you that I wasn't ready to marry you, but then I was upset when you left town. I honestly don't blame you for leaving after the way I hurt you. I know that I completely shattered your heart, and I will regret that for the rest of my life.

Kira, I guess what I'm trying to say is that it took losing you for me to realize just how much I love you and how much you mean to me. I have prayed and prayed, asking God to help me find clarity, and I'm writing to tell you that I have.

Kira, I love you, and I miss you. I would do anything to try to convince you to come back home so that we can try again. I know that I have no right to ask this, but I'm writing you to beg you to forgive me and give me another chance. I thought I was ready to move on, but my heart still yearns for you, Kira.

The house I built was built for you. I'm living in it alone now, and every day I find myself imagining the life we could have had in that house if I hadn't been a complete coward. I want you in my life. No, I *need* you in my life. My future belongs to you, Kira, and I'm ready to be the man and the husband that you deserve.

I'm sorry for hurting you, Kira. I still love you, and you still have my heart. I was stupid and immature when I told you that I needed time to figure out what I wanted in my future. My future has always been you and will always be you.

Would you please give me another chance? I promise you that I won't let you down. Please come home, Kira. Let's try again.

Your mother gave me your number, but I wanted to write to you first. If you'll consider giving me a chance, then please call me, and let's talk about it.

I love you, Kira.

Always and forever,
Philip

Kira stared down at the letter as her eyes stung with tears. Then she read the letter again and again.

And then her vision blurred, and her tears began to fall as confusion and heartbreak threatened to drown her.

Rain pelted the windshield as Jayden's driver stopped his van by Ellen and Stan's back porch. He glanced into the back seat, where the special gift he'd built for Kira sat. He considered bringing it to her, but he decided it would be best to leave it in the car. He would wait to see what she said before he presented it to her.

Then Jayden turned to his driver, Drew Cooper. "Do you mind waiting?"

"Take your time." Drew shook his head.

"Thank you." Jayden pushed open the door and then hit the button on his umbrella to open it before he jumped out into the freezing, raging rain. He climbed the porch steps and slowed when his boots began to slide. The rain had converted to sleet, and the air held an edge of snow.

When he reached the back door, he knocked and then shivered as his teeth chattered. He looked out toward Stan's store and wondered if any customers were looking for sheds on a day as frigid as today.

The back door opened, and Kira peered out. Her beautiful eyes were puffy and her cheeks were red and splotchy.

Worry threaded through him. "Kira." He pulled the door open. "*Was iss letz?*"

"What are you doing here, Jayden?" Her expression was unreadable.

He was taken aback by the question and lost his words for a minute. "We aren't working today due to the weather, and I wanted to come see you." He pointed past her. "May I come in?"

She hesitated and then nodded before heading into the kitchen.

Jayden left his wet coat, hat, umbrella, and boots in the mud-room. Then he met her by the kitchen counter. "What's going on, Kira?"

She sniffed and shook her head.

"You can trust me, Kira," he insisted. "Please tell me what has you so upset."

"It's been a tough day."

He looked past her. "Where is everyone?"

"The *kinner* are napping, and *Aenti* Ellen was up most of the night with Austin, so she decided to lie down too." She pointed to the counter. "Would you like some *kaffi* or tea?"

He shook his head. "No. *Danki.*" Then he took a deep breath. He was going to say what he came here to say, and nothing was going to stop him. "Kira, I came here to tell you something."

She swallowed and wrapped her arms around her waist.

"Kira, when I met you, I thought that I was too young for you, and I wasn't *gut* enough for you. I kept my heart sheltered, afraid that I would never be enough for you. But the truth is that I'm certain God led me to you, and I belong with you." He held his hands out to her, but she kept her hands wrapped tightly around her middle.

"I love you, Kira. I've loved you for a long time. I've been try-ing to tell you how I feel, but it never seemed like the right time. Then I was afraid that if I told you, you would say it was too soon for us. Now I'm not afraid anymore. I love you and I want you to know that I'm ready to start planning a life with you, if you'll have me."

Jayden sucked in a breath as silence stretched between them.

Kira's lower lip began to tremble and then tears trailed down her cheeks. At first Jayden believed that they were happy tears, but when she covered her face with her hands and continued to cry, worry dug into his spine.

He touched her arm, and she took a step away from him. "Kira? Kira, what's wrong?"

She ripped a few tissues from a box and then wiped her eyes and nose. Then she shook her head.

"I can't stand this silence," he said. He studied her eyes, finding pain there. He longed to know what was in her heart. He wanted to help her. "Please tell me what's going on."

"I love you, but I don't know what I want."

Jayden swallowed. "What do you mean?" he asked, shoving the words past the lump expanding in his throat.

"I miss my family. I talked to Abby today, and she's expecting. She's due in August. She and her husband have been trying for years, and she finally has a baby on the way. She begged me to come home." Kira paused and sniffed. "I don't know how I can even think of staying here with you when my family needs me."

"Okay . . . Then I'll go to Indiana with you. If that's where you want to be, then that's where we'll build our life. I'm willing to go with you wherever you want to go because I love you, Kira, and I believe that God brought you here so that we can start our life together."

She studied him, and when she remained silent, Jayden's hope began to dissolve. Worry and panic clawed at him.

Kira's eyes flickered to the table and then back to Jayden. And something flashed across her face.

He spun and spotted a letter on the table. He took a step toward it, and his eyes perused the last few paragraphs.

I'm sorry for hurting you, Kira. I still love you, and you still have my heart. I was stupid and immature when I told you that I needed time to figure out what I wanted in my future. My future has always been you and will always be you.

Would you please give me another chance? I promise you that I won't let you down. Please come home, Kira. Let's try again.

Your mother gave me your number, but I wanted to write to you first. If you'll consider giving me a chance, then please call me, and let's talk about it.

I love you, Kira.

Always and forever,
Philip

Jayden blinked as all of his thought processes came to a halt and then the air rushed from his lungs. He faced Kira again, and her eyes widened as she took a step away from him.

"That letter is from Philip?" he asked, his voice sounding strange. "He wrote you?" His jaw clenched as his eyes searched hers.

She nodded.

He felt the flash of an ache in his chest. "Do you still care for him?"

"I-I don't know," she stammered.

Jayden suddenly felt as if the floor had dropped out from under him. He stumbled back away from her toward the door as he felt his world begin to crumble around him.

He had been kidding himself when he imagined a life with Kira. She still loved Philip, and Jayden never had her heart at all.

Kira never loved him. It had all been a sham.

Jayden's stomach soured as a sick, shaky feeling grasped him. "I guess that means it's over between us?" His voice sounded as tight as a rubber band.

Kira sniffed. "I'm sorry, Jayden. I'm-I'm just confused."

"When you figure it out, let me know," he said, but her words cut him to the bone. He rushed to the mudroom and grabbed his boots, coat, umbrella, and hat. Then he sprinted out the door as he felt his heart splinter into a million painful shards.

As he made for his driver's vehicle, loneliness drenched him like the rain, and he shivered, not from the cold air, but from the block of ice forming in his chest.

CHAPTER 31

KIRA STARED DOWN AT HER PLATE THE FOLLOWING DAY WHILE she sat next to Alaina during lunch after the church service. She picked at her food while conversations floated around her. Her stomach felt the same way that she did—empty and completely hollowed out.

The past twenty-four hours had felt like a terrible dream. No, a nightmare. After Jayden had left her aunt's house, Kira had dissolved into tears. Her aunt had come to her aid, and Kira told her what had happened with Jayden, and how he had told her that he loved her and wanted to plan a future with her. Then she had allowed her aunt to read the letter from Philip.

When her aunt asked Kira which she wanted—a life with Philip or a life with Jayden—Kira couldn't answer the question. All she knew for certain was that she was confused and heartbroken.

Then Kira had spent the night crying and praying. And when she'd come to church this morning, she spent the service praying some more.

"Kira? Kira?"

When she looked up, Kira found Alaina and their friends watching her with concern in their eyes. "*Ya?*"

"Please tell me what's wrong," Alaina pleaded. "You've been quiet since you arrived here this morning."

Kira took a tremulous breath. "Jayden and I broke up yesterday."

Alaina and their friends gasped and then they all began to talk at once.

"What happened?"

"Did you break up with him or did he break up with you?"

"I thought you two were in love and were going to get married!"

"Why would you break up with him? He's so handsome!"

Alaina rested her hand on Kira's arm. "Are you okay?"

"No, I'm not. Excuse me." Kira climbed over the bench and lowered her chin as she walked out of the barn and into the midday January cold.

When she huffed out the air from her lungs, she could see her breath. Hugging her arms over her coat, she looked up at the gray sky.

"Please, God," she whispered. "Help me figure out what to do next. What should I do to fix my broken heart?"

"Kira?"

When she spun, she found Fern walking out of the barn.

"I saw you leave, and you looked so upset. Tell me what's wrong, honey."

Kira sniffed. "Could I possibly come and visit with you and Omar today?"

The older woman smiled. "We would love that."

Later that afternoon, Kira sat with Fern in her kitchen while Omar relaxed in the family room and read a book.

"*Ach*, sweetie, I'm so sorry," Fern said after Kira had shared what had happened yesterday. "You've been through a lot."

Kira nodded and then lifted her mug of tea and took a sip, enjoying how the warm liquid helped to soothe her broken soul.

"But my question for you is a simple one that's not so easy to answer."

"What is it?"

"What do you want, *mei liewe*? Do you want to go back to Indiana and try to work things out with Philip? Or do you want to build a life with Jayden?"

Kira paused as a vision of handsome Jayden seized her mind. "I want Jayden, but I'm afraid."

"What are you afraid of?"

Kira dipped her chin and studied her half-eaten piece of coffee cake. "I'm afraid of giving him my heart, my whole heart."

"Are you afraid that he'll break it the way Philip did?"

Kira lifted her eyes to meet her friend's. "It's not that I'm afraid that he'll hurt me. I guess I'm more afraid of what might happen when I allow someone to love me completely. Maybe it's more a fear of the unknown."

"Listen to me, sweetie," Fern began as she took Kira's hands in hers, "you can't let fear get in the way of your happiness." She took a deep breath. "Kira, opening your heart means opening yourself up to hurt. I'm a widow, and I know how much it hurts to lose the one you love most. But, *mei liewe*, I'm grateful for the life I had with Hiram, and sometimes hurt comes with the joy."

Kira nodded and sniffed.

Fern gave Kira's hand a gentle squeeze. "This may be difficult to hear, but have you taken a moment to think about how you might be hurting Jayden now like Philip hurt you?"

Kira sucked in a breath as the truth hit her. She *had* hurt Jayden the same way that Philip had hurt her, and her heart cracked open as guilt pummeled her. "I-I didn't realize that."

"You should take a moment and think about what you truly feel for Philip."

Kira wiped her eyes with a napkin while she considered the question.

"Do you love Philip? Or are your feelings coming from the fact that you know what to expect from him?"

Kira let that question settle over her heart as more tears spilled down her cheeks.

"You need to consider how much Jayden means to you," Fern continued. "If you believe that Jayden is the one God has chosen for you, then pray about it. If the answer is yes, then go after him and tell him how much you love him, and I assume you know that God will take care of the rest."

Kira wiped her eyes and smiled as a tiny seed of hope took root in her heart. "I'm so grateful to have you for a *freind*."

"Oh dear. You're going to make me cry." Fern sniffed. "I am, too, sweetie. I am too."

"*Gude mariye*," *Aenti* Ellen sang Tuesday morning when she walked into the kitchen. "You're up early."

Kira carried a platter of scrambled eggs to the table and set it next to the platter of home fries. "I was awake, so I thought I'd get an early start on breakfast."

She'd spent all of Monday contemplating Fern's words, and she'd prayed so much that she was certain the Lord was tired of hearing her pleas.

And then in the middle of the night, the answers had come to her like the star glowing in the sky over Bethlehem. She finally understood what Fern had meant when she asked:

Do you love Philip? Or are your feelings coming from the fact that you know what to expect from him?

Kira realized that Philip never made her feel seen, and that her love for Jayden was beyond what Philip and Kira shared. Jayden was her true love. He was the one who understood her and the one who put her first. He was the one God had led her to, and he was the one with whom she wanted to build a future and a family. And she wanted to build those things here in Pennsylvania.

As much as she missed her family in Indiana, she now had a new family in Pennsylvania. Michelle and Savannah had become like her sisters, and Fern and Crystal were mother figures in her life. And her new friends were a tremendous blessing to her.

And beyond that, she felt like a part of her community that she cherished. She wanted to see Alaina get married and witness her cousins and T. J. growing up. She wanted to get to know Crystal's new baby and to see Jayden build his little sister and niece their first dollhouse.

It had become clear to Kira that gaining a new family didn't mean losing her old family. And she had recalled her aunt's wise words about when she decided to settle in Pennsylvania instead of returning to Indiana:

I still have my family in my life. I talk to my siblings and parents, and when I have time, I write them letters. But the love that Stan and I have with our kinner *is the most important love in my life. There's room in my heart for my entire family, but Stan and the* kinner *have the biggest part of my heart.*

And that was when Kira came to understand she could have both families in Indiana and Pennsylvania, but growing up and becoming an adult meant leaving home and making a new one—whether it was down the road or across the state. She could make Pennsylvania her new home, as well as go home to be there for Abby's baby's birth and visit her new niece or nephew.

But the truth that settled in her heart was that Jayden was her future. He was the one whom God had chosen for her, and now she had to ask him to forgive her and to accept her heart as her gift to him along with her promise to never hurt him again.

She felt light-headed when she imagined confessing her love to Jayden. She just hoped it wasn't too late.

Kira grabbed a pair of tongs and began filling a third platter with bacon.

"What can I do to help?" *Aenti* Ellen asked.

Kira pointed toward the table. "Would you please make a plate for each of the *kinner*?"

"Of course."

While *Aenti* Ellen took care of the children, Kira brought a basket of rolls to the table.

"Oh, this smells amazing," *Onkel* Stan announced as he entered the kitchen. "Kira, you've outdone yourself." He kissed his wife's cheek and filled three mugs with coffee and set them on the table before he took his usual seat.

Kira and *Aenti* Ellen sat, and after a silent prayer, they began filling their plates.

"What are your plans for the day?" *Onkel* Stan asked Kira.

"I was going to ask you if you would call your driver for me."

Aenti Ellen stirred cream and sugar into her mug. "Where are you going?"

"I was hoping to go see Jayden," she said.

Her aunt's dark eyes widened. "Are you going to tell him that you want to work things out?"

"*Ya*, I am."

Onkel Stan looked out the window and grimaced. "It's supposed to snow today."

"I'm hoping that he'll be home due to the weather. If not, then I'd like to wait for him if that's all right."

Her aunt smiled. "I think it's a wonderful idea."

Kira nodded as her heart thudded. She just hoped Jayden would be happy to see her.

Snow peppered the windshield as Kira's uncle's driver steered the van up the driveway leading to Duane's house. The grass and trees were covered in snow and the roofs of the buildings were also white.

"I think the snow is picking up," Dottie said as she stopped the van by the porch. "How long are you planning to stay?"

Kira picked up her tote bag. "I'm not sure."

"Well, if the roads are bad, it might be a while before I can come back to get you."

"I understand. I'll call you, and if I have to stay, then I will." Kira pushed open the door. "Be careful."

Kira closed the door and trudged through the falling snow to the back door. Then she knocked and glanced around, taking in the beauty of the falling snow. She breathed in the crisp, clean air and sent up another prayer.

Lord, please grant me the right words to tell Jayden how much I love him. Help me apologize and show him that my love is true.

The back door opened, and Crystal stood before her, her eyes looking dull as she rubbed her belly.

"Are you all right?" Kira asked as worry gripped her.

Crystal shook her head. "Contractions started earlier, and they are getting worse and closer together. I think the baby is going to come soon." She sucked in a breath. "I don't know why they all went to work when it was supposed to snow."

"Do you want me to call your midwife?"

"*Ya*, please." Crystal pointed toward the barn. "The number is by the phone. Her name is Laverne Mast. Please ask her to hurry. Also, the number for Duane's cell phone is there. Call him too."

Kira nodded. "I will." She hurried down the porch steps and through the snow to the barn. She found the phone and a table with a list of phone numbers. She dialed the midwife first.

"Hello?" a woman's voice said.

"My name is Kira Detweiler. Crystal Bontrager asked me to call you. She's having contractions, and they're getting worse and closer together."

"I'm leaving now. Please tell her to stay calm."

"I will," Kira said. "I've actually helped *mei mamm* deliver babies, so I know what to do."

"*Gut.* It looks like the weather has gotten worse. I'll be there as soon as I can."

Kira disconnected the call and then found Duane's number and dialed.

"This is Duane," he said when he answered.

"Duane, it's Kira. Crystal is in labor."

"What?" he asked.

"I just got here, and she told me she was having contractions. The midwife is on her way, but the snow is really coming down now. I'm going to help her until the midwife gets here. I've assisted in deliveries before."

"I knew I should have stayed home today," Duane said. "We were just storing our tools. I'll be there as soon as I can."

"Don't worry. I'll take care of her," Kira said.

After hanging up, Kira walked out of the barn and blew out a puff of air when she found the snow falling even harder. She could barely see the outline of Tyler's and Korey's houses at the end of the path.

"Please, Lord," she whispered, "deliver Duane, Jayden, Korey, Tyler, and the midwife safely."

Then she trudged through the snow toward Savannah's house and knocked on the door.

"Kira!" Savannah exclaimed. "*Wie geht's?*"

"Crystal is in labor. I've called the midwife and Duane, but the roads are treacherous. I've helped deliver babies before, but I've never done it alone. Would you please assist me?"

"I'll tell Michelle, and then I'll be right there."

"*Danki.*" Kira hurried back through the snow and into the house, where Crystal leaned on the counter. "How are you?"

Crystal craned her neck over her shoulder. "My water just broke."

"I can help you if you trust me." Kira pulled off her coat and set her tote bag on the table.

"I trust you."

Kira nodded as a surge of courage overtook her. "Then let's deliver this baby."

Jayden stared out the window while the Dodge pickup truck motored slowly through the blowing snow.

"It's a winter wonderland," Tyler exclaimed from the front seat.

Jayden tried to smile, but he couldn't convince his lips to comply. For the past three days, he'd tried to pull himself from the misery that had engulfed him the moment he realized Kira was still in love with Philip, but he couldn't seem to find a way to stop his heart from shattering. The truth had gutted him, and a saturating anguish had pulled him down while he'd moped around the house and prayed for God to heal him.

On Sunday he'd told his parents that he didn't feel well in order to have an excuse to stay home from church and avoid facing his friends and telling them that he and Kira had broken up. A constant dull, hollow ache radiated throughout this chest. Yesterday he'd been grateful to go to work and take out his frustration and despondency on the nails he hammered onto the roof.

When Tyler had asked him what was wrong, he'd given an abbreviated account of what had happened, and each word of his confession had felt like a knife to his heart. He was grateful that Tyler hadn't asked any questions or given advice. Instead, Tyler had said he was sorry and hoped that Jayden and Kira could somehow work it out.

Jayden appreciated the sentiment, even though he doubted that they could ever reconcile. Instead, he was convinced it was over for good, and Jayden had no idea how he would ever recover. After all, he felt as if his heart had been ripped from his body and then trampled by his horse.

The Dodge rumbled slowly up the driveway and parked in front of his father's house. Jayden buttoned his coat and then jumped out of the truck and plodded through the snow to the house.

When he walked inside, he left his boots, coat, and hat in the mudroom and then entered the kitchen. He stopped short when he found Kira standing by the counter with Savannah.

Kira's beautiful dark eyes met his, and she greeted him with a hesitant smile.

Savannah looked between them and then muttered, "Excuse me," before she disappeared into the family room, where muffled voices sounded.

Jayden's throat dried as he stared at his ex-girlfriend. "What are you doing here?"

"I came here to talk to you." She took a step toward him. "But I wound up delivering your baby brother."

"What?"

She gave a little laugh and took another step toward him. "When I got here, Crystal was home alone, and she was in labor. I called the midwife and your *dat*, but I wound up delivering the baby before they got here. Savannah assisted."

"That's amazing." He felt his body relax as his lips turned up in a smile.

"He's perfect. Duane and Crystal named him Devon. Everything went smoothly."

"Fantastic," he said. And then her words from earlier registered in his mind. "You said you came here to see me."

"That's right."

"Why?"

Kira glanced toward the family room and then back at him. "I wanted to apologize to you and beg for your forgiveness." She held her hands out to him, and he took them in his. "I'm sorry for doubting you. I realized that when I said that Fern and Omar hadn't been together long enough to get married and that Alaina and Lewis had gotten engaged too fast, I was projecting my own fears onto them. I was worried that if I trusted my heart to you that you might change your mind about me like Philip did, but I was wrong. There is no timeline for love. Opening your heart to someone is always a risk, but it's a risk I'm willing to take. I've been a prisoner of my own fears, but through prayer God has shown me that I'm supposed to be with you."

"What about Philip?" he asked, the name tasting bitter on his tongue. "What about that love letter he wrote you begging for your forgiveness?"

"I don't love Philip. I have forgiven him and how he hurt me, but I only love you. I was so blinded by homesickness and confusion that I couldn't see what's right in front of me."

She cupped her hand to his cheek, and he leaned into her touch. "You're the love of my life, Jayden. I've loved you for a long time, but I was afraid to allow you into my heart. I want to build a life with you, Jayden." She took a deep breath. "I'm sorry for being afraid, but I'm not afraid anymore. God has been trying to show me that you're my future, and I see it now. I just hope it's not too late."

Jayden pulled her to him, and when he brushed his lips against hers, the air hitched in his chest. She deepened the kiss, sending an ache humming through his veins. She wrapped her arms around his neck and pulled him close. Her warmth seemed to pour through his body. When he released her, he worked to slow his pulse and catch his breath.

Kira smiled up at him. "I want to build a life with you here in Bird-in-Hand."

"You don't have to give up your family for me." He took her hands in his. "I'll come with you to Indiana if that will make you happy."

"Jayden, *you* make me happy. I feel as if God has called me here, and I belong here with you. I've realized that I've built a family here." She released one of his hands and gestured around the kitchen. "Your sisters-in-law have become like *mei schweschdere*, and Crystal and Fern are like my surrogate mothers. I have a new community with wonderful *freinden*, and I want to continue being a part of their life. I want to be here for Alaina's wedding, and I want to see my cousins, your siblings, and your *bruderskinner* grow up. I can have a family in Indiana as well as one right here."

All of the air left his lungs in a rush. Her confession was like a sweet hymn to his ears. "I'm so happy to hear you say that because I've always thought you fit in so well with this community."

"I agree and I realized something else today too. Delivering your baby *bruder* reminded me how much I love working as a midwife. I want to give back to my new community by working as a midwife here and helping babies come into the world."

"That's wonderful."

"Jayden, *you're* wonderful." She cupped her hand to his cheek. "My home is here with you. I want our future to be here, and I'm sorry for hurting you. You are the love of my life, Jayden."

"You mean that?" he whispered as her words wrapped around his heart like a warm hug.

"*Ya,* I do."

He pulled her against him and kissed her again, enjoying the taste of her sweet lips. Then he nodded toward the mudroom. "Where's your coat?"

"What?" The skin between her eyes creased as she laughed.

"I have something for you in my shop."

They both buttoned themselves into their coats and pulled on their boots before he led her outside and through the snow to his shop. Then he flipped on the lanterns and pointed to the dollhouse sitting on the workbench. With its two floors, the dollhouse was furnished with a bedroom, kitchen, family room, and bathroom.

"When I came to see you on Saturday, I was going to give you this. I built you this *haus,* and I wanted to give it to you as a way to ask you to plan a future with me."

Kira's eyes glittered as she covered her mouth with her hand. "Jayden, this is beautiful."

"No, you are." He took her hand in his. "I haven't asked your father's permission yet, but I want to marry you, Kira." He pointed to the house. "This represents the home I want to make with you. If your father agrees, I want to be your husband. Will you marry me?"

"*Ya,* I will." Her voice caught.

As Jayden pulled her into his arms once again, he closed his eyes and looked forward to what God had in store for them.

EPILOGUE

Fifteen Months Later

KIRA STEPPED OUT ON THE PORCH AND BREATHED IN THE warm and fresh April air. Their pasture was a lush green, and the sky above her was bright blue. Birds sang in the nearby trees while a couple of rabbits hopped by.

She smiled when she spotted Jayden leaning on the railing and looking out toward their two red barns that sat near their pasture where six horses frolicked in the warm sun. "There you are. I was wondering where you ran off to."

"I didn't run away. I walked." He pivoted to face her and grinned. "I was just out here enjoying this *schee* day." His sandy-blond beard had filled in, and she was convinced he was somehow even more handsome with a beard than he was without it.

Kira could hardly believe that she and Jayden had been married for a year now. After he had proposed, he had called her father to make sure he had permission, and of course, *Dat* said yes.

In order to join her aunt's church district, the deacon from Kira's district wrote a letter to her aunt's deacon confirming that she was in good standing with the church. After that, Kira was officially a member of her aunt's congregation, and she began wearing the same prayer covering, dresses, and aprons as the women wore in Lancaster County.

Then she and Jayden planned a wedding for April, and her family had come for the ceremony. In fact, Leah had been her attendant, and Ben had been Jayden's.

To their surprise, Omar and Fern had invited Kira and Jayden to rent Omar's farm at an affordable price. Kira and Jayden were delighted to move into Omar's house and quickly made it their home.

While Jayden continued to work for Tyler, Kira had begun serving as a midwife. She had started assisting another midwife in the community while she studied books from the library to refresh herself on the best techniques. Then after a few months, she began delivering babies on her own. She loved the work, helping women around her bring their children into the world. She felt as if she were contributing to her wonderful community. She loved her new life in Bird-in-Hand, and she kept in close contact with her family in Indiana. In fact, her parents and sisters planned to come and visit this summer, and she couldn't wait to see them.

"Why are you hiding outside when your family and our *freinden* are all inside our *haus*?" Then she pointed toward the door behind them, where his family, her aunt's family, and Omar and Fern were there visiting.

Jayden wrapped his arms around her waist and pulled her close. "I'm not hiding."

"If you're not hiding, then what are you doing?"

Her husband let out a deep sigh. "I was just thinking about how blessed I am."

"Oh *ya*?" She tilted her head.

"I have a wonderful *fraa* and now we have beautiful *zwilling-bopplin*." He touched her cheek.

"Your woodworking business has also taken off," Kira reminded him. "You have a big order for more dollhouses that will be sold in that store in town." She smiled. "I'm so proud of you."

He grinned. "*Danki*. I enjoy making *kinner* happy. This feels like my calling."

"I think it is too. You're so *gut* at it."

"You think so?"

She laughed. "*Ya*, you don't see just how talented you are, Jayden."

"I told *mei dat* I wanted to make the trains to give away at the children's hospital this season."

"You're amazing, Jayden."

"No, you are."

Just then, the door opened, and Tyler and Korey walked outside, each of them holding one of Kira and Jayden's newborn twins.

"We thought you might like a chance to hold your newborns," Tyler said with a grin.

"Savannah and Michelle told us we were hogging them," Korey admitted.

Jayden released Kira, and they walked over to their twins together.

Kira took their baby girl in her arms and kissed her head. "Hello, little Kaylene."

"Here's little Lukas." Jayden held up his son and then smiled at Kira. "*Danki* for blessing me with this beautiful life."

Kira balanced herself on her tiptoes and kissed his cheek. Then she glanced in the front door of her house and smiled at the dollhouse sitting on the coffee table. It seemed like only yesterday that Jayden had given her that house when he proposed. She turned her attention back to her handsome husband. "*Ich liebe dich*, Jayden."

"*Ich liebe dich*, Kira." Then he leaned down and kissed her, and the touch of his lips sent her stomach fluttering.

She relaxed against him as she lost herself in the feel of his lips, and bliss bubbled through her veins.

When he broke the kiss, they both looked out toward the pasture, and Kira breathed a happy sigh. She was so grateful for her beautiful life in Bird-in-Hand, Pennsylvania.

Thank you, God.

ACKNOWLEDGMENTS

As always, I'm thankful for my loving family, including my mother, Lola Goebelbecker; my husband, Joe; and my sons, Zac and Matt. I'm blessed to have such an awesome and amazing family that puts up with me when I'm stressed out on a book deadline.

Thank you to my mother as well as my dear friend DeeDee Vazquetelles, who graciously read the draft of this book to check for typos. DeeDee, your friendship is such a blessing to me! I don't know what I'd do without our daily texts. I'm so glad our kids introduced us.

I'm also grateful to my special Amish friend, who patiently answers my endless stream of questions.

Thank you to my wonderful church family at Morning Star Lutheran in Matthews, North Carolina, for your encouragement, prayers, love, and friendship. You all mean so much to my family and me.

Thank you to Zac Weikal for his help with my social media plans, my website, my online bookstore, and all of the other amazing things he does to help with marketing. Zac—I would be lost without you!

To my agent, Natasha Kern—I can't thank you enough for your guidance, advice, and friendship. You are a tremendous blessing in my life. I hope you enjoy your retirement with your family—especially your precious grandsons.

I would also like to thank my new literary agent, Nalini Akolekar, for her guidance and advice. Nalini, I look forward to getting to know you better and working with you on future projects.

Thank you to my amazing editor, Lizzie Poteet, for your friendship and guidance. I'm so grateful for your help polishing this book. I appreciate how you've pushed me and inspired me to dig deeper to improve my writing. I'm so excited to work with you, and I hope we partner together again in the future.

Special thanks to editor Becky Philpott for polishing the story and connecting the dots. I'm so grateful that we can continue working together!

I'm grateful to each and every person at HarperCollins Christian Publishing who helped make this book a reality.

To my readers—thank you for choosing my novels. My books are a blessing in my life for many reasons, including the special friendships I've formed with my readers. Thank you for your email messages, Facebook notes, and letters.

Thank you most of all to God—for giving me the inspiration and the words to glorify you. I'm grateful and humbled you've chosen this path for me.

DISCUSSION QUESTIONS

1. Kira comes to stay with her aunt and uncle after her fiancé broke off their engagement. Think of a time when you felt lost and alone. Where did you find your strength? What Bible verses helped?

2. When Jayden meets Kira, he feels an instant connection with her. As he gets to know her, he fears he's not good enough for her since he's younger than she is. He also believes Shane is a better match for her since Jayden doesn't have his own successful business. Can you relate to how he feels? Have you ever compared yourself to someone else? If so, how did you overcome those feelings of inadequacy?

3. Throughout the story, Fern Lambert, the widow Kira and her friends help, becomes a special friend and confidante to Kira. Do you have a special friend or family member you like to spend time with? If so, who is that friend or family member and why are you close to him or her?

4. Kira's aunt Ellen shares that when she chose to stay in Pennsylvania to marry her husband, she felt she had